The chief's eager face loomed above the cooking fire, over which Tavis was suspended like a deer on a spit. The giant's stout wife was at his side, clutching Brianna's rope-sheathed form in her pudgy fingers. Ribbons of early morning light were streaming down through the smoke hole, forming hazy blue halos around their knobby heads.

"That'll do you no good," Morten called. He was yelling much louder than necessary, for his words were intended as much for the hide-swaddled scout as for Noote. "Tavis won't scream."

"Will too," Noote growled. "Burning hurt."

"Maybe, but Tavis won't yell. He won't give you that satisfaction," the bodyguard maintained. "And I'm not going to make your rabbit run, either."

Noote scowled. "Not?"

"Firbolgs die with honor," Morten explained as the logs beneath Tavis began to burn. "We don't beg for mercy. We don't show pain. We just die."

"Maybe we skin you alive," Noote warned. "That hurt plenty."

FANTASY ADVENTURE

The Twilight Giants Trilogy

Troy Denning

The Ogre's Pact

The Giant Among Us
(Spring 1995)

The Titan of Twilight
(Fall 1995)

FANTASY ADVENTURE

The Ogre's Pact

Troy Denning

THE OGRE'S PACT

©1994 TSR, Inc.
All Rights Reserved.

Random House and its affiliate companies have worldwide distribution rights in the book trade for English language products of TSR, Inc.

Distributed to the book and hobby trade in the United Kingdom by TSR Ltd.

Distributed to the toy and hobby trade by regional distributors.

Cover art by Brom.

FORGOTTEN REALMS is a registered trademark owned by TSR, Inc. The TSR logo is a trademark owned by TSR, Inc.

First Printing: September 1994

Printed in the United States of America.

Library of Congress Catalog Card Number: 94-60101

9 8 7 6 5 4 3 2 1

ISBN: 1-56076-891-6

TSR, Inc.
P.O. Box 756
Lake Geneva, WI 53147
U.S.A.

TSR Ltd.
120 Church End, Cherry Hinton
Cambridge CB1 3LB
United Kingdom

In Memory of Colorado State Trooper
Lyle F. Wohlers
Who died in the Line of Duty,
November 4, 1992

Acknowledgments
I would like to thank the following people for their encouragement and support: my editor Rob, for his hard work and kind words; Ken, Sue, and Troy for giving me the chance to meet and speak with the people who read my stories; my friend Bruce and instructor Lloyd of the AKF Martial Arts Academy in Janesville, Wisconsin for their thought on battling giants; Jim W. for his enthusiasm and valuable suggestions; and most especially Andria, for her support and forbearance.

The Coldwood Forest

The Ice Spires West

Gray Wolf Valley

Needle Peak

The High Duchies

Storming Gorge

The Eternal Blizzard

Clearwhirl River

Castle Hartwick

Wynn Castle

Wendel Manor

The Cold Marches

Stagwick

The Lake

The Kingdom of Hartsvale

The Bleak

The Ice Spires

Fiefs

Cuthbert Castle

Ice

Plain

The Baronies of Wind

North

The Ice Spires South

The Frozen Moors

The Great Glacier

The Great Desert Anauroch

Prologue

The hill giant waited behind the portcullis, scowling as the blast of trumpets heralded his arrival. His hulking figure, with stooped shoulders and gangling arms, filled the archway almost entirely. A child could not have squeezed between his rotund torso and the granite walls of the inner gate, while the crown of his pointed skull came close to scraping the vaulted ceiling.

"It appears Noote passed the winter safely enough," observed Camden. The king was watching the giant from the window of the royal library. "He's as plump as ever."

"He's also eight hours early," griped Bjordrek. The chamberlain was a gray-haired man with a slender nose and a pointed beard. "Perhaps I should send him away for a few hours, Your Majesty."

Camden shook his head. "Let's be happy he managed to arrive on Brianna's birthday. That's doing well for a hill giant." Though the king tried to sound cheerful, his words seemed hollow and melancholy—even to him. Hoping to do better, Camden leaned out the window and called, "Raise the gate for my friend!"

The portcullis began to rise, the muffled clatter of its hidden chains rattling across the expanse of the inner ward. While he waited, Camden surveyed the preparations for the evening's celebration. From the spire of every tower waved a pennant of purple or gold, while the standards of the royal guard hung over the interior wall, spaced at even intervals so each company would know where to stand. Dozens of servants wandered about with brushes and pails, scrubbing indiscernible bits of grime

1

off already clean surfaces. The cobblestones, scoured three separate times during the last tenday, shined like silver.

Still, the king was not satisfied. "Bjordrek!"

The chamberlain scurried to his side. "Yes, Your Majesty?"

Camden pointed to a section of yellowed tapestry that could be seen through a window across the courtyard.

"Did I not say that everything visible from the inner ward was to be fresh and clean? The evening must be perfect for my daughter!"

Bjordrek's face reddened, whether with embarrassment or anger the king could not tell. "I shall reprove the Sergeant of the Gate myself, Your Majesty."

Camden made no reply, for Noote had ducked under the portcullis and was now striding across the ward. Fresh bearskins covered the hill giant's chest and loins, and a satchel of untanned deer hide dangled from his shoulder. He wore his coarse, black hair cropped short and ragged, while his tiny round ears seemed out of place on a head so large and lumpy.

When Noote saw the king watching him, he took the satchel from his shoulder and raised it into the air. "Noote bring present!"

Camden forced himself to smile, trying not to think of what the satchel might contain. "That wasn't necessary, my friend," he called. "Your presence will be gift enough."

The hill giant returned the smile, revealing a set of jagged gray teeth filed to sharp points, and stopped outside the king's library. Though the second floor of the High Keep was nearly twenty feet off the ground, Noote had to lower his head to peer inside. He opened the satchel and withdrew the half-frozen carcass of a snow leopard, its head smashed to a gory mess.

"Brianna like?" The hill giant displayed the dead beast by its tail. "Kill myself."

"Certainly." Camden had to fight to keep his nose from wrinkling at the odor. "It's—well, the pelt is really quite exquisite, isn't it?"

"Good." His eyes twinkling with delight, the hill giant dropped the carcass back into its sack.

The king eyed the satchel, imagining how his daughter might react when Noote dropped the squalid thing across her lap. After a moment, he returned his gaze to the giant's face and, still smiling, suggested, "Perhaps Bjordrek can take your gift and have it prepared."

Noote frowned, puzzled as to what preparations might be necessary. Nevertheless, he readily nodded. "Don't lose claws," he advised. "Make good wolf collar."

The hill giant stuffed the malodorous satchel through the window. Camden quickly stepped aside to let his chamberlain accept the gift.

"I'll take this to the tanner immediately," sniffed Bjordrek, reluctantly wrapping both arms around the heavy bag.

"Yes, that's good," agreed Camden. Although it would take much longer than a day to prepare the pelt properly, the chamberlain would have little trouble securing a suitable replacement from the royal tannery. "Perhaps you could have it made into a nice cape or shawl—or something."

"I'll see what I can do." The chamberlain went to the door, but hesitated there. "Before I go, is there anything I can do to help you relax?"

"What do you mean by that?"

Bjordrek winced at the king's tone. "Forgive me for saying so," he said timidly, "but you seem rather upset."

"If I am disconcerted, it's because of your woefully inadequate preparations," Camden snapped.

The king made no attempt to conceal the exchange, for he knew that nothing upset Noote more than being excluded from a conversation. Besides, over the years, Camden and the hill giant had developed a peculiar camaraderie, sharing with each other a great many things more personal than the king's feelings toward his chamberlain.

Bjordrek stood in the doorway, a resentful spark flaring in his eyes. He bowed and began to back away.

"Wait." The king's tone was gentler, for he could see that he had pushed Bjordrek to the breaking point. "You've done well. If I'm tense, it's because I worry about my daughter."

That much, at least, was true.

Bjordrek nodded sympathetically. "Then Brianna hasn't told even you whom she'll choose tonight?"

"No."

The chamberlain sighed. "Let us hope it won't be the scout," he said. "It wouldn't do to have the princess marry a commoner—especially that one. Can you imagine what the earls would do if a firbolg were to become king?"

"The one thing I *do* know is that Brianna won't marry Tavis Burdun." Camden's voice was as morose as it was certain. "You and the earls may rest assured of that."

The chamberlain cast his eyes toward the heavens. "At least we can thank Stronmaus for that much."

Bjordrek bowed again, then disappeared into the stairwell.

Noote cursed in the rumbling language of his race. "Noote not expect wedding!" he grumbled. "Only bring one present."

Slowly, the king turned to face the hill giant. "There's no need for concern, Noote," he said. "You know as well as I do Brianna isn't going to marry anyone."

The hill giant furrowed his heavy brow, then rubbed his leathery knuckles across his chin. His gaze grew sad and dropped toward the ground.

"Oh, yeah," he said. "Noote forget about that."

4

☙1❧
The Weary Giant

Through the open window of the enormous hall rolled a series of distant bellows, rumbling like muted drumbeats beneath the melody of the lodge musicians. Tavis Burdun rose from his seat and raised his palm toward his performers. The fipple pipe squealed into silence and the tambourine crashed to a stop, bringing the dance of the fire giant to a jumbled, stomping halt. From the streets outside came the slap-slap of a flat-footed runner. The lumbering gait was distant and erratic, too heavy for a human foot, each step echoing slightly louder as it rebounded off the rough-hewn walls of the Weary Giant Lodge.

The dancer cast an impatient glare down at the banquet table. Dressed only in a tunic and loincloth of red dragon hide, the fire giant was a lanky figure with thin legs resembling barren sumac boles, long spindly arms, and skin as black and shiny as coal. His blocky head loomed among the murky rafters more than twenty feet above, his scarlet hair and orange beard reminding Tavis of a fireball bursting high in the night sky.

"I'll finish my dance," the fire giant demanded.

"Of course, Kwasid. But give me a moment—please."

The innkeeper knew dancing was sacred to fire giants, but Kwasid would have to endure a short interruption. Tavis did not like what he heard outside, and with Princess Brianna among his guests, he had no intention of letting something unpleasant develop on the grounds of the Weary Giant.

After listening to the distant steps for a moment longer, Tavis said, "There's a verbeeg loose in the village."

"Verbeeg!" The voice came from two seats away. There sat Earl Ruther Dobbin, lord mayor of Stagwick, with a pitcher of ale and a pile of goose bones before him. "A verbeeg in my village?"

"I'm afraid so," Tavis answered. Verbeegs were one of the races of giant-kin, cousins of true giants. They were notorious thieves, for they believed that all things belonged to all people. "And it sounds as though he's heavily loaded."

Earl Dobbin considered this, his round face slowly stiffening with tension. Finally, he scowled at Tavis. "Phaw! You can't know it's a verbeeg! Why not a hill giant, or even an ogre?"

Either option would have been preferable to a verbeeg. Hill giants seldom stole anything valuable, and if they did, their chieftain, Noote, forced them to return it. Ogres were even less cause for concern. Though they were the most savage of giant-kin, for some unknown reason no ogre had committed a crime within the kingdom of Hartsvale in twenty years.

Unfortunately for Earl Dobbin, Tavis was sure of what he'd heard. "If a hill giant were running through Stagwick's narrow streets, he'd be knocking huts down with every step," the innkeeper explained. "And ogres have high arches. They move on the balls of their feet, so their soles don't slap the ground."

The earl's cheeks reddened. "I've killed an ogre or two in my time," he said. "I've seen nothing strange about their feet."

"Then you never looked, as I'm sure Tavis has." The retort came from Runolf Saemon, who sat on the other side of Tavis. A tall, wiry fellow with a hooked nose and pale eyes as blue as mountain columbines, Runolf was the only man in the room who could chastise the lord mayor in such a manner. As Sergeant of the Northern Frontier, he commanded a full company of the Border Guard, and not even Earl Dobbin would risk the king's wrath by speaking lightly against such a man. "Before Tavis came to look after this inn, he was the best scout in the Border Guard."

Tavis felt the heat rising to his cheeks. The compliment did not embarrass him, for he was well aware of his reputation. But he found it disconcerting to hear his fame vaunted by the man who had taught him everything he knew. He turned to his mentor and said, "If that's true, it's only because I had the finest teacher in the kingdom."

"Your admiration for each other is most touching," sneered the lord mayor, "but it fails to convince me you can learn so much about a marauder from his footfalls. Even if he's a verbeeg, how can you know he carries a heavy load?"

Before Tavis could point out the unsteady rhythm of the marauder's steps, Princess Brianna said, "I'm sure Tavis is a better judge than you of verbeeg gaits." Seated between Tavis and the lord mayor, the princess had endured their debate with atypical patience. "If you don't believe him, perhaps you should run along and see for yourself."

To emphasize her point, Brianna glared at the earl. From what Tavis gathered, most humans did not consider the princess beautiful. She was extremely tall for her race, with a frame as sturdy as a man's and a height just a few inches shy of seven feet. But to the former scout, a firbolg who stood over eight feet himself, Brianna was the picture of elegance. She had a striking face with clear skin, a dimpled chin, and sparkling eyes as purple as the flowers in her hair. Her long tresses were as fine as spider silk and more yellow than gold, while her figure was distinctly feminine, with long graceful limbs and gentle curves.

Earl Dobbin finally withered under the princess's stare and looked away, glancing around the hall with an air of distaste. "I wouldn't dream of leaving you in this inn alone," he said. "My guards are quite capable of dealing with the marauder—whatever his race—without my supervision."

"I'm sure that's true, but I still don't want him trying to hide in the Weary Giant." Tavis glanced down the table, where eleven orphans of various ages sat gathered around the end. All residents of the Weary Giant, they were the reason the firbolg scout had left his beloved Border Guard to become an innkeeper. "Avner, go and close the courtyard gate."

A sandy-haired boy of fifteen rose from his chair. "I'll close the gate," he said. His eyes were steely gray, much too hard and cunning for his years. "But that won't stop a thief. He'll just slip the bar or climb the wall. I would."

Tavis gave the boy a reproving frown. "Not anymore, I trust," he said. "Besides, with Earl Dobbin's guards after him, he won't have time for that."

Avner rolled his eyes. "Those oafs never stopped me."

"*Now,* Avner!" Tavis snapped, grimacing. No good could come of reminding the lord mayor that most of the Weary Giant's orphans had lived as street thieves before coming to the lodge.

With a cavalier shrug, Avner went to the door. The boy had not even stepped outside before Kwasid's voice pealed down from the rafters.

"Now I dance?"

The scout nodded, drawing an ivory-toothed grin from the giant. Against the dark background of the roof, the smile looked like a crescent moon that had slipped and fallen on its back.

The musicians, a brother and sister whose parents had perished in a blizzard, raised their instruments and once again the melodies of the fire giant's fervent song rolled through the chamber. Kwasid stomped in a circle. Each time a foot struck the ground, sparks of orange shot from beneath his ironclad boots, and platters and mugs jumped off the surface of the banquet table. The entire hall resonated to the giant's performance, the rough-hewn posts and timber rafters all shuddering in time to the beat.

Kwasid's eyes glazed over. Wisps of fire flickered upon his ebony fingertips, then he spread his arms and began to spin. Ribbons of golden flame arced through the hall's murky heights, licking at the gray rafters and roof planking. The giant's mouth opened, and he sang with the voice of fire, filling the hall with a crackling chant more eerie than it was beautiful.

The performance unnerved Tavis's guests as well as mesmerized them, but the flames did not worry the scout. He had seen enough fire giant dancers to know that their control was absolute. As terrifying as the performance appeared, Kwasid would not allow the ancient timbers of the Weary Giant to burn.

Without taking his eyes off the dance, Tavis leaned toward Princess Brianna. "I hope you're enjoying yourself." He had to speak loudly to make himself heard over the giant's crackling voice. "This banquet won't equal the ball at Castle Hartwick this evening, but the children wanted to show their gratitude for all your help."

"There's no need to thank me," she said. "As a priestess of Hiatea, I must help." Hiatea was a deity of the giants, but many humans in Stagwick also worshipped her as the goddess of nature, family, and child-rearing. "And besides, it's no trouble."

"My lady, you're too modest," Tavis said. In the few months since he had found himself in charge of the orphans, the princess had made the long ride from Castle Hartwick at every opportunity, always bearing gifts of clothing and other necessities for the children. "I suspect you'd help us even if your goddess did not wish it."

"Certainly not!" snorted the lord mayor. "The princess would never consort with rabble by choice."

Brianna graced Earl Dobbin with an acid smile. "To

the contrary, Lord Mayor," she said. "If I were to shun all the rabble in the kingdom, I should have to lock myself away from my father's courtiers and instruct my servants to admit no one but these poor orphans."

Earl Dobbin's face darkened, and Brianna returned her attention to Kwasid. The fire giant was near the end of his performance, kneeling on the floor, his torso whirling wildly and his fingertips trailing cyclones of yellow flame.

Kwasid's gyrations stopped, and he threw his chin back, arching his spine until the crown of his skull touched the floor. His eyes flared like embers, and, with a tremendous shudder, he sprang high into the air. The giant's hands streaked furiously about his body, weaving a fiery orb of such brilliance that Tavis could hardly bear to look at it.

Kwasid's voice erupted in a booming crescendo. The sphere vanished in a blazing flash of gold, leaving the fire giant standing in the center of the room with his upraised palms pressed against the hall's smoking roof. His breath came in broken gasps, as hot as forge gas and twice as mordant. The room remained entirely still, everyone at the banquet table too frightened or stunned to speak.

Before the dazed audience could gather its wits to applaud, a dull boom sounded from the courtyard. "Unbar these gates!" cried a man's muffled voice. "By the authority of Lord Mayor Dobbin, open up!"

Noting that he could no longer hear the verbeeg's footsteps echoing through the streets, Tavis rose and bowed to Brianna.

"Excuse me, Princess," he said. "Avner may be reluctant to open the gate to the earl's men, so I'd better answer it myself."

The scout stepped to the chimney, where his hickory bow, Bear Driller, hung. Runolf had helped him make the weapon, which was as famous as the firbolg himself—and a foot taller. As he took the bow and its arrow quiver off the hooks, Brianna's violet eyes flashed in alarm.

"Surely you don't need that to talk to the lord mayor's men?" she gasped.

"Just a precaution," Tavis said, pausing to give the princess a reassuring smile. The scout was in no hurry, for the lord mayor's guards had long ago learned that it angered the giant traders who stayed at the inn to have the gates of their lodging battered down. "With verbeegs about and the guard pounding at the gate, it's better to be cautious."

Runolf also rose. "With your permission, Princess, I'll go with Tavis." As he had all morning, the sergeant spoke rather softly when he addressed Brianna, an amusing contrast to the courage with which the man confronted dragons and marauding giants. Glancing at Earl Dobbin, Runolf added, "Perhaps the lord mayor would like to come along?"

The earl scowled at this suggestion. "I'll stay with Brianna, in case something unfortunate should happen."

Brianna's bodyguard, who had spent the entire banquet standing at the wall behind the princess, stepped forward. "No need for that," he grunted. "That's why I'm here."

Like Tavis, Morten was a firbolg—but the semblance ended there. With a stout frame and a height of twelve feet, the bodyguard was as large for their race as the scout was small. He had a broad nose with an orb-shaped end, brown eyes the size of gruel bowls, and a mane of red hair that would have put a glacier bear to shame. Though his face showed no emotion, his eyes were as alert as those of an eagle, and the huge sword hanging from his belt suggested that if something unfortunate happened, Earl Dobbin's help would not be required to protect the princess.

Nevertheless, Tavis faced the cautious earl. "Do as

11

you think best, Lord Dobbin." He tried to keep the spite out of his voice, trusting the princess would note the lord mayor's cowardice without his help. "I doubt there'll be trouble, and I'm sure you'll enjoy the elderberry tarts the children have made."

Tavis motioned for two of his orphans to fetch the desserts, then he and Runolf stepped out the door. The inn's courtyard lay between the dining hall and the barn, a fresh layer of straw strewn over the ground. The square was blocked at one end by the sleeping lodge and at the other by a log stockade. In the center of the enclosure stood a well and drinking trough for the animals. Avner was nowhere to be seen, but the youth had closed and barred the gate.

"We're done waiting!" cried the guard's angry voice. "Open up, or we'll batter your gate down!"

Tavis raised his brow at the threat, for it was no secret in the village that a fire giant was staying at the inn. "Be patient," he advised. "I'm on my way."

The scout started toward the gate, his eyes searching the ground for any sign of a struggle. He saw a few clumps of straw that had been kicked up when he had escorted Brianna into the inn that morning, but little else. The yellow blanket had not been disturbed since.

Tavis slung his quiver over his shoulder, then pushed the crossbar out of its hooks. The beam had barely hit the ground before a dozen of the mayor's guards pushed the gates open and stormed into the courtyard. All were humans, wearing polished leather armor with the hawk's-head crest of Lord Mayor Dobbin. Half carried crossbows so large they could not be aimed without the aid of supporting crutches, and the others carried thick-shafted pikes. They arrayed themselves in a half circle around Tavis and Runolf.

The group leader pointed his crossbow at Tavis. "Give me the thief," he ordered. "Hand over the verbeeg, or we'll tear this inn down!"

"What verbeeg?" asked Runolf.

The guard narrowed his eyes. "This time you've gone too far, Burdun! When you send your thieves to Dobbin Manor, even the princess can't save you!"

"I have no thieves," Tavis responded. "Only children and our guests, one of whom happens to be a fire giant. No verbeegs."

The guard spun away. "Search the grounds," he ordered, waving his crossbow around the courtyard. "Take the buildings apart log by log!"

Brianna's voice rang out from the inn, stopping the search before it started. "That's hardly necessary," she called. "Verbeegs are not mice. They do not hide in nooks and crannies."

Tavis turned to see Brianna leading Morten and Earl Dobbin through the inn's massive doorway. The princess walked across the courtyard, her bodyguard and the earl a pace behind, and stopped at Tavis's side. She studied the lord mayor's men for a moment, then glared down at Earl Dobbin.

"Why are your guards beleaguering poor Tavis again?"

The lord mayor swallowed, then looked to the leader of his guards. "Stinson?"

"A verbeeg broke into your manor," Stinson explained. "We chased the marauder to these grounds, and the gate closed right after he entered. Someone had to be waiting for him."

Lady Brianna studied the ground near the gate. "Your men must be mistaken," she said. "I see no verbeeg tracks."

Tavis frowned. She was right. There were no heel marks, no barren patches where the straw had been scraped away, no hint at all that a heavy foot had entered the courtyard. Yet it had been only a few hours since Morten walked through the gate. The bodyguard's tracks should still have been visible.

Earl Dobbin studied Stinson, then asked, "How sure

are you of what you say?"

"I saw it with my own eyes," the guard replied. "We were less than a hundred paces down the lane."

The lord mayor looked back to Brianna. "I must insist. This isn't the first time my men have followed a thief to this inn." The earl pointed at his guards, dividing them into groups of four. "You search the dining hall, you take the lodge. The rest of us will search the barn."

"Lord Mayor, by the grace of my father's law you have the right to run your village as you wish," Brianna hissed. "But I promise you this: if your men break so much as a mug, you won't need to come to the ball this evening. You *won't* be the earl I pick as a husband."

The lord mayor winced, for many considered him the most likely choice. Tavis did not share that opinion, and with good reason—or at least with what seemed good reason to him. During the last few months, the princess had spent more time at the Weary Giant than with all of her noble suitors combined—not all of it with the children. Of course, the scout realized that the earls would be flabbergasted if she named him as her future husband, but he still had high hopes. There were few things Brianna enjoyed more than outraging the royal court, and she had even kissed his cheek a time or two.

After a moment, Earl Dobbin regained his composure and sneered in Tavis's direction. Still addressing Brianna, the lord mayor said, "I don't know why you would take the word of a commoner over that of a noble, but I'm about to prove that this firbolg is nothing but a knave."

With that, the earl started for the barn's closed door. Brianna and Tavis walked at his side, while Morten remained a pace behind his mistress. The lord mayor's guards brought up the rear of the procession. As they approached the barn, the scout noted that the straw had not been disturbed since it was laid down. Yet, he had watched Lady Brianna lead her horse into the barn just that morning. At least a few of the yellow stems should have been bent or snapped.

The lord mayor stopped before the door and motioned for his men to open it. As the guards obeyed, Tavis discreetly used his bow to scrape away some of the straw beneath his feet. The layer below was as yellow and fresh as the one on top, and a U-shaped depression marked where a horse's foot had crushed some stems. Someone—no doubt Avner—had spread a fresh covering of straw over this part of the courtyard.

Once the door was open, the lord mayor's guards stormed inside while everyone else waited in the courtyard. A great cacophony of scraping and braying arose as they shoved mangers about and pulled startled mules from their stalls—this in spite of the fact that such areas were too small to hide a verbeeg. From the back of the building came a series of muffled thuds as two guards stomped up the loft ladder. Tavis cringed, fearing the shout of an angry verbeeg would shake the barn, but the only cries were the indignant screeches of an owl.

Lady Brianna scowled at the clamor. "Earl Dobbin, you'd better hope they find your thief," she threatened. "Otherwise, I'll see to it that my father's men visit the same treatment on your hall."

"And if I find my thief?" the lord mayor demanded. "Will you name me as your husband then?"

"*Then* I will consider it," Brianna sneered.

With that, the princess stepped into the barn. Tavis followed, Morten close on his heels. The air reeked of fresh manure and straw. The mules, most owned by villagers who lacked room to board the beasts themselves, had gathered in the back corner, around a huge mound of straw someone had pushed down from the loft. Two of the lord mayor's guards were busily pounding the stall floors with the butts of their weapons, apparently searching for secret doors that did not exist, while the other two cursed and grunted in the loft, using their spears to probe the enormous mass of hay and straw stored there.

After surveying the scene, the lord mayor picked his way to the only stall that had not been opened. Above the gate the rear quarters of Lady Brianna's horse could be seen. The mare was black with white flecks, and had a snowy tail as fine as silk. The earl studied the pen for a moment, apparently unsure whether to open it.

"Don't do it, Earl," Tavis warned. "Blizzard is very particular about who touches her."

The lord mayor studied Tavis for a moment, then a cunning smile crossed his lips. "What better way to cover the verbeeg's hiding place than to place a spirited horse over it?" He raised the latch and cautiously opened the gate.

Morten started to utter a warning, but Brianna cut the firbolg short. "Be quiet," she hissed. "The fool was warned."

The lord mayor stood aside for a moment, watching the horse carefully. Blizzard's tail stopped twitching, and she did not move, even to stamp a foot. Finally, the earl gave Tavis a confident sneer and slipped into the stall.

Blizzard whinnied—once. When the intruder did not leave, she brought her hoof down on his foot and smashed her hindquarters into his chest. He screamed in pain and shoved her away, then backed, limping, out of the pen. The mare was not satisfied. She bucked her rump high into the air and kicked out with both rear feet. Her hooves caught him in the chest. The lord mayor's feet left the ground, and he sailed across the center passage, smashed into a stanchion post, and from there collapsed to the floor, his sable cape dangling in a manure gutter.

"You see? Tavis *does* tell the truth," Brianna said. The princess, who was a skilled healer, kneeled at the groaning earl's side. After running her hands over his torso, she pulled him roughly to his feet. "Your ribs aren't broken, just bruised. You'll survive."

"But I . . . can't . . . breathe!" the lord mayor gasped.

"No wonder. You smell like a dung heap!" Brianna taunted. She shoved him into the hands of his two guards. "Take your master and wash him, so he can catch his wind."

"What about the verbeeg?" asked a guard.

"There is no verbeeg," Brianna snapped. "Now perhaps you should do as I suggested."

The earl glared at Brianna and shook his head. "Finish the search," he rasped.

The guards resumed their havoc, though they were careful to probe the floor of Blizzard's stall only from the adjoining pens. It was not long before they shoved the mules aside to search the straw piled at the base of the loft ladder. Soon, one of them thrust his spear deep into the heap and withdrew a bloody tip.

"Got something!" he chortled.

The other guards pointed their weapons at the heap. "Come out, thief," ordered one.

Something stirred, then a sharp hiss sounded from the pile, filling the barn with a foul, sulfurous stench. Crying out in disgust, the guards doubled over and began to throw up.

In the next instant, a cacophony of braying and screeching filled the air. The mules bolted for the door, joined by a swarm of rats that had scurried from beneath the mangers and several owls that had dropped from the rafters. Morten stepped in front of Brianna, forcing the stampede to divide around her and consequently protecting Tavis, Runolf, and Earl Dobbin as well. Still, the lord mayor did not escape unscathed. The horrid smell caused him to retch, and the resultant heaving of his bruised ribs dropped him to his knees in pain.

"Glacier skunk!" Tavis gasped, more perplexed than sickened by the rancid stench. Glacier skunks rarely left their mountain homes, and he had never heard of one actually entering a village.

The others in the room were less curious than alarmed. Morten swept Brianna up in his arms and lumbered out the door with Runolf close on his heels. Next went the guards, doubled over, stumbling, and stinking like carcasses left in the sun to rot. They abandoned the lord mayor readily, for glacier skunks were to the smaller striped and spotted skunks what true giants were to giant-kin. When a glacier skunk's fumes hit a man, rivers of stinging tears poured from his eyes, hot embers filled his throat, and his stomach churned like a tumbling boulder. Sometimes he coughed blood, occasionally he stopped breathing, and, worst of all, the awful stench stayed with him until a cleric cast the proper spell to remove it.

When it became apparent Earl Dobbin did not have the strength to rise, Tavis scooped him up in one arm and left the barn. After handing the man to the cowardly guards, the scout pulled an arrow from his quiver and turned toward the barn, prepared to kill the skunk if it chose this moment to come running out.

The earl grasped Tavis's arm and pulled him back. "Don't think you've won, Burdun," he hissed. Tiny beads of sweat were running down the lord mayor's pained face, and he could take no more than a shallow breath. "You'll rue this day."

Lady Brianna took the lord mayor's hand off Tavis's arm. "Why? At least he knows the difference between a glacier skunk and a verbeeg." She sneered at the earl, then added, "I'm certain this afternoon's events will make amusing conversation this evening—especially the part where Tavis carries you from the barn because your own guards left you to the skunk."

The earl's face darkened to a stormy maroon. "Tell your tale if you wish," the lord mayor spat. "But be assured that if you continue to protect this cur and his thieves, it'll be my story that draws the last laugh."

Earl Dobbin pulled free of his men and staggered out the gate. His guards loitered in the courtyard for a few moments, debating whether or not to continue the search. Finally, when their fellows returned from the dining hall and the lodge without finding any sign of the verbeeg, they decided to leave rather than search the barn again.

Once the guards were gone, Lady Brianna turned to Tavis. "I've enjoyed your party tremendously."

"I'm sorry for the interruption."

Brianna grinned. "Don't be. It was most delightful to see Blizzard plant her hooves in the earl's ribs," she laughed. "But the time has come for me to leave. There's much I must do before the ball this evening."

Tavis, his stomach knotting in anxiety, frowned at mention of the ball. "Princess, I've a question before you go."

Brianna's expression changed to one of concern. "Yes?"

"Your father didn't invite me to the ball."

"He didn't invite any commoners," the princess said.

Tavis nodded. "I understand, but I'd like to know who you'll choose this evening."

Brianna's gaze fell to the ground, and with it Tavis's heart. Tonight, the princess had no intention of outraging her father's court.

"Whomever I choose, it will be for the good of the kingdom," the princess said, taking his hand. "I hope you'll support me in that decision."

"I'll always support you," Tavis replied, trying to hide his disappointment and failing. "But I doubt an unhappy princess will be good for the kingdom."

Tears welled in Brianna's eyes. "Damn you," she said. A sad smile crossed her lips, and she wiped her cheeks. "I was hoping you'd make this easy."

"I can't do that—yet," Tavis said. The princess's watery eyes gave him hope, for the scout saw in her

19

tears what Brianna had not actually said: that no matter what name she spoke tonight, the one in her heart would be Tavis. "But it's a long time between betrothal and marriage. A lot can happen."

"What are you going to do?" Brianna demanded. "Have yourself reborn as an earl?"

"If that's what it takes, yes," the firbolg replied, smiling. "But until then, the best I can do is kill that glacier skunk so you can retrieve Blizzard."

The scout turned to ask his mentor's help in luring the beast into the open, but Runolf was nowhere in sight. The sergeant had left without a word, vanishing from the courtyard as suddenly as he could disappear in the wilderness. It wasn't like Runolf to leave so rudely, but Tavis took no offense. The sergeant may have sensed something alarming as Earl Dobbin left, and decided to follow, not bothering to excuse himself because he did not want to draw attention to his departure.

Tavis glanced back to Brianna. "Give me a moment before coming for Blizzard," he said. "It wouldn't do to have you sprayed today."

The scout took a deep breath and went into the barn. The air remained close with foul-smelling vapors, but the stench had already begun to lose its potency. Blizzard was neighing angrily in her stall, whipping her head from side to side in an attempt to snap her reins free. Tavis advanced cautiously, watching rafters and mangers as well as the straw piled beneath the loft ladder. A glacier skunk, if that was truly what had hidden itself in his barn, was a cunning predator. It could down a bull elk—or a careless firbolg—as easily as a mountain lion could.

As Tavis approached to within ten paces of the ladder, something stirred beneath the straw pile. The scout pulled his bowstring back, then patiently waited for his prey to show itself before he loosed the shaft. A smaller hunter might have fired earlier, fearing that one arrow

20

would not stop a vicious glacier skunk, but a single shaft fired from Bear Driller would stop a charging moose.

A pair of steely gray eyes peered from beneath the straw. "Is the earl gone?" whispered a familiar voice.

Tavis lowered his bow. "Avner!"

The boy crawled from the pile and brushed the straw off his body. Behind him came a wolf-sized skunk with white fur and a pair of black stripes running down its back. It had a cone-shaped head with round ears, a shiny black nose, and four curved fangs drooping beneath its lip. The beast's claws were as long as a bear's and as sharp as a lynx's, while a needlelike barb protruded from the end of its furry tail. A red smear marked where its flank had been pierced by a guard's spear.

"What's happening here?" Tavis demanded.

Avner looked away. "You always say it's important to help others." He focused his gaze on the skunk. "Basil needed help."

As the youth spoke, the skunk sat down. Before Tavis's astonished eyes, it began to enlarge. The beast's fur thinned into a curly mass of hair, while its bushy tail disappeared altogether. Its hind legs straightened out and became more manlike. The forelegs grew longer and more slender, the claws retracting to become fingers and the dewclaw spreading outward to become a thumb. Finally, the creature's fangs receded, the snout narrowed into a long, crooked nose, and Tavis found himself looking at the hairy, naked form of a verbeeg.

The giant-kin rose and offered Tavis his hand. "I'm Basil of Lyndusfarne," he said. "I'm happy to make your acquaintance."

The verbeeg, with gangling arms, bowed legs, and huge feet as flat as a beaver's tail, stood a full head taller than Tavis. He had a typical build for his race, looking gaunt and half starved, with a distended belly and stooped shoulders. A scrawny beard hung from his chin, while a thick-lipped mouth gave him an affable—and oddly sly—smile. His eyebrows were as gray as his beard and twice as thick, bestowing upon him a surprisingly sagacious aspect for one with such a steeply sloped forehead.

Tavis kept his arrow pointed at the intruder's chest and made no move to take the proffered hand. He had met enough verbeegs to know their race deserved its devious reputation, and this one's unusual eloquence only made the scout more suspicious.

When it became apparent Tavis would not lower his arrow, the verbeeg glanced down at his nakedness and blushed. "I beg your pardon," he said. "How mindless of me."

Basil reached into the straw heap and pulled out a tattered robe of untanned bearskin. The garment stank almost as much as the rancid vapors that had driven everyone out of the barn earlier, but that did not stop the verbeeg from draping it over his scrawny shoulders.

"I always forget to put my clothes back on after such changes," he explained. "It's rather a disorienting experience."

"Are you some sort of werebeast?"

Basil shook his head. "Heavens no," he replied. "I'm just a runecaster—quite harmless, I assure you."

"Verbeegs don't have wizards."

"Watch," Basil replied. He traced a symbol in the air, filling the area with flickers of golden light. The sparkles rose and circled the verbeeg's head like a crown. "Now, which do you doubt—that I'm a verbeeg or a runecaster?"

"Neither, I guess," Tavis said. "What are you doing here?"

Basil looked at the tip of the arrow still pointed at his chest. "Leaving soon, it appears," he said. "But first, I have some business with your young friend."

Avner's face went pale. "We can forget about that," he said. "I'm just glad to help."

"Nonsense. An agreement is an agreement." The verbeeg reached into the straw heap. "Thieves' honor and all that."

Tavis lowered his bow and looked at Avner. "What agreement?"

Avner's only answer was a guilty look.

With a heavy groan, Basil pulled an enormous mooseskin sack from beneath the straw. "In return for hiding me, I promised Avner half the treasure I took from the lord mayor's house," the verbeeg explained. He turned the bag over and emptied an entire library of leatherbound books onto the barn's grimy floor. "You choose first, Avner."

"Books?" the youth shrieked. "I risked my life for ink and parchment?"

Basil's bushy eyebrows came together in irritation. "My boy, knowledge is the greatest treasure." The verbeeg stooped down and selected a book. "But since you have no conception of the riches before you, I'll choose first."

From outside the barn, Brianna called, "Tavis? What's happening in there?"

Tavis spun toward the barn door, which hung ajar so that he could not see into the courtyard. "Wait a moment!"

"Why?" Brianna demanded. Her voice sounded louder, as though she were approaching the barn. "Is something wrong?"

Tavis could not think of what to say. Like all firbolgs, it was nearly impossible for him to lie. He understood the concept well enough, but the strain of uttering false words affected his race more than any other giant-kin. If he said something untrue, his voice would crack, he would break out in a cold sweat, and his guilty conscience would not let him sleep for a tenday. Therefore, he did what most firbolgs did when they could not answer a question honestly: he did not reply.

Turning to Avner and Basil, Tavis whispered, "Into the loft with you, quick!"

Avner scrambled up in a flash, but Basil was too large to move quickly. He had to climb more slowly, gripping the side rails and taking great care to place each huge foot squarely on the narrow ladder treads. Cursing the verbeeg's clumsiness, Tavis grabbed an armful of straw and threw it over the books.

"Tavis?" demanded Brianna. "Why don't you answer?"

The innkeeper covered the last book, then looked up. Brianna and Morten stood at the door, squinting into the dim barn.

"Just a moment—"

Tavis was interrupted by the crack of a snapping board. A loud thud quickly followed, then Basil moaned in pain. The innkeeper wheeled around and saw the verbeeg sprawled on the floor, the loft ladder lying in pieces around him.

"How unfortunate," Basil groaned. He pushed himself into a sitting position, then grabbed a shard of gray board. "I feared I was too heavy for the ladder."

A pair of lumbering feet thundered across the barn floor as Morten rushed to Tavis's side. The bodyguard touched the tip of his great sword to Basil's throat and said nothing. Lady Brianna followed, though her steps fell silent before she reached the scout. Tavis turned around in time to see her pull a book from beneath the straw. She opened the cover to the title page.

"*A Full History of the Dobbins of Stagwick*, by Neville Dobbin, the thirty-fifth Earl of Stagwick," she read.

Tavis took a single step toward her. "Let me explain."

"You don't have to," Brianna replied. "I can see for myself what's going on here."

The princess drew her arm back and threw the book. It caught Tavis square in the forehead, breaking the binding and scattering leaves of parchment in every direction. The blow was incredibly powerful, much more forceful than the scout would have expected even for Brianna's large frame, and he found himself stumbling backward, until at last he tripped over Basil's feet and crashed down at the verbeeg's side.

"Please, Brianna. I know this looks bad—"

"You played me for a fool, Tavis," the princess snapped. "While I was protecting you from Earl Dobbin, you were looting Stagwick—and I was blind to what everyone else saw as plainly as the sun in the sky!"

"No!" Tavis started to rise, but quickly found the tip of Morten's sword at his throat. "That's not what happened!"

Brianna shook her head angrily. "How could you do this?"

With that, she stepped into Blizzard's stall and untied the mare. "I'll send someone for the children this evening. I can only hope you haven't corrupted them beyond redemption." She started toward the door and added, "I expect you to be gone by then. It will spare me an abundance of humiliation—and save you several decades of torture in my father's dungeon."

Though Brianna's voice was cracking with grief, she did not look back.

☙ 2 ☙
Coggin's Rise

Blizzard snorted, then tossed her head and slowed from a gallop to a trot, angrily stamping the ground each time her front hooves came down. Brianna reluctantly reined her mount to a stop. She leaned forward and stroked the mare's sleek neck.

"What is it, girl?"

The horse tipped her ears forward and flared her nostrils. After testing the air for a moment, Blizzard's muscles tensed, and she became as motionless as a statue.

Scowling, Brianna pulled a silver-handled axe from its saddle sheath. A cool mountain breeze hissed down from the aspen-covered slope ahead. Though she smelled nothing but damp leaves on its breath, the princess knew her mount well enough to realize Blizzard had caught the scent of danger. She laid her weapon across her lap and, remaining as still as her horse, studied the path before her.

A canopy of small, heart-shaped leaves hung over the road. They quivered incessantly in the light breeze, flashing waxy green and dusty silver, filling the air with a rustle just loud enough to cloak the whisper of creeping feet. Supporting this shimmering vault were hundreds of papery white tree trunks, rising from a steep, boulder-strewn slope with ample cover for an ambush.

This was Coggin's Rise, named for an ancient earl who had been found on its slopes mysteriously torn limb from limb, and Brianna had learned better than to travel it recklessly. Once, she had nearly lost Blizzard when a cave bear sprang from among the boulders along the trail, and another time a marauding mountain giant had

26

chased her from the base of the hill all the way to Castle Hartwick. In spite of her eagerness to return home, she thought it wise to let her bodyguard inspect the wood.

Brianna twisted around to look at Morten, lumbering up the trail fifty paces back. After leaving Tavis's inn, she had ridden hard for half an hour, and the effort of keeping pace with Blizzard had nearly done the firbolg in. He wore his helmet pushed half off his head and his leather armor fastened too loosely to offer protection. His buckler hung across his back, slung in place by a rope strung beneath his armpits, and his feet had grown so heavy that he stumbled over the slightest obstacle. He kept his eyes fixed on the ground, and he was panting so hard the princess saw his chest heave each time he gasped for breath.

A guilty pang shot through Brianna's breast, for her anger at Tavis had overwhelmed her concern for the firbolg. Even a fire giant would have found it difficult to keep pace with Blizzard for more than a league, and the princess had forced Morten to run several times that distance. It was a good thing something had alarmed her horse, or she might have run her poor bodyguard to death. It might even be possible that an apology was in order.

Blizzard snorted again, vanquishing all thoughts of penance. A crow screeched, then the crack of a snapping branch ricocheted through the aspen trees. Catching a faint whiff of something sour and rancid, like curdled milk, Brianna twisted around to face the forest. She saw a black flash as the crow rose through the quivering canopy of leaves, but that was all. Among the white trunks, nothing stirred.

Still, the smell did not vanish, and Brianna glanced over her shoulder. "Will you hurry, Morten?" she called. "I smell something."

The firbolg's chin rose and he sniffed at the breeze, but he did not seem to smell anything. Nevertheless, from somewhere he summoned the strength to sprint. A dozen thudding steps later, he stopped at Brianna's side and braced his hands on his knees. He lifted his head and tried to catch the scent, but he was gasping so hard he could not draw air through his nose.

"I don't smell anything," he wheezed.

"The odor's not very strong," Brianna said, "but it's sour."

"Maybe bear or elk," Morten suggested. "They both stink."

Brianna scowled. "Wouldn't I know if it was an animal?" As a priestess of Hiatea, she was familiar with all the creatures of the wild, able to identify any one of them by their tracks, droppings, calls—or scent. "This is too rancid. It's more like a goatherd's cheese hut."

The firbolg went pale, the fatigue draining from his face as though he had just risen from a nap in a shady snowbank. Fixing his gaze on the woods ahead, he raised himself to his full height and tightened the buckles of his armor. "Ogre!" he hissed.

"You can't be serious," Brianna scoffed. She found herself craning her neck to look up at her bodyguard, despite the fact that she still sat upon her big mare's back. "No ogre would dare come this close to Castle Hartwick."

Evidently, the firbolg did not share her conviction. He pulled his helmet down and drew his huge sword. "Wait here," he said. "I'll scout the wood."

"We'll go together," Brianna countered. She was far from convinced that something as dangerous as an ogre lurked in the woods ahead. "I don't have time to wait."

"Better late than dead," the firbolg grunted. "Besides, the dance doesn't start until dusk. We've got plenty of time."

"I *will* have to bathe and dress," Brianna snapped. "Or do you suggest I enter the ball smelling of horse and trail?"

"You weren't worried about that before you found Tavis hiding the verbeeg," Morten replied. "You just want to get home so you can cry."

"Cry over a firbolg?" Brianna scoffed. Despite her retort, the princess felt the tears welling in her eyes. Looking away, she added, "It's the orphans that concern me. Tavis may try to take them with him."

"Why?" asked Morten. "They'd only make his life harder."

"Fire giants will trade silver and gold for human children."

Morten shook his head. "No firbolg would do such a thing."

"We have no idea what Tavis might or might not do, but it's better not to take chances." Brianna's tone was at once certain and regretful. "Besides, Tavis isn't really a firbolg. He was raised among our kind, not yours."

It was common knowledge that Tavis had been born under what the firbolgs called a "red moon," meaning his mother had died in childbirth. In accordance with the tribe's stern code of justice, the infant had been held responsible for the death and banished. A visiting bear trapper had carried the babe to Stagwick's only lodge, where the kindly Isa Wirr had taken the child to raise among the kingdom's many other orphans.

"It doesn't matter who raised him," Morten said. "Tavis's blood is firbolg. It'd freeze in his veins if he tried to sell those children into slavery."

"There's nothing I'd like to believe more." The princess had to struggle to speak around the catch in her throat. "But we can't ignore that verbeeg thief. If firbolg blood's so important, how could Tavis lie to us about him?"

Morten scowled, unable to offer an explanation.

"I know how," Brianna said. "He learned from the humans he grew up with. And when he joined the border patrol, he learned to do worse things."

Morten shook his head. "No. Tavis was trained by Runolf Saemon, and I hear Runolf's a good man," he said. "The king relies on him."

"My father relies on all his soldiers. That doesn't mean he trusts them," Brianna countered. "As for Runolf, I don't know what to make of him. He seemed to be avoiding me."

"He was nervous," Morten replied. "Like most men when they meet you for the first time."

"Perhaps, or maybe he was nervous because he knew Tavis to be a thief." The words left Brianna with a queasy, empty feeling in her stomach, but the princess had learned long ago to trust her mind over her emotions. "There are plenty of humans who think little enough of stealing to look the other way when their friend is the thief."

Morten considered this for a time, then shrugged. "You'd know better than me," he said. "But if you're so worried about the orphans, why leave them with Tavis in the first place?"

"Because Tavis Burdun has slain frost giants with that bow of his," Brianna replied. "And getting ourselves killed would not save the children."

Morten's eyes flashed in indignation. "I'm every bit that runt's match," he growled. "I'd cleave his skull in a blow."

Brianna grimaced at the image of her bodyguard's huge sword slicing through the scout's brain. "A moment ago, you were defending Tavis," the princess observed. "Now you're ready to split his head?"

"All I said was I could," Morten said, his petulant tone betraying his injured pride. "There's a difference."

"I didn't mean to insult your fighting skills." It was as close to an apology as Brianna would utter. "But whoever won, it would do the children no good to witness the combat. Tavis is the only father they know, and the sight of him killing or being killed would be a heavy bur-

30

den for such young hearts."

"Dobbin Manor has fifty men. Not even Tavis would fight so many," Morten said. "Why not demand the earl's help?"

"Because I don't want the lord mayor as a husband," the princess explained. "And it'd be just like the ruthless swine to keep the children hostage until I married him."

"How could he do that?" Morten demanded, his brow furrowed in puzzlement. "That would violate the law!"

Brianna rolled her eyes at the firbolg's naiveté. "Earls know many paths around the law," the princess said. "Which is why we must hurry. The only way to ensure the children's safety is to send a company of father's guards back before anyone—whether it be Tavis or Earl Dobbin—can take them from the inn."

With that, the princess urged her mount forward.

Morten caught Blizzard by the mane. The horse swung her head around with teeth bared, but the firbolg stiffened his arm and held her steady. The mare's mouth snapped shut two feet shy of his throat. She whinnied in anger and tried to jerk free of her captor's grasp, but even Blizzard was not strong enough to overpower the bodyguard.

"I can't let you enter the wood until I've had a look," Morten said. "If you can't wait, we'll just have to go back."

"Then make your search quick," Brianna snapped. "If you let Tavis disappear with those children, I'll replace you with a fomorian. He might not fight well, but he'd be better company."

Morten chuckled at the ludicrous threat. Fomorians were the most hideous and wicked of all giant-kin, with deformed bodies and twisted, evil personalities. Comparing one to a firbolg was like comparing a turkey buzzard to an eagle; although they had descended from the same species, at heart the two were as different as could be.

"I'll hunt the ambusher down fast as I can."

The firbolg pulled his shield off his back and buckled his helmet, then strode forward. As he entered the aspen grove, the breeze rose and the flashing aspen leaves rustled more loudly, reminding Brianna of a sound she had heard a hundred times before: the tense murmur of the earls and their wives waiting for her father to enter the banquet hall. It was a sound as full of dread as it was of hope, for such gatherings were polite forms of battle, where the prestige of great families rose and fell on the slippery course of well-told jests or foolish slips of the tongue. But in the next few moments, she reminded herself, it would be lives and limbs that were maimed, not the reputations of pompous and vain men.

Brianna watched Morten creep deeper into the wood, his helmeted head swiveling back and forth in search of the ogre. The firbolg held his buckler high, so that it covered his flank from the chin down to the ribs. He waved his right arm slowly up and down, keeping the flat of his sword turned outward as if ready to slap away a flying dart or stone. Every now and then, he stopped and raised his nose to test the air for his quarry's scent, but the princess saw no indication that her bodyguard smelled anything unusual. By the time Morten had advanced fifty paces into the grove, Brianna's patience was at an end. If something dangerous was lurking among the aspens, the firbolg would have flushed it out, and now he was just wasting her time.

Morten suddenly stopped. He spun around and raised his buckler over his head. At the same time, Brianna heard a small bowstring strum from the forest canopy. A dark shaft streaked down from the quivering leaves and ricocheted off the shield with a sharp *ping*. The firbolg let out a shout that the princess could not understand, then swung his great sword at a nearby tree. His blade bit deep, but fell far short of cleaving through the thick trunk. Still holding his buckler over his head, he threw himself at the bole, slamming his shoulder into it so hard that the aspen shuddered from base to crown.

Brianna heard the bowstring throb a second time, and another arrow bounced off Morten's shield. Searching the treetops for the firbolg's attacker, the princess saw nothing but a lanky shadow lurking among the highest branches, its true shape blurred by flashing aspen leaves.

Morten jerked his sword free and swung again at the white bole. This time, yellow chips flew in all directions, and Brianna saw a wedge-shaped void appear in the wood. The firbolg smashed his shoulder into the trunk. A sharp crack rang through the forest and, as the aspen toppled, the shadowy figure in the high branches dropped out of the tree.

The ogre looked almost as large as Brianna's body-guard, with long shoots of leafy boughs sticking out from his body at all angles. As the princess screamed a warning, the dark shape slammed into Morten's shield. The firbolg grunted and collapsed, his attacker still on top. A spindly arm raised a stone mace above Morten's head and brought the weapon down. There was a sick thud, then a barbarous chortle tolled through the forest. The mace rose again.

Brianna hefted her bejewelled axe. Before she could spur Blizzard forward, her bodyguard smashed his steel buckler into his attacker's bony face. A loud crunch shot through the grove, and the ogre pitched over backward. He rolled away, only to spring up as Morten clambered to his own feet.

The princess held her mount steady. The ogre stood with his back to her, ripping boughs of leafy camouflage off his body. His skinny torso was haggard and stooped, with hunched shoulders and gangling arms that ended in huge, gnarl-fingered hands. The brute was a striking contrast to the bloated churls that travelers from the south described when they spoke of ogres. And, judging by tales old earls liked to tell, he would also be much more dangerous. Unlike their oafish cousins of the warm lands, northern ogres were so vicious and cunning that even giants avoided them.

Brianna could have charged the brute from behind, but knew better than to try. Any attempt to help now would only confuse and upset Morten, for her father had given them both very clear instructions regarding combat: under no circumstances was Brianna to join in battle. If the danger looked too great, she was to escape while Morten sacrificed himself. It was an arrangement that seemed perfectly reasonable to the king and the firbolg, but one the princess resented deeply. She was quite capable of holding her own in a battle. Not only had she been trained with axe and sword since childhood, she was also blessed with the supernatural strength of the Hartwick line, a mysterious legacy that made her almost as powerful as firbolgs.

Brianna heard an eerie, low-pitched rattle break from the aspen grove, then the ogre charged, at the same time hurling his weapon at Morten's head. The firbolg raised his shield and sent the mace clanging away harmlessly. In the same instant, the ogre leaped into the air and flew feetfirst at the princess's bodyguard, wrapping his legs around the firbolg's burly thighs. The lanky brute gave a mighty twist, already reaching for a bone dagger hanging from his belt.

Had Morten been smaller or his attacker larger, the tactic might have toppled him. As it was, the bodyguard simply stepped back with one leg, bracing himself and at the same time breaking free of his foe. The ogre dropped to his back. Brianna heard a muffled crack as the firbolg stomped on the brute's chest, then her bodyguard drew his sword across the ambusher's throat and finished him.

Brianna nudged Blizzard forward. "That didn't take long!" she called. "Perhaps my father's guards will reach Stagwick in time to see Tavis off—"

"Stay there!" Morten ordered.

The firbolg scowled at Brianna until she stopped moving, then peered into the grove and sniffed the air. He stepped off the road and trotted deeper into the wood, fading into the white forest like a ghost. The princess sat listening to the irregular cadence of cracking sticks that marked his passage, until the muted popping and snapping grew so distant that she could no longer distinguish the sounds from the rustling of the aspen leaves.

Brianna waited with growing impatience, becoming more convinced with each passing minute that Morten was deliberately wasting her time. Coggin's Rise stood in the center of Hartsvale, far from the dangerous borderlands where giants and their kin came to raid. It was almost unthinkable that one ogre had snuck so far into the valley; she could not believe a whole party had. Still, she resisted the temptation to go after her bodyguard, reminding herself that Morten knew far more than she about this particular adversary.

Normally, that would not have been so. The princess made it her business to know her kingdom's enemies, potential or otherwise, better than she knew her friends. But in this case, it had been impossible to earn her knowledge firsthand. No ogre had entered the kingdom since the War of Harts, a three-year battle of succession in which her father had hired ogre mercenaries to vanquish the power-hungry forces of his evil twin, Dunstan. After the war, the new king had wisely paid his hirelings a generous bonus, in return eliciting a pledge that they would leave Hartsvale undisturbed as long as Camden reigned. Until today, no ogre had violated that promise.

Nor had Brianna had opportunity to study ogres outside the valley. Like most of her father's subjects, she had passed her entire life without leaving Hartsvale. The kingdom sat in an alpine valley located in the heart of the Ice Mountains, known locally as the Ice Spires. The peaks were as huge as they were forbidding, enclosing the vale inside an immense rampart of glaciers and granite that could not be climbed. Even from here, near the center of the kingdom, Brianna could see the distant white crags looming in all directions, rising up to scratch at the sky like the jagged merlons of some vast citadel.

Of course, there were rifts in the wall: narrow passes that snaked their way through winding canyons and over treacherous glaciers before dropping into distant valleys. But, aside from a handful of adventurous traders with more greed than wisdom, few dared to travel such trails. The paths were as dangerous as they were long, crossing and recrossing raging rivers, traversing sheer cliffs a thousand feet above ground, and twining through endless marshes filled with water so cold a man's lips would turn blue from drinking it.

Not the least of these hazards were the giants and their kin. They infested the Ice Spires in all directions, with the nomadic frost giants wandering the Great Glacier to the north and the fire giants plaguing the dwarves of Citadel Adbar to the south. To the west, the furtive voadkyn abided in the frigid depths of the Coldwood, while the ascetic stone giants of the east claimed the high cliffs overlooking the vast wastes of the desert Anauroch. And there were at least a dozen more giant tribes in the region, tilling the earth of the deep fertile valleys, hunting in the conifer forests on the mountain slopes, and lurking in the high desolate passes that were the only paths over sheer-faced ridges of solid granite. From Hartsvale, it was literally impossible to travel in any direction without crossing the territory of at least one giant tribe, and foolish adventurers who tried to do so without the aid of an experienced guide seldom survived the attempt.

Brianna's wait came to an abrupt end when a distant thud sounded in the aspen stand. The noise was so faint that Brianna could hardly hear it, much less tell the exact direction it came from. There was a muffled scream, then another, and finally a chorus of rasping battle cries resembling the one the ogre had made before dying. The sounds were followed by several more thuds, then Morten's deep voice bellowed out of the forest, full of bloodlust and anger.

The lady realized that her bodyguard had found what he was searching for, and from the sound of it he was outmanned by a fair amount. Though she knew her father would want her to return to Stagwick and demand Earl Dobbin's protection, Brianna planted her heels in Blizzard's ribs, urging the mare into the grove. As they passed the corpse Morten had left lying in the road, Brianna got her first close glimpse of an ogre.

Save for the tusklike teeth protruding from beneath his lower lip, the brute resembled a huge, loutish man with a jutting chin and floppy, oversized ears. From the septum of his crooked nose hung a bronze ring, while his eyes, glazed with death, had purple irises and white pupils. He wore a wolf-skull headdress that had slipped halfway off his lumpy head to reveal a mass of greasy hair pulled into a tight topknot.

Blizzard snorted, springing away as if to escape the disgusting ogre smell. Brianna guided the mare to where Morten had left the path and easily spied her bodyguard's footprints, a series of deep depressions in the mossy ground. The princess urged the mare into a gallop, keeping her gaze locked on the firbolg's trail and trusting her mount to pick a safe path. Soon, the sour smell of ogre filled the air. Brianna looked up, but the woods were so thick that she still could not see the battle.

Morten cried out in pain, then rasping battle cries rattled from several ogre throats and a series of loud blows reverberated through the aspens. First one, then a second, third, and fourth ogre howled in agony. The crack of a falling tree echoed through the stand, followed by a tremendous crash and an inhuman screech. Then the battle fell abruptly silent, and Brianna found herself listening to nothing but rustling aspen leaves and the crashing footfalls of her charging horse. She slowed Blizzard to a walk, knowing that the ogre survivors—if there were any—would be able to hear her coming now that the battle had quieted.

Morten's voice rang through the wood. "It safe, Brianna." Like his message, his tone was strained and almost incoherent, as if he were too exhausted to speak—or, more likely, was wounded. "You come . . ." The firbolg's voice trailed off.

Brianna urged Blizzard into a gallop. "I'll be right there, Morten," she called. "And thanks be to Hiatea that you survived."

Although Morten did not answer, the princess was able to follow the terrible smell of ogre bodies to the top of a rocky bluff overlooking the trail. As she approached, Brianna saw a wide band of black arrows scattered across the hillside and the bloody corpses of seven ogres strewn among the brown boulders that lay half buried in the mossy ground. Like the first ogre she had seen, they had purple eyes and topknots of greasy hair.

Her bodyguard sat slumped against the broken trunk of a toppled aspen tree, his dented buckler lying at his feet. There was a long bloody rift in the side of his helmet, his eyes were closed, and his breath came in short, shallow gasps.

As she rode over to Morten, Brianna saw that he had done his work well. A couple of the ogres had lost arms or legs to the firbolg's mighty sword and now lay in pools of foul-smelling blood so deep there could be none left in their bodies. The heads of two more lay several paces from their gaunt bodies, and a few bodies had been cleaved nearly in two. One ogre lay beneath the crown of the toppled aspen tree, his crumpled body twisted into an impossible shape.

Reaching Morten's side, Brianna dismounted. She slipped her silver-handled axe into her belt and grabbed her waterskin off her saddle, then began to examine the firbolg's injuries. A broken arrow shaft protruded from one of his massive thighs and his leather breastplate was gouged and slashed in a dozen places, but the armor had spared him any deep cuts.

Brianna unbuckled the chin strap and gently lifted off the bloody helmet. Morten's red hair was matted with blood, but that did not in itself alarm her. All scalp wounds bled freely, even those that were only superficial. She poured water over the slash to wash away the blood. To her surprise, the cut was neither large nor deep, only about as long as her thumb and so shallow that she could not even see the white bone of his skull.

Brianna frowned. "What's wrong, you great pansy?" she asked, half joking. "A little cut like that shouldn't bother you."

She placed her thumbs on his eyelids and drew them up. His pupils were both the same size and quickly retracted as if in response to the sudden daylight, but they were glassy and unfocused, like those of someone who had drunk too much wine. Brianna let his eyes close, then grabbed a nearby arrow to examine the tip. It was coated with yellow paste.

"Poison!"

Brianna took Morten's dagger and pushed the blade into his thigh. When she felt the point slip past the arrowhead, she twisted the knife and began to pry, at the same time using her free hand to pull the broken shaft out of his leg. Tossing the vile thing aside, she squeezed the puncture's red-rimmed edges to promote bleeding.

That done, she removed her silver necklace, from which hung her goddess's symbol: a golden amulet shaped like a flaming sphere. She placed this talisman inside her waterskin, then turned her eyes toward the sky.

"Valorous Hiatea, bless this water, so that it may purify this warrior's spirit and make him worthy of your healing magic."

A gentle gurgle arose inside her waterskin, then the

sides puffed out and white vapor gushed from the open neck. Brianna poured the steaming contents over her patient's injuries. Dark bubbles frothed up from the wounds, covering Morten's skull and leg with thick, brown-streaked foam. The princess waited patiently as the lather cleansed Morten's spirit of wicked thoughts and emotions.

Although the process took many moments, Brianna thought no less of her bodyguard. She had learned not to judge people by impurities of the heart. All men, even firbolgs, waged a shadow war with the evil aspects of their own natures. Whether or not they won was far more important than the struggle itself. And Morten always won his battles—even those with himself.

At last, the blessed water stopped frothing and turned more or less clear, spilling from the firbolg's wounds in red-tinged runnels. Now that Morten's spirit was ready to receive Hiatea's magic, Brianna worked quickly to heal the bodyguard. She scraped a piece of white bark off the tree stump at her patient's back and shredded it into a stringy mass. The princess laid this over the puncture in the firbolg's thigh, then pressed Hiatea's symbol onto the dressing.

"My goddess, take mercy on this courageous firbolg. Banish from his blood the vile poison of the ogre's arrow, that he may live to serve you again."

Brianna spoke the mystical syllables that actually cast the healing spell. A wave of searing energy arose beneath the princess's fingers, and when she pulled her hand away Hiatea's symbol was glowing yellow. The flames of the talisman turned orange and flickered like true fire. The bark dressing began to smoke, then erupted into a red blaze.

The magical fire whirled down into the puncture wound, then Brianna saw the veins glowing red beneath the firbolg's thick skin. Morten's eyes popped open, and he sat bolt upright. A deafening scream of pain burst from his throat and continued until the crimson glow of Hiatea's magic faded from his body. Only then did he close his eyes and collapse against the tree trunk again.

"Thank you, Huntress," Brianna whispered. "Now, let us hope Blizzard has the strength to drag him home."

The princess slipped her necklace over her head and rose. Intending to fetch a rope from her saddlebags, she turned toward her horse—then screamed.

Between her and Blizzard stood a huge ogre with skin as brown as an acorn. He was both taller and huskier than the dead ones Brianna had seen so far, almost as big and burly as Morten. He wore the skin of an enormous white bear over his shoulders and a human thigh bone through his greasy topknot. The princess could not imagine how a creature so large and awkward-looking had crept up on her so silently.

The ogre motioned at her with a single black claw. "Come, Brianna. It safe." The voice belonged to Morten, not to the ugly, stooped creature from which it issued.

Brianna pulled her hand axe from her belt, at the same time glancing at Blizzard. The mare stood a few paces beyond the newcomer, her ears tipped forward and her flanks trembling with tension. The princess shifted her attention back to the ogre.

"How do you know my name?" she demanded.

The ogre smiled, revealing a mouth filled with ugly orange fangs. "Someone tell me," he replied. "Now put axe down and come here. We not supposed to hurt you."

Brianna heard a bough of aspen leaves rustle far above. Another ogre dropped to the ground behind her, filling the air with the rancid, sour-milk odor of his race. The princess gagged, then felt an oily hand seizing her wrist. The brute slipped his other arm around her waist and lifted her off the ground.

Revolted by the beast's vile touch, Brianna brought her foot up as hard as she could, smashing the hard bone of her heel into the ogre's soft loins. At the same time, the princess whipped her head back and bashed the back of her skull into her foe's nose. She heard the satisfying crunch of collapsing cartilage, then the brute roared in pain and dropped her.

Brianna turned, swinging her axe at the height of her own head. The blade took her attacker in the arm, slicing through tendon and bone to truncate the arm just above the elbow. Again, the ogre howled. He stumbled back, his purple eyes glazed with shock and his jaw hanging agape at the astonishing force of the princess's blow. Giving him no chance to recover, Brianna leveled her foot at his knee in a vicious roundhouse kick. The joint snapped like kindling, and the ogre toppled to the ground.

The princess spun around, expecting to find the other brute already upon her. Instead, he was watching her with a bemused grin on his lips.

"I hear you strong for woman," he said.

Brianna narrowed her eyes. "Who told you that?"

Instead of answering, the ogre raised his hands and rasped the deep-throated dirge of a shaman's spell.

Brianna whipped her axe at his head. The shaman ducked, and the weapon buried itself in the bole of an aspen. The princess did not care. The attack had interrupted his spell, buying her the precious time she needed to escape.

Brianna whistled once, then called, "Blizzard, come!"

The big mare reared up and pushed forward. She brought her two front hooves down squarely on the ogre's shoulders, driving him to the ground. With an angry neigh, she bounded forward and presented her left flank to her mistress. Brianna grabbed the saddle horn and pulled herself up.

With unbelievable speed, the shaman leaped up and reached for Brianna. Pushing one foot into her stirrup, the princess raised the other and thrust it at the brute's chest. The blow landed with a solid thump, and the ogre tumbled backward.

Brianna planted her heels in her mount's flanks. As the mare sprang forward, two more ogres dropped out of the aspen trees a short distance ahead. They drew their bows back, leveling their black arrows at Blizzard's breast. The princess jerked the reins hard, turning away as the strings throbbed. The dark shafts hissed away into the forest, then Brianna found herself sailing through the air as her mount leaped a toppled tree.

To her horror, she saw two more ogres rising from hiding places behind the fallen bole. Both brutes tossed their bows aside and leaped for her mount's front legs. Blizzard crashed into them with a tremendous thump, and for a moment Brianna thought the big mare would bowl the pair over.

Then she felt Blizzard's head drop. The mare's rear hooves clattered off the fallen tree with a hollow clacking, and from between the horse's ears, Brianna saw the ground rising fast. The princess released the reins and pulled her feet from the stirrups, then pitched over the mare's head into a patch of mossy ground. She tumbled head over heels, coming to a stop only when she slammed into a granite boulder.

Brianna tried to gather her feet and rise, but the struggle was too much. She had lost her wind, and her ribs were exploding with pain as she fought to regain her breath. Her head was swimming. Her body ached in a hundred places, though thankfully nowhere did she feel the sharp agony of a broken bone.

Still, Brianna was hardly in a good position, and she would need help to escape. She raised her hands toward her necklace, but stopped when ogre feet began to surround her. Several leathery hands grabbed her wrists and jerked her off the ground. Brianna found herself suspended between two ogres, her arms drawn painfully taut and the white pupils of the angry shaman glaring into her eyes.

"You want we should hurt you?" The ogre slapped

Brianna across the face. Her head snapped to the side, and she felt a tooth fly from her mouth. "We do it good. All same to us."

The shaman hit her again, this time smashing his fist into her midsection. Brianna's stomach revolted at the abuse, and she vomited on the ground. A dozen paces away, Blizzard whinnied in anger and struggled to her feet. Glaring at the ogre's back, the mare started forward.

"No, Blizzard!" Brianna called. The command came out half garbled, for her mouth was full of blood and her cheek badly swollen. "Stand!"

When the horse obeyed, the ogre nodded his head approvingly. "That better," he commented. "Smart girl."

The shaman looked at two of his followers, then nodded at the horse. They nocked arrows and raised their bows.

"No!" Brianna yelled. "Run, Blizzard!"

Her warning proved unnecessary. By the time the pair released their bowstrings, Blizzard had leaped over the fallen tree and was galloping through the forest at top speed. The shaman watched until the mare vanished behind the white trunks of the aspen trees, then he shrugged.

"Too bad." He turned back to Brianna. "Horse taste good."

Brianna sighed, relieved that she would not have to watch the ogres butcher her beloved Blizzard, then turned her attention back to the troubles at hand.

"Someone sent you for me. Who?" the princess demanded. "Whatever he's paying, my father will double it."

The shaman looked at her loathingly, then pulled a length of thick, braided-leather cord from inside his cloak. Her two captors pinned her to the ground, then he silently began to bind her hands.

❖ 3 ❖
A Sudden Farewell

Tavis dropped his rucksack beside the well and paused to take one last look at the Weary Giant. The place could hardly be called a mansion, but the doors hung straight and storm shutters flanked every window. He was leaving the inn better than he had found it, and that gave him some small comfort.

The scout had not even considered remaining in Stagwick. With the princess herself obliged to speak against him, pleading his case before the king could only lead to disaster for all concerned. Brianna would be publicly disgraced for associating with a thief, a pall of suspicion would be cast over the orphans, and Tavis would have his hands lopped off as punishment for a crime he had not committed. The only thing to do was obey the princess's wish and leave Hartsvale as soon as possible.

"Will you truly miss this place so much?" asked Basil. The verbeeg stood next to Tavis, his sack of stolen books slung over his shoulder. "I'd think a man of your nature would find the life of an innkeeper a trifle boring."

Tavis did not look at the verbeeg. "I'll miss the children," he said. "And if you think helping those in need could ever bore me, you know nothing of my nature."

"Firbolgs!" Basil shook his head in bewilderment. "It's beyond me how such a naive race prospers."

Across the courtyard, Avner stepped from the lodge, followed by the other orphans. They had wrapped their possessions into woolen blankets and slung the small bundles over their shoulders; their feet were clad in heavy moose-hide boots Tavis had made for them. Each child carried an empty waterskin, and they all had grim, determined looks on their small faces.

"Is that all you're taking with you to Princess Brianna's?" Tavis asked. "You're going to be there a long time."

"We're not going to the castle," answered Avner. He motioned for the others to fill their waterskins. "You don't think we'd abandon you just because you got in trouble, do you?"

Tavis smiled sadly. "Of course not," he replied. "But you can't come with me."

"Why not?" Avner demanded. He dropped his bundle on the ground and untied it. "We've got everything we need: wool blankets, warm clothes, daggers—"

"The Ice Spires are no place for children," Tavis said. "Brianna can take much better care of you in her castle than I can in the mountains."

"No!" Avner yelled. "I'm not going with her. She's the one who's sending you away!"

"She thinks I'm a thief." Tavis's voice grew more stern. "And we both know why she believes that."

"So I'll tell her what really happened," Avner offered.

Tavis shook his head. "Someday, but she won't believe you now," he said. "She'd think you were trying to protect me."

"Then she's stupid," Avner sniffed.

"Why? Because she knows you'd lie for me?"

Avner looked at the ground. "I wouldn't be lying," he answered, dodging the question. "It's the truth."

"After what happened, we can't expect her to believe that," Tavis replied. "So go to the castle and do as the princess says. She cares for you as much as I do."

"But I don't care for her," Avner objected. "I like you."

"Then you'll do as Tavis says," said Livia. At fourteen, she was the second oldest of the orphans, and would soon blossom into a beautiful young woman. Already, she had riveting brown eyes and an alluring smile. Livia looked at the other children, then said, "Life's going to be hard enough on Tavis without us to watch over. If we really care for him, we'll go to Castle Hartwick."

Tavis nodded at Livia. "That's right. Knowing you're all safe will make my life much easier." He kneeled on the ground and opened his arms wide. "Now let's say good-bye."

As the children stepped forward to embrace Tavis, a loud whinny sounded in the street outside. The cadence of galloping hooves echoed through the gate, then Blizzard's speckled form streaked into the courtyard. A mantle of white lather covered the mare from her muzzle down to her breast, and her eyes were mad with fatigue. She rushed to within a few paces of Tavis and reared, neighing madly.

Tavis pushed the orphans away, then grabbed Basil's shoulder and positioned the verbeeg in front of the children. He moved toward the mare slowly, his palms turned toward the horse to show her he was carrying nothing dangerous.

"Where's Brianna?" he asked in a soft voice. "Let me come close to look at your saddle."

The mare lashed out with her front hooves, then dropped to her feet and ran to the gate. She stopped there and fixed a black eye on Tavis, snorting impatiently as she caught her breath.

"That horse seems quite mad," observed Basil.

"She's certainly upset," Tavis replied. He took his sword belt off his rucksack and strapped it around his waist, then picked up Bear Driller and slung a quiver of arrows over his shoulder. "Something must have happened to Brianna."

Tavis started toward the gate, but Avner caught him by the arm. "Think this through," the boy said. "Brianna's the one who's sending you away. It'd be unfortunate if something has befallen her, but do you really—"

"Avner, don't even say it," Tavis interrupted. He

glared down at the youth. "How could you wish misfortune on someone who's done as much for you as Princess Brianna?"

Avner's cheeks flushed. "You're right. I'm sorry." He took a slim dagger out of his bundle. "I'll come along to help."

Tavis shook his head. "Stay here and look after the others," he said. "If Brianna didn't reach Castle Hartwick, there won't be anyone coming to look after you and the other children."

Avner scowled. "I'm no child."

"And we don't need anyone to watch after us," Livia added. "We were doing that long before you took us in."

Blizzard neighed again, then stamped her feet on the ground and trotted through the gate.

"I don't have time to argue about this," Tavis snapped. Livia and the other children recoiled at his sharp tone, but Avner did not flinch. "Just do as I say one last time. You'll be rid of me soon enough."

The children dropped their gazes, and several of the younger ones wiped their eyes.

"Don't cry," Tavis pleaded. "There will be plenty of time for that after I find Brianna."

"Then you'll come back?" Avner asked, his spirits rising.

"At least to say good-bye."

With that, Tavis ran out the gate. When he turned toward Castle Hartwick, he saw Blizzard waiting at the edge of town. She whinnied, then set off down the road. Tavis followed at a trot, realizing the run ahead could be a long one.

Before he had gone very far, the firbolg heard a clumsy, flat-footed gait coming up from behind. He glanced over his shoulder and saw Basil lumbering up the road. The runecaster had left his sack of stolen books behind and carried only a small satchel over his shoulder. Tavis neither slowed his pace nor increased it, allowing the gaunt verbeeg to catch up in due time.

When Basil finally clumped up beside him, Tavis asked, "What are you doing here?"

"Avner . . . arranged . . . it," the verbeeg gasped. "He said I could have his books if I watched over you."

Tavis scowled, far from happy to hear the boy was using stolen goods to ensure his safety. Increasing his pace slightly, he said, "I hope you can keep up."

Somehow, Basil did. While Tavis trotted down the dusty road in near silence, the verbeeg pounded along at his side, gasping for breath and holding his ribs. Despite his obvious agony, never once did the runecaster ask the scout to slow down. Soon, the firbolg found himself admiring his companion's will, and even began to consider that having a magic-user along might prove useful if Brianna were in serious trouble.

Pausing frequently to look back and make sure Tavis and Basil were still following, Blizzard led the pair onward for the better part of an hour. Though they crossed several streams and the mare's mouth was frothing with thirst, not once did she pause to drink. They passed dozens of granges, small farms with huts of rough-hewn logs and pastures fenced by walls of stacked rock. Usually, neither the inhabitants nor their animals were visible, for the sight of a verbeeg, even one accompanied by Tavis Burdun, was enough to send most peasants into hiding.

The farms slowly gave way to long, rounded bluffs of brown granite and tangled heaths of low-growing spruce. Presently, they reached the base of Coggin's Rise, where the road entered a stand of aspen trees. Blizzard stopped and stared into the white forest with pricked ears and flaring nostrils.

Tavis heard nothing except a bevy of pine siskins whistling to each other. Although it was a normal enough sound for this time of afternoon, he nocked an arrow and advanced cautiously down the road, Basil and

Blizzard following close behind. The scout came to a toppled aspen at the road's edge. The bole, snapped off about four feet above the ground, had been freshly broken, for the wood still smelled of sap and showed no signs of weathering. Next to the jagged trunk lay an area of compressed ground where a very large person, probably Morten, had fallen to the ground and rolled.

Tavis pointed the tip of his arrow at the fallen aspen. "Something dropped out of that tree and attacked Morten."

Basil cast a nervous glance at the other aspens still overhanging the trail. "What was it?"

Tavis studied the surrounding area for a moment, then followed four of Morten's boot prints across the road. There, he found a mass of flies swarming over a large area of dark ground and several strange tracks that he had not seen since his days scouting for Runolf's patrol. The prints were deepest on the ball of the foot, with talon marks in front of the five toes. The heel depression was hardly visible, while the arch had left no mark on the ground at all.

"It was an ogre," Tavis said.

The scout put his arrow back in its quiver, then brushed the flies away and picked up a handful of darkened ground. He sniffed the sticky clump and smelled a rancid odor.

"This is ogre blood," Tavis said. "And from the amount spilled, I'd say the brute died quickly."

The verbeeg looked up, eyeing the quivering boughs overhead. "If he's dead, where's the body?"

"Ogres don't leave their dead behind." Tavis pointed to a single set of deep ogre tracks leading away from the road into the heart of the woods. "One of his friends took the body. When he reaches someplace safe, he'll burn the corpse so our priests can't eat it and enslave the fallen warrior's spirit."

Basil frowned. "That's ridiculous," he said. "Human priests aren't cannibals."

"No, but ogre shamans are," Tavis replied. "And they're too stupid to understand the difference."

With Basil and Blizzard still close behind, the scout rose and followed the ogre's trail away from the road. As he walked beneath the aspens where the siskins were perched, the tone of their call changed from a gentle *sweet sweet* to an anxious *bzzrreeee* until he and his companions had passed. A few steps later, he came across several of Morten's heavy boot prints heading in the same direction. He followed the two sets of tracks to the base of a stony bluff. He began to climb, then stopped halfway up the hill when Blizzard snorted softly and abruptly stopped.

Tavis pulled an arrow and crouched down. "Be ready," he said, turning to face Basil. "Blizzard seems—"

The scout stopped in midsentence, for the verbeeg had pulled a sheaf of fresh straw from his satchel and was dropping it on the ground. In the distance, Tavis could see two similar bundles marking the route they had taken since leaving the trail.

"What are you doing?" he demanded.

The runecaster's face went pale. "I was just m-marking our p-path," he stammered. "So we don't get lost."

Tavis nocked his arrow and, without saying anything, swung it toward the verbeeg's heart.

"Avner put me up to it!" Basil blurted.

"In the name of Stronmaus!" Tavis swore, lowering his bow. "Will I ever be able to trust that boy?"

Basil sighed in relief. "His behavior is perfectly understandable," the verbeeg said. "Avner's terrified of being left alone. Now that you're abandoning him—"

"I'm not abandoning him!"

"Aren't you? As valid as your reasons are, you can't expect the boy to accept them." Basil reached down to pick up the straw he had dropped on the ground.

"Leave it," Tavis ordered. "If he's following us, I don't want him getting lost with ogres about."

The scout climbed the rest of the way up the bluff. Basil came a few steps behind, but Blizzard would advance no farther. Upon cresting the hill, Tavis found a wide band of black arrows leading across the hillside to another toppled aspen tree. Like the one back at the road, it had been freshly snapped off about four feet above ground. Next to the broken stump lay Morten's body, resting facedown in a pool of his own blood.

Tavis bit his lip, but allowed himself no other reaction to the gruesome sight. During his time with the border guard, he had grown accustomed to the sight of good men lying motionless in lonely wilderness places. Though such deaths always saddened him, he had learned to control his emotions, for outbursts of grief and anger could only get a man killed when there was danger about. Nevertheless, the scout did feel a cold knot of dread forming in his stomach, and a panicked voice in the back of his head was screaming the alarm. If Morten had fallen, Brianna could not be safe.

"Diancastra save us!" Basil gasped, stepping to Tavis's side. "They killed him!"

"So it appears," Tavis replied. After studying the area to make certain no ogres were lurking in ambush, he led the way across the hilltop. "I'll have a look around. You see to Morten."

"As you wish," Basil said. "But I don't know what I can do for him. I'm a runecaster, not a necromancer."

As Basil examined the bodyguard, Tavis made a thorough inspection of the area, retracing the course of the afternoon's events. He found seven dark, rancid-smelling stains on the mossy ground, suggesting that someone—presumably Morten—had spilled a lot of ogre blood. Near several trees, he also discovered sets of deep ogre tracks. The scout realized instantly what these prints signified, for the brutes loved to attack by ambush, and dropping out of high trees was one of their favorite tricks.

To Tavis's dismay, he also found the place where Brianna had dismounted to examine Morten, another bloodstain, and the footprints of at least three ogres— one of them especially large—crossing her trail. On the bole of the toppled aspen, he noticed two gashes where Blizzard's hooves had scraped as she leaped across, and he noted the churned ground on the other side where horse and rider had fallen. Then, most disheartening of all, he discovered a gleaming white pebble that turned out to be a fractured human tooth.

Tavis was still searching for clues when Basil called out, "Morten's alive! Help me roll him over!"

The scout leaped over the toppled aspen and helped Basil roll Morten's huge body onto its back. The body-guard's head and chest were covered with blood, the beard thickly matted with the sticky stuff. His flesh was as pale as aspen bark, and a terrific hunk of flesh had been bitten from his throat. Still, there could be little doubt that he was alive. A cold sweat covered his face, and his breath came in shallow gasps so faint his ribs barely moved. Someone had even cut an arrow from his thigh and dressed the wound with shredded bark.

Tavis pulled a corner of the bandage away and saw that the wound had been scorched by the fire of Hiatea's magic. There could be no doubt that Brianna had cast the spell that nullified the ogres' poison. He put the bandage back in place and cursed.

Basil raised an eyebrow. "What's wrong?" he asked. "It's no difference to me, but I thought *you'd* want Morten alive."

"I do," Tavis replied. "But this was no chance meeting. The ogres were after Brianna all along."

"How can you know that?" asked Basil.

"The poison on ogre arrows is fast," Tavis explained. "Once it's in your blood, you collapse in about three seconds. It won't kill you, but you'll be too weak to defend yourself."

"So?"

"Morten killed at least seven ogres, but they didn't kill him, even after he was wounded and helpless." Tavis ripped a long strip of cloth from Morten's undertunic and used it to bandage the wound on the bodyguard's throat. "They let him live so Brianna would come to his aid. Then, while she was occupied with his wounds, they captured her."

"You can read all that from his wounds?" Basil asked.

The scout could not tell whether the verbeeg's tone was one of disbelief or awe. "Yes, and from other signs."

Tavis gestured at the hilltop, which was not so thickly wooded that visibility was a problem. "If there had been any ogres in the open when Brianna arrived, she would have seen them. But she didn't. She came directly to Morten's aid and bandaged his arrow wound." The scout pointed at two sets of nearby ogre tracks. "Nevertheless, two ogres surprised her here, which means they were well hidden when she arrived."

"And hiding well takes time, even for ogres," Basil said, nodding. "So they couldn't have done it on the spur of the moment. They were hoping Brianna would come to help Morten."

"Right, but I'd go even further," Tavis replied. "I'd say their shaman used his magic to lure her into the trap."

Basil raised his brow. "And how do you know they had a shaman?" This time, his voice was not doubtful, only curious.

Tavis pointed at the bandage he had placed on the fallen bodyguard's neck. "The bite," he said. "It's a serious one. If it had been there when Brianna healed the wound in Morten's thigh, she would have dressed it as well. Since she didn't, we can only assume it was made later."

"I see that," Basil allowed. "But I still don't know why you think it was a shaman."

"If an enemy has proven himself strong or cunning, an

ogre shaman eats the corpse to enslave the enemy's spirit," Tavis explained. "Morten was too big to take with them, so the shaman started to eat him here."

"Then why didn't he finish?" Basil asked. "I've never met an ogre shaman, but I know enough about magic to tell you it doesn't work unless you perform the ritual completely and correctly."

"My guess is he didn't have time," Tavis explained. "Someone's working with them, and that person wouldn't have wanted to wait around for the shaman to eat an entire firbolg. So they left Morten for dead and went on their way."

Basil considered this for a time, then nodded. "Of course, they must have a spy," the verbeeg said. "If the ogres came after Brianna specifically, then someone told them she'd be riding back from your inn today."

"And that person also warned them about Morten."

"It sounds to me as though we're talking about anyone who lives between Stagwick and Castle Hartwick," Basil said. "Let's concentrate on motives. Why do the ogres want Brianna? Ransom?"

Tavis shook his head. "They're more direct. If they wanted treasure, they'd just steal it," he said. "And the only use they have for humans is as meals or slaves— but I can't imagine why they'd single out Brianna for that. There are plenty of easier targets near the border lands."

"Then perhaps it's the spy who wants her," Basil replied. "Is there anyone who'd profit if she disappeared, or who could use her as hostage?"

"Any number of earls, I suppose," Tavis replied. "They're always trying to grab more power, but it's a rare earl who knows the mountains well enough to find an ogre camp—much less keep himself from being eaten and strike a bargain with the shaman."

"Then I fear we won't know why Brianna was taken until we learn who's behind it," the verbeeg said. He fell into a thoughtful silence, then let out a heavy sigh. "That leaves you with only one unpleasant option: Chase the ogres down yourself."

"There's nothing I'd like more," Tavis replied. Though he realized Basil was trying to exclude himself from such a dangerous prospect, at the moment the scout saw no purpose in commenting on the verbeeg's cowardice. "But we won't save Brianna by getting ourselves killed. The ogres outnumber us by five to one, and even I'm not that good."

Basil raised an eyebrow. "I take it you counted tracks?"

Tavis shook his head. "No, the battlefield's too trampled for that," he said. "But our foes are at least ten: one to bear each of their dead or wounded fellows, one to carry Brianna, and the shaman—who would consider himself above carrying anything. On the other hand, we can assume there are no more than fourteen in the party, or they would have taken Morten to eat later."

"A pleasant thought, that," Basil said. "So what do we do?"

"Go to the castle and report what we've learned," Tavis replied. He stepped over to a sapling. "But first, we'll have to prepare a litter for Morten."

"Don't bother," said Basil. "We've no need of a litter."

The runecaster removed Morten's leather breastplate and tore open the sweat-stained tunic beneath. After pulling Morten's dagger from its sheath, he shaved the hair off the bodyguard's furry chest, then he dipped his finger in the fresh blood oozing from beneath the bodyguard's neck bandage and touched the red-stained digit to the firbolg's chest.

"What will your magic do?" Tavis asked.

If Basil heard the question, he showed no sign. He lowered his bulging eyes to Morten's chest and began to draw. The process took longer than Tavis had imagined it would. The verbeeg traced his rune slowly and deliberately, taking great care to make certain each line ran absolutely true, with clean, straight edges. Whenever his gruesome ink began to run dry, he dipped his finger in Morten's blood again, and if any part of the stroke looked thinner or lighter than the rest, applied it again.

Deciding there was no use in standing around idly, Tavis returned to the place where Brianna had been captured. It took only a few moments to make sense of the jumble of ogre tracks and find a trail leading southeast. At first, this puzzled him, since the ogres' home lands lay more to the northeast. Then he realized that his quarry was hoping to throw off pursuit by circling around Castle Hartwick in an unexpected direction. The scout smiled to himself, for, with a little luck, he could cut them off—with a company of the king's men at his back.

As Tavis formulated his plan, a curious tension seemed to fall over the forest. Blizzard wandered onto the hilltop, nickering softly. Tavis looked back toward the trail and soon realized that the distant voices of the siskins had changed to a chorus of harsh *shick-shicks*. Someone was passing beneath their roosts, and from the angry sound of their calls, he was trying to be sneaky about it. The scout listened for the sounds of a man's passage. He heard nothing, not even the rustle of leaves or the snap of a breaking twig. The person stalking toward them moved with stealth enough, but he lacked any skill at keeping the forest animals from betraying his presence.

"Avner, come here!" the scout called.

"How do you know it's me?" cried the astonished youth.

"The birds complained," Tavis answered. "Now do as you're told. You've upset them enough."

"I'll be right there," Avner replied. "Just let me get something I left back at the road."

After a short silence, the scout heard leaves rustling and branches snapping as a horse trotted through the wood. The beast crested the hill a moment later, Avner's proud figure seated upon its back. As the youth came nearer, Tavis saw a hawk's-head crest embossed on the skirt of the gelding's fine leather saddle.

"Where'd you come by that horse?" he demanded.

"I found it," Avner answered.

"In Earl Dobbin's stable, no doubt," chuckled Basil. "Well done, boy."

"Don't encourage his dishonest ways!" Tavis turned toward Basil and saw that the runecaster had finished his symbol. The verbeeg was walking toward them, pulling Morten's unconscious form along at his side. The bodyguard was lying flat on his back four feet off the ground, with a red, multifarious rune shimmering upon his massive chest.

Tavis shifted his glare to Avner. "The lord mayor can have you drawn and quartered for taking one of his horses," he said. "And I'd be breaking the law if I tried to stop him."

The color drained from Avner's face, but he met Tavis's gaze evenly. "Don't worry. I wouldn't expect you to break the law." There was a bitter edge to his voice.

"You're being too hard on the boy," Basil said, joining Tavis. "He was just being resourceful. How else was he supposed to catch us?"

"He wasn't," Tavis snapped, still scowling at Avner. "He was supposed to stay behind and look after the children."

"Livia said she'd watch them," Avner replied. "I wanted to be here in case you needed me."

"What do you think I could possibly need—"

Basil's free hand clamped down on the scout's arm, cutting him off. "Don't say something you'll regret," he warned. "Besides, shouldn't we hurry to Castle Hartwick? When we report Brianna's abduction, a stolen horse will seem no big thing."

❧ 4 ❧
Castle Hartwick

At last, Tavis reached the edge of the plateau and stopped to rest, legs aching and lungs burning after the long run from Coggin's Rise. Just ahead, the road descended over the lip of an enormous cliff that dropped a vast distance into the blue waters of the Clearwhirl River. From the middle of the river's deep currents rose a sheer-sided spire of granite, hundreds of feet high. Perched upon the summit of this craggy island, like a jagged white crown atop a pillar of black stone, sat the pale ramparts of Castle Hartwick.

To all appearances, the castle was as impregnable as it was huge. Flying turrets hung from every corner, and between each pair of jagged merlons stood a ballista manned by a guard in helm and breastplate. Even the towers, scratching at the clouds like a titan's pearly lances, were constructed of granite blocks so huge a storm giant could not have toppled them.

Tavis looked back across the spruce-dotted plateau. A short distance behind him, Avner was leading the horse he had stolen from Earl Dobbin. A short length of taut rope ran between the gelding's saddle horn and Morten's chest, pulling the firbolg along as though he were a cloud. Behind the floating bodyguard came Basil, staggering and wheezing, skipping forward every now and then as Blizzard nipped at his rump.

When they finally caught up, Tavis did not give them a chance to rest. "Stay together," the scout said. "We're almost there, and I don't know how the sentries will react if they see a verbeeg coming down the road by himself."

Basil's bushy eyebrows came together. "Perhaps I

should return to Stagwick and collect my books—"

"Those are Earl Dobbin's books, not yours," Tavis reminded him. "And you won't be safe alone. There are a lot of patrols this close to the castle, and it could prove fatal if they came across you."

Without awaiting Basil's response, Tavis turned away. The road ahead ran down a narrow ledge cut into the cliffside. It passed before a small watchhouse chiseled from the living stone, then curved sharply onto a long bridge that spanned the Clearwhirl's wide chasm.

As Tavis's small company walked down the road, three sentries stepped from the watchhouse door. In honor of the princess's birthday, they had polished their armor and weapons to gleaming silver, and over their breastplates hung ceremonial tabards of red linen embossed with the king's white stag. The two youngest men carried long halberds. The oldest, a veteran with gray hair, bore a silver-sheened battle-axe identifying him as Sergeant of the Earls Bridge.

The two youngest guards came a few paces up the road, then stopped and crossed their weapons to bar the way to the bridge. The sergeant stayed behind, standing at the watchhouse door.

"Halt and explain yourself, Tavis!" the sergeant called, casting a suspicious eye at Basil. He made no mention of the strung bow in the scout's hand, for the loyalty of firbolgs—and that of Tavis in particular—was well known. "Where is Lady Brianna? Why do you have her horse and bodyguard?"

"The lady has been taken by marauders." Tavis peered over the crossed polearms, looking down the road at the sergeant. "That's all you need know to let us pass."

The sergeant shook his head and pointed at Morten's body, still floating in the air. "I can't let you cross," he said. "Not with a verbeeg runecaster in your company."

Tavis did not try to argue. The only thing that made humans more nervous than giants was giant magic.

"Then send word to the king of our arrival," Tavis said. He would have suggested that Basil wait here, but feared the verbeeg might do something foolish—such as try to return to Stagwick for his books. "Rune magic or not, he'll want to hear about Brianna."

The sergeant came up the road and took the halberd from one of his sentries. "You heard what Tavis said— and ask High Priest Simon to come," he said. "Maybe His Eminence can help Morten."

"As you order, Hauk."

The sentry turned and sprinted down onto the Earls Bridge, a magnificent structure resting on two flying buttresses mounted into opposite sides of the canyon wall. When the guard reached the other side, he slipped between the half-open gates and disappeared inside. Within moments, curious citizens had gathered atop the castle walls, thrusting their heads between the merlons to peer at Morten's floating body and Blizzard's empty saddle.

The castle gates swung open, and Hauk's sentry came scurrying out. Behind him, two members of the Giant Guard, the stone giant Gavorial and the frost giant Hrodmar, peered out of the gateway. Though the archway was fifteen feet tall, the pair had to stoop to look through the opening, filling it completely with their torsos and faces. Gavorial's gray hide and bald head seemed a strange contrast to Hrodmar's milky skin and unruly yellow beard, but Tavis knew they had more in common than appearances suggested. Like all members of the Giant Guard, they had been sent by their chieftains to protect Camden. In return, the king allowed traders from the giant tribes to use Hartsvale as a peaceful gathering place.

Once Hauk's sentry had crossed the bridge and reclaimed his halberd from the sergeant, Gavorial's sonorous voice echoed across the chasm. "Keep an arrow ready for that verbeeg, Tavis Burdun!" he called.

"The king's safety rests in your hands!"

After Tavis pulled an arrow from his quiver, the two giants withdrew inside the castle. Gavorial and Hrodmar would not be coming across the Clearwhirl, for even the Earls Bridge could not support such a tremendous weight. To enter Castle Hartwick, true giants forded the Clearwhirl on the opposite side of the island, then climbed a long and wearing path to the Giants Gate.

A blast of trumpets rang out from the castle walls, then the king and his retinue appeared. A looming figure who stood more than two heads above the earls and court officials surrounding him, Camden was built as solidly as a castle tower, with thick, sturdy legs and hulking shoulders that bulged like a bear's beneath his ermine cape. His long strides carried him across the bridge at a brisk pace, leaving his retainers to scurry along behind.

Soon, Tavis could see that Camden had already donned his ceremonial crown in preparation for the evening's festivities. It was a gaudy band of gold with seventeen bejeweled points, one for each of the giant tribes that had pledged friendship to Hartsvale. From beneath this circlet hung the king's two hair braids, while he wore his heavy beard trimmed into the neat square favored by the nobility.

Camden stepped off the bridge, brushing by Hauk and the two sentries without a word. He stopped directly in front of Tavis.

"What's this about my daughter?" the king demanded. He was even taller than Brianna and could look Tavis more or less directly in the eye. "Where is she?"

Knowing of no easy way to report what had happened, Tavis said simply, "The princess has been taken by ogres."

Camden's face did not darken with anger, or pale with fright, or even go blank with shock. It fell with despair, as though nothing could be done about what the scout had reported.

"Ogres," the king repeated softly.

The reaction puzzled Tavis, for Camden was a bull of a man, given to epic rages and stormy rantings. To see the king take the news as he had was akin to seeing a badger lie down and whimper as the hounds came to tear it apart.

Camden's small entourage arrived. The retinue stopped a respectful distance away, but two men continued forward until they were within a single pace of their monarch. One was Bjordrek, whom Tavis had spoken with on two occasions, but the other the scout had never seen. The fellow was portly and bald, wearing so much gold jewelry that he sparkled like a sun dog in the afternoon light. He carried a silver staff shaped liked a fork of lightning, the symbol of the god Stronmaus.

Camden motioned the bald man toward Morten's floating form. "Simon, see to Morten."

Calling two assistants to help him, Simon slipped past Tavis and took charge of the floating bodyguard. The trio pulled Morten down the road to an area of level ground in front of the watchhouse, then pushed him to the ground.

As the cleric rubbed the rune off Morten's chest, Tavis turned his attention back to Camden. "Your Majesty, have you received other reports of ogres?"

"Of course not!" the king snapped, his eyes narrowing. "Why ask such a thing?"

"Because it didn't surprise you to hear there were ogres in the kingdom."

Camden's face reddened, and he clenched his fists. "What are you saying?" the king yelled. "That *I* allowed my daughter to fall into ogre hands?"

The scout quickly shook his head. "Not at all," he said. "But I thought that might explain why Runolf—"

"Runolf was here?"

"He stayed the night at my inn," Tavis replied, frowning. Runolf was a good soldier, and it wasn't like him to neglect reporting his arrival to the king. "Weren't you expecting him?"

"Not . . . yet." The king's voice was weak, his lip trembling. He seemed lost in thought for a moment, then focused his gaze on Tavis. "His report wasn't due until summer's end."

Though Tavis felt certain Camden was lying, he knew better than to say so. If the king wished to keep his business with Runolf secret, it was not a scout's place to interfere.

"Your Majesty, perhaps I should finish my report," Tavis suggested. Camden nodded, and the scout continued. "Originally, there were between eighteen and twenty-two ogres, but Morten put up a good fight and now only ten to fifteen remain. Their leader's a shaman—probably a cunning one—and he came specifically to abduct Princess Brianna."

The king raised his brow. "You seem to know quite a lot about these ogres."

"Even ogres leave a trail," Tavis replied. "I should also mention that it appears one of your subjects helped the ogres."

The king's eyes widened. "Do you know who?"

"Not yet," Tavis replied. "But it won't take long to catch them. I've a fair idea where to pick up the trail."

"You?" Camden asked. "You're no longer one of my scouts."

"Under the circumstances—"

The king shook his head. "No. Tend to your other duties," he ordered. "I'm sure that's what Brianna would want."

Hauk stepped to the king's side. "Your Majesty, my duties keep me well informed of people's comings and goings," the sergeant said. "There aren't any other scouts here, at least none of Tavis's experience. He's your best hope."

Camden replied without looking at the sergeant. "It

won't delay us to summon another scout," he said. "I'm afraid it will take a few days to organize our pursuit."

"A few days!" Tavis burst out. "By then, the ogres will be deep in the Ice Spires! Give me a company of your guard, and I'll have the princess home by dawn!"

Camden's eyes narrowed. "You forget yourself, innkeeper," he warned. "I am the king, and you have heard my command."

Behind the king, a distressed murmur rustled through the entourage. One of the earls, a rough-featured man named Wendel, even dared to step forward.

"Forgive me for interrupting, Your Majesty," Wendel said. "But most of us up north are old enough to remember fighting ogre raiders, back before you bought them off." He ran a nervous hand over his gray-streaked beard, then continued, "Tavis is right. If we don't go after the ogres now, they'll disappear into the mountains. We'll never see Brianna again."

Wendel's concern sprang from more than fondness for the princess, Tavis knew. Brianna was an only child, and so far Camden had failed to produce an alternate heir to the throne—this despite a series of ever younger and more beautiful queens. Romantically inclined courtiers whispered that the king's failure was caused by grief over his first queen's death. Whether or not that was true, Brianna's disappearance would have grave results for Hartsvale. It seemed every power-hungry earl could boast some tenuous claim to the throne, so the princess's well-being was all that stood between the kingdom and a struggle for succession that would make the War of Harts seem a skirmish.

It was several moments before the king faced the earl. "I appreciate your concern, Earl Wendel, but we have little choice." The gentle words were a surprising contrast to the anger in Camden's eyes. He ran his gaze over the entire group of earls, then continued, "Before anyone goes after these ogres, I'd like to know why they took *my* daughter. If any of you can answer that question, then we can send our armies after her."

The sour tone in the king's voice made it clear that he had no true wish to hear suggestions, so the earls offered none.

Camden gave them a patronizing smile. "This is the answer that comes to my mind: The ogres want us to give chase, perhaps so a larger group can catch our armies in the open, thus weakening the defenses of Castle Hartwick."

Earl Wendel's cheeks reddened, as did those of several other men old enough to have fought beside the king during the War of Harts. Camden had used his ogre allies to execute a similar ruse against his brother, with the result that Dunstan's castle had been captured and his forces driven from the land.

"But we must do something!" Wendel said. "We can't let them take the princess!"

"Perhaps Morten will know something useful," called Simon.

The priest was kneeling at Morten's side, ready to cast his spells. His assistants had shaved the bodyguard's heavy beard away from the horrible gash on his neck. They had also peeled Brianna's shredded-bark dressing off the firbolg's thigh, revealing the jagged lips of an arrow puncture. The skin surrounding the hole was red and disfigured from the fiery healing magic of the princess's goddess, but the injury looked as though it would trouble Morten for some time to come. Both wounds were surrounded by white foam left over from the cleric's purifying ritual.

Simon laid his silver staff over the hole on Morten's leg, announcing, "He'll be ready to answer questions in a moment."

Tavis received the news with mixed feelings. Certainly, he wanted to hear what Morten could tell them about the ogres—but he was not looking forward to the bodyguard's report about what had happened earlier in the Weary Giant's barn.

Simon uttered a string of mystic syllables, and a blue flash hissed down the length of his forked staff, filling the air with the smell of fresh rain. Crackling bolts of sapphire light danced over Morten's arrow wound. The hole's jagged lips joined together seamlessly, and even the burn caused by Brianna's healing spell vanished. The spell faded, leaving only a faint blue scar in the shape of a lightning bolt to mark the injury.

Several earls voiced their high esteem for Simon's magic, but the high priest paid them no attention. Laying the forked end of his staff over the gash on Morten's neck, he raised a wineskin and began to pour. As the red fluid spilled over the firbolg's throat, he called upon Stronmaus to change the wine to blood so the veins of a brave warrior might run full once more. A dazzling bolt crackled down from the sky and struck the rod. The pommel flared blue for a moment, then the red nectar grew dark and thick as it spilled into the wound.

Morten's breath grew deeper and more steady. His eyes fluttered, then he moaned. He smacked his lips, as though the wine were entering his throat through his mouth instead of a wound. When he tasted nothing, the firbolg's eyes popped open. He twisted his head to the side and squinted up at the high priest.

"Simon?" he gasped. "What are you doing here? Where's Brianna?"

"We're at the Earls Bridge," the cleric explained, his voice soft and patient. Still pouring wine over his staff, he continued, "You suffered a wound—"

"My wounds aren't important!" Morten said. "What of the princess?"

The bodyguard pushed himself into a sitting position, but lacked the strength to stay there and promptly crashed back to the ground. "What of Lady Brianna?" he demanded again.

Camden stepped to the firbolg's side. "We were hoping

you could tell us," he said. The king waved his hand at Tavis, Basil, and Avner. "These three found you on Coggin's Rise. My daughter wasn't there."

Morten turned his head to glare at Tavis. The firbolg's eyes were ashamed and angry, as one might expect of a loyal bodyguard who had just learned of his failure, but they also seemed strangely glazed, as though the pain of his injuries had dulled his mind.

"You!" Again Morten tried to rise. "I'll kill you myself!"

Camden gently pushed the firbolg back down. "Why should you want to kill Tavis?"

Morten continued to glare at Tavis. "He betrayed Brianna," the bodyguard declared. "The knave's been using her to protect his den of thieves, and today she learned the truth."

"Tavis?" Camden asked.

Gasps of astonishment and disbelief droned through the king's entourage, with Earl Wendel's voice loudest of all. "Impossible!" he declared. "I've known Tavis Burdun for a decade. He'd never do something like that."

As the earl was speaking in his defense, Tavis heard Basil and Avner whispering to each other behind him, obviously concerned by the turn the conversation had taken.

"Stay where you are, scofflaws!" Tavis hissed, speaking over his shoulder. "Running will do no good now."

After allowing the drone to continue for a moment, the king raised his hands for silence. Looking to Tavis, he demanded, "What of Morten's charge?" Then, almost as an afterthought, he also asked, "How does it concern my daughter's disappearance?"

"Some books were taken from Earl Dobbin, and the thief sought refuge in my inn," Tavis admitted. "But I knew nothing about it until afterward, and I speak honestly when I say the incident has nothing to do with Brianna's disappearance."

"You can't believe him," Morten scoffed.

"Why not?" demanded Wendel. "Firbolgs can't lie."

"That runt's no firbolg!" Morten bellowed. He managed to push himself into a seated position and stay there. "Just look at how small and skinny he is. You can tell he was raised on human food, and on human lies!"

Camden frowned thoughtfully. "Morten might have a point there," he allowed. "But I don't see how it concerns Brianna. Even if he wanted to silence her, he hardly had the time to call a pack of ogres."

Bjordrek stepped to the king's side. "True, sire. But who else could treat with ogres?" He spoke quietly, his gray eyes fixed on the scout. "Only Tavis has the skill to find their home and survive long enough to strike an agreement."

"That's ridiculous!" objected Wendel. "Tavis is no thief, or he wouldn't have brought Morten here. It would've been simpler to leave the oaf for dead."

Morten scowled at this. "Tavis Burdun was hiding Earl Dobbin's stolen books. If that doesn't make him a thief, nothing does," the bodyguard declared. "Why he saved me, I don't know."

"It appears there are a great many things we don't know, and it may take some time to sort them out," the king said. "Until we do, Tavis and his friends shall remain at Castle Hartwick."

A knot formed in Tavis's stomach. "What of Princess Brianna?" he demanded.

"She is not your concern. Now do as I command." Camden's eyes grew hard, and for the first time he glanced at the scout's famous bow. "Or will you take arms against your lawful liege?"

Suddenly, Bear Driller felt heavier than anything Tavis had ever held in his hands. The scout had no idea whether he could loose an arrow at his own king, but he knew that obeying Camden's order would mean Brianna's loss—and he could not allow that, any more than he could lie. "I won't abandon Brianna," he said.

"Then you are an outlaw." Camden stepped back

behind Hauk's sentries, pointing a finger at the scout. "Seize him."

Bjordrek's eyes grew round. "But Your Majesty, if he—"

"No firbolg would fire on his liege." The king motioned Hauk forward. "Even a firbolg thief."

As the sergeant and his men moved to obey, Tavis nocked his arrow and in one swift motion raised Bear Driller into firing position. Basil gasped, Avner cheered, and Hauk's sentries stopped in their tracks. Several earls pulled small dress swords from their belts, and Morten managed to drag himself to his feet.

"Go on," the bodyguard said. "He can only kill one of you."

Tavis loosed Bear Driller's bowstring. The arrow hissed past Camden's head, passing so close the fletching brushed the royal ear, then shot out over the Clearwhirl's chasm. Before the color could drain from the cheeks of the astonished king, the scout was pulling another shaft from his quiver. Behind him, he heard Basil's flat feet running up the road. Avner seemed to be staying close at hand.

"I'm no thief," Tavis said, nocking his arrow. "But I'll do what I must to save Brianna—even it means defying my king."

"Traitor!" Morten shouted. "This will cost you your head!"

"Perhaps, but only after the princess is safe," the scout replied. Then, without shifting his gaze from Camden's disbelieving eyes, he began to back slowly up the trail. "Mount up, Avner. It's time to go."

No one moved to stop them.

* * * * *

Save for the cold breeze pouring down its steep channel, the ravine seemed an ideal place for Brianna's ambush. The jagged boulders along the rims would serve as excellent hiding places, and, after her allies pounced, the deep shadows of the rocky bed would make it difficult for her captors to keep track of the evasive beasts. Only the wind, blowing downhill instead of up, was wrong. If the ogres had sharp noses, they would notice the smell of mountain lion as the princess's swift friends slipped into position. But with the way the brutes stank, how could they have a decent sense of smell?

Brianna was at the mouth of the ravine, suspended from an ogre's bony shoulder by the same greasy rope that bound her hands and feet. A filthy rag had been stuffed into her mouth and secured in place with a strip of equally filthy cloth, and every time she inhaled she almost retched on the rancid odor that hovered about her captors like a fly swarm. Her flesh had grown numb from the stinging mountain cold, and the princess did not know how much longer she could endure.

There were two ogres behind the one carrying Brianna and ten ahead, many of those bearing the warriors who had died on Coggin's Rise. Several of the corpse-bearers had already entered the ravine, and the extra weight of their burdens was causing them to slip and stumble as they climbed. Regardless of the wind's direction, the princess did not think she would ever have a better chance to surprise her captors.

Brianna closed her eyes and pictured Hiatea's flaming spear in her mind. The talisman on her necklace grew warm, and she thought, *Yes, my sisters and brothers, now we hunt.*

The unvoiced call of nine vicious spirits answered Brianna's summons, pouring from the goddess's talisman into her breast. The princess suddenly felt hungry and vexed, filled with a fiery rancor that made her ache to rake open bowels and bite necks apart. She opened her eyes and ran her gaze over the dark mountainside. Somewhere up there, nine of Hiatea's most ruthless hunters were slinking toward the gorge, as quiet as shadows and as hard to see as the wind.

The ogres continued to climb, oblivious to the death waiting above. For no good reason, Brianna found herself holding her breath as she watched. Every so often, a warrior would pause to rest or catch his balance. The princess's heart would leap into her throat and pound like a drum until the brute resumed his ascent, usually after a sharp grunt from the climber behind him, but there was no sign that the warriors had caught the scent of her allies. Finally, the ogre in front of Brianna's stepped into the ravine mouth and reached up to grab a handhold.

That was when the whole line came to a halt. The princess craned her neck to see the cause of the delay. She found only the hunched backs of several ogres, spread along the shadowy ravine like so many boulders.

The ogre shaman's voice rolled down the ravine. "What wrong, spy?" he demanded. "Why stop?"

When the spy did not answer immediately, Brianna felt cold fingers of despair slipping around her heart. It would do her no good to attack until *all* the ogres were in the ravine, so the warriors close to her would be too busy fighting to worry about their prisoner. The princess could not spring her trap before then, or the brutes would organize a defense and prevent her from escaping. Unfortunately, the traitor Runolf—Brianna thought of the man that way to keep her hatred of him from tempering—was about to force her hand.

Runolf had joined the ogres at dusk, as the brutes ended a chilling two-hour wade down the Clearwhirl. After receiving a gruff greeting from the shaman, the traitor had led the group through a dark spruce forest and into the icy hinterlands of the north valley, guiding them without incident to this ravine at the edge of the Ice Spires' forbidding wilderness.

And now it appeared that in addition to leading her

kidnappers to safety, Runolf would ruin Brianna's only hope of escape. He was clearly a good enough scout to know mountain lions never hunted in packs. They were stealthy creatures as solitary as they were vicious, often fighting to the death even when male and female came together during mating season. Assuming the traitor realized that more than one beast lurked above his head, he would also know someone had used magic to summon the pack.

The ogre shaman finally grew tired of waiting for Runolf's answer. "Climb, spy," said his muted voice. "Take us Needle Peak."

"This is as far as I go, Goboka," came Runolf's answer. "You know the rest of the way—probably better than I."

Goboka, the shaman, was silent for several moments, then his voice asked, "Why afraid? What danger ahead?"

Brianna resisted the urge to call her attack. If the ambush was foiled, she would lose nothing by waiting until Runolf actually told the shaman about the mountain lions. On the other hand, if the traitor had merely decided to turn back, her plan still had a good chance of working.

"The danger ahead is minor," said Runolf. "But I've risked enough on your behalf. You can face it alone."

Brianna heard Runolf's boots scraping on the rocks as he started down the ravine. She thought Goboka would kill him on the spot, but soon saw the shaman's warriors pressing themselves against the craggy wall to let their departing guide pass.

The princess did not know quite what to make of the sudden desertion. It seemed likely that the traitor knew about her ambush, but for some reason of his own had decided to keep the secret. As for Goboka, Brianna felt certain the shaman was merely biding his time until Runolf left the crowded confines of the ravine, where his smaller size would prove a valuable advantage against the looming ogres.

As Runolf came near, he gazed into Brianna's eyes and gave her a brief nod. The princess noted no suggestion of apology or shame in his expression, only a tight-clenched jaw like she had once seen on Morten's face as he went off to execute a treasonous earl. Brianna tried to curse him. She managed no more than a garbled rasp around her gag, but the meaning was plain enough. The traitor looked away and stepped past.

Goboka's voice instantly boomed down the ravine, "Kill him!"

The last two ogres stepped abreast of each other and reached for their hand axes, but Runolf was ready for them. Throwing himself between them, he drew his weapon and lashed at the heel of the attacker nearest his sword arm. The brute's ankle came apart in a spray of blood and, bellowing in pain, he dropped to his knee.

The second ogre's axe arced down at Runolf, who avoided death only by hurling himself at the poor brute he had just injured. He struck the groaning warrior full in the chest, bowling him over and in the same move tucking a shoulder to start a somersault. The traitor rolled right up his foe's huge body, slashing the throat of the astonished ogre as he passed over, and came up standing on the ground. He spun and charged, his flashing blade beating back the brute he had not yet killed.

Hoping to use Runolf's distraction to good advantage, Brianna closed her eyes and pictured Hiatea's flaming spear in her mind. The talisman on her breast grew warm, and she thought, *Hunt, my friends! Slay the ugly ones!*

The mountain lions sprang from their hiding places, bounding along the rim of the ravine, descending into the dark gorge as silent as owls. The beasts hit their targets with raking claws and snapping teeth, filling the ravine with the pained cries of dying ogres.

The two brutes nearest the ravine mouth fell instantly, their necks crushed by their attackers' powerful jaws.

Several more warriors were tumbling down the steep channel with mountain lions still clinging to their backs. Farther up, a few had actually managed to keep their feet, and were spinning in wild circles, bellowing madly and wildly flailing their arms in an effort to halt the vicious claws slashing their backs. Brianna could not see what had become of Goboka, but she did hear his angry voice bellowing off the craggy walls as he struggled with one of the murderous beasts.

A low growl sounded from the murky ravine, then a dark shape came leaping out from a crag's shadow. Brianna's ogre let her slip to the ground, at the same time using his free hand to meet the mountain lion with a powerful backhand smash. The beast crashed into the mountainside, then righted itself as the ogre pulled his hand axe off his belt. The mountain lion eyed the weapon warily, then flattened its ears and snarled.

As the warrior and the mountain lion faced off, Brianna rolled onto her back and spun around so that her bound feet pointed at the ogre. She waited until he stepped forward to attack the mountain lion, then thrust both heels at the ogre's leg. The kick caught him at the ankle, sweeping his foot from beneath his body. He teetered on one foot for a moment, then crashed down, his skull smashing the rocky ground with a terrific crack. The brute's eyes rolled back in their sockets, and the axe fell from his grasp.

The mountain lion gathered itself to spring.

No, me first! Brianna ordered.

The princess lifted her bound hands. The lion leaped over, severing the greasy rope with a single snap of its powerful jaws. Brianna pointed at her feet, and the mountain lion bit through those bindings too.

Seeing that its job was done, the lion whirled around and jumped on the stunned ogre. It gave a tremendous snarl, then bit through his throat. At the same time, the bloodthirsty beast raked his abdomen with the claws of its rear feet, spraying entrails and foul-smelling blood everywhere.

Brianna rose and saw that her allies in the ravine had not been so successful. Although many of her foes had fallen to the initial assault, the ogres had not taken long to recover from their shock. She saw at least three mountain lions lying motionless on the ravine floor and did not know how many more had fallen in murky shadows where she could not observe them. The two live beasts she could see were on the defensive, reduced to dodging axe blows and countering with quick slashes as they slunk between their attackers' legs. Goboka was scrambling down from the top of the ravine, scowling angrily at the scene below.

Clasping one hand to her amulet, Brianna pointed at Goboka. "Big ogre—kill!"

At her command, the two visible cats whirled around to claw their way up the steep ravine. They were quickly followed by the female that had freed Brianna and one other that had been lurking in the shadows. One of the lead cats fell to a warrior's timely axe blow, but it looked as though the others would survive to reach the shaman.

Brianna did not wait to see the outcome. She turned to rush away from the ravine—and saw that Runolf had not yet cleared the way. He was still fighting the last ogre, though he had the brute pressed against the mountainside and appeared likely to win the battle.

"Go ahead and clear the way," Brianna whispered. "I'll deal with you after the battle."

The princess grabbed the hand axe dropped by the ogre that had been bearing her, then hurled it at Runolf's foe. The weapon flew straight and true, skimming just over the traitor's head to bury itself deep into the breast of its target. The brute's eyes opened wide, and his hands dropped to his side. Runolf finished the warrior quickly, driving his sword up through the heart.

Pulling his sword free, the traitor looked at Brianna,

who was charging toward him at a dead run. For a moment, Runolf did not seem to know quite what to do. He raised his sword, as if preparing to fight, then he shook his head and stood aside.

"Hurry," he called, waving at her. "Goboka's free."

The shaman's deep voice rumbled down from the ravine, uttering the guttural name of his wicked patron, the god Vaprak. Brianna cringed but did not look back, knowing what the invocation meant. Until now, Goboka had been too busy fighting mountain lions to use his shaman's magic, but that had changed.

Runolf's mouth fell open. "Stronmaus save us!" The traitor took an involuntary step backward, then caught himself and rushed toward Brianna. "Milady, forgive me." he called. "Had the decision been mine, I wouldn't have betrayed you."

Brianna started to demand whose choice it was, but a half dozen mountain lions bounded past her. For an instant, the princess did not understand what was happening—then she noticed the dark blood streaking their coats, and the gruesome wounds in their bodies. Goboka had raised her allies from the dead and turned them to his own will.

One lion threw itself on Runolf's sword, tearing the blade from his hand with its momentum. The rest of the zombie beasts fell on the traitor in a pack, tearing him apart with eerie calm. There were no snarls or any sound at all, save for the cracking of bones and the sick, wet sound of tearing flesh.

Clutching her amulet in one hand, Brianna spun around to face Goboka. The princess was too late to cast a spell, for the last of the undead mountain lions had already sprung into the air. The thing crashed into her body with a tremendous blow, forcing the air from her lungs and knocking her off her feet. The lion landed with its paws pinning her to the ground, then closed its cold teeth around her throat. It bore down until its fangs just broke the skin and little rivulets of blood dribbled down her neck.

"Not speak," ordered Goboka's voice. "Lion tear out throat."

Brianna obeyed. She listened in terrified silence as the shaman's heavy feet scraped down the ravine and stomped toward her, knowing that she could do nothing except hold very still and wait for Goboka's wrath.

The shaman kneeled at Brianna's side, then reached under the mountain lion. He slipped a filthy talon down her breast and hooked it under Hiatea's amulet, then broke the silver chain and pulled the blood-flecked necklace from around her neck.

"Nasty magic."

The shaman tossed her amulet aside, then pushed the dead beast off the princess. He summoned one of the survivors of the ambush, then said something in their own guttural tongue that made the warrior's purple eyes widen. The brute picked Brianna up and tucked her under his arm with such force that she feared he would crack her ribs.

Goboka grunted his approval, then went over and sat down cross-legged among the scattered remains of the traitor. "Bad man," he said. "Get what he deserve."

The shaman grabbed an arm and began to eat.

᠉ 5 ᠊

The Border Mountains

A small hand tugged gently on Tavis's cape. "I see Morten and the earls down in the valley," came Avner's hushed voice. "We'd better go."

"In a minute," Tavis replied, not bothering to look down the mountainside. The boy's news was no surprise to him. After raising Bear Driller to the king, the scout would have been shocked only if Camden had *failed* to send someone after them. "As long as you can see them, we have plenty of time."

Tavis and his companions stood just below timberline, on a windy shelf of tundra where they had come across a smoldering funeral pyre. Thin ribbons of greasy, rancid smoke still curled up from the scorched bones, vanishing into the gray dawn like the last vestiges of departing spirits. The skeletons were so large that a raven had crawled inside one rib cage to peck at the charred remains of a heart, while the femurs were the size of verbeeg clubs. The skulls were brutish and huge, with sloping foreheads, massive brows, and jutting jaws with long, curved tusks. Some of the heads even had the charred remnants of topknots clinging to their crowns.

"They're ogres," Tavis announced. As he spoke, the scout's eye fell on a shoulder blade lying near the base of the pile. It was much smaller than the others, and the fire had not cracked or scorched it nearly as much. "At least most of them are."

Tavis picked up the scapula. There were several long gouges in it suggesting that an ogre had used his tusks to scrape the meat off the bone.

"Whose was that?" Avner gasped. Both the boy's

79

stolen gelding and Blizzard stood behind him, their nostrils flaring at the acrid stench of the charred bones. "Brianna's?"

Tavis's heart began to pound, but he tried to remain calm. "I can't tell from a single bone," he said. "But it's clearly too small to have been an ogre."

"Then perhaps we should concentrate on our own escape," suggested Basil. "There's nothing we can do for Brianna now."

"We don't know that." Tavis's voice was sharper than he intended. "The bone might belong to someone else."

"What makes you believe that?" Basil asked.

"Every now and then, I've noticed partial tracks of what looks like a soft-soled shoe or boot," Tavis replied. "The ogres have been sticking to hard ground and the sole is smooth, so the print doesn't reveal much—not even the size or shape of the foot. But I do know this: ogres don't wear shoes."

"The tracks could belong to the princess," Basil suggested.

"Or they could belong to the spy who betrayed her," Tavis countered. "Either way, I'm not leaving here until we know for certain whose bones those are."

"We're as certain as we have time to be," Basil said. "Our pursuers have spotted us, and now they're redoubling their efforts to catch up."

The verbeeg pointed down the mountainside. Though the scarp was not quite vertical, it was steep and barren enough so that Tavis could see the valley below, where the silvery ribbon of a shallow stream meandered across a lush carpet of pointed conifer trees. More than a dozen earls were urging their horses across the brook, their lances held high and their breastplates flashing like mirrors in the morning sunlight.

On the stream's shore stood Morten, gazing up at the rocky shelf where the scout and his companions stood. If the bodyguard's wounds still troubled him, he showed

no sign of it. As each earl neared the shore, the burly firbolg looked away from Tavis to pull both horse and rider
up the steep bank.

"Maybe they're not coming *after* us," Avner said.
Despite his words, the boy's voice was doubtful. "Maybe
the king changed his mind and sent them to help."

Tavis shook his head. "No, they're coming to take us
back," he said. "If Camden were after the ogres, he
would have sent more than a few earls."

"This isn't fair!" Avner griped. "If the king's so willing
to chase us down, he ought to send a company of castle
guard after his own daughter!"

"You're absolutely right," Tavis replied, rubbing his
chin. "Since Brianna disappeared, Camden's been doing
a lot of things that don't make sense."

"He's too distraught to think clearly," said Basil. "Anxiety clouds human judgment to unwarranted extremes,
and your addled king is no exception. I fear he's chosen
us as his scapegoats."

"Then let's double back," suggested Avner. "I saw a
good place to set up an ambush."

"So we can become murderers as well as thieves?"
Tavis growled.

"Better their lives than ours," Avner countered. "It's
the only way to save ourselves."

"We're trying to save Brianna, not ourselves," Tavis
said, his voice still cross.

"It's too late to save her." Avner pointed at the bone
heap. "Even you can't put her back together."

"We can try," Tavis replied. "That's the only way we'll
find out who this really is."

"But Morten and the earls—"

"Will have to climb the mountainside just like we
did—and they're wearing armor," he said. "It will take
them at least an hour. If you two help, we can sort
through this mess by then."

"And if we discover this is Brianna?" Basil asked.

81

"What will you do?"

"I'll lead you and Avner to safety before I give myself over to Camden," Tavis replied. "After involving you in my trouble with the king, I owe you that much."

Avner scowled at this, but Basil quickly stepped over to the heap and began to pick up bones. "Then by all means, let's begin work," said the verbeeg. "An hour isn't much time."

The trio soon had the pile scattered across the ledge, gathering the bones into three separate groups: human, ogre, and those they weren't sure of. Tavis reduced the size of this last category by adding some of the unscorched bones to the human pile, since many of those that were obviously human also showed little sign of heat damage. Still, their skeleton lacked critical portions of the legs and back. Even the skull was missing, making it impossible for the scout to say whether the dead person had been as tall as Brianna.

"Well?" asked Basil, impatient.

Tavis shook his head. "I can't tell," he said. He picked up the human pelvis. "The hips look narrow for a woman's, but I can't be sure," he said. "I've never tried to identify someone from a pile of bones before."

"Don't waste too much time puzzling it over," Avner said. "I can't see Morten and his friends anymore."

"They're probably circling around to come up behind us," Tavis said absentmindedly. "Armor's heavy, so they'll stay mounted and try to traverse their horses up the slope. And the forest back there will offer cover from my arrows."

"You'd actually shoot them?" Basil asked.

"He fired on Camden, didn't he?" Avner's voice was proud.

"I fired past his ear," Tavis pointed out. "But even if the earls realize my miss was deliberate, they won't be sure I'd show them the same courtesy. They'll approach with caution. We have plenty of time."

Returning his attention to the human's bones, the scout pulled the shattered sternum from the pile and began fitting broken ribs to it. "These ribs were broken off like someone pulled them off one by one," he observed. "And they all have tooth marks."

Avner's jaw fell agape. "The ogres ate her?"

"The shaman ate someone." Though Tavis's voice sounded calm, his mind was spinning with dreadful thoughts, all of them racing toward the same opinion Avner had just voiced. Doing his best to hold back the terrible conclusion, he continued, "But it doesn't make sense that it was Brianna. Why bring her all the way up here to eat her? He could have done that anywhere along the way."

"I may have an answer," Basil said. He had stepped over to the pile of ogre bones and pulled their skulls from the heap. "There are fourteen heads, but we decided earlier that only eight died on Coggin's Rise. Someone killed six more here."

Avner stared at the human remains in obvious awe. "Brianna did that?" he gasped.

Basil nodded. "It would explain why the shaman devoured her here. If she didn't die during the fight, he decided she was too dangerous to keep alive." The verbeeg gestured at the human bones. "Either way, there she lies."

Tavis shook his head, struggling against his panic. "No," he said. "There are no signs of a fight, and I don't see how Brianna could have killed so many ogres without help."

"You're ignoring the evidence," insisted Basil. "What happened is plain enough. Now do as you promised and take us to safety—before our pursuers arrive to make that impossible."

"If you're so worried, stop wasting time by arguing," Tavis replied, unaccustomed to having his conclusions challenged by those he was guiding. "Even if it means letting Morten catch us, I intend to find out whose bones those are. Now come on. Let's see if we can locate the battleground."

With that, the scout turned and led the way up the mountainside, following the ogre trail. The brutes' footprints ran in both directions, as though they had gone up and down the slope several times. This puzzled Tavis for a time, but when they passed a hedge of gnarled, cold-stunted spruces and stepped into the stark barrenness above timberline, he realized what had happened. The six unexplained ogre deaths had occurred somewhere above the tree line, where there was no wood to make a funeral pyre. The surviving warriors had been forced to carry their dead back down the slope to burn them. That did not tell him much about the human skeleton, but the scout felt confident he would learn more when he found the place they had actually died.

"Where are you taking us?" Basil demanded, puffing mightily as he struggled to catch up with the scout. "We'll be trapped up there!"

"Our quarry must have known a route through," Tavis replied. Although the slope above ended at the base of a thousand-foot cliff with no visible breaks, the scout was not concerned. Runolf had taught him long ago never to place his faith in how a mountain looked from below. "Or do you think the ogres came up here by accident?"

This quieted the verbeeg, and Tavis continued his climb. Behind him, the two horses began to nicker and snort, for the terrain had grown treacherous as well as steep, with shaky rocks and loose ground that their hooves were ill equipped to travel over. The scout told Avner to release his gelding, and the beast promptly started back down the slope, but Blizzard continued to follow the small company toward the stony wall above.

Tavis soon saw a steep ravine cutting down through the cliff face. A short distance from the bottom of the rocky gulch were nine dead mountains lions. Most of the beasts lay bunched together on the hillside, and all had been terribly mutilated during the course of a desperate fight. Dried blood had stained brown much of the rocky ground between them and the gorge mouth, while the deadly struggle had left small furrows of dark soil churned up and dozens of stones overturned.

"Brianna is a priestess of Hiatea, is she not?" asked Basil.

Tavis nodded.

"Well then," the verbeeg added, "if this doesn't convince you she's dead, nothing will."

Avner frowned. "What are you talking about? I'm as anxious as you to put some distance between us and Morten, but I don't see any proof that the princess is dead."

"Basil's talking about the mountain lions," Tavis explained. "They're solitary creatures. They never run in packs."

"So?"

It was Basil who explained. "Brianna summoned them. That's how she killed six ogres." The verbeeg cast a nervous glance down the mountain, then said, "Perhaps now we can leave."

"We still have plenty of time," Tavis said. "And those bones could be the spy's."

Basil snorted his derision. "Why would the shaman eat his own spy?" he demanded. "That has to be Brianna back there."

"What you say makes sense," Tavis allowed. He had a lump in his throat that felt like it might choke him, and he wasn't sure that he cared if it did. "But I must be sure. You go on ahead while I look around."

"Go ahead where?" Basil demanded.

Tavis gestured up the ravine.

"I stand a better chance against Morten than trying to climb that mountain—especially alone," Basil hissed.

"Don't you have a rune that could help?"

"Of course. I have runes that will transform me into mountain goats, birds, even snow apes—but that cliff is a high one. What happens when I change back to a clumsy verbeeg in the middle of the ascent?" Basil asked. "I'm better off staying here to help you look."

The verbeeg turned his eyes to the ground and wandered away to search the hillside. Tavis went to the largest group of dead lions and kneeled down. The area was littered with bone shards and scraps of cloth, while the rocky ground beneath the beasts was coated with stale blood—some of it forming pools so deep that it still had not dried. The scout rubbed his fingertips in the sticky mess and raised the digits to his nose. The syrup smelled vaguely of iron and spoiling meat, and from that he concluded it had probably come from a human. It didn't stink enough to be ogre, and the amount of it on the claws and feet of the mountain lions suggested it had come from their prey and not themselves.

Tavis pulled a scrap of cloth from the blood pool and rubbed it between his fingers. The fabric was wool, coarsely spun but tightly woven—the same material from which his own cloak had been made.

Basil came over and squatted down at the scout's side. "I'm sorry to show you this." The verbeeg opened his hand. In his palm lay a tiny flaming-spear amulet attached to a silver chain. "This is the symbol of Brianna's goddess, is it not?"

Tavis pocketed the scrap of cloth he had picked up, then took the talisman. The amulet itself was in good condition, but the chain had been broken and several links were coated with dried blood. "Show me where you found this."

Basil led him across the hill, to where a single dead mountain lion lay on its side. Although the beast had been badly mutilated, there was little sign of blood in the area.

"It was below this lion." The verbeeg led the way

down the hill, then stopped and waved his hand over the rocks. "I can't remember where exactly, but this was the general area."

Save for a few rocks Tavis and his companions had turned over during their descent, the area looked undisturbed.

"Did you see any blood?" Tavis asked.

The verbeeg shook his head. "No, but you saw those stains."

"They don't matter." The scout allowed himself a deep sigh of relief, then slipped Brianna's talisman into his cloak pocket and smiled. "The princess will be pleased to have her amulet back. I'll be sure to tell her you were the one who found it."

"You've lost your wits!" said Basil. "That's blood on the amulet's chain!"

Tavis nodded. "True. Brianna probably suffered a cut, or perhaps the blood came from someone else," he said. "But those are the spy's bones down there, not hers."

Basil narrowed his eyes. "You're just saying that so—" Realizing the folly of accusing the firbolg of lying, the verbeeg let the allegation drop in midsentence. "How do you know?"

Tavis reached into his pocket and removed the scrap of fabric he had recovered earlier. "I found this back there." He pointed across the hill to where he had found the mountain lions lying amidst the scraps of bone and pools of blood. "That's where our human was killed—by Brianna's creatures."

Basil pointed at the fabric in Tavis's hands. "And I suppose that scrap confirms this?"

Tavis nodded, passing the cloth to him. "Coarse wool like this didn't come from the clothes of a princess."

Basil's gray eyebrows came together. "Perhaps the ogres gave her a cloak."

"Ogres don't spin wool," Tavis countered.

"I mean to suggest they stole it for her," said the verbeeg.

"Did you see any dead men between here and the castle?" Tavis demanded. "Or perhaps you think they'd simply take a man's cloak without bothering to kill him?"

"If they took it on the way in, we wouldn't have come across the body," Basil insisted.

"The ogres wouldn't have done that," the firbolg answered. "As they snuck into the valley, they'd avoid killing. A dead man's companions might notice his absence and sound an alarm."

"Speaking of alarms, it's time for us to go," said Avner.

The youth pointed down the mountainside, to where the small company's pursuers were just coming through the stunted spruce hedge at timberline. Still carrying their lances and heavy shields, the earls remained mounted, kicking and cursing their horses as they forced the poor beasts up the treacherous slope.

"If they're going to chase me, those earls would do well not to abuse their mounts."

Tavis removed Bear Driller from his shoulder and loosed an arrow. Although the distance was far too great for most archers, the scout was able to place his shaft a few paces directly behind the lead rider. The near miss caused all the earls to draw up short and jump off their mounts. They took cover among the rocks, leaving Morten to clamber up the slope alone.

"What's wrong with that firbolg?" demanded Basil. "How can he be so certain you won't fire at him?"

"I don't think he cares," Tavis replied. "After losing Brianna to the ogres, he'd rather take an arrow than fail his king again."

"Then let's go," Basil said. "I've no desire to let any firbolg reclaim his honor at my expense."

"That won't happen," Tavis said. The scout led the way to the mouth of the steep ravine. "Once we're up there in the gorge, even Morten won't follow."

"Why not?" Avner asked.

"Because he's not going to redeem himself by committing suicide," Basil said. "Which is exactly what he'll be doing if he tries to come after us while a clumsy verbeeg's up above him. I'm sure to send half the rocks in the ravine tumbling down on him—if I don't fall and crush him myself."

"That's not exactly what I had in mind, but Morten's too smart to risk an ambush up there," said Tavis. The scout would have suggested that Basil paint himself with the same rune he had used to levitate Morten, but the process would take far too long. "Unfortunately, we're going to have difficulties of our own. I can't help you both."

"Help me? Up that?" Avner scoffed, looking up the ravine. It was little more than a rock chute, so steep that, had there been a stream running through it, it would have been a waterfall. "That's a stairway compared to some of the walls I've scaled."

Avner stepped in the ravine and began his ascent. He moved swiftly and surely, never taking more than one hand or foot off the rock, or lingering in one place more than a moment. The youth found handholds on the tiniest knobs of rock and braced his feet on stone faces so sheer it was hard to imagine what kept them from slipping. Tavis had seen many excellent climbers in his time—himself among them—but the boy put them all to shame.

Once Avner had ascended a short distance, Tavis nodded to Basil. "Your turn," he said. "You're big enough that you can climb the ravine like a chimney. Press an arm and a leg against each side, then move them up one at a time. I'll be right behind you in case you need help."

The verbeeg licked his lips. "You're sure I can do this?"

"Would you rather wait for Morten?"

Basil reached into the ravine and drew himself up.

Before following, Tavis nocked another arrow and turned around. He found his view of the mountainside below blocked by Blizzard's white-flecked frame. The mare was pacing back and forth, nervously nickering and glaring up the ravine.

"Sorry girl," the scout said, using Bear Driller's end to push her away. "You'll have to trust me from here. You can't follow where the ogres are taking Brianna."

The horse stomped her hoof, then withdrew a few paces. On the mountainside below, Tavis quickly found Morten, still charging up the slope and now easily within arrow range. The scout drew Bear Driller's string back, then aimed the tip of his arrow at the bridge of his target's nose.

The bodyguard's eyes widened in alarm, and he threw himself face first to the rocky ground. Tavis quickly adjusted his aim, then released his bowstring. The arrow hissed away. A loud ping echoed across the mountain as the steel tip struck the back side of Morten's breastplate, then the shaft ricocheted away.

Tavis smiled, then whispered, "That shot should slow down even an angry firbolg."

* * * * *

Needle Peak loomed across the valley, a granite minaret rising a thousand feet above the field of gray boulders surrounding it. Behind the spire lay the silhouette of the next mountain ridge, a jagged wall of stone and ice. To the pinnacle's south, the rocky meadow ended at the brink of a vast, murky abyss. From these gloomy depths came the dull roar of an unseen river, its frothing waters filling the air with a fine mist that bent the sun's light over the canyon in a stunning arc of red and yellow and blue.

The rainbow was the only colorful thing in the vista ahead. To the north of the pinnacle, the field ended beneath a wall of loose boulders and pearly ice, the terminal moraine of a large glacier. The snow field curved away for miles, slowly climbing toward a cirque in the mountain ridge.

Somewhere in the unseen valleys ahead were trees, or so Brianna had heard, but she could see only the gray and white ramparts of mountain chain after mountain chain, each higher and more icy than the last, until the peaks grew so lofty and snowy she could no longer tell them from the clouds. The princess had never before ventured beyond the borders of her father's kingdom and gazed on the vast expanse of the Ice Spires. The sight filled her heart with a despair as dark and deep as the abysses hidden ahead.

A dozen paces down the couloir, Goboka stopped. The ogre shaman lifted a boulder off the bottom of the narrow trench, then began a careful examination of the stone. Brianna's ogre—or more accurately, the one carrying her across his shoulders—stopped to wait, bracing one hand against the couloir wall to keep from sliding down the steep slope. The other survivors of Brianna's ambush simply sat down, holding themselves in place by kicking their heels into the loose scree. Both warriors were lightly burdened, one carrying a handful of waterskins and the other Runolf's head. The head was all that remained of the unfortunate traitor, for Goboka had eaten the rest.

With an impatient grunt, the shaman dropped the boulder he had been examining and reached for another. Brianna found herself silently cursing Goboka's delay. When they stopped moving, the smell of the ogres grew immeasurably worse, to the point where her jaws ached and her stomach churned. Not even the bitter wind could carry the awful stench away fast enough, and she could not recall ever wanting anything quite so much as she now wanted to retch.

But that was impossible. Even if the ogres had not gagged her with one of their filthy rags, the princess could not have stopped her teeth from chattering long enough to do the job. They were high in the mountains, where the sun's rays were as frigid as ice and a stabbing, bitter cold crept into the lungs with every breath. To make matters worse, as a way of discouraging another escape attempt, Goboka had burned Brianna's cloak with the bodies of his dead warriors. She wore nothing more than the tattered remains of the cashmere dress in which she had attended Tavis's party. Even the slightest breeze numbed her flesh, and up here the wind howled loud enough to shame an entire pack of dire wolves.

Brianna twisted around to look up the mountain, praying she would see her father's men climbing over the rocky notch above. She could not understand what was taking them so long. Even if she had not been missed until the ball started, the ogres would have had less than a three-hour start on her saviors. With the advantage of the swift royal horses, the rescue party should be closing in by now.

At least Brianna hoped they were. Already her bones ached with cold, and her joints felt too stiff to move. If her rescuers did not arrive soon, there would be nothing left to recover but a frozen body.

When no guards appeared, Brianna reluctantly forced herself to look down the steep couloir again. Watching for rescuers only made her wait more agonizing.

At the front of the ogre line, Goboka picked up a long, narrow stone with a sharp point on each end. With a mighty thrust, he drove one end deep into the ground, planting the stake in the center of the couloir, where the walls stood within twenty paces of each other and the pitch was so steep stones sometimes rolled down the hill with no visible impetus. The shaman tested the pillar to make sure it was steady, then took Runolf's head and placed it on top of the post.

The shaman said something in the deep, guttural voice he used for casting spells. Runolf's eyes popped open. They were not dazed or glassy, as those of a dead man, but seemed fully alert and alive. The traitor's gaze roved over the couloir and came to rest on Brianna's face. There was an expression of terrible anguish in the depths of his eyes, but also something more, as though he was more sad for the princess than he was for himself.

Brianna could not look at Runolf's face without remembering how he had asked forgiveness and claimed the decision to betray her had not been his. Then whose decision had it been, Runolf? Was Tavis involved? Did his betrayal of her include more than abusing her good name? The princess would have liked to call down and ask all these questions of the traitor, but of course she could not. She had a gag in her mouth, and even if she had not, who was to say Runolf could answer. He was Goboka's creature now, and the sadness in his eyes might have meant anything—or nothing at all.

Goboka looked across the valley and raised his hands to his mouth. A loud, wavering cry erupted from his throat, cutting through the wind to crash against the cliffs of the distant mountains. For a moment, there was no answer, until an excited murmur slowly bubbled up from the remote fields beneath Needle Peak. The gray stones stirred, and at first Brianna could not understand what she was seeing. Then the distant shapes began to arrange themselves into ragged formations, line after line, rank upon rank. A strange thunder rumbled across the valley, growing more rhythmic with each repetition, until she could make out a single, guttural word rising from the throats of a thousand ogres: "Bree-an-a! Bree-an-a!"

❋ 6 ❋
Runolf's Couloir

The disembodied head of Runolf Saemon sat thirty paces down the slope, fixed atop a small rock spire lodged between the craggy walls of the steep couloir. The sergeant's face was pale with death, his cheeks hollow and his lips the color of ash, but his eyes still seemed very much alive. They were as blue as mountain columbines, with twitching crow's feet at the corners and watchful pupils fixed on Tavis's face.

For a long time, the scout sat on his haunches in the windy notch above the couloir, waiting for Basil and Avner to join him.

More than anything, Tavis wanted to avoid thinking about the gruesome scene below, but his mind would not allow it. His thoughts kept returning to what he saw, searching for an acceptable theory to explain why it was Runolf Saemon's head waiting down there.

There was only one conclusion for Tavis to reach: His mentor had been part of Brianna's abduction from the beginning. Runolf had been the guide who led the ogres past the outposts of the Border Guard. Later, he had been their spy, sneaking away from the party at the Weary Giant to warn the kidnappers of their quarry's approach. And now, having been ripped apart by Brianna's mountain lions, the traitorous sergeant continued to serve the brutes as some sort of undead watchman.

The only thing Tavis did not understand was why.

The scout fixed his eyes across the valley, where a long file of dark forms was climbing the glacier north of Needle Peak. A cold wind was blowing from that direction, and on its breath Tavis caught faint whiffs of the

94

rancid, sour-milk odor of ogre flesh. Sometimes, he thought there was a more fragrant scent, one he remembered from the princess's visits to the Weary Giant, but his imagination was only playing tricks on him. Brianna was certainly with the ogres, but her perfume would long since have worn off.

The scout's stomach burned with a hollow pain he had felt not too long ago, upon learning of the death of his adoptive mother, Isa Wirr. This time, he could not say for whom he was mourning. Was it for Brianna, hopelessly lost in the midst of a thousand foul-smelling ogres? Or was he grieving for Runolf, whose unfathomable betrayal had left him feeling even more lost than the princess?

Tavis forced himself to look down the couloir and met his mentor's gaze. Runolf's eyes were filled with shame and regret, two emotions Tavis had never before seen on the man's face. In life, Runolf had been one of those rare humans as confident in his own moral code as firbolgs were in their laws, a dedicated man who always upheld the strict codes of duty and honor to the letter. How the ogres had corrupted a man of such character, the scout could not imagine. Perhaps when he knew that, he would also know why they had taken Brianna.

"Runolf, I know you led the ogres into Hartsvale," Tavis called down. "The thing I don't understand is why. Tell me."

"That I cannot do," replied the head. "But I will say this: Remember what I taught you about three-toed tracks."

Tavis remembered. He had still been a young boy, standing barely a head higher than his mentor. Something was eating serfs off Earl Ateal's lands, and Runolf's patrol was assigned to hunt it down. They searched for days without finding any sign of the mysterious killer, until Tavis discovered a set of strange prints left by long, narrow feet with three toes and two claws. The tracks did not look large enough to be dangerous, and like all young firbolgs, his curiosity sometimes got the better of him. So he followed them.

The trail ended on top of a rocky cliff. Tavis spent almost an hour trying to pick it up again, even going so far as to climb partway down the cliff to see if the creature lived in a hidden crevice. It never occurred to him to look up, at least not until he heard the muffled flutter of a winged creature diving through the air.

Tavis pressed his face tight against the rocks, expecting to feel the talons of some angry raptor digging into his flesh. Instead, the strum of several bowstrings sounded above. A terrible, manlike cry echoed off the cliff, then a blast of bone-chilling cold washed over his back. A heavy body crashed into the rocks beside him, lashing him with a leathery wing, and fell away an instant later. When the young scout looked down, he saw a white dragon plunging along the cliff face, its body peppered with the arrows of Runolf's patrol.

Runolf came to the cliff edge and looked down at Tavis, who was frozen in place—whether from fright or the cold blast of the dragon's breath, the firbolg did not know.

"What did you learn from that?" Runolf asked.

"I thought I was the one doing the stalking, but I was wrong," Tavis replied. "The dragon was hunting me."

"True enough, but that's not what I mean," Runolf said. "I want you to think about what happens when you go off chasing things you don't understand. The mountains are as cruel as they are mysterious, and they won't suffer curious fools for long."

With that, Runolf backed away from cliff edge and led his patrol away. It had taken most of the day before Tavis could move his frozen body enough to climb up and follow.

After considering the disembodied head's warning, Tavis called down the slope, "Is that what happened to you, Runolf? Did you get involved in something you didn't understand?"

Runolf's mouth twisted into a bitter sneer. "I understood it—more than I wished. I understood so well I dared question my duty." He lowered his eyes, directing them toward the stump of his severed neck. "And this is my punishment."

"What could make you question your duty?" the scout asked, puzzled. "Why would you ever betray the princess?"

Runolf looked more ashamed than ever, but did not answer the question. "Leave Brianna to her fate," he said. "Interfering will only bring harm upon yourself."

Tavis could not believe what he heard. Over the years, he had fought all manner of beasts with Runolf, and never had his old friend warned him off. In fact, the sergeant had always recited his motto before each battle—*Forget your fear and remember your duty.*—and advised each man to keep it close to his heart.

"You were doing your duty, weren't you?" Tavis surmised. "You questioned it because you couldn't betray Brianna!"

"Go back," Runolf warned.

"Who commanded you to be the ogres' guide?" the scout demanded. Even as he asked the question, he realized his mentor would have taken such an order from only one person. Before Runolf could reply, Tavis gasped, "The king!"

"That must remain secret!" Wisps of golden light began to cloud Runolf's eyes. "I'm sorry to do this, but duty demands it."

The misty glow in Runolf's eyes began to spin, forming a pair of tiny yellow cyclones. The two whirlwinds began to lengthen, hissing like dragon's breath as they shot up the couloir.

Tavis turned and threw himself down the other side of the mountain, landing on a broad scree slope. Above him, Runolf's attack struck the notch with a thunderous crash, rocking the mountainside and filling the sky with a yellow flash. The scout began to roll, tumbling head over heels. Before he could stop himself, a muffled growl rumbled down the mountainside, then the entire scree slope broke free and began to slide.

No stranger to avalanches, the firbolg spread his arms and legs to stop his tumble. When he finally managed to stabilize himself, he was lying on his back with his head pointed downhill, still being carried down the mountain with the sliding scree.

Tavis jerked his knees toward his chest. The action flipped him into the air, with the result that he landed facedown on the avalanche. Although small stones and gravel were now pelting his head, at least he was descending feetfirst in a more controlled position. He began rolling to the side, across the landslide, and soon found himself within reach of a rock outcropping. After a few painful instants of clawing and kicking, he caught hold of a crevice and dragged himself out of the slide.

"What happened?" called a familiar voice.

Tavis looked up and saw Basil clinging to a boulder above. The scout had slid so far that he was more than a dozen paces below the runecaster, who still had a considerable distance to climb before reaching the notch above Runolf's couloir. The verbeeg's breath came in gasps as loud as the wind rasping through the crags above, for the steep climb was rendered even more difficult by the mountain's thin air.

"The ogres left a sentry on the other side of the notch," Tavis explained. A bolt of alarm shot through his breast as he noted that Avner was not clinging to the cliff near the verbeeg. "Where's Avner?"

Basil pointed down the slope. "When the slide started, Avner was about there," he said. "I didn't have time to see what happened to him."

Tavis looked down and saw that the avalanche had scraped the hillside clean, leaving a sheer scarp of dusty schist in its wake. There were several large crags onto which the boy could have scrambled to safety, but the scout did not see Avner clinging to any of them.

"Avner!" he yelled.

The boy's head popped out of a crevice. "Is it safe?"

Tavis breathed a sigh of relief. "It's never safe up this high, but at least the slide's over."

Avner scrambled up the rocky face like a mountain goat, his broad smile suggesting that he preferred the barren rock to the loose footing of the scree.

As Tavis waited for the boy, he studied the mountain below. The slide had scraped the slope clean, not stopping until it reached a flat at the base of the hill. On the other side of this small plateau, the mountainside once again grew steep, dropping away into one of the many canyons through which the scout and his companions had passed since leaving Hartsvale. It was a deep, gloomy gorge, made darker by the conifer forest creeping up its walls.

Tavis knew Morten and the earls were somewhere down there, for he had glimpsed them earlier as they passed through a clearing. The earls had abandoned their horses, along with their lances and heavy shields, to stumble along on foot. It had been difficult to tell more from a distance, but the scout had seen several silver glimmers as the sun flashed off polished steel, suggesting that they had kept at least some of their armor.

Although Tavis was not happy to know the king's men were still following, he was far from concerned. Even with Basil and Avner along, the scout knew plenty of tricks to increase his lead—and over the last few days he had employed only a few of them. But sooner or later, he would catch the ogres, and then he would have to slow down to rescue Brianna. It would be then that his own pursuers caught him. He only hoped they would be slow enough to arrive *after* the task was completed.

Avner joined Tavis and Basil on their outcropping,

then the trio ascended to the notch above Runolf's couloir. They stopped just below the summit, lying on their bellies and being careful to keep their heads down.

As they peered through the gap, Basil exclaimed, "By the rock beneath my belly! That must be the entire ogre nation!"

The verbeeg was looking across the valley at the long file of ogres climbing the glacier north of Needle Peak.

"I don't know that it's the entire nation," Tavis replied. "No one knows how many ogres live in the Ice Spires. But there are certainly more than a thousand over there."

"A thousand or a hundred thousand, it's the same to us," Avner said. "How will we ever rescue Brianna from all those ogres?"

"We'll steal her," Tavis replied. "You seem to be pretty good at that."

"The best." If Avner noticed the irony in Tavis's voice, he showed no sign. The youth pointed down the couloir at the disembodied head of Tavis's former mentor, now encased by a dome of golden light. "But I've never had to sneak past a head before. What is he, some kind of spirit guardian?"

"Yes, and there will be no sneaking past him," Basil said. The verbeeg's hand dropped to his satchel, then added, "Fortunately, I have a rune that will repay him in kind for what he did to us. An avalanche won't destroy him, but it should bury him deep enough for us to pass without trouble."

Tavis shook his head. "I'd rather capture him."

"Capture him?" Avner hissed. "We'll be doing good just to get by him alive. Basil's plan sounds good to me."

"No," Tavis insisted. "He knows too much about Brianna's abduction. I want to interrogate him."

"You're mad!" Avner said.

"Whether that's so or not, I'm the leader of this rescue party." Tavis turned to Basil, then asked, "Can you force him to answer my questions?"

The verbeeg sighed. "I do have a rune that will grant me control over undead spirits, but I must paint it on his forehead."

"On his forehead?"

"It's not as difficult as it sounds," Basil informed him. "The shaman assigned your friend's spirit to watch this pass. When he can no longer see to do that, he can't draw on the shaman's magic."

"Are you saying we have to blind him?" Tavis asked.

"That's what I was thinking of, yes," Basil replied.

"If I could get that close, I wouldn't need you!"

"Runes are not spells," the verbeeg explained. "You can't hurl them about like spears."

Tavis considered the problem for a moment, then asked, "Is there any chance my arrow would actually destroy him?"

"Not unless a cleric had blessed it," Basil answered.

"Then I may know a way to blind him," Tavis said, nocking an arrow. "Wish me luck."

He crawled up into the rocky notch and took aim. The globe around Runolf's head began to spin, forming a whirlpool of golden light. Tavis exhaled in a steady breath, releasing the bowstring at the moment his lungs had completely emptied themselves.

The arrow flew straight for one of Runolf's eyes, then passed into the spinning light. For a moment, the scout thought the shaft would find its mark, but the wood stuck to the whirling glow as though snatched from the air. The arrow swung around the back of the disembodied head like a stone in a sling, and Tavis knew what would happen next.

He yelled, "Get down!"

Tavis pushed Avner's head down and dropped over the notch. He began to slide, the rocky scarp painfully gouging his flank as his own arrow sizzled past a mere hand's breadth above his head. He braced his feet on the slope and halted his descent, then looked back to see his arrow arcing down toward the small plateau.

"So much for that idea," said Avner. "How about giving Basil's plan a try?"

"Even if I didn't want to interrogate him, what makes you think an avalanche would work?" Tavis countered. "Judging by what we've seen of Runolf's defenses, I don't think the shaman overlooked an obvious trick like that."

The scout scrambled back up the cliff and peered over the top of the notch. Runolf remained atop the stone spire, a yellow halo enveloping his head and golden flames crackling in his eyes.

"Avner?" Tavis asked. "What would you do if you had to steal a key from the pocket of a big sentry—back when it was necessary for you to do such things?"

The youth considered the problem for a moment, then said, "If there was no way to knock him unconscious, I'd sneak up as close as I could, then have someone else distract him while I picked his pocket."

"That won't work here," Basil said. "You cannot sneak up on spirit guardians, and they have no pockets to pick."

"No, but we can distract him," Tavis said. "Maybe we can get close enough to grab him."

"And then what?" Avner demanded. "Grabbing a wildcat's tail will get you clawed faster than anything else."

"Not if you do it right," Tavis said. He turned to Basil and asked, "Are you sure you can cause that rockslide?"

The verbeeg rolled his eyes at the foolish question. "Would you like me to prepare the rune?"

When Tavis nodded, Basil opened his satchel and pulled a hammer and steel chisel from it. He selected a flat rock, then set the chisel blade on it and began to tap.

While Tavis waited for the runecaster to finish, he slipped his bow over his shoulder. After a quick glance at the waists of his companions, he motioned at Avner's belt.

"Let me see that," he requested.

The youth promptly undid his buckle and handed the belt over. "What do you want with it?"

"You'll see."

The belt was surprising new, made of black-dyed cowhide as stiff as shoe leather. Tavis slowly flexed the strap back and forth. It was almost too rigid for what he had in mind, but its bulk could turn out to be an advantage. The scout detached Avner's dagger scabbard and returned it to the boy, then grabbed a rock and began to pound the belt to make it more flexible.

"Hey!" Avner objected. "That's a new belt!"

"And where did you come across a new belt?" Tavis demanded. "I don't recall making it for you, and we certainly didn't have the spare coins to buy it."

"Forget it," Avner sighed. "There's always more where that came from."

This time, Tavis looked up. "There'd better not be."

The firbolg resumed his work, pounding each section of belt until the leather grew as soft and flexible as cloth. Beside him, Basil continued to tap his chisel, filling the air with a soft chime as erratic as a bell swinging loose in the wind.

Runolf's voice sounded from the other side of the notch. "Whatever you're doing, Tavis, it won't work," he called. The words were difficult to make out, for the yowling wind softened the consonants and swallowed the vowels. "My spirit serves Goboka, and only his death will release it."

Basil looked up. "That's fine with us," he said, speaking more to Tavis and Avner than to Runolf's head. "What we have in mind has nothing to do with freeing you."

The verbeeg put his hammer and chisel back in his satchel, then showed Tavis the stone he had been working on. The glowing rune etched on its face was surprisingly simple, just three blue lines capped by a white crescent.

"I'm holding it upside down," Basil said. "When you turn it over, it'll set the whole hill to sliding."

Tavis raised his brow. "And if I turn it over again?"

"It'll stop the landslide—but I don't know how quickly," the verbeeg replied. He handed the runestone to Tavis, then added, "I suggest you be very careful."

Tavis smiled. "This should work fine." With the runestone in one hand and Avner's belt in the other, he inched up toward the notch. "I'll go over and bring Runolf's head under control. Wait here until then, but be ready to paint the rune that gives you control over undead."

"I'm coming with you," Avner announced.

Tavis shook his head. "This is too dangerous—"

"If it's so dangerous, we should just bury him," Avner said.

"I can always do that later," Tavis replied. "I'll let the avalanche take him if I get into trouble."

"With two of us, you'll be less likely to get into trouble," Avner countered. When Tavis showed no sign of yielding, the boy's eyes grew hard, and he added, "You can let me come with you or after you. We'll stand a better chance if we work together."

Remembering how well the youth had obeyed his orders to wait at the Weary Giant, Tavis reluctantly acquiesced. "Then take this." He passed the boy's belt back. "Runolf will concentrate on me, so you'll have a better chance of actually reaching him."

"That makes sense," Avner replied. He held the battered belt up. "But what do I do with this old thing once I get there?"

"I should think that would be obvious," Basil said. "Use the belt to blindfold him until I can paint my rune on his forehead. If he can't see, he can't perform the task for which he was created, and his link with the shaman will be interrupted."

Avner's eyes lit in understanding.

"We'll go down opposite sides of the couloir," Tavis said. "I'll start the avalanche to distract Runolf, and we'll go down behind it. Then I'll try to stop the slide right before it buries him, but if either of us gets into trouble, I'll just let the slide take him. You understand?"

"Nothing could be simpler."

With that, the young thief hoisted himself upward. Tavis scrambled into the notch after the boy, then the two rose to their feet. Runolf's halo dimmed, the flames in his eyes burning more brightly as he regarded Avner's small form.

"How dare you bring a child into this!" the head stormed.

"I came on my own," Avner yelled down. "And I'm as old as Tavis was when you made a scout of him."

"And that's as old as you shall grow," Runolf replied in a melancholy voice. His golden halo began to dim, then he added, "It's not in my power to show mercy—even to a boy."

The scout turned his runestone over. The scree slope came loose with a tremendous crack, sliding down the couloir in a single huge cascade. Tavis waited an instant, then shoved Avner toward the far wall.

"Go!"

Tavis leaped into the couloir on the tail of the avalanche, springing toward the wall opposite Avner, hoping to draw all of Runolf's attacks upon himself. The tactic failed miserably. The sergeant's eyes rotated in different directions, one following Avner and the other the scout. A fiery stream of energy arced from each of the golden orbs, crackling and sizzling up the narrow couloir.

Tavis ducked. The blazing beam flashed past, licking the back of his cloak with golden flames, and struck the craggy wall. A deafening bang echoed through the couloir. The scout's nostrils filled with the acrid smell of scorched rock, and he felt a heavy shard of stone slam into his shoulders, pitching him forward. He found himself flying down the slope and clutched the runestone to his breast. He glimpsed Avner, on the opposite wall of the canyon, sliding along behind the avalanche. The boy's clothes were smoking and his mouth was wide open with fear, but at least he was descending feetfirst and on his back, and that was all Tavis had time to see before he crashed face first into the sliding scree.

The scout went shooting down the couloir as though he were falling headlong down a frozen waterfall. He tried to look down the couloir to find Runolf, but all he saw was a billowing cloud of dust. A tremendous weight began to gather around his legs, and he realized that the landslide was overtaking him. He kicked himself free, trying to push himself down the slope faster than the scree, but did not turn the runestone over immediately. He and Avner would be easy targets without the avalanche to cover their descent and keep their adversary busy.

Tavis forced himself to wait five long heartbeats. He had to keep kicking his legs free to keep the rumbling heap from hurling his feet over his head and send him tumbling down the mountain. Rocks of all sizes clattered past, gouging his arms and legs, sometimes even bouncing off his flanks or back. The scout pressed his face into the gravel, shrugging his shoulders up to protect his head as best he could.

At last, Tavis counted five heartbeats. He raised his head and looked toward the center of the couloir, but still could not see anything except billowing dust. Nevertheless, he turned the runestone around—then immediately wondered if that had been wise. The scree beneath his chest began to drag against the mountain and slow, but the gravel behind him continued to press forward, pouring over him in a pelting, scouring tide of stone and dirt. Desperate to keep himself from being buried alive, the scout rolled onto his back and jerked his knees toward his chest.

The motion flipped Tavis over in a backward somersault, but did not deposit him facedown on the slide as it had done on the other side of the notch. Instead, it merely righted him, so that he stood on his feet with his back facing downhill and the landslide rumbling down in his face. The scout braced his elbows against his chest and touched his forehead to the runestone, forming a small air pocket in front of his mouth and nose. Then the scree washed over him, robbing him of all distinction between his body and the gravel that had swallowed it. The sky vanished into roaring, choking darkness. For a moment, he was vaguely aware that he was moving, but soon even that sensation vanished, and all he could see were the blue and white lines of the glowing runestone.

Some time later, Tavis's chest trembled with the effort of coughing. He did not hear the sound, only felt it, but it meant he had survived. More than that, it meant his attempt to create an air pocket had succeeded—though that was difficult to believe, with all the dirt and dust clogging his nose and throat. Though a tremendous pressure crushed down on him from all sides, he felt strangely weightless, almost separated from his body.

Tavis tried to move, first his head, then his torso, and finally each limb. He strained with all his might, pushing and pulling, pressing outward in every direction. Nothing happened, except that he felt the heat of his own breath fill the tiny pocket in front of his face. How much longer would his air last? A minute—maybe two or three?

As he contemplated this horrible question, Tavis realized he still might be able to move one set of muscles. He tried to wiggle his fingers, and discovered that he could wobble the runestone back and forth. Something that might have been a whoop of joy rose from his chest, but he could not hear it to be sure. The scout did not care. He slowly worked his fingertips over the runestone's surface, spinning it a tiny amount with each effort.

Dust fell in his eyes. The scratchy grains burned horribly, but all he could do was blink and try to wash them out with tears. He kept turning the stone. The gravel around him shuddered. The scout felt himself slip along with it, dirt and stones dropping onto his face.

Tavis turned the runestone once more, and then his body trembled as the whole hillside crept into motion. The scout stopped working the stone and tried to kick his legs and flail his arms, as though trying to fight free of the Clearwhirl's cold currents. Dirt and pebbles streamed through the gap between his arms, covering his chest and spilling into his mouth.

Suddenly, Tavis's elbow broke loose. Cool air rushed in, and gray light filled his tiny world. Dropping the runestone onto his chest, the scout pushed his free arm out of the hole and clutched at the dirt, pulling himself upward as the scree continued its gentle slide.

His head slipped into the light. A harsh, rhythmic rasping filled his ears: the sound of coughing. Tavis twisted his body uphill, freeing his other arm, and pulled the runestone out of the hole. He turned the crescent uphill, and the scree slowly stabilized. Holding his chest and head out of the dirt, the scout waited, coughing and wheezing, for the gravel to stop moving.

"Tavis!" Avner shouted. "There you are!"

Tavis looked toward the voice and saw the boy balancing on the surface of a large boulder. He looked dusty and bruised, but did not appear to have suffered any serious injuries. He still held both his belt and dagger. There was no sight of Runolf or the spire on which the disembodied head had been resting.

"Where's Runolf?" Tavis asked. Being careful to keep the crescent turned uphill, he laid the runestone aside and began digging himself free.

"After all your talk about capturing him, you buried

the spirit guardian anyway," muttered Basil. The verbeeg's report was barely understandable, for he was clambering down a barren face of schist where there had been scree a few moments earlier. "I believe he's just about even with Avner, though it's difficult to be certain—there was so much dust."

Avner smiled. "What a relief," he said. "I wasn't sure this blindfold idea was going to work anyway."

The boy let his sentence trail off, for a circle of light had formed beneath the talus just a few paces in front of him. The ground heaved upward. Golden rays streamed into the air, hissing and writhing like snakes.

"Oh, dear," said Basil. "This could be a difficulty."

Tavis braced his hands on the ground and worked his hips from side to side, at the same time trying to kick himself free. "Avner, get away!"

The youth leaped off his boulder, but did not retreat as Tavis had commanded. Instead, he put the dagger between his teeth and crept forward to the edge of the heaving ground, the belt stretched taut between his hands.

Tavis's legs came free all at once, sending him tumbling down the hill. He stopped after his first somersault, then jumped to his feet. Already, he could see the crown of Runolf's halo rising from the scree. The scout drew his sword.

"No! Attack with the stone!" Basil called. The verbeeg stepped away from the schist scarp, covering the remaining distance to the scree pile in a single jump. "Its magic will slice through what steel cannot."

The head's eyes appeared at ground level, looking up the hill toward Basil. The golden halo dimmed, and golden flames licked the stones in front of the spirit guardian. Avner stood less than a pace away, at Runolf's side where his peripheral vision would detect the slightest movement. The young thief froze instantly, standing so still even his nostrils did not flare.

"Over here, traitor!" Tavis called. Though it pained him to ridicule his mentor, it was the best way he could think of to prevent Runolf from noticing Avner.

"Who do you call traitor?" Runolf demanded. He rose the rest of the way out of the ground, slowly spinning around to face Tavis. "I have done my duty!"

"By delivering your princess into the hands of ogres?" Tavis demanded. "I think not."

With that, the scout dropped his sword and snatched the runestone off the ground. He flung it in Runolf's direction, and the head's halo flashed brilliant yellow, sending Avner stumbling two steps back. In the next instant, a spray of blue and white sparks filled the air as the runestone sliced through the protective sphere. The rock struck a glancing blow off Runolf's chin, then clattered to the ground, its runes dark and gray.

Runolf fixed his eyes on Tavis. "I was no traitor," the head said. "You must know I always performed my duty."

"To whom?" Tavis scoffed. "Vaprak, the ogre god?"

Avner sprang forward even as Tavis spoke. The boy slipped his belt over Runolf's brow in an instant, then pulled the head off the pedestal and laid it facedown in the scree.

"Well done!" called Basil. The verbeeg rushed down the hill with brush in hand. "But keep that belt tight. If Runolf spies us for even an instant, the shaman's magic will return to him—and we'll pay with our lives."

"Don't worry," said Avner. He looped the strap around Runolf's head once more, then buckled it tight. "I'm not going to let him see anything."

Once Tavis arrived, the youth carefully passed Runolf to him. The scout waited for Basil to arrange his tools, then turned Runolf over so the verbeeg could paint the brow. A faint glow of yellow shone around the edges of the blindfold, but otherwise Runolf looked more or less normal for a disembodied head, with pallid flesh and a scalp as shriveled and dry as unoiled leather. He did not say anything or struggle at all, but seemed properly quiet and still for a dead man.

Basil touched his brush to Runolf's brow. A wisp of yellow steam began to hiss from the spirit-guardian's mouth, but the lifeless head still did not resist or object. The runecaster worked slowly, showing no anxiety as he traced his lines. He did not use ink or paint. Rather, magic flowed from the brush itself, the tip trailing glowing green pigment wherever the runecaster drew it. The process took many minutes, and by the time the verbeeg had finished, the distance between Runolf's temples was completely covered with an intricate tangle of sticklike lines.

Basil lifted his brush and wiped the tip on his cloak, then returned it to his satchel. "It's safe. I've usurped the shaman's magic—at least temporarily," he said. "Remove the belt, and Runolf's spirit will be ours to command."

Tavis turned the head facedown, then did as asked, keeping the blindfold ready just in case Basil's magic was not as effective as the verbeeg claimed. Runolf's flesh seemed to come alive beneath his fingers, once again growing supple and full. When the head did not try to attack, or show any objection to the runecaster's magic, the scout slowly turned him over. The pall of golden radiance that had covered Runolf's eyes was gone, replaced now by a shimmering yellow mist that was slowly evaporating into the air.

"Tavis," Runolf said. There was neither anger nor regret in his voice, only acknowledgement and recognition. "What I have done I did not choose."

"I know, Runolf," the scout replied. "And in my heart, the things I'll remember are those you did choose: to teach me well, and to serve your king in good faith."

"Thank you," he said, his face showing his relief. "You know you were a son to me."

Tavis nodded. "And I hope I made a proud father of you," he said. "But now we find ourselves facing each other like enemies, and you must tell me why."

"I'm not your enemy," Runolf replied. "And if you're loyal to Camden, you'll turn back and never mention what you've seen."

"The king has given me no commands, so I am free to pursue Brianna, and I will," Tavis replied. "But you must tell me why he gave his daughter to the ogres."

"I beg you, do not ask. To answer is to violate my duty—and yours."

"But I have asked," Tavis replied.

Runolf clamped his mouth shut, fighting against the command. The golden mist poured from his eyes in billows, and the glowing runes on his forehead shined as bright as flames. He began to tremble, and Tavis feared the strain of the internal battle would destroy the head.

Finally, Runolf's lips parted, and a low, croaking voice issued from his throat. "Payment," he said. "It was the price Camden paid the ogre shaman, Goboka, for helping him win the War of Harts."

A cold knot of outrage filled Tavis's stomach. "Camden sold his daughter for a kingdom?" he gasped. "A man who could do that is no king!"

"Not a firbolg king, perhaps," replied Basil. "But most other races—especially men—are easily capable of such betrayals. In fact, among my own people, treachery is considered a virtue for the ruling class."

"I'm not interested in the dishonest ways of your people," Tavis growled. "Nor am I interested in serving a king who holds power in such esteem that he betrays his own flesh to secure it."

"You're judging him too harshly," said Runolf. "When Goboka offered the ogres' help in return for Camden's firstborn daughter, the promise was an easy one to make. Brianna had not yet been conceived, and girls are rare among the Hartwicks."

"So I have heard," Tavis replied. Brianna herself had once explained that her husband would be the first king not descended by direct male lineage from the original Hartwick king. "The princess told me she was only the tenth girl-child in her line, and the first woman to become sole heir to the throne."

"Then you know the king never intended to give away his child," said Runolf. "But now, he must honor the promise. To refuse would mean war with the ogres, and thousands would suffer in Brianna's place."

Tavis's knees grew weak, his thoughts spinning in his head. Still holding Runolf in his hands, he sat on the ground and felt tears running down his cheeks. "Why?" he asked. "What do the ogres want with her?"

"I don't know," Runolf replied. "Neither does the king."

"A more interesting question is *how* this Goboka knew Brianna would be born," said Basil. "After a thousand years of kings, it seems strange he should ask for a princess shortly before one becomes the first female heir to Hartsvale."

"Goboka set him up!" Avner exclaimed. "I'll bet the ogres arranged the whole war, just so he'd need them. I've helped—er, I've seen—charlatans use tricks like that to cheat people at the village fair."

"That thought has crossed the king's mind, I assure you," Runolf said. "But it makes no difference. If Goboka has the magic to do such a thing, then refusing to honor the promise would be even more dangerous."

Basil shook his head. "This shaman's magic is powerful, but not that powerful. He couldn't do such a thing without help—very powerful help." The verbeeg fell silent for a moment, then asked, "Do you know where the ogres were taking Brianna?"

Runolf's face went rigid. "They didn't tell me," he said in a strained voice.

"That's not what I asked you," Basil pressed. "Do you know where they're going?"

The mist in Runolf's eyes suddenly grew hot, then

shot out in two great plumes of searing steam. Tavis dropped the head and scrambled away, his chest and arms throbbing with pain from the scalding he had just received.

"What's happening?" the firbolg demanded.

"The shaman's fighting my magic," Basil said. "Amazing!"

The verbeeg backed away, motioning for his companions to do the same. Then he looked back to Runolf's head, which was now completely engulfed in the golden steam. "Where are the ogres taking Brianna?" he demanded.

The runes on Runolf's brow flared, filling the boiling cloud with a brilliant green glimmer.

"I overheard a name," came the croaking reply. "Twilight Vale."

The steam cloud began to whirl, draining back into the eyes of the disembodied head. Basil's runes flashed like lightning, and a deep, sonorous roar rumbled from Runolf's mouth.

"Let's move!" Tavis yelled.

The companions turned and rushed for the couloir walls, grasping for handholds even as they leaped onto the stony ramparts. With a tremendous crack, Runolf's head flew apart. A wall of sheer force slammed into their backs, driving the breath from their lungs and pinning them tightly against the crag.

Tavis did not care. His face pressed against the rock, he clung to his handholds with a death grip. Behind him, the talus shuddered, then, with a deafening roar, it released its hold and went crashing away.

As the dust began to billow out of the valley below, the scout looked toward Needle Peak. There, standing a little apart from the long ogre line with his eyes fixed on the couloir, was a single burly figure: Goboka.

❧ 7 ❧

Silent Ravine

A trio of mule deer flashed past Tavis's shoulder, their hooves pattering almost silently across the needle-covered ground. They ran up the ravine for a short distance, white rumps flashing behind gray pine boles, to where the small valley bent sharply to the north. Here, the doe suddenly pulled up short, then darted into the mouth of a rocky gulch. The three beasts vanished from sight as quickly as they had appeared, leaving the forest as still as it had been a moment earlier.

Tavis continued to walk, forcing himself not to look back. The skin between his shoulder blades felt cold and clammy, a sure sign that his senses had detected some danger his mind could not yet identify. His first thought was that Morten and the earls were catching up, but he did not hear snapping sticks or rattling armor or alarmed birds, or any other sounds to suggest an ungainly firbolg and eighteen overburdened humans were tramping through the wood behind him. In fact, an unnatural hush had fallen over the entire valley, and he heard nothing but the wind whispering through the pines.

It had to be ogres. Few things silenced a forest like a pack of ogres, and even mule deer were not so skittish that the doe would have led her fawns so close if she had not been terrified. Somehow, an ogre patrol had slipped in behind Tavis and his companions. This alarmed the scout, not because it surprised him, but because he had expected Goboka to try exactly this maneuver, and he had *still* failed to notice it happening.

Tavis was also puzzled by how all three deer had survived long enough to come charging past. Ogres customarily killed every creature they found in their path, which was why the forest grew so quiet upon their approach—most beasts had developed the good sense to hide or flee at the first rancid whiff of ogre flesh. Yet the deer had been fleeing into the wind, which meant the doe would not have smelled the brutes until they were upon her. In this thick forest, she would not have seen or heard the ogres until they were easily within bow range. So how had she and her fawns escaped alive? None of them should have survived the brutes' poison-tipped arrows, much less all three. Ogres were better hunters than that.

Tavis pulled his bow off his shoulder and stepped behind a tree. He looked back down the gully, at the same time nocking an arrow, and found the astonished faces of Basil and Avner staring back at him.

"What are you doing?" Avner gasped.

"Take cover!" Tavis hissed, genuinely surprised the fleeing deer had failed to alarm the pair. "A pack of ogres snuck in behind us. They're coming up the ravine right now, hoping to plant their arrows in our backs."

Avner threw himself to the ground and crawled behind a boulder. Basil stepped behind a tree next to Tavis. They peered down the ravine, their eyes searching the maze of gray bark for some sign of movement.

"I don't see anything," Avner whispered.

Neither did Tavis. Save for a few pine boughs swaying gently in the wind, the wood was as still as ice. The scout raised his eyes toward the forest canopy, just in case the ogres were employing the same trick they had used on Coggin's Rise. He saw nothing in the green needles, not so much as a lurking squirrel or the silhouette of a frightened porcupine. The brutes could hide well enough on the ground, but even they were not so stealthy they could move through the treetops without leaving some sign. If there had been any warriors lurking among the branches, the scout would have seen signs: broken limbs, overturned nests, clawed bark, or something similar.

"Perhaps you were mistaken," Basil suggested. "This forest is empty."

"Too empty," Tavis said. "Listen."

Basil cocked his head to one side, then shrugged his shoulders. "I don't hear anything."

"Me either!" Avner said. "I don't hear any singing birds."

"Or chattering squirrels, or whistling rockchucks," Tavis said. "We aren't alone here."

Basil began to fumble through his shoulder satchel. "How much time do we have?"

"Not enough for you to draw a rune," Tavis answered. "The ogres are fairly near, or those deer wouldn't have passed so close to us."

Avner swallowed hard. "So we have to fight?"

"Not yet," Tavis replied. "If we let the ogres pick the battle site, we're doomed."

"Then how do we escape?" Basil asked.

Tavis glanced up the ravine. He did not see any ogres ahead, but that, of course, was not as telling as the fact that the doe had turned into the side gully. Besides, if Goboka had sent a pack of warriors to sneak up from behind them, it seemed likely the shaman had also sent a second party to block their route, and the curve ahead was just the place to set such an ambush.

"They intend to drive us like game. The beaters will come from that direction." Tavis pointed down the ravine. "They'll try to chase us into an ambush just around that bend." The scout pointed up the gully at the curve.

"That's no answer to my question," Basil said, irritated. "How do we escape?"

Tavis was about to tell the verbeeg to run for the side gulch, but stopped when the distant crack of a snapping branch sounded from somewhere down the ravine. A faint metallic chime instantly followed the noise, then the forest fell silent again.

Basil stepped from behind his tree. "Ogres don't trip over sticks, and they don't wear armor," he said. "That was an earl."

"No doubt. But that doesn't mean I was wrong. The ogre beaters are still behind us. Morten and the earls are behind them." The scout pointed to where a loutish silhouette with a jutting chin and floppy ears had just slipped from behind the gray trunk of a huge pine.

Basil looked over his shoulder just in time to see the figure rush down the ravine a few noiseless steps, then vanish from sight behind another tree. The verbeeg's face paled, and he quickly returned to his own cover.

"It's not as bad as it seems," Tavis said. "We're almost out of their range."

Ogre bows were powerful enough by human standards, but they were no match for Bear Driller. Although the brutes were certainly strong enough to pull a bow as large as the scout's, they placed their faith in stealth and poison, and therefore preferred smaller weapons that were easier to fire in the tight hiding places from which they so often ambushed their prey. It was a strategy that worked well enough against unwitting opponents, but it had disadvantages in open combat.

"Being *almost* out of range isn't very reassuring," Basil said. "I'd much prefer to be entirely out of range."

"Me, too," Tavis agreed. "We'll run for it. I'll go a few paces up the ravine, then turn around to cover you."

"Turn around?" Avner hissed. "You'll be presenting your back to the ambushers up ahead!"

"I've got to present it to somebody. Besides, the ambushers will hold their attack until the beaters drive all three of us into close range," he explained. "You two move together. Dodge between trees and don't waste time looking back."

With that, the scout darted two dozen erratic steps up the ravine, changing directions each time he passed a tree, until he heard the soft thump of an ogre arrow striking a nearby pine. Had the range not been so great the shaft would be lodged in his head instead of the bole. He stepped behind a tree, then drew his own bowstring back and looked down the gully. There was no sign of the ogre who had fired at him.

"Now!" Tavis yelled.

Basil and Avner leaped out and charged up the ravine together for perhaps five steps, then split and took cover behind two separate trees. The ogres did not show themselves, though Tavis knew they were watching.

Basil left his cover first, moving two trees toward Avner, then changing his course and rushing in the opposite direction. The young thief followed. When both were in the open, three ogre beaters slipped from their hiding places and drew their bowstrings.

Tavis fired and pulled another arrow from his quiver. His first shaft struck home before his foes could release their volley, ripping through an ogre's shoulder and whirling him around. The brute howled in agony and released his shot into the air, then hit the ground with a gaping hole where the scout's large arrow had passed through his body.

The bowstrings of the two surviving ogres hummed. Their black arrows came arcing through the forest, the brutes having raised their aim to compensate for the distance. The fate of their companion had clearly disturbed them, for both shafts wobbled through the air with all the grace of pheasants in flight. The scout released his second shot. The string of his mighty bow pulsed with a loud, basal throb, and his arrow streaked away, passing beneath the two ogre shafts in midflight. One of the poisoned arrows dropped a full ten paces shy of its target, while the other careened harmlessly past Avner's head.

Tavis's arrow, driven by a much more powerful bow, struck in the next instant. The shaft tore through its target's stomach, moving with such velocity that it did not even knock him off his feet. The astonished brute simply dropped his weapons and reached for the hole that had suddenly appeared in his abdomen.

Without waiting to see him fall, Tavis nocked his third arrow. By the time he raised it to fire, the last ogre had ducked behind cover and was no longer a target. The scout waited for Avner and Basil to hide again, then turned and darted up the ravine toward the side gully.

This time, Tavis made it clear to the bend before a chorus of bowstrings sounded down the ravine. He threw himself over the trunk of a toppled pine, crashing through its brown-needled boughs. He looked out from beneath the tree and saw a half dozen black shafts drop several paces short of his hiding place.

Tavis rose to his knees and lifted his arrow over the tree, but he was too slow to find a target. He saw nothing but a handful of gray blurs as the ogres ducked behind their cover.

"Come on!" Tavis yelled. He knew that he was now within range of the ogre ambushers lurking behind the band, so he stayed low and listened carefully for any noises that suggested they were moving to attack earlier than he expected.

Basil and Avner rushed forward, crossing and recrossing paths as they ran up the ravine. This time, none of their foes were foolish enough to expose themselves to Tavis's arrows. The scout began to hope he and his friends might escape into the side gully unscathed, then somewhere up the ravine, an ogre ambusher made the uncharacteristic mistake of stepping on a loose stone.

Avner pulled his dagger from inside his tunic, calling, "Tavis, your back!"

The youth hurled his dagger. As the blade sliced through the air, Tavis spun around. He saw two ogres stepping around the bend, less than twenty paces away. Both were drawing their bowstrings back to fire.

Avner's dagger soared past Tavis's head and sailed

straight at an ogre's throat. Normally, such a small blade would not fell an ogre, but the boy's aim was so true the knife took the creature right in the gullet, burying itself to the hilt. The brute released his arrow prematurely and collapsed, a surprised squawk gurgling from his mouth.

Tavis aimed at the second ogre, releasing his arrow as the brute released his. The scout did not wait to see his shaft strike. As soon he felt his bowstring scrape free of his fingers, he rolled to one side, crashing through the lifeless limbs beneath the fallen tree. The ogre's arrow clattered into the dry boughs and skipped away.

Pulling another arrow from his quiver, Tavis crawled out of the tangle of branches. He looked up and glimpsed his attacker's form standing in the same place he had been a moment earlier. The scout nocked his arrow and fired—not realizing until the shaft was in flight that he had already killed his target. The brute was pinned to a tree, the fletching of Tavis's first arrow protruding from the center of his chest. The second shaft split the first, driving through the ogre's body in the same hole.

The hum of ogre bows sounded from down the ravine, then Basil and Avner came diving over the toppled pine. Tavis spun around and saw a flurry of black shafts flying in their direction. Looking past the immediate danger, he spied a dozen loutish beaters scurrying up the ravine. Tavis allowed the ogre arrows to fall harmlessly to the ground, then nocked an arrow.

The ogres stopped running and dived for cover. Knowing it would take a moment before the beaters could fire, the scout spun around to face the ambushers. He glimpsed three more silhouettes slipping behind tree trunks.

"Up there!" Tavis gestured toward the side gully.

Basil and Avner sprinted into the gulch. Tavis followed more slowly, pointing his arrow first uphill, then downhill. The ogres made no move to prevent the escape and did not even show themselves. There could only be one reason for the lack of pursuit, Tavis realized. The brutes no longer saw any reason to risk their lives, which meant they believed they had herded their quarry into a trap.

Confident the ogres would not pursue him into the narrow confines of the side gulch, Tavis paused to look around. This gully was a small one, lined on both sides by sheer cliffs of black-streaked gneiss. Like the ravine from which he and his companions had just come, it was filled with towering pines, though the trees here looked less healthy. They were overcrowded, and the small area prevented them from extending their branches fully. Avner and Basil were still sprinting up the center of the gulch, heedless that it was an ideal place for an ambush.

Not wishing to call out and let the ogres know he had anticipated their trap, Tavis fired his arrow up the gulch. The shaft hissed past Basil's shoulder and lodged in a tree, bringing both the verbeeg and Avner to a halt. They turned around and peered at the scout, their mouths gaping open.

Tavis motioned for them to remain where they were, then put his bow over his shoulder. Next, he took his dagger and opened a lengthy but shallow cut along his forearm. Once the wound began to bleed profusely, he walked up the gulch, dripping blood on the ground as he went.

When the scout reached his companions, Avner looked at him as if he were crazy. "What are you doing?"

"Making it easy for the ogres to follow us," Tavis replied. "After they find this blood trail, they won't pay as much attention to other signs. That'll give us a chance to escape."

"We haven't done that yet?" Basil asked.

"No, we've been forced into a trap," Tavis replied. "Somewhere around a corner ahead, a couple dozen ogres are waiting to shower us with arrows."

The scout allowed his companions to consider this

while he studied the surrounding terrain. He spied a series of three boulders close enough together that Avner could leap from one to the other, then said, "Now, here's what I want you to do."

After Tavis had explained his plan, Basil asked, "Do we have time for all that?"

The scout nodded. "The ogres won't be anxious to come after us. They've suffered losses enough to know they won't get past Bear Driller in these confines," he said. "By the time they come to see why we haven't wandered into their ambush, we'll be gone."

The scout started up the gully. Making certain to drip plenty of blood along the ground, he led his companions to within a pace of the first boulder. Instead of jumping onto the stone at this point, Avner and Basil walked past, following Tavis another twenty paces. The boy stopped there, but the verbeeg continued up the gully.

Thirty paces later, Basil also stopped. He slowly backed down the gully, placing his feet in exactly the same places as he had on the way up. When he reached Avner, he hoisted the boy onto his shoulder and continued his retreat to the three boulders Tavis had pointed out earlier. After Avner brushed his feet off, the verbeeg deposited the youth on the first boulder. The boy hopped across the three boulders, then climbed a tree and crawled across a branch onto the cliff top.

For Basil, escaping the gorge was more difficult. Like Avner, he brushed the loose soil off his feet, then crossed the boulders to the side of the gully. Unfortunately, he was too heavy for the pine's thin branches and too clumsy to climb straight up the cliff face, so he had to backtrack a short distance to where a dead tree had fallen against the cliff side. He ascended the gray trunk, then joined Avner.

As his companions made their escape, Tavis picked up a stick, then ripped a strip of cloth off his tunic. These two items he used to make a tourniquet around his arm.

Once that was done, he continued up the gulch, slowly turning the stick so that the blood trail gradually diminished. When he came to a jumble of boulders, he crossed the pile about halfway, then tightened the tourniquet until the blood ceased to drip altogether. After cleaning the bottom of his boots to make certain he did not leave any loose soil to divulge his change of path, he moved toward the side of the gorge, being careful not dislodge any of the stones he walked across.

The scout crept along the base of the cliff until he came to a sickly tree growing too close to the wall. He braced one foot against its trunk and one against the rocky face, then slowly climbed out of the gorge. By the time he reached the top, his tourniquet had loosened and blood was dripping into the canyon, but he did not worry. It would be quite some time before the ogres realized he had laid a false trail, and it would take them even longer to discover how he and his friends had escaped.

Tavis removed the tourniquet and applied a more proper bandage, then scurried down the ridge to join his friends. Together the trio started to traverse the ravine's north side, climbing toward Needle Peak, but the scout quickly realized they could not remain concealed by taking this route. The valley took a sharp turn southward. They could not travel any farther without exposing themselves.

Tavis motioned for his companions to wait. Hunching over until his chest almost touched his knees, he crept down the hillside. He stepped carefully, avoiding dry-looking twigs, loose rocks, even clumps of dry pine needles that might crackle under his weight. It had been many months since he had moved so slowly in such an awkward position, and his muscles soon began to ache from the strain. The scout ignored his discomfort, knowing that if he relaxed and did something that made a substantial noise, the ogres would hear it.

A few minutes later, he came to a place where the hill

fell away sharply, giving him a clear view of the ravine below. He was directly above the bend where the side gulch opened into the main gully. He knelt behind a pair of close-growing saplings, using the dense foliage as a screen, and began to search for ogres.

Tavis saw one warrior immediately, lying facedown on the uphill side of a decomposing log. It took him a little longer to find the others. Although they had not selected their hiding places to camouflage themselves from someone in Tavis's location, the brutes were sitting so motionless that, in their gray cloaks, many of them looked like stumps and boulders.

Even after he had found five warriors, Tavis continued to study the ravine. The ogres' stillness puzzled him. By now the brutes were certainly curious about the silence in the side gulch. They should have been cautiously venturing into the small gully to investigate. Yet here they were, still lurking in ambush, as though the beaters were driving more prey toward them.

After a moment's consideration, Tavis realized why. They had set their trap again—this time for Morten and the earls.

The scout studied the valley below, then decided he had found all the ambushers. He pulled four arrows from his quiver, planting them tip-first into the ground, and nocked a fifth. Normally, he would have set out six shafts for five targets, just in case he missed once, but two of the ogres were standing in line, and he always took advantage of any chance to save arrows.

Tavis peered through the small gap between the saplings he had selected as cover, then took careful aim at a lobeless ear protruding above a small boulder. It was his most difficult target, for not only was it on the other side of the ravine, it was all he could see of the ogre.

Drawing his bowstring back, Tavis exhaled. He stared at the ear, blocking every thought from his mind until he was aware of nothing but his target, then he pulled his fingers away. The string throbbed and sent the arrow sizzling through the air. The shaft skimmed over the rock and struck home with a muffled thud, then both ear and arrow disappeared from sight.

In one swift motion, Tavis pulled the next arrow from the ground, nocked it, and fired at his easiest target, the ogre lying behind the decomposing log. The shaft caught the brute just as he was raising his head, ripping through the back to pierce the warrior's heart.

The scout's next arrow was in the air before the warrior died, catching the third ogre through the head as he rose from behind a juniper bush to gape at the arrow in his companion's back. The fourth and fifth stepped away from their trees, spinning around to search the hillside. Despite the obvious panic in their purple eyes, the brutes remained silent, determined not to alarm the prey their companions would soon be driving up the ravine. That suited Tavis fine. He drew his bowstring back, waited until the ogre in back stepped behind his companion, and loosed the shaft.

Tavis nocked the last arrow he had set out, but there was no need. The shaft passed cleanly through the first ogre's throat, then ripped into the breast of the one behind. This warrior did not die instantly, but with an arrow lodged in his lung, his feeble gurgles would not alarm the beaters driving Morten and the earls up the ravine.

The scout paused just long enough to make certain there were no more ogres lurking below, then returned to his companions and told them what had happened.

"So now we're free to leave?" Basil asked.

Tavis shook his head. "No, Morten and the earls are still coming up the ravine," he said. "If we go now, the ogres may drive them into the ambush yet."

"And if we don't, whoever survives the battle will definitely attack us," Avner objected. "I say we leave our enemies to each other and go while we can."

"Morten and the earls aren't our true enemies," Tavis

replied. "They're only doing what they believe to be right. We can't condemn them for that."

"I don't see why not," Avner grumbled. "They condemned us for a lot less."

"We aren't leaving them to the ogres!" Tavis snapped. "Do you understand that?"

Avner met the firbolg's gaze with an angry glare. "I understand."

"Good," Tavis said. "Go down to the ravine and hide until Morten comes."

"Then what?" the youth asked. "Surrender?"

"Make sure he sees you, then lead him away from the side gulch and up the valley," Tavis instructed. "Basil and I will set up an ambush of our own. We'll pull you aside, then I'm sure Basil can do something to temporarily disable Morten and the earls." The scout cast a hopeful glance at the verbeeg.

"I can put them to sleep for a lengthy time," Basil said.

"Good," Tavis replied. "We'll treat the ogres less charitably."

"What? You're not going to spare *everyone* who's trying to kill us?"

Tavis scowled his reply.

Pulling a sling from inside his tunic, Avner reluctantly started down the hill.

Tavis shook his head in disappointment. "As much as I love that boy, I don't think he'll ever learn."

"He's learned much already, but his teacher was cruel indifference," said Basil. "If it's any consolation, I do believe he loves you more than he loves his own life."

"Perhaps," the scout acknowledged. "But I doubt you could say the same about his love of gold."

With that, the scout started across the hillside, angling toward an outcropping of rocks a short distance up the ravine.

Basil followed a step behind. "Now that we're alone, there's something I've been meaning to discuss with you."

"Can't it wait?" Tavis asked. "This lull in the fighting won't last long."

Basil shook his head. "I don't want to discuss it in front of the boy. Besides, it won't take long," he said quietly. "How much do you know about the Twilight Vale?"

"I never heard of it until Runolf spoke its name."

"That's not surprising," Basil answered. "True giants consider it a sacred place. They keep it secret from all but their own kind."

"Then how do you and the ogres know of it?"

"I read about it in a tablet I borrowed from the stone giants," Basil explained. "As for the ogres, they clearly have their own ways. But the reason I raised the subject is what happens in the vale."

"What?"

"The true giants gather there once each year. The chieftains resolve their grievances in peace, the warriors drink from magical springs, and the shamans receive guiding omens from the vale's guardian, the Twilight Spirit," Basil explained. The verbeeg looked away, obviously uncomfortable, then continued, "And they conduct ceremonies of tribal union."

"Union?" Tavis asked.

"Matings between important members of different tribes," the verbeeg explained. "To guarantee good relations."

"That's ridiculous!" Tavis had to restrain himself to keep his voice low. "Brianna would never mate with an ogre!"

Basil ran a hand over his sloped brow. "Her consent wouldn't be necessary, nor did I say it was an ogre she's going to mate," the verbeeg replied. He was looking more uncomfortable by the moment. "The Twilight Spirit arranges these unions for the good of all giants. Goboka might be taking her there to see a chief from any tribe."

"A human and a giant?" Tavis scoffed.

"It's no more ridiculous than a cloud giant and hill giant, and I've read of such unions," Basil replied. "The spirit's magic is most powerful."

Tavis considered this for a moment, then shook his head. "It still makes no sense," he said. "Ogres aren't true giants, they're giant-kin, like you and me. Why should Goboka care what the Twilight Spirit wants?"

"Goboka is extremely powerful for an ogre shaman, both in magic and political power," the verbeeg explained. "Who do you suppose helped him get that way?"

"The Twilight Spirit," Tavis concluded. "And in return, the spirit received a small and stealthy ally to send after Brianna."

Basil nodded. "There are some tasks giants just can't do—at least not if you want them done quietly."

Tavis sighed, frustrated. "That still doesn't explain *why* the Twilight Spirit wants Brianna."

Basil scowled in thought. "We already know Goboka foresaw Brianna's birth far in advance. That's why the Twilight Spirit sent the ogres to dupe Camden," the verbeeg said. "Maybe he also saw something that did not bode well for his giants."

The scout nodded. "And Brianna is the key to protecting them," he said. "The question is, what from?"

Basil shrugged. "My magic isn't that powerful," he said. "If you really want to know the future, you'll have to find the Twilight Spirit and ask him."

"I'd rather find Brianna and avoid the Twilight Spirit," Tavis said. "But first, we have some ogres to ambush."

With that, the scout lengthened his stride and did not say another word until they reached the cliff where he intended to ambush the ogres. Basil took out a brush and set to work on his sleeping rune, while Tavis climbed up the hill to keep watch.

When the runecaster finished his symbol, there was still no sign of their quarry, so he climbed up the hill to join Tavis. They waited for several more minutes, and the scout began to fear something terrible had gone wrong with his plan. Then he finally saw Avner coming up the ravine and began to breathe easier. Tavis nodded to Basil, and they both ducked down behind a boulder to wait.

The scout soon realized Morten and his band were not coming. Avner showed no particular concern as he ran through the forest, never looking back to check on the progress of his pursuers. Nor did Tavis detect the sound of any cracking sticks or clanging armor, both of which he would have heard in abundance if the clumsy earls had been rushing up the ravine. He tossed a rock down to catch Avner's attention, then rose and showed himself.

Making no more noise than a good scout would have, the boy climbed the hill to join Tavis. "Morten wouldn't follow me," he reported. "I did everything but sling a rock at him, and he just ignored me."

Tavis was puzzled by the report. Even if Morten suspected a trap, he would have followed the boy long enough to see where he was going.

"Are you sure they saw you?" the scout asked.

Avner nodded. "I was in a tree," he said. "I shook the branch I was sitting on, and he looked right up into my eyes. I jumped down to be sure he knew it was me and not an ogre, then I started running. He never followed."

"Did you see where he went?" Tavis asked. "He didn't take the earls into the side gulch, did he?"

Avner shrugged. "If he did, there's not much we can do for him now," the youth replied. "Let's get out of here before the ogres—"

A distant clunk cut the boy off. The sound was followed by a surprised shout, then more clanging and yelling.

Tavis started toward the sound. "I'm going to help Morten."

"What?" Avner shrieked. "You'll get us killed."

"Not *us*. You stay here. If I don't come back, hide here.

You can start back to Hartsvale in the morning."

"So the king can have me arrested?" the youth scoffed. "No way."

"Then go where you please," Tavis snapped. "We don't have time to argue about it now."

The scout sprinted down the hill, his long legs carrying him across the ravine as swiftly as a wolf. Basil followed along, his heavy footfalls only slightly muffled by the thick layer of pine needles covering the ground.

"I welcome your help, Basil," Tavis said. "But maybe you should follow at a slower pace. You won't be much good to anyone if you're too tired to fight."

"And I'm too clumsy to take the ambushers by surprise." The verbeeg smiled at Tavis's diplomacy, then began to fade back. "I'll come as quickly as I can without alarming the ogres."

Tavis continued forward at a sprint, guided by the clanging of armor and the angry battle cries of Morten and his companions. The ogres made no sound at all. So ingrained were their habits of stealth that they usually fought in complete silence, rarely uttering a sound except when they suffered a grievous wound—and sometimes not even then. Soon, as the scout crested the bank of the ravine, he saw the crescent-shaped rim of a box canyon on the slope ahead. Clambering among the boulders and spruces along its brink were almost two dozen ogres, all firing black arrows down into the gulch. From the panicked cries echoing from the hollow, it appeared their shafts were finding targets all too often.

Tavis stopped just outside the range of their bows, then leaned his quiver against his knee. He did not remove any arrows from the case because once his foes realized where he was, he would have to move in a hurry.

As the scout nocked his first shaft, an ogre suddenly clutched his breast and spun around, stumbling away from the canyon. Though the distance was too great for the scout to be certain, it looked like the fletching of a short quarrel was protruding from between the brute's bloody fingers. Apparently, the earls had their crossbows.

Tavis took aim and fired, shooting at the ogres on the far side of the gulch first. His arrows tore through three targets before the pack realized it was being attacked, then he hit two more of the brutes as they tried to figure out where the arrows were coming from. A large warrior in a wolfskin headdress began barking commands. The scout silenced him by ripping his throat open with a well-placed arrow.

The leader's death spurred the war party into reacting. As one, they spun and launched a volley of arrows. Without bothering to hide, Tavis killed another of his foes before the black shafts fell out of the air, lodging in the ground about fifteen paces short of his position. The scout fired again. His arrow struck home, spinning the victim around so that he fell over the edge into the gulch. Several cheers rose from the hollow, then a flurry of bolts claimed the last few brutes on the far side of the canyon.

Realizing the danger of being caught in a crossfire, the ogres on the near side dived away from the rim, taking shelter behind what cover they could find. There were only ten of them here, and Tavis quickly reduced that number to eight by picking out holes in their cover.

When the sounds of battle continued to rise from inside the gorge, Tavis realized that he had solved only part of the problem by drawing the pack on the brim of the gorge away. The group that had been acting as beaters had followed Morten's party into the gulch, and no doubt still had the men pinned against the cliffs.

That was a problem the bodyguard and his earls would have to handle by themselves. The eight survivors on top of the gulch had gathered their wits enough to begin an assault against Tavis. As the scout watched, they jumped to their feet and rushed forward.

Tavis calmly stood his ground long enough to kill two more, then grabbed his quiver and retreated over the bank of the ravine. Once he was out of sight, he ran along the slope, silently traversing it toward the box canyon for about a hundred paces. Then, when he judged he had moved past the ogres' flank, he climbed the bank and peered over the top.

The scout saw immediately that his maneuver had not fooled the ogres. Two of them were still moving toward where he had jumped over the bank, but the other four were nowhere in sight. They were no doubt lurking somewhere nearby, waiting for him to show himself.

Tavis fired and ducked. He heard a muffled thump as his arrow struck its target, then several of the ambushers' shafts flew over his head. The scout grabbed a rock and threw it across the slope, hoping the sound would convince his enemies he was on the move again. Then he nocked another arrow and stuck his head up, killing the second ogre he had seen earlier.

Two of the unseen warriors returned fire immediately, one of their arrows passing so close that Tavis felt its coarse feather brush his skull. He yelled as though wounded, then drew his sword and laid it on the slope beside him. He heard the ogres' feet pattering over the pine needles as they rushed forward to finish the kill. The scout nocked another arrow and laid the tip over the edge of the bank, not raising his head to look. Runolf had lectured him many times on the importance of using more than his eyes to pick targets, explaining that he would sometimes find himself fighting on cloudy nights or in lightless caves. It was a lesson that Tavis had learned well, and one that had saved his life more than once.

The scout lifted his arrow slightly, as if he were rising to fire. He heard the snap of an ogre's bowstring, then a single shaft sailed overhead and disappeared into the ravine below. Tavis waited, listening to the soft steps of the approaching enemy. When it seemed they had to be almost on him, he turned the tip of the arrow toward the loudest set of footfalls and released the bowstring.

Because of his awkward firing position, the shot was not particularly powerful, but it had force enough to create a moist thump as it sank into an ogre's abdomen. The target collapsed to the ground with a muffled thud.

The footsteps of the victim's companions faltered. Tavis dropped his bow, then pushed the tip of another arrow above the bank. This time, the action drew the fire of two alarmed ogres. Smiling at their skittish reactions, the scout grabbed his sword and clambered over the bank. He found himself two paces away from the three surviving ogres. One was just drawing his bowstring back to fire, and the others were frantically trying to nock fresh arrows.

Tavis twisted sideways, pushing his sword arm forward and also moving his torso out of the arrow's path. The tip of his blade slipped between the ogre's ribs in the same instant the brute released his bowstring. The poisoned arrow sizzled past the scout's breast. He lunged forward, driving his sword deeper, until foul-smelling blood began to froth from the ogre's mouth.

Tavis stepped back and braced one foot on the warrior's hip, jerking his sword free of the dying brute. He spun around to face the last two survivors—only to discover they had nocked their arrows and were even now drawing their bowstrings to fire. The scout could kill one of them, but the other one would slay him.

"Tavis!" screamed Avner's voice. A small stone came whispering through the air and struck one ogre in the head. The blow did not kill the warrior, but it stunned him enough to prevent the brute from completing the pull of his bowstring. "What are you doing?"

Tavis started to slash at the other ogre, but even as the young thief spoke, a huge boulder arced down upon this brute's head. The stone struck with a crack, then thumped to the ground. The warrior's knees buckled, and he released his arrow into the air. The scout spun, using a backhand stroke to behead the ogre Avner's stone had stunned.

"When I said go on ahead, I didn't mean you should kill all the ogres yourself." Basil dropped a second boulder he had picked up, then walked over with Avner at his side.

"You could've gotten yourself killed," Avner complained.

"I thought I told you to stay at the cliff," Tavis said.

"Lucky for you I don't listen too well," the boy countered.

Realizing he could hardly argue with the statement, Tavis retrieved his bow and quiver, then turned toward the gulch. The sounds of fighting had grown faint and sporadic, suggesting that the battle was almost at an end. Fearing that he knew who was on the losing side, the scout rushed over to the gorge's rim.

The battle had come down to only five figures: Morten, Earl Dobbin, and three ogres. The firbolg was standing directly between two of their foes, swinging a huge, double-headed battle-axe first at one, then the other. The ogres had picked up a pair of fallen earls to use as shields, but were rapidly falling back under the bodyguard's withering attacks.

Earl Dobbin was not faring so well. He had collapsed to one knee and was swinging his pitifully small sword at the last ogre's legs, barely managing to duck the wild swings of his foe's large club. The other earls lay scattered among fallen ogres, either dead or unconscious from the bite of poisoned arrows.

Tavis dispatched the ogre attacking Earl Dobbin first, then quickly killed one of the brutes fighting Morten. The bodyguard finished the other himself, cleaving the warrior's heavy skull with a single, terrible blow of his battle-axe.

The ogre had hardly hit the ground before Morten was glaring up at his savior. "Tavis!" he thundered.

"Come down here!"

The scout shook his head. "Not yet," he said. "Not until you and I come to an agreement."

Morten snorted. "The only thing I'll agree to is splitting your head."

"Really?" Tavis replied. "I should think you'd be more interested in saving Brianna—I am."

This calmed the angry firbolg a little. "Tell me where she is," he demanded. "I'll make your death an easy one."

Earl Dobbin rose, his face red with fury. "You don't have the right to make such an agreement!" he said, grabbing the bodyguard's burly arm. "The king sent us to bring these thieves back to Hartsvale, not to rescue his daughter!"

Morten jerked his arm free. "Brianna was my responsibility. If I can save her by letting a few thieves die an easy death, then so be it." The firbolg continued to glare at Tavis. "Now tell me."

"Right now, the princess is somewhere on the Needle Peak glacier with about a thousand ogres," Tavis explained. As he spoke, Basil and Avner came up to stand at his side. "They're taking her to a place called the Twilight Vale."

Morten scowled. "Where's that?"

"The Twilight Vale lies somewhere in the shadow of the Great Glacier, far north of the Ice Spires," Basil explained. "But if you want to return Brianna to Hartsvale, I'd suggest you free her long before then."

Morten narrowed his eyes. "Why's that?"

"The Twilight Vale's sacred to the giants," Tavis explained. "We don't know why the ogres are taking Brianna there, but if they succeed it'll be impossible to get her back."

Morten considered this for a moment, then asked, "Where'd you learn all this?"

"We happened upon the guide who helped the ogres kidnap Brianna," Tavis explained. "Basil interrogated him."

The scout said nothing about the roles of Runolf and the king in the princess's abduction. As much as Morten wanted to save Brianna, Tavis did not think the bodyguard would defy Camden's wishes to do so.

Morten considered Tavis's information for a moment, then nodded in satisfaction. "Good enough. I'll make your death quick," he said. "Now, will you come down here peacefully, or do I have to hunt you down?"

"I'll let you take me back to Hartsvale or kill me on the spot," Tavis offered, "but only after we rescue Brianna."

Basil quickly stepped forward. "Please understand that he's speaking only for himself," the verbeeg said. "Avner and I have no intention of letting you kill us at any time."

"Doesn't matter," Morten replied, shaking his head. "I couldn't accept Tavis's deal, even if it included you all."

The scout frowned. "Why not?"

The bodyguard snorted in derision, then waved his hand at the carnage in the gulch. "You let me lead eighteen good men into this, and now you expect me to place my faith in you?"

"Let you!" Tavis exploded. "We tried to stop you. If you had followed the boy, you'd all be alive and well."

Morten frowned in confusion. "What boy?" he asked. "We never saw any boy!"

"You didn't see Avner at the mouth of the gulch? He dropped out of a tree and ran up the ravine!"

Morten shook his head. "We saw nothing but bodies and a blood trail leading up here. We were afraid the ogres had trapped you here. There was no boy."

His head reeling with the implications of what the bodyguard had just told him, Tavis stumbled back from the edge of the gulch. He spun around and found Avner slowly backing away. The boy's face was pale with fear, and tears of shame were welling in his eyes.

"You lied," Tavis said. His voice was not as angry as it was astonished and hurt. "You lied to me."

❧ 8 ❧
The Glacier

The nickering returned, a series of soft, chattering snorts somewhere above the rim of the icy crevasse. Brianna's talisman, dangling from a piece of rune-inscribed bark in Tavis's hand, slowly spun in the darkness and pointed toward the sound. The tip wavered there a moment, then whirled back in the direction it had been pointing earlier. The silver spear began to sweep back and forth, never holding its position more than a second.

"Phaw! We can't trust that amulet," Morten growled, keeping his voice low. He wore a fresh bandage around his neck, for the last few days of hard travel had sapped his recuperative powers so much that the wound on his throat had begun to fester. "We know where Brianna is. Let's just go get her."

Tavis did not answer. His eyes were fixed on the heavens, searching for the source of the strange nickering. He could see only a narrow wedge of purple starlit sky, for the scout and his rescue party were climbing through a lateral crevasse, an abyssal ice canyon that ran the entire length of the Needle Peak glacier. Gleaming blue walls loomed to both sides of them, impossibly high and so close together that any of the three giant-kin present could have touched both sides by extending his arms. In the bottom of the rift, cold, dead air hung heavy around their numb faces, while the frigid torrents of a tiny melt-water stream gushed over their frozen feet.

Despite the cold, Tavis's face was flushed with excitement. At dusk, Avner had climbed a few hundred feet up Needle Peak to survey the glacier. He had seen the ogres making camp not far above, at the base of a huge ice wall. Several brutes had been erecting an ice-block hut, and the youth had seen a smaller form, almost certainly Brianna, lying in the snow nearby. After hearing the boy's report, Tavis and his companions had decided to sneak up the lateral crevasse to rescue Brianna.

It had been shortly after they started the long journey up the glacier that the nickering began. The sound was soft and plaintive, so hushed that at times Tavis thought it might be nothing but the distant groans of flowing ice—until he looked down and saw Brianna's talisman swinging toward the sound.

Tavis turned to Basil and raised the wobbling amulet. "This happens each time we hear that snorting," the scout said. Although he did not say so, he recognized the sound as that of a horse—most likely Blizzard. "Why does the talisman spin?"

"His m-m-magic's f-f-failing," chattered Earl Dobbin. He and Avner were suffering more from the freezing cold than the three giant-kin. "What do you expect from a ch-charlatan?"

The scout ignored the comment and waited for Basil's reply. If it had been up to Tavis, the lord mayor would have returned to Hartsvale with the other earls who survived the ogre ambush, but Morten wouldn't hear of it. The burly firbolg did not trust Tavis or his companions and had agreed to work with them only if Dobbin came along to balance the odds. Even when Basil had pointed out that Dobbin's peers were all suffering from injuries and could use a healthy man's assistance on the journey back, Morten had insisted that the lord mayor come along.

Casting an angry glare at Dobbin, Basil said, "I assure you, I am no charlatan. The talisman is wavering for good reason."

A terrible thought occurred to Tavis. "Has Goboka vexed your rune?" the scout asked. Given that the shaman's warriors had failed to return from their ambush, the ogre would be a fool not to assume his pursuers would try for Brianna tonight. "Can he do that sort of thing?"

"A powerful shaman like him? Of course he can," Basil replied. The verbeeg paused, then smiled proudly. "That's why I didn't use a rune that would lead us to Brianna herself. I employed one that's designed to locate lost property. I doubt Goboka has thought of that."

"What nonsense are you babbling?" demanded Morten.

"Simply put, the talisman isn't pointing at Brianna," the verbeeg explained. "It's pointing at her belongings—in this case, her clothes and, I believe, at her horse." He cast his eyes toward the crevasse rim, where the soft nickering continued.

"That's ridiculous!" Earl Dobbin scoffed. "No horse could follow over the t-terrain we've c-crossed!"

"Lord Mayor, I'd think you, of all people, would know better than to underestimate Blizzard." Tavis could not quite keep from sneering as he made the observation.

"I do," the earl replied. "But Blizzard is a horse, not a mountain goat. Even she could not have—"

An alarmed whinny sounded from above, interrupting the lord mayor. Tavis looked up in time to see the black shadow of a horse leaping across the crevasse, then something clattered off the ice overhead. As the silhouette vanished from the night sky, a slender shaft of wood tumbled down the canyon walls and splashed into the icy stream. Morten grabbed the stick as it floated past.

"Ogre arrow," grunted the bodyguard.

Tavis fixed his gaze on the rim where Blizzard had been. "But no ogre," he observed, noting that there were no gleaming eyes peering over the edge. "You'd think the warrior would be curious about why Blizzard was lingering by the crevasse."

"Unless he already knew," suggested Basil.

Tavis looked down at Brianna's amulet. The silver spear had stopped wavering, its tip pointing considerably away from the route ahead. Given that they had traveled less than halfway up the icy canyon, the angle seemed much too great. They still had at least a mile to go, so if the ice shelter had been built anywhere near the crevasse, the talisman should have been pointing almost straight up the gorge—at least if Brianna was inside the structure.

"You're suggesting Goboka's ice hut is meant for us?" Basil nodded.

"For us?" asked Morten. "What for?"

"To l-lure us into his t-trap, you oaf," said Earl Dobbin. "We should t-turn back for t-tonight. We can warm ourselves by a nice f-fire and try again in the morning."

"Our chance will be gone by then," said Tavis. "Besides, if I'm right, we may be able to turn the ogres' plan against them."

"And if you're wrong?" demanded the lord mayor.

Tavis shrugged. "We'll know soon enough."

The scout resumed the journey, sloshing up the tiny stream in the bottom of the crevasse. So frigid was the brook that only its swift current prevented the water from turning solid. A thick layer of slush rolled along its icy bed, making the footing so treacherous that Tavis had to hold on to the canyon walls to keep from falling. Nor was the going any easier where the rivulet slowed, for the eddies and pools were covered by thin blankets of ice that shattered beneath the giant-kin's great weight, and he often found himself standing up to his thighs in water so cold it made his bones ache.

Morten and Basil suffered the same discomforts as Tavis, but, for the two humans, wading up the icy stream was an even greater challenge. They stumbled about as if they had lost all feeling in their legs, and more than once Morten or Basil had to catch one of them before he pitched headlong into the frigid waters. That Earl Dobbin continued to wear his breastplate and helmet did not help matters, for the steel was covered with a thick coating of hoarfrost that added to the armor's burdensome weight.

Despite their difficulties, they made steady progress. Tavis paused every now and then to look up and see if they were being watched, but he saw no eyes—ogre or equine. The angle between the crevasse's route and the tip of Brianna's talisman steadily increased. By the time they had ascended the glacier far enough to see the dark silhouette of the ice wall looming above the rim, the silver spear pointed almost directly at the side of the canyon.

Tavis stopped and gathered the others close. "Avner, where would you say that ice hut is in relation to us?"

Despite Avner's obvious discomfort, the mere fact that the scout had condescended to ask him a question caused the boy's eyes to light. It was only the third time Tavis had spoken to him since learning how the youth had abandoned Morten and the earls to the ogre ambush.

"It'd be about th-there," Avner said. He pointed almost directly up the crevasse. "They were b-building it right on the edge, at the b-b-b-bottom of the ice wall."

Avner's arm and Brianna's talisman were pointing in completely different directions. "Goboka's keeping Brianna someplace else," Tavis said. "He built the ice hut to lure us up this crevasse."

"Isn't that wh-what I said?" demanded Earl Dobbin. "You sh-should have t-turned back when I suggested it!"

Tavis shook his head. "The trap was already sprung," he said. "By then, a pack of ogres was in the crevasse, coming up after us."

The earl's eyes widened in alarm. "And you said nothing?" he yelled. "You're in this with the ogres!"

"Keep your voice down," ordered Morten. The bodyguard placed his tremendous bulk in front of the earl and eyed Tavis. "You said you have a plan. What is it?"

"How much time have you spent under glaciers?"

Morten frowned, as did everyone else. "I try to keep my head *above* the snow," the bodyguard grunted. "Why?"

"Because if Goboka's using the ice hut as a decoy, he

needs someplace else to hide Brianna," the scout explained. "And I have an idea where to look."

Before Morten could ask more questions, Tavis continued upstream, stopping about two hundred sloshing paces later. It was here that the meltwater stream flowed into the crevasse, trickling out of an ice cave near the bottom of the rift. A chill breeze seeped from the mouth of the grotto, gnawing at Tavis's soaked legs with its stinging breath.

Noting that the tip of Brianna's talisman was pointing directly into the cavern, Tavis stooped over to peer inside. The passage was about five feet in diameter, as smooth as glass and about half filled with the swift, silent currents of the meltwater stream. The first few paces of the cave gleamed with the same cool radiance as the canyon walls. But as the grotto snaked its way toward the glacier's heart, the blue light gave way to an inky gloom more chilling than death.

"We'll need to light a torch," Tavis said.

"I've got something better," offered Basil. The verbeeg reached into his satchel and withdrew a small poplar stick carved with a single rune. A brilliant yellow radiance shined from the tip of the wand, filling the bottom of the crevasse with a flickering light of gold. "It won't go out, even if it's soaked."

Fearing the bright light would let the ogres know their position, Tavis grabbed the wand and stuck it under his cloak.

"I'm not g-going in there," objected Earl Dobbin.

"Then stay here and fight the ogres," growled Morten. The bodyguard's gaze was fixed on Brianna's talisman, which continued to point unerringly into the ice cave. "I'll follow Tavis in there—after he answers a couple of questions."

Tavis nodded. "If you wish."

"First, how'd you know we'd find a cavern here?" Morten narrowed his eyes, still distrustful of the scout.

"Have you been here before?"

"No," Tavis replied. "But crevasses don't usually have streams."

"Then where'd all this come from?" the bodyguard demanded, kicking at the icy meltwater.

"Do you know what a nunatak is?" the scout asked.

Morten shook his head, but Basil had a ready answer. "It's a projection of rock protruding above the glacier surface," the verbeeg said. "It gathers heat from the sun, which tends to melt the surrounding ice and create a hollow area around the stone."

"Right," Tavis said. "And what happens to all that water?"

"It flows away," Morten growled. "What else?"

"Right again, but it doesn't run over the top of the glacier," Tavis explained. "It's already below the surface when it melts, so it seeps down and melts a path under the ice. So when I saw a stream in the bottom of this crevasse, I knew there had to be an ice cave somewhere up here. Next question?"

The bodyguard did not hesitate before replying. "You said earlier you knew where to look for Brianna. Tell me."

"If you want," the scout said. "I think Goboka's keeping her in a nunatak hollow—perhaps even one that feeds this stream."

Morten raised his brow. "How can you know that?"

"Because she'll freeze if he leaves her in the open," Tavis replied. "And it would be more difficult to lure us into an ambush if we saw his warriors building a second ice hut or digging a snow cave. The hollow of a large nunatak offers the best natural shelter."

"It s-seems to me a small c-crevasse would do as well," said Earl Dobbin. "I've been on enough glaciers to know there are plenty of those."

Tavis shook his head. "After the trouble he took to kidnap her, the shaman won't risk Brianna's life on something so unpredictable," the scout said. "Even crevasses that have stayed open for decades can close in an instant."

The earl cast a nervous glance at the icy walls of their own crevasse, but no one else showed any concern about the risk that their own rift would close.

"Besides, a nunatak hollow should be warmer than a crevasse," Basil added. "At night, the stone will release much of the heat it absorbs from the sun during the day."

"And you think you can find the right nunatak by going into this ice cave?" Morten addressed his question to Tavis.

The scout gestured to Brianna's talisman, which continued to point into the cavern. "What do you think?"

Morten nodded, then checked to be sure the rope and other gear hanging from his belt were secure. "I suppose it's our best chance," he said. "But if something happens—"

"We'll all die together," Tavis replied. "And all your threats won't save any of us."

The scout slipped Brianna's amulet into his cloak pocket, then crawled into the low cavern on his hands and knees. As impossible as it seemed, the meltwater inside the grotto felt even colder than that in the crevasse outside—perhaps because now both his arms and legs were submerged up to the elbows and thighs. The gentle breeze made matters worse, for its breath was as frigid as a frost giant's, cutting through Tavis's damp cloak like daggers of ice.

When the tunnel began to grow so dark he could no longer see, the scout pulled one hand from the frigid currents and drew Basil's light-wand from inside his cloak. He placed the stick between his teeth, then paused long enough to look back. Earl Dobbin had apparently forgotten his earlier refusal to enter the cavern, for he was close behind Avner, who was following directly behind Tavis. The youth was short enough to stand upright in the small cavern, but the lord mayor had to stoop over to keep from scraping his ice-covered helmet on the ceiling.

The lips of both humans were trembling, and the scout knew they could not long withstand the freezing conditions of the meltwater grotto. Unfortunately, there was little he could do to help, except hurry upstream and hope Brianna could save them with a clerical spell after she was rescued. The only way Tavis could help would be to start a fire, and even if that were possible, the smell of smoke would draw the ogres to them in short order.

They continued upstream for many long, bitter minutes. Occasionally the water rose as high as the shoulders of the giant-kin, forcing them to crane their necks to keep their chins above water. The two humans were not strong enough to battle the cold currents alone, so they grabbed Tavis's belt and allowed him to pull them forward. Then, when the brook grew shallow again, they pried their frozen fingers open and waded forward under their own power, the icy breeze cutting through their wet clothing like the claws of a life-stealing wraith. Soon, the draft had stolen so much heat from Earl Dobbin's body that he lost control of his muscles, pitching headfirst into the dark waters. He would have drowned had Morten not been close by to pull him out.

Seeing that Avner's eyes had glazed over and his lips were the color of sapphires, Tavis realized the boy was also perilously close to collapse. The scout loosened his cloak, then instructed the youth to crawl under it to ride on his back. The firbolg doubted his body heat would restore the youth, but at least it might prevent him from collapsing until after they rescued Brianna.

Morten removed Earl Dobbin's frozen breastplate and started to cast it aside, but Basil took the armor from him and sat down in the water.

"You g-go on ahead," the verbeeg said. "I'll c-catch up later." It had grown so cold inside the cave that even giant-kin were beginning to stutter.

Tavis frowned, remembering that the runecaster had

tried to slip away once or twice before. "If you've d-decided to wait this out, this isn't the p-place to do it," the scout advised. "Assuming an ogre pack is following us up the c-crevasse, it won't take them long to realize we didn't continue past the ice cave. They'll come looking for us in h-here."

"Don't w-worry, I'm still on your s-side," Basil replied. The runecaster opened his satchel and withdrew a steel stylus. When he touched it to the breastplate, the tip began to glow, illuminating Basil's homely features. "I j-just thought I'd leave a little p-present in the water."

Earl Dobbin cast an indignant glance toward his breastplate, but when he tried to protest, all that spilled from his frozen lips was an incoherent mumble.

"Don't be too l-long," Tavis said, starting up the stream again. "We won't have t-time to wait for you."

The scout's warning had more to do with their human companions than with his fear of the ogres. Avner's shivering form felt cool and wet against his back, and he knew the boy was starting to freeze to death. Although Tavis had not removed Avner's boots or gloves, he had no doubt that the youth's hands and feet were already white with frostbite. Soon, as the boy's body grew too weak to warm itself, the cold would creep up his limbs into his torso. When its icy fingers gripped his heart, he would give a deep sigh and the life would exit his body on one last steamy breath.

Soon, they came to a fork in the ice cave. From the smaller tunnel, running more or less straight up the glacier, came the muffled gurgle of water flowing over a field of stones. From the other passage came the distant roar of a small waterfall. Tavis pulled Brianna's amulet from inside his cloak and dangled the chain between his fingers. The silver spear spun around aimlessly, the tip unable to settle on a direction.

"You let the verbeeg t-trick you!" Morten accused.

"He didn't trick us," Tavis replied, examining Basil's

rune. The scout took the amulet's chain off the bark, then turned the scrap so Morten could see the smeared symbol. "The water washed away his magic."

The bodyguard snorted. "Now what?" he demanded. "This is a big g-glacier, and we d-don't have much time."

"It'd take a fairly large nunatak to make a hollow large enough to shelter Brianna," Tavis said. "It will be the biggest stream that leads us to her."

"And if you're wrong?" Morten growled.

"I'm not," Tavis answered.

Brianna's amulet had been pointing more or less in this direction before Basil's rune disappeared, so the scout felt every bit as confident as he sounded. He returned Brianna's amulet to his pocket, then used his dagger to make several large gouges in the icy wall to show Basil which way they had gone. He followed the largest branch of the stream toward the distant roar of the waterfall, occasionally stopping to listen or sniff at the wind. The passage forked several more times, and Tavis always chose the one with the largest stream flowing out of it. Eventually, the din of the waterfall became so loud he could no longer hear Morten sloshing along behind him. The stream grew so shallow that it barely covered the scout's hands, and the tunnel flattened out to the point where he had to crawl on his belly to keep from scraping Avner against the icy ceiling. He began to catch whiffs of a sour, rancid smell on the chilling breeze, and he knew they were near their destination.

Tavis stopped and slipped Basil's wand into his cloak. Once his eyes adjusted to the darkness, he saw a halo of purple starlight streaming down around the black silhouette of an enormous rock outcropping. They had found their nunatak.

The scout pulled Avner off his back. Although he could not see the youth in the blackness of the tunnel, the boy's skin felt icy to the touch, and his breath came in shallow, weak sighs. They did not have time to wait for Basil before they attacked. If the two humans were to survive, they had to free Brianna—and quickly.

Pulling Avner along with one hand, he crawled through the icy stream on his belly. Morten followed his example, and by the time they stuck their heads out of the ice cave, both firbolgs were shivering from the cold. The scout felt sick to his stomach, and it took a supreme effort of will to wiggle his fingers.

Still, Tavis felt optimistic, for the air was thick with the rancid smell of ogre. An erratic curtain of meltwater was pouring off the ice wall over his head, and in the dim light he could make out the craggy features of a granite scarp less than a body's length away. The scout crawled into the small hollow between the nunatak and the glacier, pulling Avner's chill form behind him. He could feel a frail warmth radiating off the boulder, but he knew it would not be enough to save the humans.

Tavis climbed to his feet and looked up the narrow chasm. To one side loomed a wall of glacier ice, the creamy glimmer of moonlight shining through the silvery sheets of water that cascaded down its face. To the other side rose the shadowy scarp of the nunatak, as steep and craggy as any precipice in the Ice Spires. Near the top of this gloomy cliff, about fifty feet above the scout's head, sat the loutish figures of two ogre warriors.

The brutes were squatting at the opposite ends of a long ledge, with the yellow glow of an oil lamp brightening the cliff at their backs. In the flickering light, Tavis could barely make out a fur-swaddled form lying outstretched between the two ogres. From his angle, he could see little more than one flank of the tightly wrapped bundle, but that was enough to make his heart pound harder. The figure looked about seven feet long— just tall enough to be the princess.

Tavis pulled Bear Driller off his shoulder. "Morten, we've found Brianna," he whispered. "Just like I promised."

❧ 9 ❧
Rescue

Keeping his eyes fixed on the ogres, Tavis pulled two arrows from his quiver. Before he could nock the first shaft, he felt a huge hand come down on his shoulder. The scout looked back to see Morten shaking his head.

"You m-might hit Brianna." The bodyguard whispered so softly Tavis could barely hear him.

"How else can we k-kill those g-guards before they realize we're here?" the scout asked, his teeth chattering. Although the nunatak hollow was not so cold as the ice caves, neither was it warm enough to counteract the effects of the freezing waters they had been in. "If you have a b-better idea, l-let me know."

Tavis tucked his hand into his armpit to warm it, allowing Morten a chance to study the figures above. The bodyguard seemed more occupied with shivering than thinking and did not suggest any alternatives. When the scout's fingers felt warm enough to control the bowstring, he nocked an arrow.

"No!" Morten hissed. "It's t-too dangerous."

"It's the safest choice we have," Tavis replied. He drew his bowstring back, then glanced at the massive hand on his shoulder. "I won't hit Brianna—unless you throw my aim off."

The bodyguard reluctantly took his hand away, then Tavis released the bowstring. The arrow shot toward the ogre on the far side of Brianna, the rustle of its flight muffled by the sound of the waterfall. The shot took its target under the jaw, slamming the brute's head against the rock wall. His limp body slipped off its perch and fell into the chasm below.

The second ogre gave a startled jerk and leaned forward to see what had happened to his companion. Tavis's arrow caught him in the mouth. The brute's head snapped back, then he slumped down on the ledge. The swaddled figure next to his corpse did not even stir.

"It's a g-good thing your aim is true," Morten said. "If you had hit Brianna, I would have k-killed you."

With that, the bodyguard started to climb.

"Wait," Tavis said. He pointed at the coil of rope hanging from Morten's belt. "Let me have that. I'll t-tie a line around these two in c-case we must leave in a hurry."

Without saying anything, the bodyguard took the rope off his belt and threw it to Tavis.

"Climb up to the glacier and keep watch," Tavis suggested. He kneeled at Avner's side to loop the end of the rope around the boy's chest. "I'll wake Brianna."

"So you can c-claim the honor of rescuing her?" Morten scoffed. "I think n-not."

"We haven't rescued her yet," Tavis snapped. There was a grain of truth to the bodyguard's comment, but the scout's main reason for sending Morten to the top was hardly selfish. "It's time to prove all those threats you make aren't empty. There are bound to be more guards outside, and sooner or later they'll notice what's going on down here. If you're half the fighter you claim, you can hold them off better than I."

"I'm twice the warrior I claim," Morten snarled. He tugged at his battle-axe to be sure it wasn't frozen into his belt, then resumed his climb. "But try to keep things quiet. There's no use starting a battle until we have to."

Tavis finished tying the two humans into the line, then fastened the other end of the rope to his belt and followed the bodyguard as far as the ledge. After pushing the dead ogre into the chasm below, he pulled himself onto the broad shelf and sat down. The figure beside him was so completely swaddled in furs he could not be certain it was human. The ogres had wrapped the occupant in several layers of bearskin, then tied a greasy rope around the whole thing to keep the bulky cocoon from unraveling. Altogether, the sheaf was close to eight feet long. The only opening was a small breathing hole, but the scout could not see inside it.

Behind this cocoon sat a crude heater that the ogres had made by filling the top of a firbolg's skull with bear fat and lighting it. The resulting flame was orange and rank, exuding an oily smoke that had already stained much of the cliff above it with a grimy black soot.

Tavis started to loosen the rope, then thought better of it. If he startled Brianna, she might cry out in surprise and draw the ogres down upon them. He grabbed the bear-fat lamp and held it over the hole. Inside was a small mouth that appeared to be human—at least judging by what little he could see, which consisted entirely of two cracked, chapped lips. The rest of the face remained completely hidden, rendering it impossible to guess how the princess might react when he untied the bundle.

The scout glanced up and saw that Morten had reached his station. The burly firbolg sat with his back to the cliff and his feet braced against the glacier, holding him in place. His mighty battle-axe rested across his lap, and in his throwing hand he held his dagger. The bodyguard glanced down and waved an impatient hand toward the cocoon.

Tavis slipped his hand into the breathing hole, intending to keep Brianna from crying out in alarm. As she exhaled, he felt the hot, damp air of her breath against his palm, then a set of teeth clamped down on the delicate flesh between the thumb and first finger.

Stifling a scream, the scout tried to pull his hand back, but found it held in place by a pair of powerful jaws. The teeth began to work back and forth, cutting their way toward the delicate tendons of the thumb. To keep from smashing his free fist into the cocoon, Tavis had to remind himself that it was Brianna inside—though he was beginning to have his doubts.

The scout set aside the skull-lamp, then pulled his dagger, quickly cut the rope, and ripped the skins open. The face inside was gaunt and haggard, with wind-burned cheeks and dry, red skin. Glacier-glare had reduced the eyes to a pair of sunken, bloodshot pits, while the brilliant mountain sun had burned the nose to a deep shade of ruby. Despite its condition, Tavis found the face more beautiful than ever. It belonged to Brianna.

The princess opened her mouth, pulling her teeth away from the scout's bleeding hand. "You!" she croaked.

Tavis smiled. "That's right. I've come to save you."

Brianna considered this for a moment, then began unwrapping herself. She moved slowly, as though greatly fatigued, her fingers trembling as she struggled to grip the filthy bearskins. Nevertheless, when Tavis reached out to help, she angrily pushed his hand away.

"How much is the reward?" she demanded.

"Reward?" Tavis echoed, stunned by the acid tone in the princess's voice. "You think I'm doing this for gold?"

Brianna rolled her eyes. "Please, I know better," she said. "How much is my father paying you for this?"

"Nothing!" Tavis snapped. "The king—"

The scout stopped himself in midsentence, realizing that now was no time to tell the princess about her father's betrayal.

"What about the king?" Brianna demanded. If the haughty tone in her voice was any indication, the princess was recovering fast. "Finish what you were going to say."

Tavis shook his head. "The king didn't offer to pay me anything," he said. The scout pulled Brianna's amulet from his cloak pocket, then pressed it into her hand. "And you can have this back—free of charge."

The princess's mouth fell open. "Where'd you find it?"

"The same place you lost it," he replied curtly.

Tavis turned away and untied the rope from his belt,

then sat down on the ledge to pull up Avner and the earl.

"What are you doing?" the princess asked, peering over his shoulder. The bitterness had gone from her voice, but it had not been replaced by any hint that she felt sorry for how she had treated him so far.

"I'm hauling up two people who risked their lives on your behalf," Tavis said.

As the scout fed the rope through his hands, slivers of fiery light began to flicker across the ledge. He glanced back and found Brianna clutching her talisman to her chest, the red glow of her goddess's magic slipping from between her fingers.

"Save some of your healing magic," he said. "These humans are dying of cold and need your help—if it isn't too much trouble for Your Highness."

"Of course not." If the princess noticed the reproach in Tavis's voice, she showed no sign. "Who are they?"

"Avner and Earl Dobbin."

"Really!" Brianna considered this news for a moment, then asked, "And what did my father promise them?"

Tavis did not bother to answer, and before the princess could say anything more an alarmed war cry sounded from above. The scout looked up to see Morten flinging his dagger at something across the glacier.

"Morten?" Brianna gasped. "What's he doing here?"

"He came with us," Tavis explained.

The scout redoubled his efforts to pull his companions up, but raising two humans over such a distance was not an easy task, even for a firbolg.

Brianna sat down beside him, then reached for the rope. "I'll bring them up," she said. "You help Morten."

Tavis did not yield the line. "They're too heavy."

"Don't be ridiculous," the princess said. She grabbed the rope about a foot below Tavis's hands, then began to raise the humans almost as fast as the scout had been doing. "After all, I *am* a Hartwick."

"So I see," Tavis said, standing. Like almost everyone in

Hartsvale, he knew of the supernatural strength of Brianna's father and male ancestors, but this was the first he had heard that the princess shared the gift. "I wonder what other secrets you and the king have been keeping."

Without waiting for a reply, Tavis climbed up to help Morten. By the time he reached the top of the chasm, the bodyguard had already disappeared onto the glacier. From the constant chime of clanging weapons, it sounded as though the firbolg was hard-pressed to defend himself against the ogre pack.

Tavis braced his back against the granite cliff and peered over the lip of the glacier. Directly ahead lay two dead ogres, one with a dagger through his throat and the other missing a head. Morten stood a short distance away, surrounded by the whirling clubs and darting spears of more than a dozen of Goboka's savage warriors.

What the scout saw on the other side of the glacier concerned him more than Morten's situation. The shaman's huge figure was just cresting a ridge of moonlit snow. He was coming, with a large troop of warriors at his back, from the direction of the ice hut. Tavis didn't understand how Goboka had reacted so quickly to his failed plan. The ice hut was on the far side of the glacier, too far away for the shaman to have heard the fight between Morten and the sentries guarding Brianna.

The scout drew his sword and thrust the tip into the soft snow, using it as a handhold while he pulled himself onto the glacier. A dozen paces away, Morten continued to battle the ogres, spinning first in one direction and then the other, his battle-axe slicing through the air in long graceful arcs. With their primitive weapons, his foes could not penetrate his whirling guard, but neither could the bodyguard assault them. As Morten tried to bring his axe to bear, three of the brutes moved forward to strike at his flanks, forcing him to redirect his efforts into driving them back. The ogres were locked into combat just as tightly as the bodyguard. Two of them lowered their clubs and reached for their poisoned arrows, only to have Morten assail them with a vicious series of cross-strikes.

Once he felt the glacier beneath his feet, Tavis hefted his sword and silently rushed across the snow, announcing his arrival by slicing into an ogre's neck. The target's head flew off and crashed into another warrior, who was so startled that he howled in alarm and dropped his guard. Morten took quick advantage of the brute's surprise, cleaving him down the center with a single axe-blow. The battle turned against the ogre pack then, and the flashing blades of the two firbolgs made quick work of their enemies. Within moments, more than a dozen of the brutes lay motionless, their lifeblood draining out to form dark stains on the glacier's milky surface.

"You're no idle braggart," Tavis said. He kneeled down to clean his bloody sword in the snow. "That was fine axe work."

"You helped," Morten grunted. He looked toward the horde of ogres approaching across the glacier, then said, "I wasn't expecting them so soon."

"Me either," Tavis said. "It'll complicate our escape."

"What of Brianna?" the bodyguard asked. "Can she run?"

"The princess is well enough," Tavis said, using snow to numb the painful bite she had left on his hand. "But her ordeal has certainly taken its toll on her manners."

"I'm sure the king will show enough gratitude for both of us," said Brianna's voice. "But I have no intention of growing maudlin just because I'm free from the ogres. I'm hardly fool enough to believe that you—or Earl Dobbin—saved me out of the goodness of your hearts. And why you brought Avner along, I'll never understand. This is no place for a child!"

The scout spun around in time to see the princess crawling out of the nunatak hollow. She had wrapped a foul-smelling bear skin around her shoulders, securing the improvised cloak in place with a small piece of rope.

Tucked into this makeshift belt was the dagger Tavis had left beside her on the ledge, and from one hand dangled the rope to which the humans were tied.

Morten rushed to her side. "Milady, are you well?"

"Better than you were when I last saw you," she replied. "But you look fine now. What happened?"

Morten looked away, as though ashamed that he had not died in the battle with the ogres. "Tavis and his thieves took me to the castle," he explained. "Simon healed me."

Brianna glanced toward Tavis. "My gratitude." For the first time, there was a hint of warmth in the princess's voice. "I'll see to it that Father rewards you."

"I doubt that will be as easy as you think," Tavis replied. "But right now, we have more pressing concerns."

The scout pointed across the glacier. Goboka was now so close they could see the moonlight gleaming in his eyes, and his horde was close behind. Most of the ogres seemed to be armed with clubs or spears, but those running closest to the shaman's immense form carried their bows in their hands. Apparently, the shaman hoped to ensure Brianna's safety by allowing only his most trusted marksmen to fire arrows.

When Brianna saw the charging pack, she handed the coil to Morten. "Pull that up," she ordered. "Fast."

"How are the humans?" Tavis asked. "Are they well enough to run?"

Brianna raised her brow, regarding the scout as though he had lost his mind. "It was all I could do to save their lives," she said. "They were practically ice blocks."

"We'll carry them," Morten said.

With an effortless jerk, the bodyguard pulled the two humans onto the glacier. Brianna had swaddled them both in furs, so that Tavis could tell them apart only by the relative size difference between the boy and the man. The princess cut the rope binding them together, then passed Avner to Tavis and Dobbin to Morten.

"What about Basil?" Morten asked, throwing the earl over his shoulder.

"We won't save him by waiting here," Tavis replied, hefting Avner onto his own shoulder. "He can catch us later."

"Who's Basil?" Brianna asked.

Tavis turned away from the ogres and started to run, at the same time explaining, "The verbeeg you saw in my barn."

"*He's* a part of this?"

The princess had hardly finished her question when a tremendous shudder rumbled up from the heart of the glacier. Tavis's feet slipped from beneath him, and he dropped to his side, his fall cushioned by the soft corn snow on top of the glacier. Brianna and Morten also fell. The bodyguard landed atop his burden, drawing a muffled cry of anger from Earl Dobbin.

"Did Goboka do that?" Morten gasped.

Tavis looked back and saw a great crevasse opening across the glacier, more or less above the ice cave through which they had crawled. Dozens of ogre warriors had already disappeared into the rift, and more were spilling into it as the abyss widened.

"It wasn't the shaman," Tavis reported. "My guess is that Basil's rune caused that explosion."

Morten stared at the growing crevasse in awe, then shook his head and picked up the bundle containing Earl Dobbin. "We can't tarry here."

As Tavis considered Basil's absence, a growing knot of concern formed in his stomach. Nevertheless, he gathered Avner's bundle and rose to his feet, then started across the glacier. Whatever the verbeeg's fate, they could not help him anyway.

The scout quickly realized that he and his companions would never escape by trying to outrun the ogres. To survive, they had to make their pursuers slow down—and he knew just the place to do it. He angled up toward the great ice wall that had stopped the ogres in the first place.

"Are you trying to get us killed?" Brianna demanded. Her eyes were fixed on the sheer ice cliff ahead, which loomed like a bank of clouds rolling down from the valley above. "We'll be trapped. We can't scale that wall!"

"I don't intend to. I'm just trying to get us into that ice fall." The scout pointed to the base of the ice wall, where the glacier tumbled down a hundred paces of steep slope in a jumbled heap of mansion-sized blocks and jagged spires. "If we can't escape the ogres in there, we aren't going to."

Tavis continued up the glacier. When he reached the bottom of the ice fall, he pulled Bear Driller off his shoulder and glanced back to check on the ogres. They were still out of range, but wouldn't be for long. The scout turned uphill and began to climb, probing the snow ahead with the tip of his bow.

"Follow my trail exactly," Tavis said, panting from the exertion of running through snow. "Ice falls have lots of crevasses."

The scout was counting on that. Ice, like water, flowed faster on steep slopes, which caused more crevasses to open. These rifts were smaller than those on gentler grades, and therefore were more easily concealed beneath thick layers of snow. With any luck, the scout had more experience than his pursuers at negotiating such mazes of hidden danger, so the ogres would be forced to follow in his footsteps in a snakelike column— at least until he decided it was time for them to scatter.

Within a few steps, Tavis began to see long, faint shadows ahead. He twined his way around each of these areas, for the differences in color marked sagging surfaces where the snowpack hung suspended over the unseen maws of hidden crevasses. Often, the scout stopped running long enough to push Bear Driller into the snow ahead. Usually, the tip struck a solid surface of ice, but every now and then the bow would sink as though he had plunged it into water. When that happened, the scout would retrace his path a few steps down the mountain, then carefully probe his way around the end of the concealed chasm until he could resume the climb.

Soon they reached a thicket of seracs, looming ice spires that had fallen off the ice wall and imbedded themselves among the crevasses. The seracs resembled nothing so much as a city of craggy blue towers, unkempt and jagged, inclining in every direction and at impossible angles. Some minarets lay almost upon their sides, with no more distance than a human's height between their peaks and the glacier surface. Other towers stood bolt upright, as straight and proud as any steeple in Castle Hartwick.

Tavis led his company a few steps into the seracs, then paused to look back down the slope. The ogres had reached the base of the ice fall, and the first warriors were already rushing up the trail he had blazed through the crevasse-field. Although they were easily within Bear Driller's range, the scout did not take Avner off his shoulder to reach for his arrows. Goboka had been wise enough to hang back, with his own archers at his side, and let his warriors lead the charge.

"We're running out of room," Morten growled. "Shoot!"

"Not yet," Tavis said. "It's better to wait until there are more of them behind us."

The scout turned and began to thread his way through the seracs. When the small company reached the base of the ice wall, Tavis and Morten deposited their burdens behind a fallen serac, then the two firbolgs and Brianna retraced their steps to a small clearing that afforded a relatively unobstructed view down the glacier. The first ogre was just entering the serac thicket, and behind him came a long winding file of his fellows. They were all following Tavis's trail, which, now that it could be seen from above, often seemed to pass unnecessarily close to dozens of crevasses, both hidden and open to plain sight. Only Goboka and his archers had not yet entered the ice fall. They still stood well out of range, watching the others climb until they saw what was going to happen.

Tavis took a handful of arrows from his quiver and stuck them in the snow at his side. "Now it's time to shoot," he said.

The scout let his first shaft fly, then began firing as fast as he could nock arrows. First the lead warrior fell, then the second and third. Suddenly the ogres at the front of the line were scrambling for cover. As they scurried off Tavis's trail, they began to drop into crevasses in groups of three and four, leaving nothing behind but the empty air where they had been standing only a moment earlier.

Tavis shifted his aim farther down the trail, to where the ogres were not yet scattering. He began to pepper the entire line, sometimes putting a single arrow through the bodies of two warriors. The brutes stampeded away from the attacks, scattering in every direction. They vanished into the crevasses a dozen at a time, as often as not forced over the edge by the press of their panicked fellows. Many of those who did not perish simply threw themselves to the ground and cowered in the snow. The scout aimed a few more arrows at these targets, and soon they were up again, rushing about with the rest of their peers.

Goboka's angry voice echoed up the ice fall, yelling commands at his warriors in their own guttural language. A few of the brutes heeded his words and began trying to calm their comrades. Tavis concentrated his fire on these would-be leaders and prevented the ogres from regrouping. The survivors began to take shelter in shallow depressions and behind blocks of ice, but showed no inclination to resume the journey up the dangerous icefall—at least not while Bear Driller was showering them with arrows.

When it became apparent that the scout had stopped the ogre warriors, Goboka spoke a few words to his archers. They arranged themselves in a three-abreast column. The shaman stepped into the middle of the group and ducked down to prevent himself from becoming an easy target. The entire line started up the trail Tavis had blazed, those in front using their bows to probe for crevasses along the edges of the path.

The scout did not bother firing at the column. He did not have enough arrows left to kill even half of them, and he would only empty his quiver in vain if he tried to frighten them off the path as he had the first group.

"This makes no sense," Morten growled. "Why doesn't the shaman use his archers, or cast a spell at us?"

"Because of Brianna. He won't risk killing her by accident," Tavis explained. "He wants her alive as much as we do."

"Then let's count ourselves lucky and run for it," the bodyguard urged.

Tavis shook his head. "Not yet," he said. "If we run now, the others will regain their courage and prevent us from climbing off the glacier."

"They're doing that now," Brianna said. She cast an angry glance at the ice cliff behind them. "Or hadn't you noticed?"

"You're looking the wrong way," Tavis said. He pointed along the base of the icy cliff, to where a jagged rib of granite rose from beneath the glacier to ascend the canyon wall. "All we need is time enough to get up that ridge."

"That's no simple climb," Morten said. "The ogres will catch up and pull us off before we're ten feet up."

"Not without their shaman, they won't," Tavis said.

The scout motioned for his two companions to follow, then dodged a short distance down the steep slope to a huge serac. The block was tipped almost horizontally across the slope, directly above the route Tavis had blazed up the crevasse-field. Morten instantly understood the plan. Without being asked, he braced his hands against the side and began to push.

Goboka also realized the scout's intentions. As Tavis laid his hands on the ice, the shaman shouted a harsh command. Dozens of bowstrings snapped. A volley of arrows sailed up the hill to clatter harmlessly off the spire's far side.

Tavis pushed. A loud crack sounded from the serac's base.

A deep, rumbling voice echoed through the night air: the shaman casting a spell. The scout pushed harder, drawing an involuntary scream of exertion from his lungs. Another crack sounded from the bottom of the tower—then Tavis heard Brianna utter a spell. A sharp sizzle filled the night air as the princess called Hiatea's name and a bolt of red flame shot down the slope toward Goboka's head.

The shaman's voice fell silent in the middle of a word and he kicked at the snow. A white spray erupted from beneath his feet, coalescing into an icy shield just as Brianna's spell streaked down from above. The fiery bolt crashed into the frosty circle with a deafening blast, then both spells sizzled away in a cloud of steam.

"Now, push!" Morten yelled.

Tavis braced his boots against the snowy slope and, placing his shoulder against the serac, drove forward with all the strength in his legs. With a thunderous boom, the icy tower broke free. As it tumbled away, both firbolgs pitched forward and slid down the glacier on their faces.

Tavis thrust his hands deep into the snow, arresting his fall before it had the chance to build momentum. He looked up and peered over Morten's huge back as the serac tumbled down the slope. The scout couldn't see on the other side of the spire, but the rumbling of the block of ice couldn't overpower the shrieks of the terrified ogres, and Goboka's angry scream was the loudest of all.

Tavis rose to his feet, then reached down to help Morten do the same. "*Now* we can run."

❧ 10 ❧
The High Forest

A series of clumsy, flat-footed steps pulsed through the open ground of the montane forest. The footfalls were as enigmatic as they were fleeting, bouncing from the bole of one tree to another, until the palpitations seemed to come from many directions at once and no place in particular. They were also distant, so feeble that Tavis barely heard them drumming above the incessant lisp of the wind. Still, the ungainly rhythm was unmistakable. Basil was out there somewhere, running across an outcropping of bedrock.

Slipping his fletcher's tools and a handful of osprey feathers into his belt pouch, Tavis laid aside the arrow he had been crafting. Gathering his bow and the handful of arrows he had already made, he stood, trying to guess from the maddening echoes where he would find Basil.

Beside the scout, Brianna was tending to the festering wound on Morten's neck. She had already washed the yellow ichor away and purified the gash with blessed water, and was now placing her goddess's talisman on the gash.

"I don't know what good this will do." Morten kept his voice to a soft whisper, for the wind had been carrying faint whiffs of ogre to them all morning long. "Simon already healed it once."

"It's not uncommon for bite wounds to fester," Brianna replied, equally softly. "We may have to do this many times."

The princess uttered her incantation, drawing a sharp hiss from the bodyguard as Hiatea's fiery magic poured from the talisman into the ulcerous sore.

On the other side of Brianna, Avner and Earl Dobbin were dozing in the midmorning light, sitting with their backs against a sun-baked crag of black basalt. Between them lay the remains of that morning's meal, a pile of raw squawrat that Tavis had dug up as they crossed a meadow.

The outcropping was not a large one, rising less than a quarter as high as the towering pines around it, but it made an ideal resting place. Not only did it catch the warm rays of the morning sun, it stood just high enough so that Morten could peer over the top to inspect the group's back trail—as he had been doing all morning, until Brianna awakened and decided to heal his throat wound.

A broad expanse of lodgepole pines surrounded the crag, their thin bare trunks as straight as horse lances. Though the boles were not densely packed, their sheer number created the impression of a gray, foglike wall through which any manner of evil spirit might walk at any moment.

"Wait here," Tavis whispered. "I'll be back soon."

As the scout moved to enter the depths of the gray forest, Morten's large hand clasped his shoulder.

"Where are you going?" Morten asked. All that remained of the wound on his neck was an ugly red scar resembling a huge boil. "This is no time to go wandering."

"Don't you recognize those steps?" Tavis whispered back. "It's Basil."

"How can you be certain?" Brianna demanded. Even as she asked the question, the verbeeg's distant footfalls faded away, and there was no other sound in the forest except the wind slipping through the pine boughs. "I can hardly hear them."

"He's moved onto softer ground," Tavis explained. "But I'm certain it was Basil. I recognized his gait."

Brianna and Morten exchanged doubtful looks.

"Basil's done as much to rescue you as anyone," Tavis reminded her.

The princess's expression became fretful. "That's not

the issue," she said, still speaking softly. "It's whether you really heard him."

"You think I'm lying?" Tavis gasped.

"No, of course not!" Brianna's reply was quick and emphatic, but no sooner had she uttered it than she gave the scout a sideways glance and added, "Not this time, anyway."

"Not ever! I've always been truthful," Tavis insisted. "I had nothing to do with the theft of Earl Dobbin's books!"

"Then why did the princess find them in your barn?" whispered the lord mayor, opening his eyes to join the conversation. "And why are you now willing to risk your life—indeed, all of our lives—to go off searching for the verbeeg who took them?"

Brianna quickly interposed herself between the scout and Earl Dobbin. "We don't need to discuss your books now." She scowled at the lord mayor, then added, "At the moment, I don't care if Tavis and his verbeeg took your ancestral jewels. The important thing is to return to my father's castle, and Tavis Burdun is the only person who can get us there alive."

The words left Tavis with a hollow, anguished feeling in the pit of his stomach. It seemed clear the princess had placed her trust in him only because she had no other choice—and she had said nothing at all about believing his words. If he could not persuade her of his innocence in the theft of Earl Dobbin's books, how could he convince her that her own father had betrayed her to the ogres?

The scout sighed at his quandary, then asked, "Princess, if you don't think I'm lying, why the doubts about what I heard?"

"Because the shaman's a mimic," she said. "That's how he lured me into his trap the first time."

"Thanks for the advice," Tavis said. He did not bother to question whether the shaman had survived the battle on the ice fall. That the ogres had regrouped was evidence of that, for the brutes were a notoriously shiftless and disorderly race that would not have mounted such a sizable pursuit without a strong leader. "I'll be careful."

"You're still going?" Morten asked.

Tavis nodded. "Even a mimic can't duplicate what he hasn't heard—at least not precisely," the scout explained. "And if Goboka has heard Basil's feet slapping against bedrock, there's a good chance Basil's still alive. Whether those footfalls were real or not, I have to take a look."

"I'm afraid it's too late for looking," said Earl Dobbin. The lord mayor's gaze was fixed on the forest, and he was scrambling to his feet. "We have a—"

The drone of a flying arrow cut the lord mayor off. A black shaft suddenly appeared in his thigh, and he cried out in pain.

Already nocking an arrow, Tavis spun in the direction from which the shaft had come. He did not see any ogre warriors, of course, but noticed a few trembling stalks in a huckleberry thicket.

The scout drew his bowstring back. A pair of huckleberry leaves suddenly fluttered to the ground, and a black dot appeared outside the bush: an ogre's arrow coming dead on. Tavis released his own shaft then twisted away, at the same time swinging Bear Driller vertically through the air.

With a sharp clack, the bow struck the shank of the ogre arrow. A tiny, stinging jolt ran through the scout's hands, and he saw a curving black streak as his foe's missile sailed away to shatter against the basalt crag.

Tavis's own arrow penetrated the thicket with a sound like tearing cloth. There was a thud and a strangled gasp, then a hush fell over the forest. The scout nocked another arrow, already searching for his next target.

Among the lodgepoles, nothing else moved. Keeping his eyes on the forest, Tavis squatted beside Earl Dobbin, who had fallen to the ground. "How many were there?"

The question went unanswered, for the ogre's poison

had already done its work and put the lord mayor fast asleep. Brianna pulled her borrowed dagger and set to work digging the arrow from the earl's leg.

"We'll leave when you finish there," the scout said.

Tavis stepped over to Avner, who had not stirred during the ogre's attack. If the youth felt any guilt for the disgrace he had brought upon his guardian—or the deaths he had caused by failing to warn Morten about the ogre ambush—it did not show. He was still sleeping, his expression as innocent as that of a newborn babe.

"Wake up." The scout kicked the sole of the boy's boot harder than necessary. "Time to go!"

Eyes half open, Avner leaped to his feet. "Got you covered!" he mumbled. The youth was already pulling his sling from beneath his cloak. "Where they at?"

"Come and gone, boy," chuckled Morten. The bodyguard passed a waterskin to the youth. "Wash the sleep from your eyes. We're going to need you alert."

Tavis turned back to Brianna. She had bandaged Earl Dobbin's wound and was about to cast a healing spell.

"Let him sleep for a while," Tavis suggested. "I doubt the lord mayor suffers pain quietly, and groans will attract ogres."

Brianna considered his advice, then hefted the lord mayor over her shoulder. Tavis slipped past her and, with an arrow still nocked, started off at a silent trot. He did not need to look to know the princess was following a dozen paces behind, for he could hear a muffled cadence of dry pine needles crackling beneath her soft steps. Morten's steps were louder, a basal reverberation that Tavis sensed more than heard. Avner was the most difficult to keep track of. Despite having to run to keep pace with his large companions, the boy moved so silently that, if Brianna's pace had not faltered now and then as she tried to avoid his heels, Tavis could not have been certain the young thief was behind him.

A short time later, the scout stopped so the others could

catch up to him. He studied their back trail for a few moments, then pointed southward. "Keep going in that direction until I return," he whispered. "I won't be long."

"You still mean to go after Basil?" asked Morten. The bodyguard cast a nervous glance into the forest. "That's foolhardy. The woods are swarming with ogres. They could kill you, and where would that leave us? Only you know the way."

"The ogres won't kill me, but even if they do, you don't need me to find your route," Tavis said. "There's only one way to go. Down the valley."

"But it's too obvious," Brianna objected, laying Earl Dobbin's unconscious form on the ground. "The ogres will block that direction. We have to go another way."

"We can't," Tavis replied. "We can't retrace our steps without running a gauntlet of ogres. And we can't go north without venturing onto the Great Glacier."

"That's not f-for me," Avner said, shivering at the mere remembrance of how cold the Needle Peak glacier had been. "I'd freeze to death the f-first night."

"Only if a frost giant didn't find you first," said Morten. He looked back to Tavis. "But why not go west?"

"Hill giants," the scout explained. "The Gray Wolf clan claims the next valley from crestline to crestline."

"The Gray Wolf clan?" Brianna repeated. "Their chieftain has visited Castle Hartwick many times. Noote will protect us."

Tavis shook his head. "Hill giants aren't very noble, and the ogres will outnumber the Gray Wolves by five to one," he said. "This Noote's more likely to turn us over to Goboka than to fight him on our behalf."

Brianna remained determined. "How many times have you met Noote?" she demanded.

"I haven't," Tavis admitted. "But I know hill giants."

"And I know Noote," Brianna countered. "I've spoken with him several times, and he's always been very kind."

"But he was visiting the king," Morten reminded her.

"It only makes sense to be nice to the princess."

"That's my point," Brianna said. "If he values my father's friendship, what better way to earn it than by saving me?"

Tavis groaned, thinking of what the chieftain would do if he knew of the king's bargain with Goboka. The prospect was not as unlikely as it seemed. As the leader of a hill giant tribe, there was a good chance Noote would know the Twilight Spirit wanted the princess. In that case, the chieftain would certainly turn her back over to the ogre shaman—or take her to the Twilight Vale himself—and earn Camden's gratitude for doing it.

"What's wrong, Tavis?" Morten demanded. "You look like you've seen a storm giant."

The scout could only shake his head. Looking at Brianna, he said, "We can't trust Noote to help. You must believe me."

"Why?" she demanded. "What do you know?"

"You wouldn't believe me," he said.

"Perhaps not, but after that incident in Stagwick, you've hardly earned the right to demand my blind faith," Brianna countered. "You've nothing to lose by speaking."

Tavis took a deep breath and stepped out of Morten's reach. "Your father gave you to the ogres," he said, "in payment for their help in winning the war against his brother."

"Liar!" Morten boomed.

The bodyguard reached for his sword, but Brianna restrained him. "Don't be so rash," she chided. Looking back to Tavis, she demanded, "What game are you playing now? If you're worried about splitting the reward, let me assure you Noote's help won't cost you a silver."

"There isn't going to be any silver—at least not from your father," Tavis replied. "As outrageous as it seems, what I say is true. Runolf told me."

Brianna glared at Tavis reproachfully. "I warn you, such ridiculous stories will accomplish nothing."

"It's not a story," said Avner. "Runolf's head told him. I

170

heard it myself."

Brianna kneeled in front of the boy, taking his face between her hands. "You don't have to lie for Tavis anymore," she said. "He won't hurt you."

"I'm not lying!" the boy protested. "And neither is Tavis."

"Goboka was taking you to someplace called the Twilight Vale," the scout explained. "To mate, either with himself or some giant."

Brianna rose, her expression growing hard. "Are you saying that my own father would have me raped by an ogre?"

Tavis fixed his eyes on the ground. "Or something worse."

"You must think me a terrible fool," she snarled. "How can you think I'd take the word of a thief over that of a king?"

"Runolf was no thief," Tavis insisted. "He was a loyal scout."

"Runolf was a traitor, but he wasn't the one I called thief." The princess snatched Earl Dobbin off the ground and threw him over her shoulder. "We're heading west, toward Noote's lands. You have my permission to go find your friend, but don't bother to rejoin us if you intend to keep disparaging my father."

Frustrated, Tavis let his chin drop. "I'll make you a bargain," he said. "You continue west until I find Basil. Once the ogres pick up your trail and think you're heading toward the hill giants, they may grow careless and leave a path open to the south. Then, after Basil and I rejoin you, I'll say nothing more about your father and we'll turn down the valley."

"And if the way is not clear?" Brianna asked. Her face remained angry and tense, but the princess's voice betrayed her relief that Tavis showed no real inclination to abandon them.

"We'll have no choice except to risk the hill giants," the

171

scout allowed. "And you'll stand a much better chance of reaching Noote's lodge with me as your guide."

To Tavis's surprise, it was Morten who spoke up to accept the agreement. "That sounds fair enough, except for leaving us alone," he said. "If the ogres pick up our trail, your place is with the princess."

Tavis raised his brow. "Can't you look after her?"

"Of course, but that doesn't relieve you of your duties," Morten insisted.

Tavis studied the bodyguard's bearded face and was surprised by what he saw there. Instead of peering down his nose with his customary sneer, Morten met the scout's gaze evenly, his expression one of hope and need rather than disdain.

"You're afraid!" Tavis burst out.

"Don't be ridiculous," Morten replied. "Death means nothing to me."

"But failure does," the scout surmised. "You've lost the princess once, and you're afraid it'll happen again."

Morten's cheeks reddened, and he inclined his head in acknowledgement. "I can only *kill* our foes," he said. "You can avoid them."

Tavis silently cursed the bodyguard's deficiency, but said, "I'll stay."

The princess furrowed her brow. "What about your friend?"

"Basil can look out for himself." Morten said. He spoke too quickly, frightened Tavis would change his mind. "The life of a verbeeg thief is of no importance."

"It is to me," Tavis said, his voice bitter at Morten's callous attitude. "But don't worry, I know where my duty lies."

In accordance with the plan, Tavis led the way west. Though he probably could have persuaded Brianna to turn south right away, traveling toward the giant lands would misdirect the ogres. It would also put some distance between the scout's company and their pursuers. Just as important, this was the direction in which Basil was most likely to flee. As Morten had pointed out, Tavis's primary duty lay in protecting Brianna, but he also had a secondary obligation to the runecaster. If he happened to run across the verbeeg's trail while guiding the princess, he might be able to meet both responsibilities at once.

The forest floor remained flat and open, save for the scattered heaths and waxy carpets of kinnikinnick. Every now and then, when a thicket looked too dense or they came across a crag of rock jutting up from the ground, the scout would stop and listen, slowly creeping up on the suspicious terrain until he was certain none of Goboka's warriors had circled in front of them.

Tavis did not even try to hide their trail. Had he been alone, he could easily have passed through the forest without leaving any spoor the ogres could follow, but his companions were hardly capable of traveling over even open ground without leaving traces of their passage. As inexperienced trackers, they probably couldn't name even half the many marks a creature left as it moved across the ground, much less avoid leaving those signs themselves.

Eventually, the ground developed a slight upward slope, and the looming white wall of a snowy ridge began to peek over the treetops. The breeze grew damp and fresh, the heavy scent of pine displaced by the chill touch of faraway ice fields. Soon, the distant roar of rushing waters rose among the lodgepoles, and the scout knew they were nearing one of the cold rivers spilling down from the Gray Wolf Mountains.

Tavis brought his small procession to a halt. "We'll use the river ahead to make our break south," he said. "It's time to convince the ogres that we're heading for hill giant country."

"How?" Morten asked.

"You'll carry Avner," Tavis said. "He's light enough that he won't make a difference in the depth of your tracks; the ogres will think he's suddenly taking care to leave no spoor."

"What about the rest of us?" Brianna asked. "Morten can't carry us all."

"You and Morten try to avoid leaving tracks. Stick to solid ground and walk on rocks when you can. Stay away from thickets and dust," Tavis said. "There will still be plenty of signs, but it'll look like you're trying not to leave any, and that's what's important. My own trail will all but disappear, and we'll take a crooked path, laying a false trail heading northwest. The ogre trackers will think we're trying to lose them."

"And how do we really lose them when the time comes?" Avner asked, climbing onto Morten's back.

"We'll lay another false trail on the other side of the river, then float away," Tavis explained. "There won't be any signs for the ogres to follow."

"Good plan," grunted Morten.

"Of course," said Avner. "Tavis will get us back to Hartsvale. He knows everything."

"Not everything," Tavis corrected. He didn't know how to make Brianna trust him, and until he could do that, nothing else mattered. "I know the mountains, but that's not everything."

With that, Tavis turned and resumed the journey. Moving more slowly now, the scout led the group on an erratic course that took them more or less northwest. Whenever the mood struck him, he would make a sharp turn, sometimes heading east, sometimes west, and occasionally even back the way they had come. Always, he kept a sharp eye out for any disturbance caused by the large, flat foot of a verbeeg, and he listened carefully for the sounds of someone clumsy moving through the forest.

Tavis did not confine his steps to hard ground or rocks as he had advised Brianna and Morten to do. Nor did he take a pine bough and brush away his tracks as foolish humans sometimes did, for such nonsense only made it easier to follow quarry. The sweeping action wiped the actual footprints away well enough, but it also left the ground so disturbed that the trail became as easy to follow as a deer path.

Rather, Tavis moved with careful, light steps, keeping to the pine needles covering the forest floor, placing his feet down as slowly and gently as he could. With each step, he listened intently to the sound of his supple boot soles settling on the ground. Every now and then the soft crack of a snapping twig or the muffled crackle of crumbling pine needles came to his ears. Whenever he heard such a sound, he stopped to retrieve the object that had made the noise, slipping it into his cloak pocket. Then he would look over his back trail to see if he had left any other obvious signs of passage. Occasionally, he would spy a small dip where his foot had rested too long in one place, but these depressions did not worry him. The pine needle carpet was spongy enough to return to its normal state long before their pursuers came.

Soon the scout's wandering path came to a steep bank that descended to the river's refuse-littered flood plain. Solitary boulders, carried ashore by winter ice, lay interspersed among jumbles of old weathered logs strewn over the small flat. Here the forest's regal lodgepoles gave way to trees more suited to the boggy ground, shabby black spruces carrying as many tangles of dead gray branches as they did live green boughs.

The river itself was close to a hundred paces wide, racing down a broad, cataract-strewn channel lined with driftwood and round, moss-blackened stones. Where the waters were not a churning mass of froth and foam, they appeared dark and cold, moving with a strong, steady current that would carry the group swiftly down the valley and, if their ruse was successful, away from the ogres.

The scout sent Morten and Brianna directly down the bank to a log pile that, via a tangled network of crisscrossing boles, led to the river's edge. After wiping his soles clean, Tavis descended the slope by climbing down the barren trunk of a fallen lodgepole and, upon reaching a place where the dead bark still clung to the bole, he jumped to a nearby boulder. That was where, in the wet ground at the rock's base, the scout saw the track.

It was a hoofprint. The horse's leg had sunk close to a foot in the black mud, leaving a round, postlike hole half filled with water. A long line of similar craters led to the river's edge. By the slow rate at which they were filling with seep water, Tavis estimated the tracks were between thirty minutes and an hour old. Given the harsh terrain of the surrounding mountains and the proximity of a clan of hill giants—who prized horse meat as a delicacy only a little less desirable than halfling flesh—the scout did not think it likely a wild horse had left the print.

Tavis scampered across a network of stones and toppled tree trunks to the rocks on the river's shore. Here, the prints no longer sank deep into the ground, but on the stones he saw several rusty red streaks where an iron horseshoe had scraped over the surface.

Brianna and the others peered over his shoulders. "What are you looking at?" asked the princess.

"Your mare's trail." Tavis pointed to the signs he had discovered. "She seems to be moving upstream."

"Blizzard?" Brianna gasped. "Here?"

"She's the one who led us to Morten in the first place," Tavis said. "And she's been following us since. We saw her on the Needle Peak glacier shortly before we rescued you, and here she is again."

Brianna's face lit up. "Can we catch her?"

Tavis hesitated before answering. Recovering the horse might help him win Brianna's favor, but it would also increase the ogres' chances of tracking them downstream.

"Finding Blizzard right now wouldn't be wise," he said. "As intelligent as she is, I don't think we could convince her to float down the river with us. And if she starts following us along the shore, the ogres will spy her in an instant. That would ruin our whole plan."

"We can change plans," Brianna suggested.

"No," Morten said. The bodyguard cast a wary glance at the raging river. "This is the best plan. The ogres will never expect us to float down that."

"I'm sure there are other ways," Brianna insisted. "Blizzard's a very special mare."

"Not that special," Morten objected. "I won't put you in greater danger for the sake of a horse."

"You're not *putting* me anywhere," Brianna snapped. "This is my own choice."

"That may be, but what of the danger to Avner and Earl Dobbin?" Tavis asked. Although he was thinking more of the princess's welfare, he knew Brianna would find this objection difficult to overcome. "Are you also willing to risk their lives on behalf of your mare?"

Brianna fixed a cold glare on the scout and did not answer. Her icy expression suggested she understood Tavis's strategy, but the knowledge did nothing to lessen the validity of his point. She searched her mind for a suitable alternative, finally lowering her gaze when it became obvious there wasn't one. Without speaking, she turned away from Blizzard's trail.

Tavis wanted to offer her some reassurance about the horse's welfare, but to do so would have been to lie. Even if there had not been hundreds of murderous ogres in this valley and a clan of horse-eating giants in the next, Blizzard had to be close to starvation by now, and montane forests were not good grazing grounds.

The scout went over to a log tangle and snapped eight-foot sections off three treetops. He handed one of the makeshift staffs to Brianna and Morten, keeping the third for himself.

"We'll wade upstream until we find a safe place to cross," he said. "Use these to brace yourselves, or the water will sweep your feet from beneath you."

Morten examined the thick end of his staff, then looked toward the broken treetop from which it had come. "Won't the ogres find the fresh breaks and know we've gone into the river?"

"That's right," Tavis said. "When they see we've made staffs, they'll know we're wading upstream—they might even think we're following Blizzard."

The scout walked into the river until it was about knee-deep. Although the snow-fed waters were cool, they were not as bone-chilling as the streams of the Needle Peak glacier. He was not a good judge of how well humans tolerated cold, but he hoped that they would be able to endure the frigid currents for a short time.

Nevertheless, he took the precaution of turning to Brianna. "You and the other humans will grow cold after we get wet, and we won't be able to stop and start a fire."

The princess nodded. "I was just thinking that."

Brianna took off her amulet and uttered an incantation. The silver spear began to glow. Once it had turned fiery red, she touched the talisman first to her own forehead, then to Earl Dobbin and Avner's, raising a spear-shaped welt on each brow.

Ignoring the boy's yelp of pain, the scout started upstream. He moved quickly and carefully, using his staff to brace himself each time he moved a foot over the round, slick rocks of the riverbed. Occasionally, one of the stones shifted or turned over, but he did not bother to stop and return it to its original place. The ogres might notice a void or change in color that told them it had been moved, but such signs would be few and far between. The swift current would destroy most of the other marks of their passage, so the scout doubted that his foes would realize he was deliberately leaving a trail for them.

After about two hundred paces, they reached a pool of slow-moving water. Tavis told his companions to cross the river, then continue another hundred paces upstream. There, Avner and Earl Dobbin were to remain in the water while Brianna and Morten traveled into the forest, carefully trying to leave no signs of their passage. After about ten minutes, the princess was to return to the river walking backward. Morten would continue on for another five minutes, then do the same thing.

"Just be careful not to step on your own tracks when you back up," Tavis said, finishing his instructions. "That's the only thing that will let the ogres know what you're doing. Otherwise, as long as you avoid soft ground, you won't leave enough prints to make them realize you've passed over the same place twice."

"What will you be doing?" asked Morten.

"Get something to hold as we go down the river," the scout said. "The current's too fast to swim on our own."

"Then perhaps I should wake Earl Dobbin while I'm waiting for Morten," Brianna suggested, eyeing the churning waters in the center of the channel. "It could be difficult to hang on to him."

Tavis nodded. "Do what you can to keep him quiet."

Morten did not move to cross the river. "All this will take time," he complained. "The ogres will catch us."

The scout shook his head. "Not likely. That's why we laid a crazy trail. It'll take the trackers a few minutes to find our path each time it changes direction—especially if they have a lot of their own warriors trampling the signs."

This seemed to satisfy the bodyguard, so Brianna passed Earl Dobbin's unconscious form to him and began to swim. Avner followed in her wake. Morten simply waded across the dark pool, holding the lord mayor above his head and tipping his chin back to keep his mouth above the surface of the cold water.

Once the princess and the others had reached the other shore safely, Tavis started to wade again. Because the river was not as violent here as below the pool, he moved into deeper water, where the dark currents would prevent the ogres from seeing anything he happened to disturb on the riverbed. Half swimming and half wading, he continued upstream long after Brianna and Morten had stopped to lay their false trails. Occasionally, he approached the shore close enough to look for verbeeg tracks, but saw none.

When he had finally gone far enough to be certain the ogres would no longer be coming up this side of the river, the scout went ashore. He found two of the largest logs he could move and pulled them to the river's edge. After tying the boles together with two short lengths of rope, he slipped his wading staff under the bindings and guided the makeshift raft into the dark waters.

The swift currents carried him downriver in a fraction of the time it had taken to wade up it. He soon saw his companions waiting just above the slow-moving pool where they had crossed the river. Brianna had already revived Earl Dobbin, who looked pale and frightened. The earl stood on one foot, bracing himself on Brianna's arm, as though his leg hurt too badly to support any weight. His stance might have seemed reasonable, had Tavis not been able to see, even from the middle of the river, that the princess had already called upon her goddess's magic to close the arrow hole.

The scout waved, and they came out to meet him, Avner and the princess swimming. Morten waded, carrying the lord mayor on his back and using both his staff and Brianna's to steady himself in the deep waters. As the four reached the logs, Tavis directed the humans to the back end of the raft. Taking one of the wading poles from Morten, he positioned himself and the bodyguard near the front, and then they were floating out of the pool. The current swept the raft down a swift-flowing tongue of black water, launching it toward a churning wall of foam.

"Hold fast!"

The two firbolgs each locked an arm under the front binding and barely got their legs pointed downstream before crashing through the froth. The raft bucked so hard Tavis thought it would jerk his arm from the socket.

Pitching side to side and threatening to fling its passengers into the churning waters, the raft shot into a boiling, roaring cataract filled with boulders as large as stone giants, bottomless craters of bubbling water, and eddies spinning like tornadoes. The descent became a crazed, lung-burning struggle to keep the logs pointed downriver. Tavis and Morten used the staffs to fend off jagged rocks that popped up to snap like bear teeth at the flimsy raft. They kicked madly in a vain, useless effort at control before the current spun them around, reducing the scout and his companions to so much flotsam tumbling down the channel with all the other debris.

The journey only grew worse as more water poured in from side streams. The canyon grew deeper, the channel steeper, and the raft began to roll, dousing them for long minutes in the angry river only to whip them back into the air so they could draw breath and endure the icy beating a little longer.

How long the torture continued, Tavis could not say. But he started to hear a certain sonorous undertone in the roaring waters, and the logs rolled with less frequency. Soon, the cataracts grew gentle enough that the raft stopped spinning and began to drift backward down the river. The current slowed, and the river broadened. The scout kicked against a passing rock—he had long since lost his staff—and slowly spun them around.

Ahead of them lay a basin of swift, dark water. On the other side of the pool, the river disappeared, as did its banks and the forest rising above its flood plain. The world just seemed to end, dropping away into nothingness, with only blue sky and distant mountains beyond.

Tavis pulled his arm out of the rope that held the raft together. "Swim!"

The command was useless, for even the scout could not hear the word he had just screamed over the roar of the waterfall. Nevertheless, he found himself trailing behind his four companions as they splashed and kicked, in seeming silence, away from the raft.

Though the river's bank was not distant, Tavis thought they would never reach it. The closer they came to the rocky shore, the faster it seemed to slip past. The scout swam with all his might, trying to angle upstream away from the deafening plunge, yet he felt himself drawn inexorably backward. He caught up to the others, but that small accomplishment brought him no relief. In the corner of his eye he could see nothing but blue sky.

Then Morten stopped swimming. Though he was submerged up to his chest in dark waters, he stood like a granite pillar against the current. He reached out and clasped Brianna's hand. She stopped drifting and clasped Avner, and then Earl Dobbin was clutching madly at the boy's legs, his mouth gaping open in a scream that no one could hear above the din of falling water.

Tavis reached for the lord mayor's ankles. He felt cold water slipping between his fingers. The scout glanced over his shoulder and saw the dark edge of nothingness creeping toward his feet. He cupped his hands and pulled with all his might, at the same time kicking with both legs. He surged forward, felt the water drag him back, and plunged his feet toward the river bottom.

The scout felt soft mud sucking at his boots, then found himself struggling to keep his balance in neck-deep water. Pulling against the current with his arms, he walked toward shore, carefully anchoring each foot before he moved the next. The water grew shallow, and soon he found himself standing on shore, a half dozen paces from where his companions lay gasping on the boggy ground.

Tavis started to collapse, but stopped when he saw Avner yelling at him and pointing at his back. The scout slowly turned and saw, less than a pace away, the sharp edge of a cliff. Far below, the silvery ribbon of the waterfall emptied into a pool strewn with craggy boulders that had tumbled off the top of the precipice in times past.

And down there, leaping from one jagged stone to another in a frantic attempt to cross the river, was Basil.

Tavis raised his arm to wave, then saw a black shaft come streaking out of the trees on shore. The arrow skipped past the verbeeg's shoulder and disappeared into the river, then a lone ogre stepped out of the forest. The scout pulled Bear Driller off his back and reached for an arrow—only to discover that his quiver had been ripped from his back in the raging river.

With his useless bow in hand, Tavis watched the ogre below nock another arrow. Basil dived into the water and saved himself as the shaft shot past, but the refuge was only temporary. His attacker was already pulling another arrow from his quiver and leaping onto the rocks.

Realizing the runecaster could not stay underwater forever, Tavis stepped over to Avner. He tried to ask for the boy's sling, but when he could not make himself heard over the waterfall, simply pulled it from inside the youth's cloak. Grabbing a stone off the ground, he returned to the edge of the cliff.

The ogre was standing on a boulder in the middle of the river, peering down into the water. Tavis placed his stone in the sling and whirled the strap over his head, then hurled the missile at the brute below.

The rock splashed into the water a dozen paces behind its target. The ogre loosed his shaft, then Basil came up for air. By the time his foe could nock another arrow, the verbeeg had disappeared once again beneath the water.

Tavis grabbed another rock off the ground, then felt Avner's hand tugging at his wet sleeve. The boy took the sling and placed a fist-sized rock into the pocket. He stepped over to the cliff edge, began whirling the strap above his head, and waited. When the ogre drew his bowstring back to fire, the young thief whipped his missile forward. The stone streaked down and struck the brute squarely in the back of the head. The warrior pitched face first into the water.

Basil came up for air again, cocking his head in puzzlement as the dead ogre drifted past. The verbeeg touched his hand to the back of the corpse's head, then seemed to realize where his help had come from and looked toward the top of the waterfall. Tavis waved, motioning for the verbeeg to come up and join them.

Basil shook his head, then turned downstream and began to swim. He looked over his shoulder and waved one last time, then dived back under the water.

As Tavis stood puzzling over the verbeeg's sudden desertion, a volley of ogre arrows sailed out of the trees below, arcing up toward him. He did not even bother to step back, for the distance was too great, and he knew they would all fall short.

Goboka's burly figure stepped from beneath a giant hemlock's heavy boughs, a crackling red javelin in his hands. The shaman glared at Tavis for a moment, then hurled the spear into the air. The scout leaped back, barely ducking out of the way as the missile streaked past in a blur of red and orange.

The javelin struck a black spruce, splitting the bole in two as it passed through. The shaft buried itself deep in the trunk of another tree, then hung there with crimson sparks sputtering from its end.

Along with Brianna and the rest of his companions, Tavis threw himself to the ground. He landed at the princess's side. They lay on the ground for a moment. Then, with an explosion audible even over the din of the waterfall, the tree erupted into a giant pillar of flame.

Tavis felt Brianna's hand on his shoulder. "I guess you *don't* know everything," she yelled, holding her mouth close to his ear. "Now we try my plan!"

❧ 11 ❧

The Hanging Moor

After a grueling all-day ascent with the ogre horde clambering close behind, Brianna crested a small cliff and saw a hill giant hulking in the distance. She knew then her small company would soon be safe.

It didn't matter that the entire length of a hanging moor and a deep alpine canyon separated her from the giant. The meadow's tundra would be easy to run upon, and the gorge was narrow enough to yell across, so she would simply sprint over to the chasm's edge and demand the hill giant's help. Then he would escort the princess's party into Gray Wolf lands, and even Goboka would not dare violate Noote's dominion by following. At least that was Brianna's hope, for she saw no other means of escape.

The hanging meadow sat like a broken saucer upon the mountain's flank. On its uphill side, a sheer wall of granite soared into the sky, its distant crown lost in the pearly vapors of a low-hanging cloud. The downhill side was encircled by a craggy precipice, falling more than thirty feet to a steep slope of talus stones and puny bristlecone pines. This scarp descended several hundred paces to timberline, where a wall of spearhead spruce abruptly rose to replace the ground-hugging pine thickets.

There, just emerging from the majestic spruce forest, was Goboka's horde. The warriors were spread out in both directions, cutting off any hope of trying to descend back into the valley below. Unless the companions could fly, their only hope of escape was to descend into the gorge at the far end of the moor.

"Well?" called Tavis. "Does it lead anywhere?"

"Yes, to freedom!" Brianna turned around and lay on the moor, reaching down to help her companions up the small cliff. "There's one of Noote's hill giants ahead."

Tavis's lips tightened in irritation, but it was Morten who spoke. "We'd better think this over," he said. "That giant's liable to attack before you can explain who you are—especially when he sees you with giant-kin."

"That's why I intend to approach him alone, while you and Tavis wait here," Brianna said. "I know how giants and giant-kin feel about each other."

The animosity between the two groups was not bitter enough to be called hatred, but it was as old as the giants themselves. According to the ancient stone giant songs, both true giants and giant-kin had sprung from the loins of the lusty mother-goddess Othea, but they had not been sired by the same father. The true giants were descended from Othea's husband, the great god Annam, while the giant-kin were scions of her illicit lover, a minor deity named Ulutiu. As with many such families, the sibling races were jealous and resentful of each other, but they could also be helpful when it was mutually beneficial—and Brianna felt sure she could make it worth Noote's trouble to tolerate a pair of kin.

Unfortunately, her firbolg companions seemed reluctant to test the hospitality of hill giants. Neither one of them was making a move to climb the cliff, or to help Earl Dobbin and Avner up.

"We don't have time to debate this," Brianna said. She pointed down the mountain, to where the ogres were gathering themselves into packs of ten and twelve. "If you know another way out of here, tell me."

Tavis's only reply was to point up the mountainside.

Brianna craned her neck back. She saw only a vertical wall of granite, scoured by gales of blowing snow and draped with thick curtains of ice.

"I can't scale that!" burst Earl Dobbin. "Not with an

injured leg."

"And probably not with two good legs," the scout replied. "But Avner's an excellent climber. He'll lower his rope for you." The scout pointed at the coil of rope the youth carried over his shoulder.

"I understand being nervous about asking hill giants for help, but you can't be serious!" Brianna continued to stare at the cliff. Now that she had been looking a little longer, she could see that the ice curtains were in fact hanging glaciers—most ready to come crashing down at any moment. "We'd freeze to death up there, even if we survived long enough to climb out of arrow range."

"Morten and I'll hold the ogres off," Tavis said. "By the time they get past us, you'll be out of range."

"Leave you behind?" Avner gasped. "I won't do it!"

"You won't have to," Brianna said. She continued to look at Tavis. "How can you think climbing that cliff's safer than asking help of the hill giants?"

"Because it is."

Brianna found her gaze locked with Tavis's, for he was staring at her with the steady, confident expression that he always used when he wanted her to trust him. It was a look that made her ache to believe him, and whenever he used it she found her heart pounding with the desire to forget what she had seen back in Stagwick.

"Tavis, if there's some reason the hill giants give you a special fright, tell me now," Brianna said. "Otherwise, I *will* seek their help."

Tavis looked at his feet. "I can't. I promised not to bring it up again."

"Then don't!" Brianna snapped, surmising he was referring to her father. She shook her head in disgust and gathered her feet to rise. "Give me a minute with the giant before showing yourselves."

"Wait!" Tavis cast a sideways glance at Morten, then said, "If I can't convince you, maybe Morten can."

"Me?" the bodyguard gasped.

"All I ask is that you tell her what happened at the Earls Bridge."

"If that's what you want and Brianna will listen."

"Make it quick," the princess said.

Morten shrugged. "Tavis shot an arrow at your father," he said. Then, in a helpful voice, he added, "But I don't think he meant to hit him, or surely the king would be dead."

"You did what?" Brianna gasped, staring at the scout in astonishment.

Tavis did not return her gaze. "Tell her *why,* Morten," he said. "And what the king did about it."

Morten's eyes lit with understanding. "They were arguing about how to rescue you," he explained. "Tavis wanted to lead a company after you right away, but your father wanted to wait for more troops. Then Tavis said he'd track you alone and the king forbade it, so he shot an arrow past your father's head and left anyway."

"And then His Majesty sent us to bring this recreant to justice," Earl Dobbin added. "As well he should have."

Brianna felt a cold lump forming in her stomach. "We're wasting time." She glanced down the mountain and saw that the first ogre packs were already well above timberline. "What's the point of all this?"

Tavis shook his head and looked away. "Can't you see that for yourself?"

"I can," said Avner. "The point is that your father didn't send anyone to rescue you. And the only reason he sent the earls was to stop Tavis from freeing you."

The cold lump in Brianna's stomach began to swell, until it seemed an icy ball of anger filled her entire abdomen. "Avner, you'll have to learn that kings often do things that don't make sense to other people," she said, forcing more patience into her voice than she felt. "Even if my father did not share Tavis's opinion about the best way to rescue me, that does not mean he betrayed me."

The princess turned her angry glare upon the scout.

"In fact, it's quite possible that the king's plan would have worked better—had it been given a chance." She pointed to the ogre packs scrambling up toward them. "It's clear enough that your plan has not been entirely successful—so I suggest you and Morten do something to hold off the ogres until I can arrange for our safe passage to Noote's palace."

With that, the princess turned away. She had taken barely three steps before a series of crashes echoed up from the mountainside. Brianna looked over the edge of the moor to see a half dozen boulders bouncing down the slope at the ogres. Even if they didn't trust hill giants, Tavis and Morten were doing their best to give her time to strike a bargain with this one.

Brianna started to run, looking back toward the gorge at the far end of the moor. The hill giant had not moved. He sat squatting on his heels, his armpits resting on his knees and his gangling arms swinging in the long, listless sweeps of a bored child. His eyes, as dim as they were gray, stared blankly into the canyon below, while his mouth hung open in a slack-jawed gape of tedium. The untanned bearskin covering his shoulders did not prevent him from shivering in the cold wind, and every so often Brianna heard a ghastly rattle that could only be the chattering of his huge teeth.

The princess reached the end of the moor and stopped. The gorge between her and the hill giant was no more than fifty paces wide. "Hello!" she called, yelling into the wind. "Over here!"

Without raising his eyes, the giant held a finger to his plump lips. "Quiet!" His order boomed across the gorge many times louder than the princess's call. "Hunting."

Reluctant to argue with a giant, Brianna carefully leaned forward and looked into the gorge. It was one of those narrow ravines many times deeper than it was wide, with cliffs of sheer granite capping its talus-covered slopes. A silvery stream meandered through the patchy forest of spearhead spruce carpeting the canyon floor. Aside from a few nuthatches flitting between roosts, the princess did not see anything that looked even remotely like prey.

A wolf's howl echoed somewhere down the rocky gorge. It was answered by another, much closer. Brianna studied the canyon floor more closely but saw no sign of the beasts that had caused the noises.

"What are you hunting?" Brianna asked. "Wolves?"

The giant scowled. "No, stupid," he growled. He twisted his mouth into a gluttonous grin and licked his lips with a fat gray tongue. "Horse."

The wolves howled again. Brianna's heart fell, certain that it had to be her mare the beasts were chasing. She heard the distant clatter of hooves on rock. The sound was sharp and distinct, leaving no doubt that it had been made by steel-shod feet. The hill giant grabbed a boulder off his pile and stood, raising the huge stone over his head. In the bottom of the gorge, a white-flecked streak came galloping out of a stand of spearhead spruce, pursued by the gray forms of nearly a dozen huge wolves. The sentry gave a long, piercing whistle, and the beasts instantly fanned out, forcing the horse toward the wall where their master stood waiting.

"Blizzard, no!" Brianna yelled, her voice echoing through the valley. "Come!"

The mare stopped and, with a joyful whinny, pricked up her ears. She looked half starved, with a snarled mane and dozens of open cuts on her flanks. The horse began to circle, following the sound of her mistress's voice as it bounced off the canyon walls. The wolves surrounded her immediately, but contented themselves with snapping and snarling and did not close in for the kill. Blizzard looked up and saw Brianna standing atop the cliff. With a determined neigh, the mare charged the wolf blocking her way. When she reared up to lash him with her hooves, the beast wisely dodged aside and allowed her to escape.

Bellowing in anger, the hill giant hurled his rock into the gorge. His pets scattered in all directions, just in time to avoid being sprayed with debris as the boulder shattered in their midst. Blizzard cast a wide-eyed glance over her shoulder, then continued across the valley. The wolves rushed after her, regrouping as they ran.

Casting an angry glare at Brianna, the hill giant grabbed a small boulder and raised it over his head. Though the princess was not sure whether he intended to hurl it at her or her mare, she pointed up the canyon.

"Blizzard, go!" she yelled. "Run!"

"Quiet!"

Startled by the giant's roar, Blizzard turned and galloped up the canyon. The angry hunter bellowed again, scattering his wolves once more, and hurled his boulder into the gorge. His aim and range were incredible, for the stone sailed straight down and would have intercepted the mare had she not dodged into a spruce stand at the last second. The wolves sprinted into the trees after her, their howls of frustration echoing through the gorge.

"Stupid, stupid girl!"

The hill giant grabbed another boulder, and this time, Brianna knew, it was intended for her.

"Wait!" Brianna yelled. "I'll make it up to you. I can give you something better."

The sentry checked his throw. "Better than horse?" He cocked one side of his heavy brow. The expression looked more gruesome than inquisitive. "How?"

"I'm your chief's friend—"

Before Brianna could continue her explanation, the hill giant burst out laughing. "Why Noote want little girl for friend?" he demanded. "Too small for the rut!"

Brianna felt the blood rising to her cheeks. "I'm not that kind of friend," she said. "I'm Princess Brianna of Hartwick. Noote and my father are comrades." She didn't think it wise to say friends. "I want you to take me to see your chief."

Still holding the boulder over his head, the hill giant scowled. "How that better than horse?" he demanded. "Maybe good for Noote—not for Rog."

Knowing that the ogres would not allow her much time to complete her negotiations, Brianna hazarded a glance down the mountainside. At the other end of the moor, the ogres were still scrambling up the slope, making more progress than she would have liked against the torrent of boulders Morten and Tavis hurled down upon them. Closer to the princess, the brutes had opted for a different strategy. They were staying below timberline, slipping through the spruce shadows as they ran abreast of her route. This puzzled the princess for a moment, until she realized that they were trying to enter the gorge lower down, after which they would quickly move to cut off the last escape route.

Brianna looked back to the giant. "If you bring me to Noote, he'll be happy with you." In spite of her growing concern, she forced herself to remain patient. She would not win Rog's help by trying to pressure him. "He'll reward you."

This sent Rog into such a fit of hysterics that he dropped his boulder, almost crushing his own foot.

"All right, then!" Brianna called. "I'll reward you myself. How would you like *five* horses?"

Rog stopped laughing and picked up his club. "Where?"

From the other end of the moor came the clatter of ogre arrows striking stone. Brianna glanced back to see Earl Dobbin and Avner scrambling toward her across the tundra.

"Those humans!" the giant protested. "Not horses."

"I'll send the horses to you," Brianna promised. "Okay?"

The hill giant's eyes narrowed in suspicion. "You not

even let Rog eat one horse. Why give him five?"

"Blizzard is special to me," Brianna said. "It would be like watching me eat one of your wolves."

Rog's lip curled into a disgusted sneer, and the princess knew she had touched an emotional cord. "I'll give you ten horses," she offered. "But you have to say yes right now—and call your wolves off my horse."

"Yes!"

Rog tightened his lips against his yellowing teeth and gave a rising whistle that rang through the canyon. A dozen indignant howls protested the call. The hill giant repeated his summons, this time following it up with a threatening bellow. The wolves yelped, then Brianna spotted their gray forms slinking back down the gorge.

Rog tossed his club into the canyon, then sat down and braced his hands on the edge of the cliff. He turned around and carefully lowered himself until he was dangling by his fingers. Although the precipice had to be thirty feet high, the hill giant was so tall, and his arms so long, that his feet almost reached the bottom. He dropped into the gorge and fell over backward, tumbling down the talus slope head over heels. Halfway down, he slammed into a spruce trunk, shaking a torrent of brown needles down on his head, and came to stop. As though nothing unusual had happened, the giant stood up and brushed himself off, then retrieved his club and crossed the valley to climb up the slope on Brianna's side of the gorge.

The princess turned around to check on her companions. Earl Dobbin and Avner were almost upon her. By the steady rumble of rolling rocks, she could tell that Morten and Tavis remained at their posts, still hurling boulders down at the ogres. Meanwhile, down at timberline, a steady line of Goboka's warriors were sneaking through the spruce forest toward the gorge.

"Tavis!" Even as she yelled the name, Brianna found herself wondering why her first instinct had been to call the scout's name instead of her bodyguard's. "You too, Morten! Come now—or you'll be cut off!"

The princess heard one more set of boulders crash down the hill, then the rumbling began to quiet. Confident that the firbolgs had heeded her warning, Brianna faced the gorge again. She found Rog standing at the base of the cliff, his arms raised toward her.

"Jump," he called. "Rog catch good. Better than most hill giants."

Though the hill giant's words hardly inspired faith, Brianna had no time to indulge her reservations. She simply stepped off the cliff and hoped for the best, fairly certain that at least Rog *intended* to catch her. The princess dropped through the air for a single queasy instant. The back of her shoulders slapped the edge of the giant's leathery palm, but the rest of her body missed entirely. The momentum of her fall whipped her forward. Her head flashed past four massive fingers that were slowly curling inward in a futile effort to grasp her before she tumbled away, and she found herself pitching face first toward the rocky talus slope below.

The hill giant's second hand rose from his side and appeared beneath her. She slammed facedown into the palm, coming to a stop with a loud and painful grunt. A moment later, Rog's thick fingers curled around her body, almost crushing her ribs as they locked her in his grip.

"See? Rog's hands good." The hill giant set her on the ground near his feet.

"They got the job done," Brianna allowed, still gasping from her impact. "But hold your hands like this for my friends."

She cupped her palms together to show the hill giant what she meant. He stooped over—way over—and squinted at her hands with a single red-veined eye. Most giants suffered from farsightedness, but Rog's condition was worse than most. He hardly seemed able to separate her from the rocky slope.

"But what if Rog miss with first hand?" the giant asked, cupping his palms together.

"Hold still," Brianna advised. "They'll jump into your palms."

The hill giant looked doubtful, but put his hands together as she had instructed and raised them toward the cliff top. "Your friends, not mine," he said, shrugging.

As Earl Dobbin leaped from the cliff, Brianna heard a soft growl, then felt a cold nose nuzzling her neck. She turned around and found herself staring up into the yellow eyes of the leader of Rog's wolf pack. When she had seen the beast from atop the cliff, she had not realized how huge it was. The thing was almost as large as Blizzard, its thick fur matted so densely that a dagger could not have pierced it. The creature's muzzle was slender and pointed, with slavering black lips and fangs as long as daggers. Bounding up the hill behind the beast were its eight fellows, all close to their leader's size and just as wicked-looking.

As the creature glared at her, the princess realized that she had been mistaken about its species. The thing was not a wolf, but its cousin, a *dire* wolf—twice as large, nasty tempered, and not nearly as smart.

When the dire wolf began to snarl, Brianna quickly lowered her eyes so it would know she wasn't challenging it, then raised her hand to Hiatea's amulet. *Me little no threat,* she thought, using her goddess's magic to project the message to the beast. *Big wolf leader wolf. Don't hurt.*

The message seemed to satisfy the wolf. It merely snapped at her face a couple of times, then quickly retreated before Rog noticed what was happening. Brianna breathed a sigh of relief, then repeated the message as the hill giant lowered her two human companions beside her.

Rog was just raising his arms again when Tavis's

panicked voice drifted down. "Here we come!"

In the next instant, both Tavis and Morten came soaring over the top of the cliff, followed instantly by a flight of dark arrows. As the shafts sailed across the gorge, rattling harmlessly off the far wall, Rog's eyes opened wide as bucklers. He tried to position his cupped palms first under the scout, then under the bodyguard. Finally, he gave up and threw a hand out toward each one. The firbolgs hit the giant with a mighty crash, then all three figures went tumbling down the slope amidst a cloud of dust. The dire wolves bounded after them howling in glee, trying in vain to catch up and join the fun.

Taking her lead from the beasts, Brianna grabbed her human companions by the wrists and started down the slope. "The ogres can't be far behind."

"They aren't," Earl Dobbin assured her.

The three humans approached the bottom of the hill just as the dire wolves caught up with Rog and the two firbolgs, who were still rolling across the rocks toward the small stream. The beasts leaped into the fray with snapping jaws and wagging tails.

"Off, Anouk!" commanded Rog. "Back, Elke!"

If anything, the hill giant's orders only made the wolves more determined to continue the tussle—until one of the beasts suddenly sprouted a dark shaft in its flank. The creature yelped in pain and limped from the jumble, collapsing less than ten steps away. The other dire wolves scattered instantly, breaking for the nearest stand of woods. Brianna and the other two humans followed their lead.

"Firbolgs!" Rog yelled, finally getting a look at his companions. The hill giant scrambled to his knees, then began squinting at the ground in search of his club. "Hate firbolgs!"

"We don't think much of giants, either!" Morten yelled back.

The bodyguard pushed Rog over, then reached for the

battle-axe tucked into his belt. Tavis simply rolled away, content to have the hill giant's immense bulk off his body.

"Morten! Rog!" Brianna yelled. "Leave that till later. We have real problems!"

The princess pointed up the slope, to where a pack of Goboka's warriors were drawing their bowstrings. Rog and the firbolgs hurled themselves in three different directions. In the same instant, a chorus of strums sounded from the ogre bows, then a flurry of arrows clattered to the ground where the trio had been wrestling a moment before.

"Go!" Tavis yelled. As he rose, the scout grabbed a handful of black arrows from the ground. "Take cover!"

Neither Morten nor Rog needed to be told twice. Morten scrambled away on his hands and knees, then found protection by slipping over the bank of the small stream. Rog launched himself toward the nearest stand of spruce, crashing into the trees at Brianna's side.

"Ogres!" he gasped. His face was as pale as snow. "Now Rog want a hundred horses!"

❦12❧
Rog's Gate

Crouched behind a boulder barely large enough to conceal him, Tavis nocked one of the black arrows. The shaft was too short for Bear Driller's draw, so it would not have as much power as one of his own arrows. But, having lost his quiver to the river, it was the best the scout had. He could still generate enough force to pierce his enemy's thick hide, and, thanks to the poisoned tip, nothing more was required.

Tavis poked his head up, heard the expected chord of humming bowstrings, then ducked back down. A host of black shafts scraped over the top of the boulder and rattled to the rocky ground behind him. The scout jumped up and raised his pilfered arrow toward the gorge rim, where a pack of ogre warriors stood clustered three-deep. He aimed at one of the brutes in the second rank and released his bowstring.

The shaft sailed toward the cliff top at an agonizingly slow pace. It seemed to float more than fly, allowing the target and the two warriors in front of him plenty of time to see that it was coming for them. They tried to dodge, but the pack stood so tightly crammed they could hardly move. The arrow nicked the shoulder of one of the ogres in the front, then sliced across the chest of the original target as he tried to twist away, and finally lodged in the arm of an astonished warrior in the third rank. None of the injured ogres fell, and the rest of the pack were already pulling arrows from their quivers to counterattack.

Tavis dived over the dire wolf the ogres had injured with their first volley, cursed silently as he rolled across jagged rocks, and came up running. He heard bow-strings snap as the fastest of his enemies loosed their arrows. The scout hurled himself over a fallen log into a stand of trees. He did not see where the shafts landed, but none hit him.

Tavis crawled beneath the low-hanging boughs of a spearhead spruce, then stood up behind its bole and nocked another ogre arrow. When he peered around the trunk to take aim, he saw that the three warriors he had wounded earlier were in various stages of collapse, one teetering at the cliff's edge, one holding himself off the ground with his hands and knees, the last lying uncon-scious with the arrow still lodged in his arm.

The scout fired again, picking, as he had before, a tar-get in the second rank. The arrow gashed two ogres before shattering against the mountainside. This time, Tavis had plenty of time to watch his targets collapse, for those who had not been wounded finally understood the strategy of his glancing shots and were scrambling to open some space between themselves. The poison did not drop the wounded ogres immediately, for they had received only minute doses as the tip grazed them. Still, the toxin was powerful. Their knees began to wobble, then abruptly buckled, and both dropped in the same instant—one knocking the teetering warrior over the cliff.

The five uninjured warriors kneeled at the edge of the precipice, arrows nocked and ready. They seemed con-tent to hold their fire as long as their quarry made no move to escape. The ogres had no reason to press the attack; reinforcements would arrive soon enough.

Tavis fired another arrow. He waited long enough to see his target drop flat and narrowly escape death, then the scout ducked back behind his spruce trunk. Four ogre shafts answered his attack, two of them passing so close they peeled the bark from his cover. The arrows had not even planted themselves in the ground before Tavis was sprinting from his stand of trees.

"This way!" He leaped over the fallen wolf and dodged toward the stream where Morten had taken cover, motioning for Brianna and Avner to follow him.

The ogres' bowstrings snapped, and the scout threw himself headlong into the water. After splashing into the middle of the icy stream, he climbed to Morten's side and peered over the bank. Along with Avner and Earl Dobbin, Brianna was still hiding in a stand of trees with the hill giant.

Tavis nocked an arrow. "I'll cover you!" he yelled. "Hurry! We've got to get out of here!"

Avner stepped from his hiding place to obey Tavis, and the ogres drew their bowstrings back to fire. Then the hill giant's long arm lashed out and snatched the boy up.

"Stupid firbolg!" the giant yelled, glaring at Tavis. He pointed up the canyon, toward the headwaters of the tiny brook. "Gate to Noote's lands upstream!"

Morten started to crawl in the direction the hill giant indicated.

Tavis caught his arm. "Listen to me," he said. "We can't trust Noote."

"We have no other choice." As he spoke, the bodyguard was staring over Tavis's shoulder. "Have you seen what's coming up the valley?"

Tavis twisted around to look. At first, he did not understand what concerned Morten. The valley looked liked any high alpine canyon, with a silvery brook, small patches of tundra meadow, and thick stands of spruce.

Then, on a talus slope about two hundred paces below, something changed. At first, Tavis could not say exactly what. Nothing moved on the hillside, no stones clattered, and the wind came from the wrong direction to carry on its breath any whiff of hidden ogres. But the scout knew better than to doubt the gnawing in his stomach or the hair prickling on his neck. He watched.

At the edge of a spruce stand, a black rock suddenly vanished into the darkness beneath the tree limbs. Tavis blinked, not quite able to believe what he had just seen. The shadows swallowed a second stone, this one white, then a third and a fourth, and the scout realized the whole talus field was disappearing before his eyes. The entire copse of trees was advancing up the gorge, creeping along so slowly that it hardly seemed to be moving at all.

The gnawing in Tavis's stomach changed to queasy dismay. He had seen ogres creep forward behind screens of shrubbery before, but knew better than to think he was seeing that. Ogres could not carry seventy-foot spruces, nor could hundreds of them coordinate their movements well enough to move an entire stand so precisely and imperceptibly. Only Goboka's magic could do that.

Morten was right. Tavis and his companions would have to go with the hill giant now, and hope they could part company later—before he took them to Noote.

The scout nocked an ogre arrow in Bear Driller, then gathered five more—all he could reach—and gave them to Morten. "We'll have to run for it," he said. "Hand those to me as we go."

The bodyguard sneered at being relegated to the position of assistant, but, lacking any missile weapons of his own, took the arrows. "Follow my lead. I'll take five steps and turn left, then three steps and break right, and do the same thing once more," Morten said. "If we're not dead by then, you're on your own."

The two firbolgs scrambled up the bank. Tavis fired at the top of the cliff. Goboka's warriors stood their ground and counterattacked, determined to keep the pair from reaching the copse where Brianna and the hill giant were hiding. The scout's arrow pierced the throat of one brute, then the other ogres released their own bowstrings. Tavis and Morten made their break, narrowly avoiding injury as ogre shafts clattered to the ground beside them.

Avner's sling whistled from the spruce stand. A stone

streaked up and glanced off an ogre's shoulder, then Brianna voiced a spell. One of the shafts in the brute's quiver changed into a snake and buried its fangs into his arm. Morten slapped another arrow into Tavis's palm. The scout fired again, the ogres shot back, Avner's sling whistled, and the battle evolved into a flurry of flying shafts and stones.

By the time the firbolgs made their last break, only one ogre remained. He suddenly retreated from the edge of the cliff, and Morten leaned over to rest his hands on his knees.

"Runt, I've got to admit it," the bodyguard panted. "You're a fine archer."

The scout paid the compliment no attention, and not only because the pounding of his heart in his ears made it difficult to hear. Ogres did not abandon their posts, at least not when their shaman was nearby. If the warrior had retreated, it was because there was no longer any need to hold his quarry at bay.

Tavis looked down the gorge and saw that Goboka's magical copse was no longer gliding up the canyon. Rather, the stand was sweeping toward them with all the speed of a wildfire, the roots of the majestic trees slithering over the rocky ground like tentacles. The spruces themselves were swaying madly, their boughs fluttering and snapping like battle flags, and their boles groaning like bloodthirsty banshees.

"Run for the gate!" Tavis yelled.

Brianna and the other humans were already fleeing up the gorge, but the hill giant was not moving. Instead, he remained at the edge of the copse, staring at his unconscious dire wolf.

"Greta!" he wailed.

Tavis could not tell whether the giant was crying out in remorse or commanding his stricken wolf to rise. The scout thrust his bow into Morten's hands, then turned back for the pet. He had no love for dire wolves—he considered them little more than cowardly bullies—but if rescuing the giant's pet would help their dimwitted guide think more clearly, it was worth the risk.

The scout hoisted the beast by its legs and could not help noticing that the thing was a male. "And that churl called *me* stupid," he muttered. "Greta indeed!"

Tavis hefted the wolf across his shoulders, then turned and ran toward his companions. Greta was a heavy load and slowed him considerably, but the broad grin on the giant's face left no doubt in the scout's mind that he had avoided a lengthy delay by picking up the beast.

"Go on!" Tavis yelled. He did not dare stop to look back down the valley, but knew that they had no time to waste. Goboka's magical copse was coming fast, perhaps faster than any of them could run. "I'll bring Greta!"

The hill giant plucked the three humans off the ground, then stepped into the stream and splashed up the valley. Although the big oaf was rather ungainly and awkward, his long strides covered the ground quickly. Even Morten could not quite keep pace, though he was scrambling along the bank at his best sprint. It was no wonder that Tavis, burdened by Greta's extra weight, quickly fell behind and lost sight of his companions in the rough terrain of the stream channel.

That was fine with Tavis. The hill giant was putting distance between Brianna and Goboka, which seemed a fair trade for bearing the wolf. But the scout could not keep his end of the bargain for much longer. Already his lungs burned with exhaustion, his thighs ached with weariness, and his head pounded from the exertion. He struggled on, determined to outrun the shaman's copse not for his own sake, but for that of the princess. Only he understood the true danger to Brianna—that posed by her treacherous father—and if he allowed himself to die she would never be safe.

The rush of falling water began to hiss through the cramped canyon. The scout looked up to see the slender ribbon of a waterfall spilling over the lip of a high granite wall. Although the tiny cascade was a mere trickle compared to the rumbling monster that had nearly claimed the party earlier, it rose more than a hundred feet high, and Tavis saw no way he could scale such a high cliff with a dire wolf on his back.

The scout stopped at the base of the waterfall, his legs quivering, his breath coming in burning gasps. No one had stayed to help him, but dropping Greta was out of the question. Not only was he afraid of angering the giant, he had said he would bring the beast, and a promise was a promise. A terrible, rancid odor began to thicken the mountain air, and, cringing at the thought of what he would see, Tavis turned to look down the gorge.

It was worse than he expected. Less than fifty paces down the stream loomed a wall of blue-green spruces, madly rocking from side to side as they waddled up the gorge on their gnarled roots. Many of the trees were leaning forward, stretching their spiny boughs out to seize Tavis, while others were spreading out to flank him and make sure he didn't escape.

Tavis dropped the dire wolf and reached for his sword.

"No, stupid firbolg!" The hill giant's voice came booming down from above. "Bring Greta."

A coil of greasy rope splashed into the stream. Tavis looked up to see the hill giant straddling the top of the waterfall. Morten and the humans were nowhere in sight. Snatching the wolf, the scout jumped into the water. Holding Greta under one arm, he barely managed to slip the line around his chest before the loop tightened and he was yanked off the ground, a steady spray of cold water crashing down on his head.

Several spruce trees lunged forward and scratched their prickly boughs across his legs. Tavis kicked so madly that he almost dropped Greta, but his efforts did not keep a limb from twining itself around his ankle. The scout's ascent ended with an abrupt jerk. His leg nearly popped from its socket, and the rope bore down so hard that his breath left his chest in a single huff of agony.

From the top of the waterfall, the hill giant let out a deep grunt and continued to pull. The loop around Tavis's chest tightened until he feared it would crush his ribs, and the joints in his leg felt as though they might burst apart. Greta began to slip out from beneath his arm. He dug his fingers into the wolf's fur, knowing that if he dropped the beast, the giant would drop him.

Tavis looked down and could hardly believe what he saw. The hill giant had pulled him, with an entire spearhead spruce dangling from the limb wrapped around his ankle, more than halfway up the waterfall. The tree's roots were waving in mad circles, as though the thing were actually frightened, and it was reaching up with several other limbs to secure a better grip on the scout.

Screaming in anger, Tavis drew his sword and hacked at the branch around his ankle. His blade cleaved it in a single blow, slicing through with a sick pop that sounded more like he had cut bone and tendon than wood. The tree dropped away, its limbs and roots flailing madly, and splintered against the rocky streambed with a tremendous crash.

Then, as the hill giant tugged Tavis to the top of the waterfall, the spearhead's color changed from needle-green to flesh-gray. Its trunk flattened into the oblong form of a chest, its roots twisted themselves into a pair of legs, and its branches withered into two gangling arms, one ending at the wrist. The tree began to shrink, its tip coalescing into a brutish head with the jutting chin and squinting, purple eyes of a dead ogre.

Tavis looked at his own leg and saw that the branch clinging to his ankle had become the brute's severed hand. Before he could kick it away, the scout felt himself being swung over the cliff. He was gently lowered and placed on a granite bank beside the waterfall, then the hill giant took Greta from him and stroked the wolf's fur.

"Thank you, stupid firbolg."

"You're welcome," Tavis huffed. He pulled the ogre's hand off his ankle and flung it over the waterfall. "But call me Tavis, not stupid firbolg."

The giant smiled down at him, showing the stubs of a dozen brown teeth. "Rog." The finger he used to jab his burly chest was the size of short sword. "Friends?"

Tavis returned the grin, and not just out of politeness. Hill giants were not known for repaying debts of honor, but if Rog felt grateful enough to offer his friendship, perhaps he would make a good ally.

"Yes, friends." Tavis did not raise his arm to shake hands, for hill giants interpreted such gestures as an attempt to steal something. "May our fellowship endure as long as the mountains."

"Longer!" boomed the hill giant.

"Then may it last as long as there is sky above and ground below," Tavis corrected.

Glancing over the waterfall into the gorge, the scout saw that Goboka's magical copse was rapidly changing back to its true form. All of the spruces had shrunk to proper size for ogres. Each tree stood on two crooked legs instead of a tangle of roots. Half of them were rushing forward, their boughs twining together to form long gangling arms, while the rest seemed to be plucking bows and arrows from the midst of their branches.

As Tavis watched, a huge crow stepped from behind an ogre-tree near the back of the stand and glared up at him with an eye as black as an abyss. It cackled angrily, then stretched its wings.

"Rog, we'd better run for your gate," Tavis said. "I have a feeling there's more ogre blood than crow blood running through that bird's veins."

Rog's eyes went blank. "Huh?"

The crow launched itself into the air.

"That bird's really an ogre shaman," Tavis explained.

He stepped away from the cliff edge. "And if we let him catch us in the open, neither one of us will live long enough to appreciate our new friendship."

"Tavis not worry," Rog said. "Gate here."

The scout turned around and saw the small pond from which the waterfall flowed. To all sides of the pool rose sheer walls of stone, their dark faces streaked with runnels of water trickling down from the shelves of blue ice hanging upon every ledge. There was no gate anywhere, at least that Tavis could see, nor any other passage out of the tarn valley.

Tavis was about to ask about the gate, and his companions, when he noticed the rest of Rog's wolf pack swimming near the base of a cliff. They were circling outside a black crevice that the scout had, at first, taken to be merely a streak of dark stone, but which he now realized was a fissure in the mountainside.

With Greta tucked under one arm, the hill giant stepped into the icy water and waded toward the crevice. After sheathing his sword, Tavis followed. The bottom disappeared from beneath his feet, but the swim was a short one, and he quickly found himself trailing Rog's wolves into the fissure. He paused inside the entrance to look back across the pool and saw Goboka, in crow form, rising above the waterfall.

Tavis turned around and resumed his swim, following the wolves into a narrow channel of dark water. The cove continued about fifty paces before coming to a gently sloping bank of dry granite. The scout's companions sat upon this craggy shore, waiting for him.

Brianna held what passed for a torch among hill giants, a burning sapling so large she had to support it with both hands. By the brand's light, Tavis could see that they had entered a fault cave, a sort of crack in the mountain between two unimaginably huge blocks of rock. Unlike limestone caverns that wandered along the winding courses of ancient underground streams, fault caves ran in straight passages and sharp angles.

This one was no exception. Beyond his companions, the scout saw a long, narrow corridor leading toward the heart of the mountain. Rog had already finished his long swim and was starting to crawl up the passage on his hands and knees. The tunnel was large enough that even Morten could stand in it, but the massive hill giant could barely squeeze through. His great rear-end was dragging against both walls at once, while his broad back was perilously close to becoming lodged in the confines of the crack's narrowing ceiling. The giant could not have turned around if his life depended on it.

Ahead of Tavis, the first wolf crawled out of the pool and shook, spraying Brianna and the others with icy water. A moment later, the scout's feet touched bottom and he began to wade forward, waiting his turn in line. Morten slipped around the wolf and held Bear Driller out to Tavis.

"Here's your bow, runt." The bodyguard was not ridding himself of an unwanted burden so much as promptly returning another warrior's weapon. "Glad the ogres didn't get you."

"I wanted to wait for you," said Avner, "but Rog wouldn't put me down."

"Which is just as well," added Earl Dobbin. He stepped deeper into the passage, trying to keep himself from being sprayed as the wolves continued to crawl from the icy waters. "Our goal is to save Princess Brianna, not your wretched master."

"She's not safe yet."

As Tavis uttered his warning, the crow sailed low over his head and dropped down on the granite shore. Before the scout could utter another word, Rog's wolves leaped for the bird, snapping and snarling, knocking Morten into Tavis and sending both firbolgs sprawling in the pond.

The crow sprang into the air, but did not fly away. Instead, the bird darted to and fro, its talons slashing noses and its beak shredding ears. Cowards that they were, the dire wolves retreated the instant they suffered an injury. Within moments, the entire pack had brushed past Brianna and the other humans to flee down the passage, licking their wounds and yelping for their master.

"That's some crow," Morten observed, raising himself out of the cold waters.

The instant he could stand, Tavis lashed out with Bear Driller, catching the bird's neck between the tip and string of his bow. He quickly pulled the thing down, but it slipped free and dived past him into the water.

"That's no bird. It's Goboka." The scout plunged his hands into the water, searching for the submerged crow. "Go on. Once you're out of the tunnel, tell Rog to seal it behind you—whether or not I've caught up."

Earl Dobbin took Brianna by the hand and started up the corridor, but Avner drew his dagger and stepped toward Tavis.

"I'll stay to help—"

Morten cut the boy's offer short by snatching him up and starting up the corridor. "Don't stay long," the bodyguard advised. "The giant said the gate isn't far ahead. We don't need much of a head start."

Tavis acknowledged the warning with a grunt, then slipped Bear Driller over his shoulder and drew his sword. He was tempted to wait for the bird to surface, but this was no ordinary crow, and he had no idea how long it might remain submerged. He began to blindly slash his blade through the dark water, hoping that he would at least keep Goboka too busy dodging to counterattack.

A chorus of mad, deep-throated growls suddenly echoed down the corridor. Tavis whirled around and, by the distant light of Brianna's torch, saw Rog's wolves spinning around to attack.

"No!" thundered the giant's voice. "Down!"

The dire wolves paid no attention to their master and leaped for the first person in line, Earl Dobbin. The lord mayor's hideous screams filled the passage as he disappeared beneath a mad flurry of fur.

"Bad wolves!" yelled Rog. "Stop!"

Morten dropped Avner to the ground, then grabbed Brianna and pulled her behind him. Tavis scrambled from the pool. Earl Dobbin's screams fell abruptly silent. In the dim light cast by Brianna's torch, the scout saw the wolves tearing at the lord mayor's body, their slavering jaws ripping it into a dozen separate pieces.

Morten grabbed Brianna and pushed her back toward Tavis, then spread himself across the tunnel. He swung his axe, and a pair of dull thumps reverberated down the corridor. Two wolves yelped in pain, then abruptly fell silent.

"Stop!" Rog's grief-stricken wail filled the passage.

Morten's foot lashed out, crushing another beast against the wall.

"Tavis friend!" yelled Rog. "Make stupid firbolg stop!"

"Sorry, Rog," Tavis called, sprinting down the corridor.

The scout did not have time to explain that the beasts were being controlled by the ogre shaman, for Morten was swinging his axe again. The bodyguard killed another pair of wolves, but two more slipped past in the confusion.

Before the wolves had a chance to attack Brianna or Avner, the princess swung her huge torch like a club. She dropped one beast dead in its tracks and caught the other on the backswing, setting its fur ablaze. So powerful was her blow that it darkened her torch and sent the wolf tumbling down the passage.

The flaming brute landed directly in front of Tavis. It sprang up instantly, snarling and snapping. The scout tried to bring his sword up, but the red-eyed monster, stinking of scorched fur and the rancid breath of a carnivore, was already on him. He threw his free arm up to keep the beast from ripping his throat out, then felt its momentum bowling him over.

Tavis let himself fall, dropping to his back and planting a

foot squarely in his attacker's abdomen. His whole arm exploded into searing pain as the fangs sank deep into his flesh, but the scout ignored the agony and kicked as hard as he could. The beast rolled over him and he followed, leading with his sword. The blade pierced the creature's sternum with a wet crackle. The wolf's fur, smothered beneath its huge body, quickly stopped burning, and the scout found himself lying in darkness.

"Tavis?" came Avner's voice.

The passage had grown eerily quiet, save for Rog's distant demands for someone to open the gate. The scout looked behind him and saw only a few faint embers glowing on Brianna's extinguished torch. Otherwise, the corridor was as black as a grave.

"Is anyone hurt?" asked Brianna.

"Aside from the lord mayor?" countered Morten.

The sound of sloshing water echoed through the passage. Tavis needed no light to know that a huge, burly ogre was rising from the pool.

"Tavis?" Avner repeated. "Is that you?"

"No, it's Goboka," Tavis whispered over his shoulder. "Morten, take Brianna and Avner!"

"Do you need a light to fight by?" asked Brianna.

"No, just go," Tavis whispered. "And that means you, Avner. I'll have enough to do without worrying about where you are."

"If that's what you want," the boy responded. "But you better make it out alive."

"I'll do my best," Tavis replied.

The scout waited until his companions' footsteps began to echo down the corridor, then rose and crept forward, moving as silently as possible to keep Goboka from tracking him by sound. Because ogres were as blind in the darkness as firbolgs, Tavis considered himself at an advantage. He was an experienced blind-fighter, while the shaman could not use his magic without revealing his position. Tavis continued forward, holding his sword before him, warm blood dripping off his mauled arm, ready to spring forward the instant Goboka uttered the first syllable of an incantation.

The shaman did not make that mistake. He remained as silent as Tavis.

The scout did not worry. No matter how silent Goboka remained, he could not hide completely. A sour, rancid odor filled the cave, and it was growing stronger by the moment. Tavis pressed himself against the cavern wall and raised his sword, waiting for the slightest sound that would give the shaman's position away.

Something came hissing at Tavis's head. The scout swung his sword and leaned away, failing to avoid the four leathery knuckles that caught him in the cheek. His head snapped back, his blade clanged off the stony wall, and he fell reeling to the ground.

Tavis rolled. A foot crashed against the stone where he had been lying, and he swung his sword's hilt up into the darkness. The pommel smashed into something solid, and he felt the ogre's knee buckling. Tavis pushed off the ground, bringing his legs beneath him and slashing down as Goboka's great mass fell.

The blade clanged against bare stone.

This time, Tavis sensed nothing before he was hit. The shaman's fist caught him square in the chest, driving the wind from his lungs and hurling him back through the darkness. The scout landed on a lifeless lump of fur somewhere down the passage—he could not tell where—still gripping his sword in both hands.

The scout forced his aching body to rise. He slowly backed away, sliding his feet along just above the cave floor. His chest *hurt*, hurt like it had never hurt before. There had been no snapping or cracking when his foe's blow landed. So why did it hurt so much?

The ogre smell seemed weaker now. Tavis hoped that meant Goboka was far away, but he also knew it could mean he was getting weaker. He had fallen unconscious before, and he remembered his senses beginning to fade just before he passed out.

But his hearing seemed fine. As he continued to back along the corridor, he heard Rog's thundering voice behind him: "Gate! Open gate now!"

Tavis's heel touched the warm body of another wolf. He stepped over the furry corpse and silently continued down the corridor. If he had entertained any hopes of killing Goboka today, they were gone. Now he was just trying to escape alive, without losing Brianna.

"Blood tastes good." The whisper was deep and guttural, and it came from the floor right in front of Tavis. "Even firbolg blood."

Of course! The shaman was following his blood trail. Tavis stepped forward, slashing diagonally at the voice.

His blade skipped off the stone with a loud clatter.

"Wrong!"

The word seemed to come from behind him, but the blow that snapped his head back definitely came from the front. Tavis slammed to the ground on his back, then threw his legs over his head and rolled. The momentum carried him several more tumbles up the passage, then he came to a rest on his stomach. A few paces ahead, Goboka pounced, slashing at the stony ground where he had expected to find his quarry.

The scout silently cursed himself for striking at the voice. Brianna had warned him that Goboka was a mimic, so it was no surprise that the ogre could also throw his voice. Many shamans used such tricks to impress their followers when the spirits were not communicating.

Two could play that game. Tavis picked himself up and dropped his sword on the ground, making certain it clanged nice and loud. Then he drew his dagger and took three quick steps back, stopping when he felt the hot breath of one of his companions across the back of his neck. Realizing that only Morten was tall enough to breathe down on him, the scout reached back and tapped the firbolg's hip. Once the bodyguard knew where he was, Tavis felt sure he would help.

Goboka fell completely silent, but the scout could smell his rancid body coming closer. In his mind's eye, Tavis saw his foe creeping forward, running his fingers over the ground in search of the blood trail, hoping the dropped sword meant his enemy had finally collapsed. Could the shaman also sense how close he was to his true quarry, Brianna? The scout hoped not.

"Open gate!" Rog's booming voice filled the corridor.

Goboka's talons scraped sharply across the floor, then clinked against Tavis's sword. The ogre burst into a mystic chant. The scout smiled and flung himself forward, striking at the darkness just beneath the shaman's droning voice.

A thunderous clap echoed through the corridor, then, with a deafening clatter of chains, bright, glaring sunlight rushed into the narrow passage. Suddenly Tavis could see his dagger blade slashing through the air—and so could Goboka.

The shaman threw himself against the wall, narrowly dodging the gleaming steel. He brought Tavis's sword up to counter. The blade bit deep, lodging itself between two ribs and hurling the scout across the corridor. His whole body burned with pain, and he felt himself slam into a rocky wall. Still struggling to continue the battle, the scout rolled, bringing his dagger around in a desperate effort to deflect the final, killing stroke.

Morten's burly form flashed past, axe raised high and eyes burning with ire. The bodyguard's blow missed, but he followed it up with a series of furious assaults. Goboka, off-balance and blinded by the light streaming into his eyes, had no choice except to fall back.

Avner and Brianna were at Tavis's side instantly, the princess already tending his wounds and the youth trying in vain to pull the wounded firbolg into the light. The scout did not think the boy would succeed, for inside his mind the dark curtain was falling fast.

⇒ 13 ⇐
Dale of the Gray Wolves

The iron plate rose into place with a deep, rumbling boom, and Rog slipped the enormous crossbar onto its supports, locking Goboka on the other side of the gate. The two hill giant guards released the hoisting chains and let them crash against the cliff, shaking the timber platform so hard Brianna feared the rickety thing would come apart. The ends of the chains slipped through a pair of slots, then hung beneath the huge shelf, dangling in the wind.

On this side of the mountain, the fault cave opened high on a wind-scoured wall of cold, sheer granite. Aside from a timber road that hung suspended from the stone face, the cliff was so smooth and clean it could have been cut by the axe of Stronmaus. It stretched for hundreds of feet in both directions, abruptly ending at a craggy rib with nothing but empty air beyond. Below— far, far below—lay a wooded dale encircled by precipices similar to the one upon which the companions stood. In the center of this valley the hill giants had hacked a muddy clearing from the forest and erected a small village of rough-hewn lodges. Though the buildings were probably as large as castles, from so high up they seemed as small as shepherds' lean-tos, and the giants wandering between them looked no larger than sheep.

Brianna went a short distance down the timber road, then laid Tavis beside the cliff. Though his swollen cheek had almost closed one eye, the princess suspected that other injuries were more pressing. Taking the dagger from the scout's good hand, she cut his cloak away.

Tavis's body was strong and lean, with a powerful

neck and shoulders. His chest was also larger than Brianna had expected, muscular and sharply defined, while his stomach was so flat and sinewy it looked like a stone giant had chiseled it from a granite slab. It was the kind of torso that the princess's eyes might have lingered on for a very long time, had she not seen several other things that concerned her deeply.

Where his skin color had not been tainted by the effects of his wounds, the scout was as pale as alabaster. His sternum had turned black and swollen up to form a dome as big around as Brianna's fist. There was a gash in his side so long and deep that she could have hidden the dagger in it. Most troubling of all was the steady stream of blood oozing from his mangled arm. If she did not halt that flow, Tavis would be dead within minutes.

"Will he be all right?" demanded Avner.

"I'll do what I can," Brianna replied. She found it difficult to speak around the catch in her throat. "But I am young, and Hiatea has not blessed me with her most powerful healing magic—and only two of her lesser remedies."

"You can't let him die!" Avner burst.

"The princess will do all she can," Morten said, coming up behind the boy. "You'll only make the task more difficult by disturbing her."

Brianna slipped her amulet from around her neck, then opened her waterskin and placed her goddess's flaming spear inside. "Valorous Hiatea, bless this water with your magic so that it may boil the enemy's contagion from the wounds of this . . ."

Brianna hesitated, trying to think of the kindest thing she could honestly say about Tavis. Hiatea was not profligate with her magic, seldom granting it to aid those who had proven themselves unworthy of her attention, and the princess feared that her goddess would not heed her call to aid the firbolg. To her surprise, she found herself terribly alarmed by that possibility, so much so that unsummoned tears were rolling down her cheeks.

"Bless this water so that it may scald the evil from this warrior's blood," she continued. "Many times has Tavis Burdun's bravery saved my life and that of an orphaned child. He has served you in that much, at least."

Avner demanded, "Does your goddess let people die just because she thinks they've done bad things?"

"We'll talk later," Brianna replied, hardly hearing the boy.

"But Tavis didn't know—"

"Later!" Morten grunted. He plucked Avner up and carried him across the platform to where the boy would not interfere with the princess's work.

Brianna brushed the tears from her eyes, then spoke the mystic syllables that would actually shape Hiatea's purifying magic. A gentle gurgle arose inside her waterskin, then the sides puffed out and white vapor gushed from the open neck. The princess sighed in relief. Her supplication had convinced the goddess of Tavis's worthiness.

The princess removed her talisman and poured the boiling liquid over her patient's injuries. White bubbles frothed up in the open cuts, though not to the extent she had expected. She had assumed the scout's blood would be so full of wicked contagions that it would continue to lather until her waterskin ran empty. Instead, the fluid quickly cleared and began to stream from his wounds in red-tinged runnels. Brianna bit her lip, puzzled. When she had healed Morten back on Coggin's Rise, even his blood had frothed more than Tavis's.

The scout's eyes popped open. "Bri . . . an . . . na!" he croaked. The effort of speaking drained even more color from his face. "Giants!"

Noticing that his gaze was fixed over his shoulder, Brianna looked up to see that the three hill giants had come to watch her work her magic. In one hand, Rog still held Greta's limp form, but no other wolves were near, for the rest had perished inside the fault cave.

Brianna returned her attention to Tavis. "Don't you remember? Rog is our friend; we're safe with him."

Given the power of the shaman's magic, the princess was not entirely sure that was true. But if Goboka did find a way past the gate, Brianna could only hope Rog and his two friends would be able to dispatch the ogre.

Tavis grabbed her head and pulled her ear close to his mouth. "No. Can't . . . trust . . . giants!"

"Be quiet," the princess said gently. "You're not strong enough to talk."

Brianna placed her silver spear on the scout's mauled arm, then closed her eyes and uttered the mystic syllables of her healing spell. A wave of searing heat pulsed from the silver spear, and Tavis cried out.

Brianna opened her eyes again and looked down to see her amulet flickering with orange fire. The arm itself was hidden by a pall of gray smoke, though the princess could see tongues of yellow flame dancing where there had been runnels of blood before. Hiatea's magic continued to sear the mangled limb for several moments, Tavis groaning in pain as the heat burned his flesh. At last, the flames died and the smoke cleared, revealing a hairless arm covered with swirls of raw, scorched hide.

By way of comforting Tavis, Brianna said, "Don't worry, it'll look better after I heal it a few more times. At least the bleeding's stopped."

The scout hardly seemed to notice the arm. "Just make me strong enough . . . to protect you." Then, so quietly that even the princess could barely hear him, he gasped, "In case you're wrong . . . about Noote."

Brianna held her gaze on Tavis's. The scout's persistence was beginning to convince her that he believed what he was saying. Perhaps Basil or Runolf, or both of them, had lied to *him*. That would certainly explain his fanatic accusations against her father and Noote.

"We'll worry about that later." Brianna took a hooked needle from her satchel and ran a coarse black thread through its eye. "Right now, I must concentrate on you."

"But—"

The scout's objection changed to a hiss of pain as Brianna pinched the gash on his stomach closed. Before he could protest further, she slipped the tip of her needle through a flap of skin and began to stitch the wound shut. Tavis allowed her to work in silence, perhaps because he found it impossible to speak through clenched teeth.

The princess had to concentrate to keep her attention focused on the task at hand. Her thoughts kept wandering back to what had happened when she purified Tavis's wounds. The lack of froth suggested the scout was exactly what she had originally believed: a rather naive, self-sacrificing firbolg incapable of treachery. Yet, that could not be so. Even if she dismissed his accusations against her father, she had seen with her own eyes that Tavis was a thief. The two incidents were contradictory, and she did not understand how she could have witnessed them both.

Brianna finished closing the wound and returned the needle to her satchel. In spite of her efforts, brightly colored blood continued to ooze from between the gash's puffy lips. She laid her talisman over the cut, then decided to make a quick inspection of the bruise on Tavis's chest before using her last healing spell. The wound on his stomach was probably a greater threat to his life, but the bruise might mask some internal injury that would kill him more quickly.

The princess placed her hands on both sides of the black circle and pushed down, steadily increasing the pressure. Despite Tavis's howl of pain, she was pleased by what she felt. The sternum had not moved and probably was not cracked. Next, the princess grabbed the dome of swollen flesh and worked it back and forth between her fingers, drawing even louder cries from the scout. The lump felt soft and watery, with no sign of anything solid inside.

"If you're . . . trying to kill me, just slit my throat," the scout growled. "It'd hurt less."

"Don't be such a coward," Brianna chided. "This is nothing but a bruise. You're not going to die from it."

With that, the princess touched Hiatea's talisman and cast her last healing spell. The spear's silver flames flickered to life, sending a wave of searing heat deep into the scout's abdomen. He gasped in pain, his eyes rolling back in their sockets as a thin line of yellow fire shot from the slash. The flames continued to burn for a moment, then, beginning at one end of the gash, slowly died away, leaving the lips of the wound melted together. The black thread remained untouched by the magical blaze, for it would be some time before the skin alone was strong enough to keep the cut from ripping open.

Once the spell was finished, Tavis's eyes rolled back into their normal positions. He was even more pale than before Brianna had healed him, with a cold sweat running down his brow.

"Now will you listen to me?" he asked.

"If that will make you feel better," Brianna said, giving him an overly sweet smile. She laid her talisman upon the scout's bruised chest, taking care to position it directly over the scout's heart. "Just let me do one more thing."

Brianna closed her eyes, preparing to cast a spell that would prevent any lies from slipping his from lips.

"No!" Rog's voice shook the entire platform. "Wait!"

Brianna opened her eyes to see the hill giant laying Greta at her side. The ogre's arrow still protruded from the beast's flank, while his fur was matted and dark with drying blood.

"First fix Greta." The hill giant locked a threatening glare on the princess.

Brianna's stomach knotted in panic. She could cast no more healing spells today. But if she explained that to the hill giant, Tavis would wonder what spell she intended to cast on him. The princess took a deep breath, then said, "I'm sorry, Rog. It's more important that I use this spell on Tavis than on Greta."

"Liar!" Rog stooped over and pressed a huge finger to Tavis's bruised chest, drawing a groan of pain from the scout. "Him not die from little bruise. *You* say that."

"Still, this spell is for him," Brianna said.

"No, use it on Rog's wolf," Tavis insisted. He took her amulet off his chest and returned it to her, at the same time pulling his lips to Brianna's ear. "We want him on our side."

"I doubt Hiatea will grant her magic on behalf of a dire wolf," Brianna countered.

"Why not? She's the goddess of the hunt as well as the family," he pointed out. "And dire wolves are nothing, if not hunters."

"But—"

"Save Greta!" Rog insisted. "Rog's other wolves all dead. You not tell him about ogres!"

"There wasn't time," Brianna objected.

As the princess spoke, Morten stepped to her side, axe in hand. Brianna knew he would be hard pressed to defend her against a single giant, let alone three.

Rog seemed to know this better than the princess. He dropped to his hands and knees, in the process brushing Morten aside and nearly knocking him from the platform.

"Not matter," Rog growled. The hill giant, eyes narrowed, hovered over Brianna. "How you feel if Rog not watch where he step and squish horse? Same thing, huh?"

"There's nothing I can do for Greta," Brianna said. Her jaws ached with nausea, for her lungs were filled with the giant's breath, a foul odor that smelled like rotting swamp grass and rancid meat. "Maybe tomorrow—"

"Cast the spell on the wolf!" Tavis urged. "Or do you want to get everyone else killed along with yourself?"

"Tavis not worry," Rog said. "Tavis friend—save Greta."

It did not escape the notice of either Brianna or her bodyguard that the hill giant had limited his reassurances strictly to the scout. Morten stood and carefully moved forward to place himself near the princess.

At the same time, Brianna lowered her head until her lips were next to the scout's ear. "I need you on my side," she whispered. "If I cast my spell on the wolf, all it'll do is howl in its sleep—if it does that much."

"What do you mean?" Tavis demanded.

"I've run out of healing spells for today," Brianna replied. She spoke loudly enough so the hill giant could hear also. "The spell I was going to use on you was true speaking—so I'd know you were telling the truth."

Tavis's jaw dropped. "You can do that?"

Brianna nodded. "As long as you don't resist—which is why I haven't tried it before now," she explained. "I was trying to take you unaware."

The scout shook his head in astonishment. "Women!" he hissed. "I'll never understand you. Why didn't you just ask?"

"You'll *let* me cast the spell on you?" Brianna did not know whether she was more astonished or confused. Even the most honest of men were reluctant to give someone complete access to their innermost thoughts. "And I can ask you anything?"

The scout nodded. "If Rog lets you live that long," he said, glancing above her.

Brianna looked up and saw the hill giant's head still poised above her. His lips were twisted into an angry snarl, and his brow was furrowed in confusion.

"Can't save Greta?" he demanded.

"Then kill humans," suggested one of his friends. "Don't taste good anyway."

Rog's second friend reached out and plucked Avner off the platform. "If stupid girl can't save Greta, then Kol crush boy!"

Avner's face, all that showed above the giant's thumb,

went as pale as Tavis's. "Maybe we can get more wolves?" he suggested.

Rog shook his head stubbornly. "Take years to train new bully wolf. Raise from pup, teach to like Rog, to make others obey," he complained. "Without Greta, Rog no hunter. Him just stupid guard."

The other giants frowned at this. "What wrong with that?" demanded Kol, the one holding Avner.

"Yeah, Sart like being stupid guard," the other confirmed. "Sleep on same floor every night, rut whenever Sart like."

Rog's face reddened as he realized he had insulted his friends. Glancing over his shoulder, he said, "Nothing wrong with being stupid guard—for you. Rog not stupid. Him smart, have own pack."

This did not alleviate the tension. "Not after Greta die," smirked Sart.

"Yeah, then Rog stupid, too," added Kol.

Rog's face went pale. He looked back to Brianna and pointed at the dire wolf. "Fix Greta!"

"Maybe you can do something without a spell," Tavis said. "The ogre poison only knocks its victims unconscious. It doesn't kill them. With luck, Greta may not be injured that badly."

Brianna needed only a glance to know the scout's hopes were without foundation. Though she had never tended a dire wolf before, she could see the arrow had lodged itself deep in the intestines. The ogre poison had done the beast a service by knocking it unconscious. Such wounds were terribly painful and, without a prompt healing spell, invariably fatal. The princess could do nothing. Removing the arrow would only bring death sooner, and counteracting the poison would revive the wolf only so it could suffer a horrible death.

"Fix Greta now!" Rog insisted.

Brianna began to prod and poke the wolf's belly, desperately trying to buy time to think. Her stomach was churning with fear, not as much for herself as for the boy, and there was something else, too: guilt. She had been wrong to doubt the scout, and her mistake could cost Avner's life—as well as hers and Morten's. The princess still did not understand what had happened back in Hartwick, but she now accepted that somehow she had interpreted events incorrectly. No thief would allow a truth-speaking spell to be cast on him, yet Tavis had been more than anxious to subject himself to it and clear his name. She owed him a big apology—if she could figure out a way to keep herself and her friends alive that long.

Their only hope was Tavis's friendship with Rog, Brianna decided. If anyone stood a chance of reasoning with the hill giant, it would be the scout. The princess looked up and caught Tavis's eye, then shook her head ever so slightly.

The motion did not escape Rog. "Do something!" he boomed.

Tavis pushed himself to his feet, bracing himself against the cliff face to keep from reeling. "Rog, listen—"

"No!" The hill giant pushed the scout back down, then looked over his shoulder at Kol. "Drop stupid boy over cliff!"

Kol extended his arm over the edge of the platform. Brianna caught her bodyguard's eye, then flicked her head toward Avner. Morten obeyed instantly, moving to intercept Kol with a raised axe. Rog lashed out and caught the burly firbolg by the ankle, then lifted him high into the air.

"Fat firbolg next!" he declared.

At the edge of the platform, Kol began to open his fist one finger at a time. A wicked grin creased his mouth, then he teased, "Rog gonna be stupid, too!"

Avner's eyes were opened wide with fear and his lips were trembling uncontrollably, but the boy seemed far from resigned to his fate. Although he could move no more than his head, the youth's eyes were wildly searching for a means of saving himself.

"Rog, do you think I'll keep my promise if you let Kol kill that boy?" Brianna asked. She did not know whether the hill giant would consider ten horses worth the price of his wolf pack, but it was her last hope. "Do you think I'll send all those horses?"

Kol's fist closed instantly, once again holding Avner secure. "Horses?"

Sart scowled in Rog's direction. "You didn't tell us nothing about horses!"

Brianna stood, breathing a silent sigh of relief. "I promised to give Rog ten horses if he'd help me."

"With what?" demanded Kol, eyeing Rog suspiciously.

"To go see Noote," Rog growled. He scowled down at Brianna. "And Rog say a hundred horses!"

Kol pulled Avner back from the edge of the platform. "A *hundred* horses?"

"That's right," Brianna replied. "But there won't be any if we're hurt."

Sart and Kol nodded to Brianna. "We not let Rog hurt you."

"Them's Rog's horses!" The hill giant tossed Morten toward the wall.

The bodyguard hit with a loud thump, then dropped to the timber road at Tavis's side, gasping for air as he tried to recover his breath.

Rog stepped toward Kol. "Give boy!"

Kol backed away, placing Sart in front of himself and holding Avner out of reach. "Share!" he yelled.

"Rog lose wolves!" Rog thundered back, stopping in front of Sart. "Not Kol! Not Sart!"

With that, the hill giant loosed a vicious right hook that landed with a deafening boom. Sart slammed into the cliff, dropping with such force that the sound of splintering timbers echoed off the granite wall. Fearing the platform would collapse, Brianna, in a futile search for handholds, turned to clutch at the smooth cliff.

"Rog, I'll bring horses for everyone!" Brianna yelled.

Rog was too angry to pay her offer any more heed than he did the shaking platform. He stepped past Sart and tried to snatch Avner. Kol shoved him away, then stepped back. He was now standing directly in front of the fault cave gate, with less than a pace of platform left behind him.

"Leave Kol alone!"

"Give boy here!"

Rog lunged for the hand holding the boy, and Kol twisted away. For an instant it looked like Avner's captor would dodge aside and send his attacker plunging over the edge, then Rog caught himself by smashing an elbow into his foe's temple. Kol's eyes rolled back in his head, and his knees buckled. He collapsed backward, the hand clutching his prize still extended, and tumbled headfirst over the edge of the platform. Avner's muffled voice cried out in alarm, the hoisting chains rattled briefly, then Kol's echoing death scream drowned out both sounds.

"Avner!"

Brianna leaped to her feet and charged toward the end of the platform, but quickly found her way blocked by Sart's enormous form.

"Kol killer!" Sart threw himself forward, driving his shoulder squarely into the other giant's back.

Rog roared and stumbled forward, one enormous hand scraping at the sheer wall of the cliff as he tried to brace himself. "Stop! Stop!"

Sart's feet continued to pound the floor of the platform, driving Rog back, closer to the edge. Brianna was too horror-stricken to think. She didn't know what to do—didn't know what she could do—to stop the titanic struggle before her, or even whether she should after Avner's loss. Her companions seemed as horrified and dumbfounded as she. They were staring at the battle with gaping mouths and making no move to rise.

"Rog sorry!" Rog yelled. "Rog share!"

With a final, thunderous grunt, Sart shoved the other giant toward the edge. Rog's terrified voice rumbled through the entire platform, then, arms flailing wildly, he followed Kol into the valley below.

Sart stared after Rog only until a distant crash echoed up from the bottom of the cliff. Then, his breath coming in great gusts of foul-smelling wind, he turned back to Brianna and her companions.

"Now Sart take you to Noote," he said, a rapacious grin on his lips. "Get horses for himself."

*   *   *   *   *

As the peasant's wagon trundled across Earls Bridge, a chorus of trumpets echoed from the summit of Castle Hartwick's lofty ramparts. A sonorous thud sounded from inside the walls, then the gates began to creak open.

"Stop here and let me out," ordered Earl Wendel. The earl issued the command from the bed of the peasant's wagon, where he lay with two of his unconscious fellows. The other seven survivors of the ogre ambush waited in more carts back at the guardhouse, where the sentries had halted them for fear of overloading the bridge. "I won't meet my king in an oxcart."

The peasant halted the wagon as ordered. "You shouldn't be walking, milord," he protested. "Your wounds are too serious."

"I think I can make fifty paces." Wendel could not quite keep the sarcasm out of his voice, for his two arrow wounds, one in the shoulder and the other in the thigh, had not stopped him from dragging one of his fellows out of the mountains on a sledge of pine branches.

The earl climbed down from the wagon and limped toward the gate, where he saw Gavorial's enormous face glaring out at him.

"Where's Tavis?" demanded the stone giant.

"We don't have him," Wendel replied.

"Why not?" The muffled question came from behind Gavorial, but that did not stop Wendel from recognizing the voice as Camden's. "Did you kill him?"

"No, Your Highness."

Gavorial abruptly retreated from the gateway, then the king himself came storming onto the bridge, his chamberlain and young queen, Celia of Dunsany, trailing close behind. Wendel stopped a few paces in front of the oxcart to wait for his liege.

Upon reaching the earl, Camden demanded, "If you didn't kill Tavis Burdun, what are you doing here?" The circles beneath the king's eyes were as dark as charcoal, and his lower lip was bloody and chapped from constant biting. "Where is he?"

"Somewhere beyond the Needle Peak glacier by now," Wendel replied, alarmed by Camden's demeanor. Only a madman would be more worried about avenging his wounded pride than his kidnapped daughter. "He saved us from an ogre ambush, then promised to surrender on his own—after Morten helped him rescue Brianna."

An angry light flashed in the king's eyes. "You allowed that?"

"We had no choice." Wendel motioned to his wounded fellows in the oxcart. "None of us could stand at the time."

Camden glared at the wagon for several moments, his expression growing as dark as a mountain storm. Suddenly, he looked back to Wendel.

"You can stand *now*!" he yelled.

The king shoved Wendel hard, sending him crashing to the ground at the feet of the peasant's ox.

"Go back and do as I commanded!"

The queen, a golden-haired girl standing barely up to Camden's elbow, placed herself between Wendel and the king.

"Please, milord. Earl Wendel and these other men have already suffered much on your behalf." As Celia spoke, she kept her eyes fixed on Camden's feet, clearly frightened to look her own husband in the eye. "You're being unreasonable."

"Unreasonable!" Camden roared.

Celia grimaced, but nodded. "Aye," she said. "These men need to rest—and to see Simon."

The king scowled at her, then stepped past the quivering peasant to peer at the unconscious figures in the back of the wagon. "So they do."

Suddenly, Camden's voice seemed as gentle as a meadow breeze. Wendel found the abrupt mood change more frightening than he had the king's anger.

"They'll stay at Castle Hartwick until they recover," the king declared. He seemed to grow thoughtful, then added, "And I'll have to do something else about Tavis Burdun, won't I?"

Celia breathed a sigh of relief. She reached down and took Wendel's arm, helping him to his feet. "Please forgive him," she whispered. "The strain has affected his temper."

"It's affected more than his temper," Wendel replied, eyeing the king nervously.

"Ssshhh!" Celia hissed. "There's no telling what he'll do if he hears you."

But there was no danger of that, Wendel saw.

Camden had already turned to face his nervous chamberlain. "Bjordrek, do you think Noote is home by now?"

The chamberlain nodded. "M-most certainly," he said. "He left the day after Brianna's disappearance."

"Good. Needle Peak isn't far from Gray Wolf lands." Camden grabbed his chamberlain by the shoulders and shoved him toward the gate. "Go and tell Simon to prepare one of his message birds. I must ask Noote to do something for me."

⇒14⇐
The Fir Palace

When Sart herded Brianna and her companions into the Fir Palace, as he insisted upon calling Noote's over-sized lean-to, the princess felt like she had stepped into some vast, sour-smelling vault where the gods held wicked spirits in purgatory. The air was hazy and damp, filled with the stench of unwashed bodies and the acrid smoke of the distant cooking fire. A roaring din of brutal laughter, bellowing voices, and lewd, bestial groans reverberated through the entire place. Around the perimeter of the room lounged great mounds of flesh that could only be hill giants, their faces and features lost in the flickering shadows draped along the walls.

"Go," Sart urged. "Noote way down there."

The giant thrust his arm over their heads, pointing. The air was so murky that Brianna could see only a few paces beyond the hand, much less clear to the other end of the cavernous room. Nevertheless, she led the way forward, determined to find Noote and interrogate him. The chief was cunning for a hill giant, but he was not a quick thinker. The princess felt confident it would not take long to learn everything he knew about her abduction.

Winning the hill giant's help could be more difficult. Because Tavis had been so willing to let her cast her *true speaking* spell on him, Brianna had decided to accept his warning about Noote and the Twilight Vale—though she still believed the scout was mistaken about her father's involvement. Now the princess was trying to think of some way to convince the chieftain to take her to Castle Hartwick instead of returning her to the ogres or taking her to the Twilight Vale himself.

230

The safest thing would have been to avoid Noote altogether, but the princess had spent all afternoon and most of the evening, the length of time it had taken to climb down from the gate, trying to persuade Sart to lead them through the valley. The giant had steadfastly refused, even when Brianna pointed out that Noote might demand some of his horses. Although he had not said as much, Brianna suspected Sart anticipated trouble explaining what had happened to his two fellows, so he wanted some captives handy to blame for the deaths.

As Brianna progressed through the room, curious hill giants loomed out of the shadows to peer down at her and her companions. The princess could not tell the males from the females, for their brutal faces were entirely androgynous, with uniformly heavy brows, flat noses, and blocky chins. Nor was facial hair any help. They all seemed to have a little on the upper lip and chin, though never enough to grow a beard or mustache. And their bodies were uniformly lumpy and bulky, lacking any of the customary curves or angles that suggested their sex.

A few of the giants snapped belittling comments at Sart. "Stupid Sart! Firbolgs not good slaves!" Others pointed at Tavis, who was being carried in Morten's arms, and cried, "That one no good! Can't walk, can't work!"

Others seemed more alarmed by Brianna's presence. "Hide girl!" they warned. "Noote says don't take humans, stupid!"

Occasionally, a hand would snatch out at the princess, but Sart would promptly slap it away, explaining she had come of her own will to see Noote. This invariably drew some ribald remark about "the rut" and caused a thunderous outbreak of laughter.

Brianna soon realized that the hill giants were not just visiting their chief. They all appeared to live in this one chamber. Some were eating—what, she could not tell—and others were sewing hides, repairing weapons, and tending to all the many chores of everyday life. Here and there some of the giants were even lying on their backs snoring—as often as not within ten paces of a bellowing argument or a thundering chorus of laughter.

Brianna was even more puzzled by their love of wrestling. Everywhere she looked, giants were rolling on the ground in groups of two and sometimes more, their arms locked around each other's torsos, their hands clawing at each other, growling and groaning, screaming and . . . Suddenly falling silent, two nearby giants rolled apart with stupid grins on their faces, and the princess saw that they hadn't been wrestling at all.

"The rut," Morten commented, his voice thoroughly disgusted. "Savages!"

Brianna had to agree.

Morten nudged her, and Brianna realized she had stopped moving and was simply staring at the two giants. With her cheeks burning, she quickly resumed her pace, taking care to keep her eyes fixed straight ahead—though she wasn't sure why. The hill giants certainly didn't seem to care if anyone watched. In fact some were being observed with all the rapt attention of an athletic contest, and she half expected to hear the spectators wagering on the outcome.

About halfway through the chamber, they came to an abhorrent mound of flesh standing about twice as tall as the princess. There was one overly long leg dragging on the ground behind him, one incredibly short leg dangling from his hip, and one that seemed just about the right size propped beneath his tailbone. He had a pale, hunched body, stooped shoulders, and no neck whatsoever. His head was bald and wart-covered, with floppy, pointed ears and red, bulging eyes lacking brows or lids.

Brianna's first impression was that a hill giant child had fallen into the fire and melted, then somehow survived to crawl back out. But once she recovered from her shock, she realized the figure was only a fomorian slave. Every member of this strange race of giant-kin was born hideously and uniquely deformed, though few quite as grotesquely as this fellow.

The fomorian, secured by a lengthy chain to a post, stood next to a large cooking fire. Over the roaring flames were suspended a dozen roasting spits, each skewering the charred remains of what might have been a deer. At the far end of the fire lay a tremendous pile of skinned animal carcasses, while at the closer end, where a huge black pot bubbled at the edge of the blaze, there was a much larger mound of pine cones.

As Brianna and her companions approached, the fomorian hopped along in front of the spits, using his single arm—which stuck out of the center of his chest—to crank each handle a quarter turn. When he reached the end of the line, he paused long enough to grab a shovel and throw a scoop of pine cones into the boiling pot. Then, before the princess realized what he was doing, the fomorian snatched her up in his slimy hand and hopped toward the carcass pile at the other end of the fire.

With both hands, Brianna grabbed the cook's huge thumb and pushed back against the joint. A garbled rasp of pain spewed from the fomorian's throat, then his hand opened, and the princess dropped to the dirt floor. The slave's lidless eyes glared down at her, clearly astonished by her unexpected strength, then he cautiously stooped down to pick her up again.

"Not her, Ig!"

Sart cuffed Ig in the back of the head. The fomorian whirled around and leered up at his tormentor. Brianna could not tell whether his twisted face was scowling or pouting, but Sart paid the ugly expression no attention.

"Humans not for eating!" the hill giant said.

Ig shrugged his stooped shoulders, then hopped, rather reluctantly, toward Morten.

"Not us, either!" the bodyguard grunted.

Ig looked up to Sart for confirmation. When the hill giant nodded, the fomorian sighed, then hopped back to his duties at the cooking fire.

"Let's go—before we get mistaken for vermin and stomped," Morten growled.

The princess led the way to the other end of the lodge, where another fomorian was halfheartedly performing a dance of debauchery. Though just as bald and warty as the cook, her abnormalities were mostly monumental exaggerations of curves typical to the females of most giant races. In a morose attempt to beguile her audience, she was spinning in a little circle, shaking her chest and swiveling her hips, raising a choking cloud of dust by stomping the beat to an eerie song of dismay that rumbled from her lips.

If the hill giants fathomed the sad beauty of the fomorian's dance, they showed no sign. They lounged around, bellowing lewd comments, mocking her deformities, and rutting with each other. In the center of this crowd, sitting cross-legged on the dirt floor and tossing hunks of charred meat at the woman's cleavage, was the dull-eyed, corpulent giant who Brianna had once been foolish enough to believe would save her: Noote.

Beside the chieftain sat an especially large and flaccid giant wearing a silver necklace that Brianna's father had once sent as a gift to Noote's wife. On the queen's shoulder—assuming she was the queen—sat one of the talking birds Simon had enchanted to serve as messengers, a raven with a silver band around its leg. It crossed Brianna's mind that her father may have sent the bird to ask the hill giants' help in rescuing her from the ogres. But if that were so, she certainly saw no sign that the chieftain had done anything to honor the request.

On the side opposite Noote's wife sat another female— at least the princess hoped the giant was female, considering where the chieftain's free hand was resting. If the queen disapproved of her husband's actions, she showed no sign, and was in fact engaged in her own dalliance with a fellow beside her.

Brianna had a sinking feeling in her stomach. It was not just a faint apprehension of trouble, but a pain more like a granite ball grinding its way through her digestive tract. During his visits to Hartwick Vale, Noote had always struck her as a rather noble savage, crude and primitive, but basically good at heart. Now, she saw that she had been as mistaken about his character as about Tavis's. Not only was the giant cruel and debauched, he was a slave-taker and a hypocrite as well. If her father knew what occurred inside the Fir Palace, the princess felt sure Noote would not have been such a frequent and welcome guest in Castle Hartwick.

Brianna closed her eyes and took several deep breaths, girding herself against her rising fear. Now more than ever she realized Tavis had been right about the hill giant. Not that it mattered. Even if they had wanted to, they could not have avoided both Rog and the ogres, or that was what the princess told herself. She could not allow herself to consider the possibility that the scout had been right to suggest climbing straight up the mountain. Even now, that plan seemed too crazy to have worked—but was it? If she had followed the scout's advice, perhaps they would be camping somewhere above Hartsvale tonight instead of trusting their lives to the unpredictable mercies of hill giants. Perhaps Avner and Earl Dobbin would still be alive—Brianna shook her head, trying to shut out the visions of their deaths. She could live with the guilt of causing the lord mayor's death, but not Avner's. That burden was too heavy to bear. If she allowed herself to think about it, she would not have the strength to negotiate for Noote's help—and, as slim as it was, that was the only hope for her or her companions.

The princess opened her eyes, then circled around the fomorian's gyrating mass, narrowly avoiding being knocked off her feet as an immense hip swung past her head. She led the way forward until she had cleared the dust cloud raised by the dancer's feet, then stopped in front of Noote's colossal bulk. Brianna craned her neck and found herself looking up into a pair of cavernous nostrils. The chieftain remained entirely oblivious to her presence, flinging an entire haunch of venison high over her head, then laughing uproariously when it became lodged between his slave's pendulous breasts.

"I'm glad you don't behave this way in Castle Hartwick!" Brianna deliberately allowed her anger to creep into her voice as she yelled. Their best hope lay in keeping Noote off-balance. If she could convince him that she was in control of the situation, that his only choice was to do as she ordered or face her father's wrath, he might not pause to consider that he was in charge in his own palace. "Perhaps next time you visit, we'll let you root for your food with the swine."

Noote's jaw dropped, and his gaze flickered around the room for a moment, then he finally realized where the sound was coming from and looked down at Brianna. His face was even more brutal than that of most hill giants, with narrow black eyes, a broad flat nose spreading from one cheek to the other, and a mouthful of jagged gray teeth that had been filed to sharp points.

"Princess!" he gasped. Noote's eyes flicked above Brianna's head to the fomorian dancer, then his face turned a deep shade of crimson. He grabbed another hunk of venison and threw it at the slave, bellowing, "Put skins on!"

The fomorian quickly trundled toward the wall to obey, her face betraying her relief at the interruption.

"Please, don't let me interrupt." Brianna cast a pointed glance at the hand still lying in the lap of the giant next to Noote. "It's apparent you weren't expecting me."

The chieftain pulled his hand back to his own lap and shoved his companion away. "Act nice!" he bellowed. He leaned across his queen and also pushed her friend away. "Joke over!"

"What joke, Noote?" the queen asked.

Noote's face deepened to a shade of maroon so dark it was almost black. "Rutting jokes," he hissed, nudging her in the ribs. "This Princess Brianna."

All around him, hill giants furrowed thick brows in confusion. Their murmurs filled the chamber like the drone of Camden's guards gathering in the courtyard for an unexpected assembly.

"Quiet!" Noote demanded.

A few nearby giants fell silent, but that only increased the curiosity of those farther away, and the clamor actually grew louder. Noote's wife glanced around, seeming more irritated at having her bacchanalia interrupted than at the noise, then glared down at Brianna. The queen was uglier than her husband, with sagging red bags under her eyes and a plump, oval-shaped mouth smeared with black soot—whether for decoration or by accident, Brianna could not tell.

"Who?" the queen demanded.

Noote leaned over and whispered in her great ear, fingering the silver necklace she had been sent by Brianna's father. The queen's eyes opened wide, and her expression changed from one of irritation to one of surprise.

"Quiet!" she thundered.

The lodge fell instantly silent. The queen whispered something to Noote. Brianna could not quite make out her words, but she could hear the breath of the giantess rustling in the chief's ear like wind in a box canyon.

Noote whispered something back to his wife. This time Brianna heard something about stealing and ogres, and the couple exchanged a few more whispers. Finally, Noote nodded, then fixed his attention on his unexpected guest.

"What doing here?"

"I escaped from my kidnappers. I should think that

you'd have guessed that yourself." Brianna allowed her gaze to flick up to the raven sitting on the queen's shoulder. "My father did send a message telling you about it, didn't he?"

Noote glanced at the bird, then looked back to Brianna. "Just come tonight." He glanced over the princess's head and cast a thoughtful eye at her companions. "Him say two firbolgs trying to rescue you. That them?"

"Yes," Brianna replied. Although her tone was calm enough, thoughts were racing through her mind with the speed of swooping falcons. It was apparent that Noote's queen was the real power behind the throne, and the princess was hardly prepared for that. She did not even know the giantess's name! Forcing herself to keep her eyes on Noote, the princess continued, "And now I need an escort back to Castle Hartwick."

Noote furrowed his brow and turned to consult with his queen. They exchanged a few whispered comments, then the chief looked over Brianna's head to Sart.

"Where they come from?" he demanded, gesturing at Brianna and her companions.

"From High Gate." The sentry looked at Noote as though the chief had lost his mind. "Where you think?"

Noote hurled a charred boar's head at Sart, then growled, "Who chasing them? Ogres?"

Sart nodded. "Yeah. Lots of ogres. Ogres kill Rog, but I fight 'em back and close gate." The giant glanced down at Brianna with a hopeful expression. "Right?"

Brianna gave Sart a reassuring smile, but she was thinking to herself that the giant would have been much better off if he had taken them directly to Castle Hartwick. The princess glanced at Morten and nodded for him to put Tavis down. Once she saw that the bodyguard understood her instructions, she looked back to Noote.

"That's not what happened at all."

"Lying girl!" The giant stomped forward to silence the princess.

Morten hurled himself at Sart's knees, knocking the astonished sentry to the floor. The two figures grappled, a thick cloud of dust billowing up to hide the combat.

"Stop!" Noote yelled, rising. "Not time for fighting!"

"Sit down, Noote!" Brianna motioned for the chieftain to resume his seat, then, in a more gentle voice, added, "Morten's not going to hurt your guard."

As the princess had hoped, her comment drew a raised brow from the queen, who grabbed her husband's arm and pulled Noote roughly back to the ground. The struggle continued for only a few moments more before it abruptly ceased. When the dust cleared, Morten was sitting astride Sart's throat with the giant's own dagger pressed against his throbbing jugular vein.

"I wouldn't take a deep breath," the firbolg warned. "This blade's kind of heavy, and it might slip."

Sart pressed his lips together and held his breath.

Brianna looked back to her hosts. "Now, as I was saying, Sart's version of what happened at the High Gate isn't quite accurate." She motioned to Morten and Tavis, then added, "Actually, Rog and Kol were killed in an argument over some horses I promised to send to Rog."

Noote's eyes opened wide. "Kol dead too?" he thundered, glaring at Sart. "Who at High Gate?"

Sart swallowed nervously. "No one," he admitted.

The chief snatched his bone dagger from his belt, but managed to keep himself from hurling it at Sart's helpless form. "Go back!" he thundered. He pointed the tip of his knife at two more giants. "You, too!"

The two new sentries jumped from their seats and lifted Morten off Sart, then the three sentries could not scramble from the lodge quickly enough. After watching the trio leave, Brianna turned back to Noote with a bemused smile.

"There's no need for such concern. The ogres won't be bothering you." Brianna motioned at her two companions. "Morten and Tavis stopped them."

At the mention of the scout's name, an astonished buzz rustled through the chamber. Tavis Burdun was as famous among Noote's tribe as he was among humans—perhaps more so, since he'd often been called upon to track down and slay their rogues. A crowd of curious hill giants began to gather, and Morten quickly pushed his way between them to protect the unconscious scout. As he did so, Brianna noticed the wart-covered face of the dancing slave peering down at Tavis from between two burly shoulders. The princess was surprised by the adoration on the slave's face, for she knew Tavis's arrows had also thinned the ranks of many fomorian tribes.

Brianna's attention was drawn back to Noote and his queen when, after a lengthy consultation with his wife, the chieftain asked, "Them firbolgs kill all ogres?"

The sneer on Noote's lip made it clear that he did not believe they had.

Brianna shook her head. "No, just one," she said. "Goboka."

She smirked hugely, deliberately twisting her face into an expression the hill giants would find difficult to read. In spite of her words, the princess was painfully aware that the shaman had only been driven away, not killed. She avoided lying when possible, but had learned on her father's knee that diplomatic necessity sometimes dictated saying things that were not strictly true.

In this case, convincing Noote and his queen that her firbolgs had actually killed Goboka served two very important goals. First, if they thought the ogre was dead, they would not be tempted to return her to him. Second, if they knew how powerful the shaman was, they might well think it wisest not to anger those who had killed him.

Much to Brianna's relief, her strategy seemed to be working. Noote and his queen had pressed their faces cheek to cheek and were whispering furiously into each other's ears. So intense was their conversation that the princess could hear certain words flying back and forth, among them "spirit," "ogre," and her father's name. Finally, after a particularly sharp exchange, the queen shoved her husband away.

"Tell me, if Goboka is dead, why do you need an escort from us?" asked the queen.

The princess's jaw dropped. It was a rare giant who could speak so articulately, and for a hill giant to express herself so fluently was unheard of. Brianna could see that she had badly underestimated the queen. By the standards of her race, at least, the giantess was a genius. Even among the earls of Hartwick, she would have to be considered shrewd—and therefore dangerous.

"Perhaps the reason you can't answer my question is that Goboka isn't dead."

The queen was probing, trying to convince Brianna that she knew more than she really did. It was a trick the princess had seen her father use often. "Goboka is dead," she replied. "Unless having his head severed and his heart pulled from his chest does not kill an ogre shaman."

Brianna added this last part in an innocent voice, as though she were really afraid that such treatment might not have killed her enemy.

The queen smiled at Brianna's response. "No, I'm quite sure you killed him if you did that," she replied. "But I'm afraid we won't be returning you to your father."

A cold ball of dread formed in the princess's stomach. "I warn you, the king will be angry if you don't help me."

The queen's smile turned into a sneer. "I think not, my dear," she said, glancing at the raven on her shoulder. "You see, he said we could take you to the Twilight Vale ourselves."

* * * * *

Avner could remember exactly when he had last been this cold—inside the Needle Peak glacier, wading up the icy stream to rescue Brianna. He had almost died.

He felt certain he was about to die now, as the wind howled along the cliff face, spraying the stone—which was already slick—with freezing sleet, coating the hoisting chain with clear ice, and stealing the warmth from his body with each clatter of his teeth. The thief could hardly bend the frozen fingers on his good hand, but that really did not matter, since it was trembling so hard that he would not trust it to support his weight anyway.

Avner was two links from the bottom of the hoisting chain, his body wedged through the loop and swinging in the freezing wind. He had no concept of how long he had been hanging there, for the last thing he remembered was his stomach rising toward his throat as Kol stepped off the end of the platform.

The sky had arced out of sight in a single flash, and he had found himself staring at the distant spires of the fir forest below. Then Kol's hand crashed into something hard and flew open. Avner felt rough iron scraping down his back and realized it was the chain. He twisted around, arms flaying madly, and nearly wrenched his arm out of its socket as he jammed his hand through a link.

The chain crashed into the cliff. Avner felt the bones in his wrist being mashed to powder as the chain ground his arm against the cliff. His entire body went limp; had his hand not been trapped, he would have plunged after Kol into the trees below. But his pain served him well, reminding him that he was still alive and might stay that way if he reacted quickly enough. With his good hand, the boy grabbed hold of the link and pulled himself up, wedging his body through the center as it twisted away from the wall. He banged into the granite several more times, less violently than before, then his pain washed over him like a dark, cold river, and he closed his eyes.

When he opened them again, and the chain was still swinging. The wind was howling, Avner's teeth were chattering, and the boy did not know whether the laughter spilling from his throat was caused by joy or hysteria. But he did know that he had to get off this mountain, and fast. By morning, the only thing lodged in this link would be a hunk of frozen flesh.

Avner wrapped an arm around the outside of the icy loop, then pulled himself up until he could work a leg through the opening and straddle the bottom. The link was just tall enough that he could sit hunched inside it. He tried to examine his injured arm by moonlight, but the shadows under the platform were too thick to see clearly. All he could tell for certain was that it was horribly swollen, and he could not bend it from the elbow down.

"I sure hope Brianna's still alive," he whispered, not quite certain why he was afraid to speak out loud. If there had been any giants on the platform above, he would have heard their footsteps echoing through the timbers.

Avner drew his dagger and cut the sleeve away from his injured arm, then used the cloth to bind his arm to his side. Next, he took his rope off his shoulder and tied a series of loops. By the time he finished, he had a makeshift ladder of about a dozen feet, easily twice as long as he needed to reach from one link to the next.

The boy passed the rope through the link above, pushing the line through one of the loops he had tied to secure it in place. He slipped his good arm, still trembling from the cold, into another loop and began to climb. The young thief moved quickly and efficiently, for many times he had used similar techniques to climb the exterior of some tower that supposedly could not be scaled—though he had seldom found anything inside worth the trouble. Once he had even used the method to climb from Earl Dobbin's well, after he had been forced to jump down the pit to elude a company of murderous guards.

To his surprise, Avner felt sad about the fate of the

lord mayor. He was not sorry the man was dead—the earl had certainly threatened to kill *him* enough times—but it seemed an era had passed. For as long as the boy could remember, he had been stealing from Dobbin Manor, and Earl Dobbin had been trying to catch him in the act. It had not been a game—the consequences of the king's law were too deadly for that—but the contest had been eminently fair. Now, with the lord mayor separated not only from his property but from his own limbs as well, there no longer seemed any point to stealing from Dobbin Manor. It was even possible the boy would be forced to rethink his ambitions—providing he didn't freeze to death on the side of this mountain first.

Fortunately, that was beginning to look less likely. Avner had only one link left before he climbed into the hoisting chain slot. He could see the iron plate that blocked the entrance to the fault cave, the moonlight glinting off the crossbar's white wood less than twenty feet above. Once he climbed through that hole and had solid timbers below his feet, he would march down the road as fast as he could. Even if it did not get him off the mountain quickly, it would at least warm him up enough to stop shivering.

Avner reached up to pass his makeshift ladder through the last link of the hoisting chain—then abruptly stopped and pulled the rope back down. Not far above, in the shadows beneath the crossbar, a pair of hands was emerging from the iron gate. They were gaunt and leathery, with knobby joints and long black talons the boy recognized as those of the ogre shaman. Even cold iron would not keep Goboka from his prize.

⇛ 15 ⇚
The Rabbit Run

The runt had it easy, Morten thought. The giants had sewn Tavis into a cocoon of waterlogged deerskin, then tied him to a spit and hung him over the fire to roast. Morten they had stripped to his loincloth and smeared with rancid bear grease. The stuff smelled worse than a glacier skunk—worse, in fact, than a glacier skunk that had drowned in a fetid bog and floated to the surface after it decayed. Every time the bodyguard inhaled, his stomach threatened to purge itself and such a wave of nausea rolled over him that his legs nearly buckled.

Morten kept his teeth clenched and his knees locked, trying to hide his distress. Not only was he determined to deny his tormentors the satisfaction of seeing him suffer, he knew that showing his misery would only encourage the giants to smear him with substances even more repugnant. As Tavis's cocoon was tied to the spit, the scout had made the mistake of groaning in pain. Noote had ordered the deerskin cut away around the victim's face, so his cries would be more clearly audible when the flames began to roast him. So far, the groan had been the only sound to escape the runt's lips, but wisps of steam were just beginning to rise from the wet skins. The real pain would come later, when the leather began to shrink and his blood began to boil.

Morten did not see how he could save the runt. Noote's queen was a shrewd woman, and she clearly intended to steam Tavis as a warm-up for the morning's climactic torture, the "rabbit run." The hill giants would be lined up along both walls of the Fir Palace, their hands fastened behind their backs. Morten would be released at the far end of the lodge. If he could run the entire length of the chamber and out the door without being kicked to death, he would be allowed to live—or so Noote claimed. If the bodyguard tried to save the scout, he would probably be killed before he had a chance to make the rabbit run.

In itself, that would not have bothered Morten. He had no interest in playing the queen's game, at least not for the stakes she had proposed. But if he could convince the giantess to wager Brianna's freedom as well, then he was determined to succeed. The run was the bodyguard's last chance to redeem himself for letting Goboka capture the princess, and he was not about to squander it on the scout.

After Ig had turned the spit for several minutes without drawing a single moan from Tavis, Noote grew impatient. He pulled the fomorian away from the flames and shoved him toward the log pile. "More wood!"

The chief, his eager face looming above the cooking fire, stood across the floor from where Morten was tied. His stout wife was at his side, clutching Brianna's rope-sheathed form in her pudgy fingers. Ribbons of early morning light were streaming down through the smoke hole, forming hazy blue halos around their knobby heads.

Ig returned with an armful of tree trunks. He dropped the load next to the fire, then put the smallest logs on the pyre.

"That'll do you no good," Morten called. He was yelling much louder than necessary, for his words were intended as much for the hide-swaddled scout as for Noote. "Tavis won't scream."

"Will too," Noote growled. "Burning hurt."

"Maybe, but Tavis won't yell. He won't give you that satisfaction," the bodyguard maintained. "And I'm not going to make your rabbit run, either."

Noote scowled. "Not?"

The logs beneath Tavis began to burn. Ig left the rest of the trees on the ground and started to turn the spit.

"Firbolgs die with honor," Morten explained. "We don't beg for mercy. We don't show pain. We just die."

"Maybe we skin you alive," Noote warned. "That hurt plenty."

"What are you, fomorians?" Morten scoffed. "I'd have thought hill giants could do better than that."

Many of the giants snickered at their captive's defiance, but the bodyguard did not care. He knew their ridicule would soon change to disappointment. Whether Tavis was thief or hero—and Morten no longer knew which—the scout was a brave firbolg. He would die silently, especially if he understood that Brianna's life depended on it.

"You might as well kill us now," Morten added. "We're not going to scream."

"You'll run, Morten," said the queen. "And Tavis Burdun will scream."

The giantess picked up one of the iron bars Ig used to stir the fire and placed the end in the glowing coals, then pulled the fomorian away from the spit and motioned for him to put more wood on the fire.

Morten smiled, then locked eyes with the queen and waited. He had spent enough time in Castle Hartwick to know that the first rule of kings, at least those who wanted to stay king very long, was to keep their earls happy. The giantess was not exactly a king and her followers were not exactly earls, but the bodyguard was willing to gamble that she understood this principle as well as he did.

Soon the steam stopped rising from Tavis's cocoon. The stitching at the seams began to stretch, the first sign that the hides were shrinking, and the leather on the bottom side started to blacken. The scout's face turned pink, but he clamped his jaw shut and showed no sign that he would yell.

"You see?" Morten said. "He's not going to scream."

A concerned murmur rustled through crowd of hill giants. "No fun," one of them protested. "Scream, stupid firbolg!"

Tavis's lips formed a smile. "It's not that hot," he said, speaking through clenched teeth.

"Roasting firbolg stupid!"

"Yeah," agreed another giant. He pointed at Brianna. "Maybe girl scream!"

"No!" the queen thundered. She pulled Brianna closer to her chest. "We're taking her to the Twilight Vale."

Brianna's face, all that Morten could see of the princess, did not change expressions. She seemed far more concerned with Tavis's plight than what the giantess might have in mind for her.

"No fun," grumbled a giant. "Noote stupid."

When the big oaf turned away and others began to follow, Morten could not help smiling. Hill giants were like spoiled human children: one could always count on them to sulk.

The queen grabbed the poker she had placed in the fire, then thrust the handle into her husband's hand. "Call the rabbit run."

Noote stepped toward Morten, waving the poker's white-hot tip through the air. "Wait!" the chieftain yelled, addressing the backs of his departing subjects. "Time for run."

The giants paused, but only a few turned to face their chief. "Him not run," said one. "Firbolg too."

Noote grinned wickedly, then lowered the poker's tip and laid it against Morten's cheek. The firbolg heard a loud sizzle, then the sick odor of burning flesh filled his nose and his entire head burned with agony. He had to bite his tongue to keep from crying out, and even then he nearly choked on the silent scream rising into his throat. The pain filled his entire head, as though the god Vulcan had swung his flaming hammer into his skull.

When the agony had subsided enough that Morten could be sure he would not scream, he said, "I have no reason to run."

"Then Noote will give you a reason," growled the queen. She was so angry that she could not quite keep her voice from making the floor tremble. "You can run, or he'll burn your eyes out."

The bodyguard felt a cold sweat break out on his brow. It would be impossible to rescue Brianna if his captors blinded him. Still, he could not let them see his fear, or the princess was doomed.

Morten shrugged. "What use does a dead man have for eyes?"

The bodyguard looked away from the poker's white tip, distracting himself by fixing his attention on the spit. Tavis's blackened cocoon was now beginning to shrivel. From what Morten could see of the scout's face, he was suffering more from the shrinking leather than the heat. His cheeks had turned that peculiar crimson of someone being choked, and the veins in his temples were bulging.

Once again, the bodyguard found himself envious of the scout. From all appearances, the cocoon was squeezing Tavis's chest so tightly that the runt could not have screamed if he wanted to. But if Morten's eyes were burned out, he would have to rely on his own willpower to keep from yelling.

Noote kneeled beside Morten, then grabbed his head and twisted it toward the poker. "You 'fraid!" the chief insisted, moving the tip closer to the firbolg's eye. "Say it!"

"I'm not afraid," Morten replied. "But I will run—if you give me reason."

Noote stopped short of pressing the poker into the bodyguard's eye socket, but he continued to hold it so close Morten could feel the heat searing his eyeball. "What?"

"The princess," the bodyguard suggested. "Put her at the other end of the palace. If I carry her out the door, then we're both free."

"Fun!" chortled a giant.

"No!" burst the queen.

"Then burn my eyes out," Morten said. "I won't run for any other reason."

This occasioned so much grumbling and scuffling of giant feet that Morten feared the vibrations might cause the chief to inadvertently blind him. Fortunately, Noote's hand remained steadier than the dirt floor, and he continued to hold the glowing iron a mere finger's breadth from the bodyguard's eye. Sensing their chief's indecision, the giants whispered among themselves optimistically.

Finally, they broke into an excited chant, "Rabbit run, rabbit run!"

The chorus made Noote's mind up for him. He rose to his feet and tossed the poker aside, then held out his hand out to his wife. "Brianna," he demanded.

The queen shook her head. "Think of what it would mean if that little vermin succeeds—"

Noote grabbed his queen by her silver necklace and pulled her toward him. "Me chief!" he growled. "Chief want girl!"

The queen refused to yield her prize, even when the other giants gave an approving cheer and stepped forward to support Noote. Morten feared the confrontation would erupt into a full-fledged combat, which bothered him only because he remained tied to the post and would be powerless to protect Brianna. The chief leaned forward and whispered something into his wife's ear. She listened for a moment, the scowl never leaving her face, then slapped the princess into her husband's hand. The resulting cheer was so loud Morten felt it in his bones.

The queen glared at Noote until the deafening sound died away, then she ran her angry gaze over the crowd gathered around the cooking fire. "If that firbolg escapes, I'll crack every one of your skulls."

The giants quickly wiped the smiles from their faces, but the enthusiasm with which they began to bind each other's hands suggested they took the threat less than seriously. So did Morten, but for a different reason. Even if he managed to run the gauntlet and squeeze out the door with Brianna, he knew better than to think Noote would actually set them free. But once they were together, with his hands unbound, their situation would be better than it was now.

As Noote passed the princess's bound figure to another giant, Brianna asked, "What about Tavis? Won't two rabbits be more fun than one?"

Noote appeared to consider this, at least for the half moment it took him to spot the queen violently shaking her head. "No," the chief said. "Him sick. No fun to chase."

"I can make him better," Brianna insisted.

"No!" Noote boomed. The chieftain returned his attention to the giant to whom he had passed the princess, then pointed toward the other end of the lodge. "Hang her on wall down there."

The giant grinned, dangling the princess by the rope entwining her body. "Gar put her good and high."

Morten fought back the urge to despair, and immediately began thinking of ways to turn this new obstacle to his advantage. If he could find a long pole or spear, he might use it to lift the princess off her hook instead of trying to climb up the wall as the giants would expect, and that would cause a short period of confusion—confusion he could use to good advantage.

Once the giant had disappeared into the gloom at the other end of the lodge, Noote stepped behind Morten. Instead of untying his prisoner, the chief pulled the entire pole out of the ground and dragged the body-guard toward the far end of the Fir Palace.

Morten glanced over his shoulder at the cooking fire. It pleased him to see his strategy working well enough to keep Tavis alive. The scout's face had turned to a light shade of purple and his eyes had rolled back in his head, but the flames still had not burned through the shriveled leather of his cocoon. With luck, the bodyguard might save the scout on his way past—and that would be another surprise for the hill giants.

That was when Morten noticed an ogre warrior walking out of the gloom. The brute was striding down the center of the passage, both hands in plain sight, his purple eyes fixed straight ahead. Walking with him was Sart, the hill giant sentry that had fought Rog, but it was difficult to tell who was the prisoner of whom. Sart's eyes were fixed on the floor and he bore no weapon in his hands, while the ogre, who was also unarmed, kept his eyes fixed proudly ahead.

To Morten, it looked like the giant had failed in his sentry duties once again, and this time the lives he had endangered were those of the firbolg and his companions. At the very least, dealing with the ogre would cost valuable minutes—minutes that Tavis would spend roasting over the fire. At the worst, it would mean a premature end to the rabbit run when Noote and his queen learned Brianna had lied about Goboka's death.

Noote did not notice the ogre, but continued to drag Morten along until they had reached the far end of the lodge. There, he stopped and turned around to face his giants, leaving the firbolg half stooped over with the long stake still tied to his back.

"Ready for rabbit run?" the chieftain boomed. Then, when he was answered by nothing more than an astonished drone, he saw Sart coming toward him and demanded, "Who at High Gate?"

It was the ogre who answered. "High Gate Goboka's now." He waved his arm around the room. "All this be Goboka's, soon."

Noote bared his filed teeth in displeasure. "What you mean, ugly pip-squeak?" he demanded. "Goboka dead!"

The ogre's jaw dropped, and he knitted his sloped brow in confusion. He studied Noote for a moment, then his purple eyes twinkled with understanding. "Liar, fat giant!" he accused. "Goboka send me to talk."

The queen's eyes flashed toward the far end of the palace, where Brianna was probably hanging by now, then she narrowed her eyes and bit her lip in thought. Morten needed no magic to know she now realized the princess had lied about the shaman's demise.

The ogre fixed his purple eyes on the queen's face, then said, "Goboka say give Brianna, or Gray Wolves all dead by dusk."

Keeping her eyes fixed on the ogre, the queen leaned over to whisper in Noote's ear. If Morten wanted to keep the hill giants from returning Brianna to Goboka, he had to do something now.

Dragging the heavy pole along with him, Morten took a few quick steps and planted his heel in the ogre's ribs, pushing the brute to the ground with a powerful thrust. "If you want Brianna, you have to race me," he growled. "Make the rabbit run!"

"Big fun!" yelled a nearby giant.

Such a clamor broke out that Noote could only scowl in frustration as he tried to hear his whispering queen. Finally, he gave up and shrugged her off.

"Grab ogre!" he bellowed at Sart. "New game today: rabbit race!"

Morten told himself that racing the ogre would make it easier to rescue Brianna. With two rabbits in the race, he would be kicked by only half as many hill giants.

But the bodyguard didn't believe it.

* * * * *

When Avner heard the footsteps echoing out of the fault cave, his weary body jerked so hard that it nearly sent him plunging into the valley below. He braced his hands against the wet timbers and carefully pushed away from the edge of the platform, at the same time trying to swallow the cold lump of panic that had risen into his throat.

The youth's concentration had been so consumed by the scene below, where the dark figures of Goboka's horde had quietly surrounded all the hill giant lodges, that he had entirely forgotten the possibility stragglers might be coming through the cave at dawn. Now he feared he would pay a terrible price for his oversight. Hiding was out of the question, since he had been peering over the edge of the timber platform, consequently lying in plain sight, when he heard the sound. Nor could he flee, since the only direction to go was down into the valley with the ogres.

Still, the youth was not about to give up. After Goboka had opened the gate, Avner had spent half the night clinging to the timbers beneath the platform, hiding from the ogre packs as they sporadically came slinking out of the cave. Only his terror and the pain of his broken arm kept him from freezing to death. Despite the ruthlessness with which their shaman was driving them, the brutes seemed as alert and as dangerous as ever, and the boy spent the entire time horrified that his teeth would start chattering and give him away, or that one of them would sense him shivering through vibrations in the platform's timber floor. But somehow he escaped detection, and they stopped coming, leaving only a pair of sentries behind to guard the cave mouth.

The young thief disposed of the first sentry by chirping softly until one of the brutes, no doubt thinking to make a meal of the birds nesting beneath the platform, stuck his head down to investigate. Avner attacked quickly and savagely, driving his dagger into his foe's exposed gullet. Leaving the blade buried there, he used his good hand to grab the stunned ogre's greasy topknot and pull him over edge. The warrior plummeted into the dark night, the knife in his throat preventing him from voicing a scream that might draw the notice of his fellows below.

The ogre had not even hit bottom before the boy was silently climbing up through the chain slots. As expected, the second sentry was kneeling close to where his partner had disappeared. Although the brute's attention was fixed on the edge, he was not foolish enough to expose himself as his companion had done. Instead, he had a shaft nocked in his bow, and was listening for more sounds from beneath the platform. Moving as quietly as only a terrified thief can, Avner crept a half dozen steps across the platform, then pulled a poisoned arrow from the warrior's quiver and plunged the tip deep into his back.

Gasping in pain, the brute stood and spun toward his attacker in one swift motion. The youth dove into the fault cave and heard his foe's arrow clatter off the rocks above his head. By the time the boy stood and turned around, the warrior was lying on the platform, knocked unconscious by his own poison. Avner replaced his lost dagger with the warrior's bone knife, then pushed the ogre off the platform. That done, he crawled inside the fault cave to take refuge from the cold night.

After all that, the young thief had no intention of surrendering to the brute now stomping through the cave. He would at least go down fighting.

With his good hand, Avner pulled his bone dagger and spun around. His target was still hidden by the shadows of the fault cave, but the footsteps continued to grow louder. The youth cocked his arm back to throw, certain he could hit his foe by sound alone.

"Hold your weapon, my friend!" called a familiar voice. "I'm sorry I fell behind, but surely I don't deserve such a stern punishment!"

Avner lowered his arm. "Basil?"

"The one and the same."

The verbeeg stepped into the light at the cave mouth and squinted out into the morning. He looked about as haggard and cold as Avner felt, with a nose blackened by frostbite and hoarfrost hanging from his bushy eyebrows.

"What are you doing here?" Avner demanded.

The verbeeg looked hurt by the question. "Surely, you haven't forgotten our bargain!" he said. "Or are you hoping to claim all those books I stole for your own?"

"You can have 'em," Avner replied. "It's just that I thought you deserted us at the waterfall!"

"That's what the ogres thought, too—or I wouldn't be here now," Basil chuckled. He stuck his head out of the cave mouth and looked around. "Where's everyone else?"

"Down there." Avner pointed into the valley. "I think the hill giants have them, but not for long."

Basil's lip twisted into a sneer of disgust at the mention of hill giants, but he did not voice any opinions. The verbeeg stepped to Avner's side and peered down.

"I've been trying to figure out what to do," Avner said, "but I can't."

"Perhaps that's because there's not much you can do—especially with that arm." Basil shook his head at the situation below, then added, "We can only hope for the best—and be ready to help if it should come to pass."

Avner looked up at the verbeeg. "What do you mean?"

"From what we can see, it appears there will be a battle soon." As he spoke, the verbeeg turned around and began to study the hoisting chains and the heavy iron gate hanging below the cave mouth. "That'll be when our friends try to escape. If they're to succeed, it will be up to us to provide a quick exit."

"How?"

Basil pointed at Avner's rope, still tied into a makeshift ladder.

"We can start by hanging that rope over the side," the

verbeeg said.

Avner looked from the rope ladder, which he knew was not much longer than Basil was tall, to the enormous drop into the valley below. "You're mad!" he said. "Even with no knots, the rope will never reach that far."

"Then I suppose we'll have to make it longer."

The runecaster sat down next to the rope and opened the satchel where he kept his brushes and quills.

* * * * *

The ogre, now stripped of his clothes and smeared with foul-smelling grease, seemed unable to comprehend what was happening to him. He stood on the other side of Noote's kneeling figure, glaring up at the bellowing hill giants lined all along the Fir Palace's gloomy walls. He paid Morten no attention, as though he did not understand he would be competing against the firbolg, and had not even glanced over at the bodyguard.

Morten hoped the dazed expression on his foe's face meant the brute would meet a quick end. It was going to be difficult enough to weave his way through the forest of bolelike legs ahead, especially when they began kicking and stomping. Save for the alley down the center of the room, which he felt sure would be the quickest avenue to death, he could see no open ground at all, only huge filthy feet with stumpy toes and broken yellow nails.

About halfway down the gauntlet, Tavis still hung over the cooking fire. Fortunately, once the hill giants had lost interest in steaming him, the fomorian cook had let the fire die down to glowing coals, and it seemed entirely possible that the scout would be alive when Morten reached him. Whether he would be strong enough to help free Brianna was another matter, but at least his presence might add to the confusion. The princess herself hung near the ceiling of the far wall, a distant cocoon of rope illuminated by a single torch the giants had placed there so the rabbits would know where they were trying to go—though few expected them to live that long.

"Ready rabbits?" Noote asked.

Without waiting for a reply or offering any other warning, the chief lifted the hands he had placed in front of the two racers. Morten reacted first, sprinting forward without so much as a sideward glance. The giants roared their delight, filling the palace with a deafening rumble louder than any thunderstorm. The sound seemed to buffet the bodyguard like a powerful wind, threatening to sweep him from his feet.

The giants began to stomp, and before Morten knew it, the dirt floor was bucking beneath his feet like a collapsing rampart. The firbolg managed two steps before he bounced so high into the air that he lost his feel for the ground. He came down at an angle, arms flailing wildly, and crashed to the floor on his back.

The hill giants yelled even louder, shaking the walls so hard that the hide coverings flapped as though a terrible wind were tearing at them. As his tormentors moved in for the kill, Morten saw their heads forming a rough circle high above. He rolled sideways, narrowly saving himself as a huge foot crashed to the floor.

The impact bounced the firbolg into the air. He tried to gather his legs and felt as though he were trying to stand while tumbling down a steep hill. He managed to plant his feet on the ground, but his body's momentum carried him past his balance point and sent him sprawling. He glimpsed the ogre tumbling through the air beside him, then landed face first on the ground.

Something heavy crashed down on his back. Morten dug his fingers into the dirt and tried to pull himself forward, expecting to feel a large heel with all the enormous weight of hill giant behind it.

Instead, the ogre's powerful jaws bore down on the firbolg's burly calf, sending sharp daggers of pain shooting up through his knee. The bodyguard howled in surprise and anger, though even he could not hear the cry above the din of the hill giants. He twisted around to grasp his attacker. The ogre pulled his head away from Morten's leg and spit a hunk of flesh from between his lips, then lowered his mouth to the firbolg's ankle.

Morten brought his foot up as hard as he could, driving the hard knob of his heel into his attacker's face. Unlike those of humans or firbolgs, ogre noses were filled with dozens of small bones, and the kick snapped them all like dry twigs. The ogre went slack; whether he was unconscious or dead did not matter to Morten. The brute was out of the race either way. The firbolg rolled, throwing the ogre's limp body off his back—then saw a giant's immense foot sweeping toward him.

The kick landed square in his ribs. The firbolg felt the air rush from his chest, then he and the ogre went sailing in different directions.

Morten crashed, back first, into the side of a giant's treelike leg. He felt something crack, like an inflexible trunk snapping in a heavy wind. A pained bellow reverberated above, louder even than the tremendous tumult of the other hill giant voices, and the fellow's knee buckled—not in a direction it normally bent, but sideways. The giant reflexively clutched at the joint, barely retaining his balance as he attempted the impossible maneuver with both hands still bound behind his back.

Morten slid to the ground, a terrible ball of dull, throbbing agony forming between his shoulder blades. The firbolg knew the impact had knocked something in his back terribly out of place, but he could not let that bother him now—not when he had such an opportunity to throw the hill giants into a confused panic. The bodyguard rolled onto his stomach and pushed himself to his hands and knees. He spun around until he saw the injured giant's good leg, then, without standing up, he gathered his feet beneath him and drove his shoulder into it as hard as he could. Again the giant bellowed, but this time he also came down.

The effect was something like a tree toppling in an over-thick stand of woods. The fellow crashed into two more giants beside him, and they also fell, unable to catch themselves with their hands tied behind their backs. This pair unbalanced two more, who had to stop kicking long enough to regain their balance.

The opening that resulted wasn't much, but it was enough for the firbolg. He jumped to his feet and clambered away, dodging and weaving as hill giant feet lashed at him from all directions. He suffered several glancing blows that almost knocked him over, and twice he was struck so hard that he actually fell and tumbled through the swarm of legs, somersaulting across insteps and ricocheting off ankles. Each time, he managed to roll back to his feet and continue running. At first, he moved across the lodge toward a side wall, as though searching for a clear alley. Then he suddenly turned toward Brianna and darted into a dense thicket of hill giant legs, where the crowd was packed so thickly that the giants smashed each other's shins more often than their target. Even when a foot did catch Morten, it did not have much momentum, and so the blow was not very painful.

By the time the firbolg neared the middle of the lodge, the hill giants ahead were beginning to bump each other aside, trying to create enough space around themselves so they could land a solid attack if the rabbit came their way. Morten dodged back toward the center of the room, running straight for the shimmering orange light of the cooking fire.

As the firbolg broke free of the thicket of giant legs, he was surprised to see Tavis no longer hung over the fire. Ig had already taken the scout's spit down and was using a bone butcher knife to cut the cocoon apart. Long strings of drool were dripping from the fomorian's mouth, and he was licking his twisted lips with a long gray tongue.

"Leave him alone!" Morten bellowed.

The bodyguard started to charge the cook, hoping that the fomorian was typical for his race and coward enough to bluff away easily. Otherwise, Morten would have to abandon the scout. He could not afford the time it would take to kill the fomorian.

The firbolg suddenly found his way blocked by the fomorian dancing slave. Although hardly as big as a hill giant, she was still much larger than Morten, and he could not easily dodge around her.

"Go!" She thrust his battle-axe into his hand. "We take care of Tavis Burdun."

Morten stared at the weapon in confusion, so stunned by the unexpected help that it took him a moment to realize the fomorian slaves had become his allies. The firbolg accepted his axe and started to step past the fomorian, intending to rush into the crowd on the other side of the lodge. Before he made it all the way around her enormous hip, the hides on the wall ahead were ripped away with a tremendous whoosh. The firbolg caught a glimpse of towering fir trees silhouetted against a blue sky, then hill giants began to spin around, shouting and screaming in astonishment. The tumult lasted only a matter of seconds before giants began to collapse, the black fletching of ogre arrows protruding from wounds that, on their huge bodies, seemed mere pinpricks.

Deciding it wiser to risk hill giant feet than ogre arrows, Morten spun around. The conditions on that side of the lodge were no better. Goboka had planned his attack well, catching his enemies in a deadly cross fire.

Noote's angry voice came bellowing from the other end of the lodge. "Forget game! Fight ogres!"

Hoping the giants ahead could hear their chief, Morten turned and ran for Brianna's end of the lodge. At first, Noote's followers seemed confused about what was happening. While their fellows dropped all around them, many continued to stomp and kick at Morten, angrily bellowing about the game being unfair when he used his axe to fend off their attacks. Then, as their unconscious fellows piled on top of each other, the giants seemed to realize the firbolg was not their greatest problem. They began to work feverishly to unbind each other's hands. Morten even began to help, cutting their hands free as he ran past.

To the bodyguard's relief, Goboka's attack was concentrated near the center of the lodge. Fifty paces down from the cooking fire, the walls remained intact, and the giants were moving toward the battle with their clubs and wooden shields. Occasionally, one of these warriors took a swipe at Morten, but the firbolg had little trouble dodging these halfhearted attacks—especially when the aggressor was invariably chastised for wasting time. They had ogres to kill!

By the time Morten reached the far end of the lodge, it was more or less empty. All the giant warriors were back near the cooking fire, bellowing insults at their attackers and trying to work up the courage to raise their shields and charge into the onslaught of ogre arrows. All that remained here, in the relatively untouched corners of the lodge, were a handful of wrinkled giants too old to do much of anything except watch the clan's whimpering children. None of them made any move to stop Morten as he approached Brianna.

"Are you all right up there?" the bodyguard called.

"Better than you," Brianna warned. "Look behind you."

The floor began to tremble as someone broke into a charge. Morten spun around to see Noote and his queen rushing toward him. The bodyguard could not imagine how they had pushed their way through the swarm of giants in the center of the lodge, but there could be no denying they had.

Cursing under his breath, Morten braced himself to meet the charge. One giant he could handle, but two—his silent complaint was interrupted by the muffled strum of a bowstring. The queen cried out in shock and began to stumble. She managed to take one more step before collapsing on her face, the black fletching of an ogre arrow protruding from one enormous buttock.

The bodyguard felt the cold fingers of panic slipping around his heart, at least until he realized that it wasn't an ogre that had fired the shaft. Tavis's crimson-skinned figure stood a short distance beyond the queen, with a scrap of filthy hide tied loosely about his waist and the fomorians standing to either side of him. The scout was trying to nock another arrow, though he was so weak that he could not stand without leaning against the leg of the female dancing slave.

"Save your strength!" Morten yelled.

The bodyguard allowed Noote to continue his charge. Then, when the hill giant stooped over to reach for him, the firbolg hurled his axe. The weapon tumbled through the air once, then lodged its blade deep in the chieftain's forehead.

Morten dove away, catching a glimpse of Noote's eyes growing blank as he pitched forward. The hill giant's body did not fall clear to the ground, instead lodging against the wall below Brianna's feet.

The firbolg picked himself up, then climbed Noote's back and stood on the hill giant's shoulders as he plucked Brianna off the wall.

"Nice axe work," the princess commented. "Now let's get out of here—and fast!"

Morten glanced over his shoulder and saw that some of the hill giants had decided it would be easier to go out the entrance than to try squeezing out the holes the ogres had opened in the center of their palace. About two dozen of the huge warriors were rushing toward the exit, bellowing war cries and whirling clubs over their heads.

"Fools," Morten commented. He began to unwrap Brianna. "Goboka will expect that."

"But I bet he won't be expecting *that*, will he?"

The princess pulled her arm free of her loosened bindings and pointed to Tavis. The scout and his fomorian rescuers were rushing straight toward the side of the room, desperately attempting to avoid the giants charging down the center of the lodge. As Morten and Brianna watched, the fomorians linked arms and lowered their shoulders, then hurled themselves through the wall with a tremendous crash.

"Let's go," Brianna ordered. She pulled the rope off her legs and tossed it aside, then started to run. "We don't want to get left behind."

⁂ 16 ⁂
Unexpected Help

A few moments after the fomorians opened the gaping hole in the side of the Fir Palace, Tavis and his companions rushed through it. The scout ran between Morten and Brianna, who had snatched up two battered hill giant bucklers to screen the trio's flanks. Although the shields were as large and heavy as tower doors, the princess's ancestral strength allowed her to carry hers as easily the bodyguard did his. The small company did not bother to guard against frontal assaults, for their fomorian allies had ripped a huge section of hides from the lodge wall as they exited, then cut a broad swath through the ogre lines by hurling this tattered canopy over the heads of their would-be attackers.

Tavis and his companions made it only three steps out of the lodge before ogre arrows began to pound the shields on both flanks. The assault sounded like some sort of crazy drumbeat, reverberating through the wood with an erratic cadence of thumps and thuds. Tiny splits appeared in the thick planks, each sprouting the dark tip of an iron arrowhead. The venomous points were not yet penetrating far enough to be dangerous, but the scout knew that soon a shaft would split one of the gray slats and pierce the flesh of a shield-bearer.

Though Tavis was not carrying either of the heavy shields, he found it difficult to keep pace with his companions. Both his mangled arm and the gash in his side throbbed with a deep, boiling pain, while Noote's torture had scalded his skin to such a degree that he felt as though wasps were stinging every inch of his body. But his thirst caused the worst suffering. The scout had lost so much sweat during the steaming that he felt like he had not drunk water in a tenday. He could hardly draw breath past his swollen tongue, and his joints burned with the fiery ache of fever. Even the spots swimming before his eyes seemed ready to sink into darkness.

Despite his weariness, the scout nocked an arrow as they stepped onto the canopy the fomorians had laid over the ogre lines. Soon, the warriors flanking them would be in position to try for rear shots. He had to be ready to answer. Trying to summon the strength to draw Bear Driller's bowstring, Tavis glanced over his shoulder—then a tremendous echoing crash rolled over him as the Fir Palace came apart, untanned hides and fir trunks flying in every direction.

At first, Tavis thought Goboka had blasted the lodge with a spell—until he saw the hill giants, following the example of their fomorian slaves, come crashing through the walls. The whole lodge seemed to be exploding, like a hive no longer able to contain its angry bees, and suddenly there were giants everywhere.

The rain of arrows pounding the trio's shields dwindled to a trickle, then died away completely as the ogres scrambled to dodge the canopies of tattered hides and splintered tree trunks being hurled at them by the hill giants. Morten and Brianna tossed the heavy bucklers aside and, dragging Tavis between them, scrambled away from the ogre lines, following the fomorians toward the nearest stand of fir trees.

As the trio sprinted into the copse, powerful jolts and heavy shocks began to rumble from the direction of the Fir Palace. Tavis glanced back and saw that the ogres had recovered from the initial shock of their foes' charge and were again firing. A handful of hill giants already lay sprawled on the ground, and several others were taking their last lurching steps. But many more were still charging forward behind their huge shields, their long legs carrying them toward their enemies with incredible speed.

A different kind of crashing began to roll across the field: the sound of massive clubs smashing anything that might conceal an ogre archer. Fir trees came tumbling down, boulders went clattering across the valley floor, hillocks of soft ground burst apart. Tavis and his companions did not tarry to watch the carnage, but continued deeper into the stand. The sudden reversal of the battle's course made little difference to them. They had to put as much distance between themselves and the victors, whether ogres or hill giants, as possible.

By the time they finally caught the fomorians, Tavis could hardly stand. His vision had narrowed to a long black tunnel, his shaking legs could barely support him, and his throat was so swollen he feared it would close up entirely. Fighting the urge to collapse, he staggered over to the bank of the tiny stream where their allies had stopped, then threw himself face first into the cold waters.

When he finished drinking, the scout found Brianna and Morten standing next to him. From outside the thicket, the constant thunder of hammering clubs and falling giants suggested the combat had grown even more intense during the few moments it had taken him to quench his thirst.

Ig and the dancing girl had crossed to sit on the opposite shore and were calmly pulling apart the rotten carcass of a deer they had apparently brought from the Fir Palace in the cook's shoulder satchel. Although the meat was so putrid that even an ogre wouldn't have eaten it, Tavis was not surprised to see the pair gorging themselves on it. The fomorian diet consisted of the most noxious, virulent refuse that they could find—and if something was too fresh, they would often take it home to rot for a time.

Brianna placed her hand on Tavis's shoulder. "If you've quenched your thirst, I should cast my spells."

The scout was disappointed to see that the princess did not meet his eyes. He started to ask if something was wrong, then thought better of it and remained silent. Of course something was wrong. Last night, Brianna had learned the truth about her father's betrayal. Tavis could only guess how that knowledge made her feel—sad, angry, lost perhaps—but he knew for certain that those emotions would be as powerful as the terrible despair he was feeling over Avner's loss.

In the back of his mind, the scout kept hearing the boy's footsteps padding through the thicket. He half expected the young thief to appear and announce that the whole thing had been an elaborate joke, but Tavis knew that would not happen. Thousand-foot falls were not jokes. Avner was gone, and all the wishful thinking in the world would not bring him back.

When Tavis made no move to lie down, Brianna gently pushed him onto his back and purified his injuries with blessed water, then laid her amulet on his stomach wound. "I'll start with this one."

"No." Tavis moved the talisman up to his sternum. The stomach wound was by far the most dangerous and agonizing of his injuries, but he didn't care. He had no intention of allowing Brianna to go the way of Avner, and he would be better able to defend her if his bruised chest did not interfere with drawing his bowstring. "If you only have two spells, cast them on my chest and my arm."

Brianna frowned. "This is only a bruise," she said, touching his discolored sternum. "It isn't dangerous."

"It hinders me when I pull my bow," the scout replied. "And right now, that's more dangerous than any wound I have."

The princess nodded, then did as he asked. Tavis could not help hissing as Hiatea's symbol began to glow with white heat, searing his already scalded skin.

The sound drew gap-toothed smiles from both fomorians.

"I thought we were on the same side," Tavis complained.

"Pain good," replied the female. She gave Ig a coy smile, then added, "Pain mean you alive."

"Then maybe you'd like some of your own," growled Morten.

"Don't mind them," Tavis said. As he spoke, the color of his bruised chest was lightening from blackish-purple to pale crimson, and he could feel the goddess's strength coursing through his bones. "That's just their nature."

"If you say so." The bodyguard stood and started back toward the battle. "I'll go see what's happening at the Fir Palace."

As Morten left, Brianna moved her talisman to the scout's arm and cast her second healing spell. To the fomorians' obvious disappointment, Tavis remained quiet as the scarred flesh on his forearm slowly smoothed itself back to normal. He felt more of Hiatea's magic flowing up through his shoulder, and even the weakness caused by his dehydration seemed to fade.

Brianna left her talisman in place for several minutes. Only after the magical glow had faded and the silver had turned cold did she take it from Tavis's arm.

"I hope that's better." She still did not meet his eyes.

The scout stood, then grabbed Bear Driller and drew the bowstring back. The effort caused a little pain in all his wounds, but he now felt more than strong enough to nock a few ogre arrows on its string.

"I should be able to kill a few ogres now," he said.

"Then you'll need some arrows," Morten said, returning from his observation post. He was carrying a full quiver of ogre arrows in one hand and stone hand axe in the other. "I took these from a dead ogre at the edge of the stand."

"The battle's still going strong?" Tavis asked. The scout noticed that Morten's throat wound was about to fester again, for it had grown red and swollen. "There's no sign that the ogres are coming after us?"

"They couldn't if they wanted to." The bodyguard handed the quiver to Tavis. "The giants are going after them like bears after dogs."

The report alarmed the scout. "What about the shaman?" he asked. "Isn't he doing anything to help his warriors?"

Morten shook his head. "Not that I can see."

"We'd better get out of here, fast," Tavis said. "If Goboka's not helping his warriors, he's looking for us."

Tavis turned to leave, but when the fomorians stood up to follow, Morten grabbed the scout by the shoulder. "Are we going to let them come with us?"

"Ooo help you," the female reminded Morten. "You help Ooo and Ig."

"Smashing palace wall easy," said Ig, stepping to Ooo's side. "But need Tavis Burdun to leave valley."

Tavis nodded. "It's a fair bargain."

"I suppose so." The bodyguard stepped close to Tavis, then spoke more quietly. "But be careful. You can't trust fomorians."

"They deserve a chance," Brianna said. She glanced at Tavis, then looked away. "I recall both of us saying the same thing about a certain firbolg—and look how wrong we were."

"This is different," Morten grumbled.

Tavis smiled to himself, then led the way through the thicket. With Ig half staggering and half hopping along behind them, there was no possibility of moving with any kind of stealth. The scout tried to reduce the likelihood of ambush by traveling as far ahead of his companions as practical, but he did not think his efforts would do much good. The fomorian's gait was so clumsy that, even with the din of battle still raging around the Fir Palace, a careful listener almost anywhere in the valley would hear him crashing through the thicket. Tavis tried not to worry about the noise, since there was little he or anyone else could do about it.

In contrast to Ig, Ooo moved with the uncanny silence typical to most fomorians. Her immense figure seemed to glide through the thicket in slow motion. She made no wasted gestures, placed each foot with precision and care. She was so graceful that the scout even began to think of her as beautiful—though in a dangerous sort of way. Tavis had seen enough carnage wrought by her race to know fomorians used their remarkable stealth for purposes as twisted as their forms.

They reached the edge of the stand. The scout motioned for the others to wait, then stood behind a fir bole and studied the ground ahead. The small field was dotted with boulders, tufts of long yellow-green grass, and bright clumps of dainty alpine flowers. There was no sign of the battle between Goboka's horde and the hill giants, but Tavis knew better than to assume there were no ogres nearby just because he did not see them.

Across the small field, a ridge of barren bedrock curved toward the cliff with the High Gate. The granite face stood at such an angle that neither the fault cave nor the timber road was visible, but the scout could see a well-traveled giant path leading up the crest of the ridge. From what little he remembered of the journey down from the gate, the trail was both long and arduous, and they would be visible for much of its length.

They could not risk ascending it during the day. Goboka would certainly see them, and with Ig staggering along in their company, they were not fast enough to flee the shaman. It would be better to wait until dark. He and Ooo would sneak up the trail first, slaying any sentries that the victors of today's battle sent to guard the gate. Brianna and the others would follow later.

As the scout turned to tell the others of his decision, a sharp thunk sounded on the tree behind him. He dropped to the ground, an arrow already nocked. Something hissed past his head and thumped into the tree bole ahead, then bounced to the ground. It was not an ogre's arrow, as he had expected. The missile was a small round rock, such as might be hurled from a sling.

Tavis's first thought was of Avner, but of course that was ridiculous. The boy was dead.

Another stone hissed overhead and bounced off the same tree, pitting the bark just inches above the mark left by the first. The slinger was either missing on purpose, Tavis realized, or had just gauged the distance to his target. The scout scrambled into a seated position, looking in the direction from which the stones had come.

Across the field, a human boy stood behind a boulder, using one arm to gesture at Tavis. His other arm was bound to his side as though it had been injured.

Tavis did not lower his bow. Avner had fallen a thousand feet, and if his body was now standing across the field waving, the scout could think of only one explanation. Goboka had animated the boy's corpse. The shaman was trying to lure them into a trap.

Tavis pulled his bowstring back.

Avner's eyes widened, and he ducked down behind the boulder. "Whatever it is, I didn't do it!"

"Avner?" Tavis gasped. The boy certainly didn't sound dead.

"What are you, blind?" The youth peered over the top of the boulder. "Of course it's me."

"But Kol . . . Rog pushed you off the platform!"

"Do I look like I fell a thousand feet?" Avner cautiously rose so that Tavis could see his entire body.

The scout had to admit that the boy looked far too healthy to have suffered the fall. Even if Kol had cushioned the youth's landing, the impact would have twisted his body into something more akin to the fomorians. Tavis lowered his bow. Even if there had been reason to loose an arrow, he could not have hit his target. He was so filled with relief that his hands were trembling.

"How did you—"

"Later. There are ogres about," the boy said. "That's why I was trying to get your attention without shouting."

"That wouldn't have worked anyway," Tavis replied, listening to Ig come crashing up behind him. "Stealth is no longer our strong point."

"Then we'd better hurry," Avner said. "I don't know how long Basil will wait. He's nervous about the ogres."

"Basil?" asked Morten, joining the scout. The body-guard sounded as suspicious as Tavis had been a moment earlier.

"He still wants his books," Avner explained. "Now, are you coming or what? It's not like I'm charging a toll."

Tavis stood and led the way across the field. Once they were past the ridge and had a clear view of the High Gate, he could see why Avner was concerned. On top of the granite ridge, well beyond the bend where the scout could have seen them from the fir stand, a dozen ogres where sprinting toward the timber road. Goboka was behind them, strolling up the hill at a more leisurely pace. Fortunately for the scout and his friends, the cliff was casting a dark shadow over their group. Even if the shaman had heard them calling to each other, it would be difficult for him to find them in the deep shade.

No sooner had the scout reached this conclusion than the shaman's head slowly turned toward their position. Despite the distance, Tavis could see a fierce purple light gleaming in his eyes, and he knew that the ogre had spied them.

"He sees us!" Brianna gasped.

"He can't!" Avner replied. "I was hiding in these same shadows when he started up the trail, and he looked right at me without doing anything. Why should he see us now?"

"Perhaps because of this," said Morten. The body-guard held his fingers out for the others to see. They were covered with yellow ichor from the sore on his throat, which had begun to fester again. "I felt the wound swelling as we escaped the Fir Palace. It started to ooze right before he looked down at us."

"You think he's tracking us through the bite?" Brianna asked.

Morten nodded. "It explains how he reacted so quickly when we rescued you on the glacier." The bodyguard fixed his eyes on the ground. "My wound was festering then, too."

Tavis cursed under his breath. "That explains why he didn't kill you on Coggin's Rise," the scout surmised. "He knew that if anyone came after Brianna, you'd be among them."

Tears of shame began to roll down Morten's cheeks. "I should have realized it earlier."

"Why? None of us did," Tavis said. He placed a reassuring hand on the bodyguard's arm. "It's not your fault."

"And it's not going to stop us from escaping," Avner added. "Goboka and his ogres have a long climb."

"And we have an even longer one—with them ahead of us," Morten countered. He looked up at the craggy ridge above. "It won't be easy to fight our way up that."

"We don't need to. Basil will lower a rope, then he's got something figured that'll get us up in no time." Avner pointed across a small field to the base of the cliff, where the mangled bodies of Kol and Rog lay in a heap below the High Gate. "All we have to do is run over there."

The youth started toward the cliff, trotting across the valley on a course roughly parallel to the trail the ogres were climbing to the base of the timber road. As Tavis and the others followed, the scout glanced up and saw Goboka watching them with a thoughtful expression. The shaman glanced toward the platform outside the High Gate and looked back to them.

Goboka pointed his finger down the trail, to where a

rocky slope spilled down from the ridge crest, directly above the small field Tavis and his companions had to cross. The shaman cried out in the guttural language of his race. A deep, pulsing vibration shot through the floor of the valley, then a deafening crack rang off the canyon walls. Huge boulders began to slip free of the scarp face and tumble down the steep hillside.

"He's trying to cut us off!" Tavis yelled. "Run faster!"

They broke into a sprint, their eyes fixed on the hillside above. The landslide built slowly, for the bedrock ridge did not crumble easily and would not have broken apart at all save for the incredible power of Goboka's magic. As the boulders went bouncing down the scarp, they occasionally knocked more rocks loose, but the result was nothing like the cascade of loose stone that had nearly killed Tavis in Runolf's couloir. By the time the small company's leaders, Avner and Brianna, reached the field's edge, less than a dozen boulders were tumbling down the slope above them.

Goboka's voice rang out again, and another tremendous crack rang through the valley. This time, his spell was more successful. Near the crest of the ridge, a curtain of powdered rock shot into the air, then a mountainous slab of granite came free and slid downslope. It began to break apart, producing a tremendous rockslide. The cloud of rock dust rolled down the scarp and spread out over the field like a gray, bitter-smelling fog.

Morten rushed up and took Tavis's arm, half dragging the scout into the choking haze ahead. "Let me help you along, runt!"

As they rushed across the field, the scout found himself gagging on the billowing dust. He could not see Brianna and Avner—though he hoped they had already cleared the danger. He and Morten veered away from the ridge as much as possible. Even so, dirt and gravel, surging ahead of the main avalanche, pelted their flanks, while boulders came bouncing past their heads with alarming frequency. Above the roar, Tavis heard the arrhythmic beat of Ig's gait crashing along behind them. Ooo was gliding along with the fomorian, cursing his three mismatched legs and herself for staying at his side.

Tavis heard a dull thud as a small boulder, no larger than a human head, ricocheted off Morten's shoulder. The bodyguard groaned and stumbled. Without slowing down, the scout leaned into his companion's flank and propped him up. Together they staggered forward until the dust began to clear and no more stones came bouncing past. A short distance ahead Brianna and Avner stood on a gentle rise, safely beyond the rockslide.

A loud crack sounded behind Tavis. Ig yelled in pain, then there was a crash as the two fomorians fell to the ground. The scout whirled around and saw the dust-blurred shape of the fomorian cook lying on the ground, his hand pressed to a dripping head wound. Ooo was a short distance away, kneeling and stunned. A churning wall of stone was roaring down the slope to swallow them.

Tavis started to rush back to help, but Morten's hand restrained him. "There's no time."

Realizing the wisdom of the bodyguard's words, Tavis shouted, "Ooo, get up! Ig needs help!"

The scout's warning roused both fomorians. Ig pushed himself up enough to prop his shortest leg beneath his body, but seemed unable to rise farther without teetering like a drunken hill giant. Ooo did better, leaping to her feet in a single graceful motion. When she turned toward Ig and saw the wall of stone boiling toward her, her eyes grew as large as moons. There was a good chance that both she and Ig could escape if she helped him, but Ooo simply turned toward Tavis.

She began to run, calling over her shoulder, "Good-bye, Ig."

Ig raised his head to look at her back. "Good-bye,

Ooo." Then, as the rockslide swallowed him up, he added, "Coward hag!"

Ooo danced past the two firbolgs with no sign of remorse for Ig's death. "Hurry!" The fomorian pointed toward the ridge above, where the ogres ahead of Goboka had drawn to within a few hundred paces of the timber road. "Not much time."

After casting a last glance at the talus pile where Ig lay buried, Tavis started across the last dozen paces to where the giants lay. Basil's voice echoed down from the High Gate platform.

"Stand clear!"

The scout looked up in time to see a dark circle of cord spinning down from above. At first, he did not understand what Basil was doing, for he had never seen a rope that could reach such a distance. But the spool kept descending, the line growing impossibly long as coil after coil unfurled, until the last loop opened and the end of the rope snapped to a stop just a few paces away.

"That's some rope," Morten observed.

"It sure is," Tavis replied.

"It's magic," Avner explained impatiently. "Come on!"

The youth led the way past the jumbled hills of flesh and bone that were the remains of Rog and Kol. He stopped about fifteen paces from the cliff face, where the rope hung with several loops tied into the last twenty feet of the line. When Tavis followed and looked up, it did not seem the cord was dangling from the High Gate so much as ascending straight into the sky.

"You two first," Tavis said, motioning to Brianna and Avner.

"No," Avner said. "Basil said the two heaviest people should go up first."

Ooo did not need a second invitation. She stepped over to the line and grabbed a loop, then quickly pulled herself up to make room for Morten. The bodyguard was more reluctant.

"That rope doesn't look strong enough to hold Ooo alone," the firbolg said, eyeing the line suspiciously.

"Don't worry, Basil's taken care of everything." Avner held a loop open for the firbolg's foot. "Just climb in."

The bodyguard secured his hand axe beneath the greasy cord serving as his belt, then placed his foot in the noose and climbed into position below Ooo.

"Snap the rope twice," Avner called. "Hold on tight."

The fomorian plucked the rope as instructed. The resulting vibration sent a deep, sonorous hum singing across the meadow, then the muted rattle of chains rolled down from the High Gate. Ooo and Morten shot upward, their quivering cries of astonishment trailing after them. A distant tolling, not unlike the knell of an alarm bell, echoed over the valley.

"What's that?" Brianna asked.

"You'll see in a second," Avner said. "But right now, we'd better step back."

By the time they did as the boy suggested, Tavis could see the source of all the clamor. The High Gate and its chains were sliding down the face of the cliff, trailing a long dark cord. Apparently, Basil had run the other end of the rope through one of the iron hooks set into the cliff above the fault cave, then tied it to the hoisting chains and cut them loose. Now the entire gate assembly was plunging groundward, serving as a counterweight to pull the immense bulk of Ooo and Morten up to the platform.

Realizing what would happen when the immense weight hit the ground, Tavis pulled Avner and Brianna behind a boulder. The gate and chains smashed down a second later. The resulting crash was so loud they didn't even hear it; their ears simply began to ache with terrible, ringing pain. They were bucked high into the air and came down sprawled atop each other. Sheets of red gore, all that remained of Rog and Kol's crushed bodies, sprayed over the top of boulder and coated the field for dozens of paces around.

Tavis looked up. Ooo and Morten, so distant that they appeared to be nothing more than blobby shadows with arms and legs, were scrambling over the edge of the platform. At the other end of the hanging road, the first ogre was just setting foot onto the timbers and starting up toward the fault cave.

The scout felt Avner tugging on his arm. When he looked down, he saw the boy's lips moving but heard nothing. The ringing in his ears was so loud he could hardly hear his own thoughts, much less someone's words. The youth gave up trying to talk and ran toward the gate, which lay smashed into a dozen pieces. Avner climbed up a hoisting chain to where the rope had been connected to the gate and began to untie it. Just above the knot he was working on, there was a series of loops similar to those in which Morten and Ooo had ridden up to the platform.

Tavis climbed up the hoisting chain before Brianna, taking the highest position on the rope himself. It appeared that Basil and the others would have to pull them up to the platform by hand. The scout didn't know how long that would take, but feared the ogres would be waiting at the top. He certainly did not want the princess to be the first one they plucked off the rope.

Once Avner and Brianna had secured themselves beneath him, Tavis jerked the line as Ooo had done earlier. The trio did not shoot into the sky as the fomorian and Morten had, but rose rapidly and steadily. At first, the ascent was rather painful, for the rope dragged them along the cliff face, scraping their skin raw. They soon learned to work together to keep the soles of their feet pressed against the stone, so that they found themselves more or less running up the granite wall.

Tavis spent most of the trip craning his neck in an effort to see what Goboka and his ogres were doing. He quickly lost sight of the warriors as the last one started up the timber road, but the shaman himself was simply standing on the ridge watching them. The scout would have preferred to see the brute waddling up the trail as fast as his stubby legs would carry him. If Goboka was not worried, then Tavis was.

As the underside of the platform grew larger, the ringing in the scout's ears grew fainter. By the time he glimpsed flashes of Basil's hands pulling the rope up through the chain slots, Tavis could hear—not quite normally, but well enough to communicate.

"Where are the ogres?" he yelled.

"Close, but we have time," came the response.

"Not enough," Tavis growled. "Without the gate, they'll catch us in the cave."

"No, they won't," Avner said proudly. "Once we're up, just start running. Leave the rest to Basil and me."

"If it's all the same to you, I think I'll have Bear Driller ready," Tavis replied.

The scout pulled his bow off his shoulder. As Basil raised him through the chain slot, he jumped onto the platform, already nocking a black shaft. He slipped past his three panting companions and took aim down the road. The ogres were less than fifty paces away, easily within arrow range, but their bows remained slung over their backs and they were carrying hand axes or warhammers instead. Tavis quickly realized the reason for their choice of weaponry. If they shot the people hauling the rope up, they would send Brianna plunging to her death—and that was the last thing Goboka wanted.

Tavis had no such concerns about the welfare of the ogres. He loosed his first shaft and dropped the leader of the pack. The others leaped over him and continued charging. As the scout nocked his second shaft, he heard Avner scrambling onto the platform. Taking his own advice, the youth rushed straight into the fault cave.

Tavis fired again, dropping another ogre. The next

two brutes kept coming, their purple eyes gleaming with bloodlust.

Brianna jumped onto the platform and rushed into the cave after Avner, yelling, "I'll make us a light!"

Tavis nocked another arrow. The ogres were less than thirty steps away.

Before the scout could fire, Basil brushed past him. "You may as well save your arrow!"

The verbeeg kneeled at the edge of the platform where it joined the hanging road, then pulled his dagger and began to carve. Tavis peered over Basil's shoulder and saw that the runecaster had already cut an elaborate symbol into the wood and was just etching the last line.

"Go!" Basil urged.

Tavis started to back toward the cave, then thought better of it and glanced toward Goboka. The shaman remained where he had been standing all along, but was now stretching one arm toward the platform.

Morten started to scream, but the cry quickly changed to a choking gurgle. Tavis swung around to see an ogre's gnarled fingers shooting from the sore on the bodyguard's throat. An eerie blue aura of magical energy was dancing over the digits, crackling and snapping like lightning. In the next instant, the shaman's entire hand appeared, its black talons straining for Basil's back. Morten began to stumble forward against his will, as though Goboka were pulling him toward the runecaster.

The bodyguard dropped to his knees behind Basil. In words so garbled Tavis could barely understand them, he gurgled, "Throw me over!"

Goboka's arm stretched forward and ripped Basil away from his work.

"Do it!" Morten urged.

The scout glanced down the road and saw that the ogres were still twenty paces away. "No."

Tavis reached down and jerked the hand axe from

Morten's makeshift belt, then brought the blade down on the ichor-covered appendage protruding from the bodyguard's throat. The blow severed the arm with a sort of wet crackle. The stump of the limb receded into the festering sore from which it had come, and a pained wail rang out from the ridge.

Tavis glanced toward the sound and saw Goboka clutching his shoulder. Even from so far away, the scout could see that nothing hung below the elbow.

"Give me that!" Morten growled.

Tavis felt the axe being ripped from his hand, then saw Morten charge down the road to meet the ogres.

"Come back, Morten!" Tavis yelled.

"I can't finish the rune with you down there!" Basil added. "You'll be killed."

"That what he wants, verbeeg," Ooo said. "Finish rune."

"No," Tavis replied. "We can cure—"

Ooo shoved her way past the scout, nearly knocking him from the platform. "No time for stupid feelings."

The fomorian snatched Basil's dagger and, as Morten crashed into the ogre pack, carved the rune's last line.

A coating of bright green moss instantly spread down the path. The timbers began to rot, dropping away in a steady stream of decomposing matter. A deep groan sounded from the wooden buttresses, then the hanging road tilted steeply, spilling Morten and the ravaged ogre pack toward the valley floor.

Ooo dropped the dagger at Basil's side. "Escape complete. Now bargain done." The fomorian stepped into the fault cave. Without looking back, she called, "Good-bye, Tavis Burdun."

❧ 17 ❧
Goboka Returns

From deep in the forest echoed a loud, sharp thump, then something began to crash through the underbrush toward them. Too exhausted to leap up, Tavis and his three companions slowly gathered their weapons and dragged themselves to their feet.

"Do we run or fight?" asked Avner.

"I can't do either—at least not well," Basil complained. "I'm too tired."

The company had been on the move for two solid days and had glimpsed the distant figure of a lone, one-armed ogre often enough to know Goboka was dogging their trail. Apparently, the rest of the ogres—if any had survived the battle at Noote's lodge—remained trapped in the hill giant valley, for the shaman had no warriors with him. To make certain, Tavis had even circled back twice and found signs of only their single pursuer.

"Maybe we should hide," Brianna said. "If we're too tired to run or fight, that's our only option."

Tavis shook his head. "The cover's not good enough."

They were standing beside a cold bog, surrounded by swamp spruce, white birch, and tamarack. The terrain was flat and level in all directions, with nothing to offer protection except fallen tree trunks and a single boulder.

"Besides, Goboka wouldn't make so much noise unless he's already seen us," the scout added.

"Maybe it's not Goboka," suggested Brianna, staring into the forest. "If he can see us, we should see him too."

"What are you implying?" asked Basil.

Brianna licked her finger and held it in the air. "That noise is coming from downwind," she said. "Whatever's coming, I'd say it smelled us."

"A bear?" Avner asked.

Two more thumps echoed through the woods. The unseen beast snorted in alarm, then seemed to regain its footing and continue crashing through the undergrowth. Tavis could now hear its footfalls well enough to realize the creature was galloping.

"It's a horse," the scout said.

"Blizzard?" Brianna gasped.

A loud whinny rang off the trees, then the horse's white-flecked head and chest came flying into view, her hooves barely clearing the jumble of logs over which she had leaped. She caught sight of Brianna and whinnied again, galloping toward the princess as fast as she could. The mare looked as haggard and tired as the four companions. Her coat was dull and rough, so smeared with dirt and mud that it was more brown than black. Her mane and tail were tangled with burrs, and she had lost so much weight that her ribs stuck out like sticks.

Brianna stepped away from the boulder and spread her arms. Blizzard did not slow down until she was almost upon the princess, and the impact as she galloped into her mistress's arms would have sent a smaller woman tumbling into the cold bog. As it was, Brianna stumbled and nearly fell, but the near mishap did not wipe the smile from her face.

Tavis found the sight of Brianna's gleaming teeth a welcome one. It was the first time he had seen her smile in longer than he cared to remember.

The princess finally released Blizzard's neck and began to stroke the mare's nose. "It looks like you've had a rough time of it, girl," she said. "You must be as ready to go home as I am."

"Home?" Avner gasped. "Back to the castle?"

The smile vanished from Brianna's lips. "That's right." She nodded. "I must face my father."

"Are you sure that's prudent?" asked Basil. "In all likelihood, he'll return you to the ogres."

"Not before I tell the earls the price he paid to win his kingdom," she replied.

"What good is that?" Avner objected. "Half of them would do the same thing! They won't defy their king to protect you."

"He doesn't deserve to be their king!" Brianna snapped. "When he made his bargain with Goboka, he didn't betray me alone. He betrayed his kingdom!"

"How so?" Basil asked.

"The king has sired no other children," Brianna explained. "If the ogres take me, there's no legitimate heir to the throne. Hartsvale will fall into anarchy when my father dies."

"And that's why we must go back," Tavis said. The scout chose not to comment on the other, more ghastly possibility: that the Twilight Spirit would help some giant get a child on her—a half-breed who would, in time, become heir to Hartsvale's throne. "We must make the earls understand the king's crime."

"Not we." Brianna took Tavis's hand between hers and looked into his eyes. "You've already done more for me than I deserve."

"Brianna, that's not possible," the scout protested.

"It is, especially given my poor behavior," the princess insisted. "I should never have doubted you, but I swear in Hiatea's name it will never happen again. Please forgive me."

Tavis felt the heat rising to his cheeks. "My lady, I already have," he replied. "All I ask in return is that you allow me to stand with you during the trying days to come."

Brianna's eyes grew watery, and she released Tavis's hand. "I only wish I could," she said. "But Avner is right about my chances with the earls. When we reach Castle Hartwick, I want you to wait in the woods. If I fail, take the boy and go find your tribe. You're a remarkable firbolg, and I'm sure there will be a place for you."

Tavis shook his head. "You know I can't do that," he said. "Now more than ever, you need a bodyguard—and I'm the only firbolg available for the job."

"But what of Avner?" Brianna demanded. "If we fail, it won't be safe for him in Hartsvale."

"It would be safer than sending him to live with firbolgs!" Basil protested. "The child wouldn't last two days in such a stern society."

"Besides, my place is at Tavis's side," Avner said.

"If Brianna and I fail, your place will be with Basil," the scout countered. "You aren't going into the castle."

Avner rolled his eyes and sighed. "If that's what you want."

"This won't be like the time you let Morten walk into the ogre ambush," Tavis warned. "I mean what I say."

"So do I," Avner replied. He met the firbolg's eyes squarely. "I won't disappoint you this time."

"I know you won't." Tavis ruffled the boy's hair, then looked back to Brianna. "See? We're all set."

"Almost," the princess said. "But there's one thing you must promise me."

"As long as it's in my power," the scout replied.

"It is," Brianna said. "You mustn't let my father return me to the ogres. Kill me first."

"I couldn't raise a hand against you!" he objected.

"What I ask is well within your power," Brianna insisted. "To deny me this promise is to break your word."

Tavis looked away, but the princess stepped around and forced him to look at her.

"I've told you what I want. Will you obey?"

A knot formed in the scout's throat, but he nodded. "My last arrow will be for you," he said. "But, if it comes to that, the first one will be for your father."

"Agreed," Brianna replied. "It will be better to end the Hartwick dynasty quickly, so that a powerful earl can seize the throne before the others start plotting and scheming."

"I'm glad you've developed a plan for what you're going to do *inside* the castle, but what about getting us there?" asked Basil. "As exhausted as we are, we can't outrun Goboka."

Tavis nodded. "You're right about that," he said. "Sooner or later, we'll have to rest—or pass out from fatigue. Either way, the shaman will catch us long before we reach Hartsvale."

"Then let's meet him here." Brianna studied the bog for a moment, then said, "Here's what we'll do."

When the princess finished explaining her plan, Tavis shook his head. "It puts you in too much risk," he said. "You'll suffocate if something goes wrong."

"We all share in the risk," Brianna countered. "And if something goes wrong, I want to suffocate. I'd rather die than fall into Goboka's hands again."

Basil passed his hand axe to the princess. "In that case, the hunted shall become the hunter."

* * * * *

From his hiding place in a log tangle, Tavis watched Goboka's bulky figure approach. The shaman could not have had much rest in past two days, but he showed little sign of fatigue. His strides were long and steady, his eyes alert, and his jaw set with determination. Even his wound seemed to be healing. From the stump of his severed arm dangled the beginnings of a new limb, complete with a tiny elbow, wrist, and hand.

Goboka stopped twenty paces from the bog. His purple eyes narrowed and glared over the gray mud at the weary Brianna, who sat in the center of the quagmire on a hastily constructed raft of three logs. The ogre's gaze flickered to the opposite bank, where Blizzard stood nickering and scraping at the shore with her hooves, then his nostrils flared. He scowled and dropped to his knees, sniffing at the ground as a wolf might.

Cursing under his breath, Tavis nocked an arrow. Goboka had stopped a good dozen steps short of the cross fire he and Basil had set up, but the scout knew their target would come no closer. Ogres normally did not have an acute sense of smell, so it seemed apparent the shaman had used magic to enhance his—and if his spell was half as powerful as a wolf's nose, it would not take him long to find his ambushers.

Tavis rose and fired. At the sound of Bear Driller's bowstring, the shaman sprang to his feet. As fast as he moved, his reflexes were not quick enough to spare him entirely. The shaft took him in the shoulder above the severed arm. Tavis was still using ogre arrows, so the impact did not even knock Goboka down, but when the ogre saw the arrow's black fletching, his eyes widened in alarm. Cursing in the guttural language of his people, he ripped the shaft from his wound and flung it away.

"Now, Basil!" Tavis yelled. The scout was already nocking another arrow.

Goboka's eyelids began to droop and he sank to his haunches, but he managed to pull a clay vial from his satchel. Without even opening it, he stuck the small bottle into his mouth and bit down. Runnels of bright blue fluid spilled from the corners of his mouth and dribbled down his chin, bubbling and hissing, sending wisps of blood-colored vapor up past his nose.

The scout released his bowstring, aiming for one of the shaman's sleepy eyes. The ogre's lethargic gaze was fixed on his attacker, seemingly oblivious to the streaking shaft. Tavis's hand dropped reflexively toward his quiver, but he found himself thinking he might not need another arrow—until, almost casually, Goboka tipped his head aside and allowed the shaft to hiss past.

Basil rose from his hiding place, also in a log tangle, and flung a flat runestone toward the ogre. With smoke and flame spewing from its edges, the rock sailed straight for Goboka. The shaman looked toward the sizzling rock, then raised the stump of his arm into the air and, with the tiny hand growing at its end, tapped the disc ever so slightly. The missile changed directions and came shooting straight for Tavis.

The scout hurled himself from the log tangle and rolled, trying to put as much distance between himself and the runestone as possible. A loud thump echoed through the forest as the disc buried itself in a log. The sizzle deepened to a rumble, became a roaring crescendo, and finally exploded with a deafening clap.

An eerie tranquility settled over the wood. The silence lasted only an instant before it was shattered by the sputter of a hundred flaming wood shards returning to earth. Tavis curled into a tight ball, listening to the lumber crashing through the tree limbs. The acrid smell of smoke filled the air as huge staves thudded into the ground all around, then he heard a branch snap above his head. The scout looked up to see the sharp end of a flaming stick dropping toward his face. He twisted away, barely keeping the fiery stake from piercing his skull.

Tavis jumped up, nocking another arrow. When he turned to aim, Goboka had vanished.

"Where is he?"

Basil slowly spun around, craning his neck in all directions. "He's disappeared, Tavis." The verbeeg's voice cracked as he registered the complaint. "I can't see him!"

"It's all right. Don't panic," the scout said.

Tavis moved cautiously forward, his eyes searching for fluttering branches or some other sign that might betray an invisible foe. Goboka's voice echoed through the trees behind Basil, chanting the mystic syllables of an incantation. Tavis turned toward the sound and found his arrow pointing at the verbeeg's chest.

"Duck!" the scout yelled.

By the time Basil could obey, Goboka had ended his incantation. The scout released his arrow and heard the shaman leaping for cover. The shaft hissed into the forest without hitting anything, but at least it would make their invisible foe think twice before he uttered another spell.

Basil's log pile shifted. The runecaster cried out in alarm and tried to scramble away, but something caught his feet and pulled him back. One of the logs began to writhe, its gray bark changing to scales before Tavis's eyes. The bole slithered around the verbeeg's waist and began twining him in its mighty coils.

The scout resisted the urge to sprint to Basil's aid, realizing Goboka was probably using the runecaster as bait. Instead, Tavis stopped well out of the snake's reach and fired his arrow. The shaft bounced harmlessly off the beast's thick scales. He tried again, this time drawing his string back until the tip barely touched the bow. Again, the shot did not penetrate.

"Where boy?" demanded Goboka's voice.

Tavis nocked an arrow and turned toward the sound, but remembered how the shaman had thrown his voice in the fault cave and did not fire. Taking care to conceal the maneuver with his fingers, the firbolg slipped the notch of the ogre shaft off Bear Killer's string, but drew the bow as if he were going to fire.

"Leave Avner out of this," Tavis said, relieved to hear the shaman trying such a trick. If it had been possible for the ogre to throw his voice while uttering a spell incantation, Goboka would not have bothered trying to make conversation.

"Let all you go," Goboka said. To give the impression that he was moving about, he had shifted the location of his words. "Give me princess."

Tavis turned his bow toward the voice and released the cord beneath his fingers. The sonorous strum of Bear Killer's snapping bowstring echoed off the trees, but the firbolg's arrow remained between his fingers.

As the scout expected, Goboka's heavy footsteps came rushing at him from behind. Tavis tightened his grip on the arrow and spun, thrusting the shaft out in front of him. He heard an astonished groan and felt the iron tip sink into something pulpy, then the shaman's huge bulk smashed into him, breaking the arrow and knocking the firbolg off his feet.

Tavis crashed to the ground beneath his attacker. The air rushed from his lungs in a single excruciating gasp, then a pair of huge hands closed around his throat. He felt hot ogre blood spilling onto his skin, then Goboka's loathsome face appeared before his eyes, the illusion of invisibility shattered once the shaman revealed his location by attacking. The brute's yellow tusks were gnashing in fury, with blue poison antidote still frothing at the corners of his mouth.

Tavis slammed his palms into the ogre's elbows, trying to break his attacker's arms and free himself of the hands that had squeezed shut the veins in his neck. The shaman roared in anger, but his sturdy limbs did not budge, and he brought his heavy brow down to smash his captive's face. The scout turned his head, keeping his nose from being shattered, but Goboka's forehead still caught him in the cheek. An agonizing crackle resonated through the firbolg's head, and his entire face erupted in pain.

Tavis's sight began to grow murky and black, as though he were climbing into a cave for a deep winter sleep. The scout fought to stay alert, turning all his thoughts toward the dwindling light at the lair's distant mouth, but the gloom continued to close in, until he could see nothing but Goboka's hideous face leering at him from the other end of a narrow, dark tunnel.

Tavis reached up and pressed his thumbs to Goboka's eyes, trying to gouge the purple orbs from their sockets before the warrens of his mind grew completely dark.

The shaman threw his head back, pulling his eyes safely out of reach—then Avner's small frame appeared in the gloomy shadows at the edge of Tavis's vision. The youth's hand was arcing through the air, driving the gleaming blade of a steel dagger down past Goboka's face. The knife struck with a deep thud. A spray of blood shot up past the shaman's cheek, and the ogre finally pulled his hands from Tavis's throat.

As the blood rushed back into Tavis's head, the murk began to lighten. The scout glimpsed Goboka's clublike arm swinging toward Avner's small form. The blow landed with a terrible crack and sent the youth sailing through the air. The boy yelled once, then fell quiet.

The shaman stood and turned to follow. As soon as the tremendous weight disappeared from Tavis's chest, the scout pushed himself up and reached out to clutch Goboka's ankle. The ogre did not even spin around. He simply swung the heel of his huge foot and caught Tavis beneath the chin. The scout went reeling down into the dreamless mists where bears sleep.

* * * * *

Brianna snatched up the small wooden javelin Basil had prepared for her and stood, more than a little frightened by what she saw on shore. The shaman's kick had left Tavis lying motionless, either unconscious or dead, while the ogre's snake had just captured Basil's second arm in its coils. Goboka himself was striding toward Avner's groaning form, apparently determined to make certain the youth did not survive to attack him again. Despite the steel dagger and two arrows that had been lodged in his bloody torso, the shaman showed no signs of discomfort—much less of debilitating injury—as he moved to finish the boy.

"Hiatea, give me your blessing," Brianna whispered. "The battle has fallen upon my shoulders now."

The princess spoke the command word Basil had taught her, then hurled the javelin in her hand at Goboka's back. With a great whoosh, the spear burst into flame and streaked away, long tongues of yellow fire trailing after it. The shaman cocked an ear toward the hissing shaft, then, without even glancing toward the sound, hurled himself to the ground.

The maneuver did not spare him. The shaft curved down and planted itself between his shoulder blades. Goboka's scream echoed through the woods. The javelin burst apart, leaving a geyser of flame to shoot from the hole in the ogre's back.

At last, something had injured the shaman. For several moments, he lay on the ground with a pillar of greasy black smoke rising from his wound, growling with pain and digging his long talons into the dirt. Brianna thought he might be dying, but that hope vanished when he raised his head and looked back toward her. His purple eyes had gone black with rage, while his lips were covered with gashes from his own gnashing tusks.

Goboka pushed himself to his feet. After glancing around to make certain his other foes would not be attacking again, he fixed his eyes on Brianna and staggered toward her.

"Princess like hurt? Goboka too. Got plenty." The ogre stopped at the edge of the bog and scowled at the syrupy mud. "Hurt you good before we go."

Brianna stared across the bog, not trying to hide her fear. "You're not going to hurt me," she said. "I won't allow it."

The princess turned and took quick steps, then leaped away from the edge of the raft. She splashed, with a syrupy gurgle, into the mud and plunged in as far as her chest, then began to sink more slowly.

Goboka's angry eyes paled to lavender, and his heavy jaw fell open. "Stop!" he ordered. "What you do?"

"I swore I'd die before I let you take me again," Brianna said. Her feet touched the boulder she and her companions had placed on the bottom when they moved the raft into position, and she slowly bent her knees so that it would appear she was continuing to sink. "And I meant it."

The princess held her chin above the mire long enough to see the shaman grab a log and come splashing toward her, then she closed her eyes and let her head sink into cold mud. Pinching her nostrils shut with one hand, Brianna kneeled down and ran her hand over the boulder until she found the line they had tied to it, then she followed the rope until she came to the hand axe.

The princess pulled the weapon loose. Her heart began to pound, rebelling against any plan that required her to stop breathing, and within thirty alarmed beats the rest of her body joined the panic. Soon, it seemed to Brianna that she had been submerged forever, though a small corner of her mind knew that no more than a minute had passed. Her lungs began to ache for air, and her mouth longed to open wide. It required a conscious act of will to keep her legs folded beneath her, for every instinct screamed at her to straighten them out and thrust her head up into the cool, crisp air just two feet above. But the princess knew what would happen if she did: Goboka would realize he had been tricked. He would react instantly, dodging or blocking her axe strike, and her chance would be gone.

The princess could not understand what was taking Goboka so long. He was obviously intelligent, at least for an ogre, and this was a simple enough thing to do. Push his log out to her raft and plunge his hand into the mud, then grasp her hair—or whatever he could find—and pull her up.

Perhaps he was casting a spell. They had talked about that possibility, but Basil had convinced them that once Brianna was submerged, the ogre would not have time to prepare a spell capable of saving her. Unfortunately, Goboka had surprised them too many times for the princess to place much faith in the runecaster's reassurances. That she was now crouching in the bog was proof enough of the shaman's prowess, for this was the last hope of victory. All of their other plans and assaults had failed to stop him.

There was nothing for Brianna to do but wait, fighting against her own instincts while her body slowly burned her last whiffs of air. Her temples began to throb, and her chest was about to burst with the urge to expel the stale breath in her lungs. In the back of her mind, a fiendish voice kept saying she would feel better if she exhaled. The princess did not listen. She knew her desperate lungs would try to refill themselves the instant she emptied them, and she still had enough control over her mind to know humans could not breathe mud.

At last, Brianna felt the mire swirling near her face. She pushed her head toward the activity and felt her brow brush a pair of talons. They twitched away, and she lost contact. The princess almost screamed, then felt the coarse pads of five ogre fingers slipping over the crown of her head. They squeezed down, the claws digging into her scalp so deep she feared they would puncture her skull.

Brianna took her fingers away from her nostrils and reached up to claw at the hand, trying to pull Goboka into the mud on top of her. She did not want to succeed, but if she allowed the shaman to pull her from the bog without a struggle, he might sense a trap.

Goboka's talons dug deeper, and he pulled. Brianna was surprised by the force the bog exerted to keep her down. The suction was more powerful than the princess had imagined possible, and she found herself worrying the ogre would not be strong enough to pull her free. She had heard many stories of moose, bears, and even dragons that had become so caught in quagmires that they starved to death within plain sight of solid ground. If such powerful beasts could not free themselves, it seemed unreasonable to think an ogre could pull her out.

Fortunately, Brianna did not have to rely on her foe. Ever so slightly, she began to straighten her legs and push against the solid surface of the boulder. She felt herself slipping slowly upward, until, with a loud whooshing sound, the suction broke and her head came shooting out of the mud.

Brianna found herself looking at the side of Goboka's log, with what appeared to be a bleeding mass of mud piled on top. At first, the princess did not know what to make of the sight, then she understood exactly what she was seeing and braced her feet solidly on the boulder. She pushed herself to her full height, so that she was standing only chest-deep in the mire, and brought the hand axe up from beneath the muck.

Goboka tried to slide off the other side of the log, but Brianna was already swinging the weapon at his throat. The blade came down with a damp, distinct thump, then she felt the satisfying crackle of a skull popping free of its neck.

The head splashed into the bog, but the rest of the shaman's bulky corpse remained on the log. Brianna shoved the loathsome body out of sight and pulled herself from the bog, already turning toward the shore where her friends lay in desperate need of healing magic.

It did not occur to the princess to give a victory cry, not until she reached the shore of the bog and saw Tavis lift his battered head.

❧ 18 ❧
Audience with the King

As the flabbergasted doormen performed the ceremonial presentation of their poleaxes, Brianna pulled Basil's runestone from beneath her grimy bearskin cape and turned its glowing symbol toward them. The eyelids of both men drooped shut, the tension drained from their bodies, and their weapons slipped from their hands. They fell to floor, landing atop each other in a crumpled heap.

The princess spun around, presenting the runestone to the six astonished sentries flanking Tavis. These guards also sank into slumber, collapsing to the floor amidst a clamor of weapons and armor.

"Can I look yet?" Tavis was holding his hands to his eyes. Avner and Basil were waiting, at Brianna's order, in the woods outside Castle Hartwick.

"Yes." Brianna turned the runestone toward the floor, then waited for the scout to uncover his eyes and handed it to him. "You keep this, in case any more of Father's guards show up."

Tavis slipped the runestone beneath his cloak, then retrieved Bear Driller from the guard who had been holding it. "I'll slip inside once you've drawn their attention away from the door," he said. "Don't worry if you don't notice. I'll be there when you need me."

Brianna smiled and touched his cheek, which was still badly swollen in spite of all the healing spells she had cast on it. "You always have," she said. "Wish me luck."

The princess turned and kicked the door, thrusting her heel into the bas-relief face of a leering satyr. The portal swung open with a resounding boom, then

Brianna stepped through a looming arch into Castle Hartwick's banquet room.

The cavernous chamber was every bit as gloomy as the interior of the Fir Palace, for the wall sconces had all been hung with red mourning curtains that turned the flickering torchlight to the color of blood. A long feasting table ran down the center of the room. Standing along its sides, staring in her direction with their swords drawn and mead dripping from their beards, were the surviving earls of Hartsvale. Most had white bandages covering the wounds they had suffered during the ogre ambush, and a few still seemed to have trouble standing.

"Put your weapons away and sit down, gentlemen," Brianna commanded. "I intend you no harm."

The princess looked toward the far end of the table where the king, his eyes bleary and his beard slick with the grease of roast fowl, sat. In the first chair on the right sat his young queen, Celia of Dunsany, barely older than Brianna, while High Priest Simon sat in the first chair on the left. Two members of the Giant Guard, the stone giant Gavorial and the frost giant Hrodmar, stood in the shadows behind him, hardly distinguishable from the great pillars supporting the ceiling.

As Brianna swept into the room, the king squinted at her as if he did not know who she could possibly be. The earls remained frozen in silence, too shocked even to whisper to each other. Only the giants seemed to accept that the princess had returned, with Hrodmar glancing nervously at Gavorial for guidance. The stone giant, patient and stolid as ever, raised a single long finger to instruct his companion to remain motionless.

Finally, Camden demanded, "Who dares burst into my hall?"

"Brianna of Hartwick, of course," the princess replied.

Brianna stepped over to the banquet table, where she would be illuminated by the candles, and paused. After her long ordeal in the mountains, she had a haggard, wind-chapped face and snarled, stringy hair, but the princess had not changed so much that even her drunken father could fail to recognize her.

"What apparition are you?" demanded the king. "My daughter was abducted by ogres!"

"Then what are you doing here?" demanded Brianna. Though she had just entered the room, she could see that strong drink had reduced the king to a pitiful, confused shadow of the father she remembered. "Why are you feasting in your hall when you should be in the mountains, tracking ogres and fighting to save me?"

This was too much for the stuporous king. "She's a ghost!" he blurted. "Away with her!"

Hrodmar started to step around the table, but Gavorial raised his hand and gently held the frost giant back. Brianna found the favor puzzling, for the Giant Guard prided itself on obedience to the king's every word. But then, it had always seemed to her that the stone giant was constantly and silently measuring the actions of those around him. Perhaps Gavorial had ignored the command because he already knew what the princess hoped to prove to the earls: that her father was no longer worthy of obedience.

When no one moved to obey, the king leaped out of his chair. "She's a ghoul, I tell you!" he yelled. "Don't let her near!"

"I'm no fiend," Brianna replied. She touched her fingers to the cheek of a nearby earl, one of the few whom she knew to be an honest and trustworthy man. "I'm quite alive, as I'm certain Earl Wendel will tell you."

The earl nodded. "Her flesh is as soft and warm as that of my own wife."

"What are you saying?" the king demanded. "Whose side are you on?"

"My king's, of course," the earl replied. He met the king's glare evenly. "I'll claim that Brianna's a fiend, if you desire—but I don't know why you'd want that. If she were my daughter, I'd be overjoyed to see her return safely."

For a moment, Camden stared at Earl Wendel as though he didn't comprehend what the man had said. Then the king seemed to realize he was making a fool of himself and sank back into his chair. He pulled off his golden crown and placed it next to his mug, then ran his hands through his tangled hair.

"Yes, forgive me. It's just that I'm . . . I've been so distraught." The king raised his gaze to Brianna, and she saw that there were tears welling in his eyes. "I *am* happy to see you alive. It's just that . . . I'm so sorry . . . but I didn't expect I ever would."

"I imagine you didn't," Brianna replied, sickened by the pathetic figure at the head of the table. "Considering your bargain with Goboka, I'm quite sure you counted me lost forever."

The king's lips began to tremble. His eyes darted around the banquet table, studying the mood of his earls. When he saw nothing but blank faces, he motioned Brianna forward.

"You must be hungry, my dear." Camden cast a meaningful glance toward High Priest Simon. As the cleric rose to offer his chair, the king continued, "Come and sit beside your father. Eat and drink."

The king had not lost his capacities entirely, Brianna realized. He was attempting to retain control of the situation by changing the subject, and by subtly exerting his authority over her. Also, closing the distance between them would transform the discussion from a public matter to a private one. The princess knew her cause would be lost if she allowed him to accomplish either goal.

"Sit down, Simon." As she gave the command, Brianna glared into her father's eyes, making clear that she was challenging his authority. "I have no intention of accepting hospitality from a man who would trade his daughter—his only heir—for a kingdom."

Camden's eyes flashed with anger. He pushed his chair back and drew himself to his full height, slamming his fist onto the tabletop. Earthenware mugs and platters bounced so high into the air that they shattered when they came down, spilling mead and greasy meat.

"I did not trade you for my throne!" he thundered.

Celia's face went as pale as bone, but the young queen seemed afraid to rise without permission. Brianna wondered if the king had become that much of a tyrant. By the deathly silence in the room, she suspected he had. Even the earls sat petrified in their chairs, their eyes fixed on Camden's shuddering figure as though he were about to explode.

"You dare deny it?" Brianna inquired. Despite her growing anger, she deliberately kept her voice as calm as possible. The contrast between her composure and the king's demented fury would only serve to convince the earls she was telling the truth. "Then why were the horses of all your companies still in their stables? What forces have you sent to rescue me from the ogres?"

This drew a quiet drone of whispering from the earls, and Brianna knew they had probably been wondering the same thing.

"I don't deny that I have made great personal sacrifices for the benefit of Hartsvale." The king's voice was suddenly as calm as Brianna's, his face so serene and collected that it was difficult to believe he had been a blustering drunkard only a moment before. He braced himself on the table and leaned forward, speaking to his earls now instead of Brianna. "Goboka has been a good friend. Not only did he help us resolve our difficulties during the War of Harts, he has kept ogres from marauding in our valley for these nineteen years."

"And the price for his help was your daughter?" asked Earl Wendel, incredulous.

The king narrowed his eyes at the earl and gave him a menacing glare. Then he answered, "Yes."

The king's mouth hung open for a moment, as though he intended to add more to his explanation, then he shifted his gaze to Brianna's face. The tears that had welled in his eyes earlier began to spill down his cheeks openly, and he made no attempt to conceal them.

"Please understand, Brianna," he begged. "I acted for the good of Hartsvale."

The princess studied the king without responding. Although his tears appeared genuine enough, the eyes from which they came were cold and hard and, most surprisingly, angry. If not for the ire in her father's eyes, Brianna might have believed that he had acted only out of a stolid sense of duty. But the king's anger bespoke something far more sinister: a spiritual barrenness that would always prevent him from ruling with the true welfare of his subjects at heart.

"You're lying, and the sad thing is that you're the only one who doesn't know it," she said. "You don't have any idea what it means to act for the good of the kingdom. You can think only of what makes your throne more secure—and the reason you're angry with me now is that my return threatens your power."

Camden's tears suddenly dried up. "I'm still your king."

"And that's all that matters to you," Brianna retorted. "That's why you promised your unborn daughter to Goboka—not to end the war, but to protect your crown from Dunstan."

"You mustn't say such things." Camden's voice was as cool as ice, and as threatening as an avalanche. "Your mother did, and look what . . ."

The king let the sentence trail off, his eyes racing over the faces of those nearest him.

"Look what happened to her?" Brianna demanded. She was beginning to understand that the man in front of her had never truly been the father she loved, or the king she had admired. He was an imposter, a thief who had stolen his throne, and perhaps a ruthless murderer who had killed to defend it. "Did you throw her into the Clearwhirl? Is that what you'll do with me?"

By the crimson color of the king's face and the throbbing veins in his temples, Brianna knew she had guessed correctly. "You killed her!"

"She was weak!" Camden retorted. "She wouldn't make the sacrifices demanded of a queen!"

"A queen is not required to give her child to ogres," Brianna countered. "Not unless she has a monster for a husband."

Though the massive banquet table weighed as much as one of Castle Hartwick's gates, Camden grabbed it and heaved it aside. Regardless of what manner of king he had become, he remained a Hartwick and was blessed with the giantlike strength of their line. The table flipped on its side, knocking several earls and Celia of Dunsany to the floor. The queen cried out in pain, but the king appeared not to notice and started across the room.

A general clamor filled the chamber as the earls leaped to their feet. They seemed entirely unsure as to what they should do, but were apparently convinced that some action would be required. A few moved forward to grab the king, others rushed to lift the table off Celia, and the remainder simply reached for their belt weapons.

"Stand your ground!" warned Gavorial.

"I'll mash any man who harms the king!" added Hrodmar. The frost giant's voice shook the entire room.

The warnings were enough to freeze the earls in their places. The king threw a chair aside, then, as High Priest Simon kneeled over Celia at the other end of the room, Camden stopped in front of Brianna.

"Apologize!"

"No."

Camden raised his hand. Brianna lifted her chin and

303

glared into her father's eyes, hoping Tavis would be wise enough not to make his presence known at this moment.

"Beat your daughter if you must," the princess said. "I'm sure it will be a good lesson for the earls."

The king checked his hand in midswing, then slowly looked around the room at his earls. They were all watching with uneasy expressions, as though considering what the king might do to them if he was willing to beat a princess in public. Camden slowly lowered his hand, then backed away from his daughter.

"You're right. It was a tragic mistake to ask Goboka's help," the king admitted. He was staring at the floor with the vacant gaze of a lost man. "Your mother was the lucky one. She didn't have to watch you grow up, knowing that she would have to give you up when you reached the bloom of womanhood."

The king raised his eyes to Brianna's face, and this time there was no anger in his gaze, only bitterness and self-pity. "Do you know what that was like, Brianna? To watch your child mature, knowing for nineteen years that you would betray her?"

"I can only imagine," Brianna replied coldly. "It must have been like growing up without your mother, believing she had chosen to die rather than raise you."

"But she did choose to die!" the king insisted. "When she refused to understand that I couldn't undo my mistake, I had no choice but to kill her. I had to protect the kingdom."

"You had to protect the king," Brianna corrected.

"They're the same. You'd understand that if you were in my position," Camden said. Then, as if Brianna had agreed with him, he continued, "You don't know what I've endured all these years. The agony has been eating me from the inside out."

"I'm sure."

The king stepped over to Brianna and took her hand. A cold sweat had slickened his palms. "I'm glad you know the truth at last," he said. "It will make it easier to understand why I must send you back."

Brianna looked around the chamber. Gavorial and Hrodmar had slipped forward to be near the king, and were thus blocking her view of Celia and the earls attending her at the head of the table. But the men she could see were staring at her father with slack-jawed expressions of disbelief. Already, she guessed that half of them believed him an unfit king. The time had come to take the offensive and convince the other half.

Without removing her hand from her father's grasp, the princess asked, "Are you worried that there will be a war with Goboka and his ogres if I don't return to them?"

The king smiled. "I knew you'd understand," he said. "For the good of the kingdom, we must both live with my tragic mistake."

Brianna smiled back. "That won't be necessary," she said. "Goboka is dead."

"What?" Hrodmar boomed.

"The shaman poses no danger to me or Hartsvale," Brianna repeated. "Tavis Burdun and I killed him."

Many of the earls voiced their congratulations, while others sighed in relief, and the rest began to murmur among themselves about what Brianna's return meant to the kingdom's future.

Gavorial's voice knelled out above the din, bringing the babble to a sudden silence. "Perhaps you killed Goboka, but what of his horde?" the stone giant asked. "Surely, the two of you couldn't have slain so many hundreds of ogres?"

"Not by ourselves," Brianna replied.

The princess glanced around the shadowy room, hoping that Tavis had slipped into position by now. Her demented father no longer posed the greatest danger, for if Gavorial and Hrodmar knew of the Twilight Spirit's involvement in her abduction, there was no telling how the pair would react to what she was reporting. Fortunately, she and the scout had discussed this uncertainty beforehand, and Tavis knew what to do.

When Brianna offered no further information about the horde's fate, it was Hrodmar who demanded, "What do you mean? Are those ogres dead or not?"

Brianna regarded the frost giant with an expression of disdain. "I'm hardly accustomed to being interrogated by my father's guards," she replied. "But if you must know, Noote's hill giants killed most of them—though we certainly slayed our share as well."

"The hill giants!"

Hrodmar looked to Gavorial for guidance, but the stone giant had none to offer. He merely regarded Brianna with his gray eyes, a thumb and single long finger rubbing his chin.

Brianna turned back to her father, determined to have the earls solidly on her side before any trouble with the giants began. "Without Goboka and his horde to concern you, the time has come for you to make amends for your *tragic mistake*, Father."

A suspicious light flashed in the king's eyes. "What are you talking about *amends*?"

Raising her voice so she could be heard throughout the chamber, the princess replied, "As your daughter and the princess of Hartsvale, I demand your abdication."

"Don't mock me, foolish girl!" her father yelled. His eyes were gleaming with a mad purple light. "In spite of my mistakes, I've been a good king!"

"Really?" Brianna scoffed. "Would that be because you murder your queens, or because you were about to deliver Hartsvale into the hands of the ogres?"

"Enough!"

The king lashed out, striking her with the back of his hand. He hit her harder than Goboka had on Coggin's Rise and sent her tumbling over the banquet table into the empty seats beyond. The chairs toppled over, spilling her to the floor, and all she could do was lie on the cold stone with the blow still ringing in her ears.

Brianna heard the table being dragged aside and knew her father was coming. She shook her head clear, then grabbed a chair back and pulled herself to her feet. The princess found Wendel and three earls standing between her and her father.

Wendel gave her a clean cloth. "Perhaps you'd like to wipe your face," he suggested. "Then I think the earls would like to hear what you have to say."

"Thank you." As Brianna stanched her bleeding nose, she discreetly searched the shadows on the other side of the room. The princess found Tavis peeking out from behind a pillar, Bear Driller in his hand.

"Traitors!" Camden yelled, glaring at the earls. Despite his accusation, the king did not call on his giants for support. Instead, he returned his gaze to the princess. In a sly voice, he said, "I see your game now. You're jealous of Celia."

Brianna did not understand her father's purpose. By now, he should have been threatening the earls, not making flimsy accusations against her. "Why would I be jealous of Celia?"

"Because you want to be queen."

"I would have been content to wait—had you allowed me that choice," Brianna replied. She turned to address the earls. "But what I would not do is bear an ogre's child, especially not when that child could one day became the king of Hartsvale."

The princess did not need to spell matters out for the earls. Since she was the single heir to Hartsvale's throne, one day her offspring would have the only legitimate claim to the throne. If that child was half-ogre, the earls would be left with a very unpleasant choice: pledge their fealty to a brutal savage, or wage a war of rebellion against the rightful heir of a thousand-year dynasty.

Brianna allowed the earls a moment to ponder what she had implied, then finished, "I'd rather die before I did that to Hartsvale."

The king applauded, cutting short any reaction from the earls. "Your dedication to Hartsvale is most appreciated—but hardly necessary." He smirked at Brianna, then said, "Happily, soon you will no longer be my only child."

"What?" Brianna gasped.

"Celia is with child," the king replied. He turned toward the far end of the room, where chairs and crockery still lay strewn over the floor after his fit of temper. "Ask her, if you like."

High Priest Simon rose from behind the toppled table, his hands dripping with blood. "The queen is in no condition to answer questions, Your Majesty." He glared across the room at Camden, then added, "And if she survives, I doubt she will be bearing you any children."

Camden's face went pale, and he whirled on Brianna. "This is your fault!" he screamed. "See what your treachery has done?"

"The princess has done nothing," said Earl Wendel. "But you—you have abdicated your crown."

"Hear! Hear!" shouted an earl. He repeated the cry, and this time many more voices joined in. "Hear! Hear!"

Camden turned to his giants. "Stomp them!" he ordered. "Smash them all!"

Hrodmar raised a foot to obey, but Gavorial grasped the frost giant's arm. "It is our duty to protect the king's life, not perform his murders," said the stone giant. He knelt at Camden's side and held out a chair-sized palm. "Come along gently, my king. There is no longer anything here for you."

The wild-eyed king looked slowly around the room, searching for a friendly face. As he looked into each set of eyes, they turned as hard and cold as his had been the last few days. When he found no warmth even in the countenance of his most trusted advisor and friend, High Priest Simon, Camden slumped into the stone giant's open palm. He pointed to a golden circlet lying on the floor near Celia, amidst the bones of greasy fowl and pools of spilled mead.

"My crown," he said. "I want my crown."

* * * * *

From among the banquet chamber's shadowy pillars, Tavis Burdun watched as Earl Wendel picked up the grease-stained crown. He did not give it to Camden, but turned instead and passed it to Brianna. "This no longer belongs to your father," he said. "Now it is yours. May you wear it in health."

"Hear! Hear!" chorused the earls.

As far as the scout could tell, none of the earls realized that he was in the room, and Princess Brianna, now Queen Brianna, was too busy accepting her subjects' congratulations to concern herself with him.

It was just as well. Crowds, even those as small as the gathering around Brianna, made firbolgs uncomfortable. Besides, as soon as the giants left, it would be time for Tavis to return to the Weary Giant. He could already imagine the mess the place had become under Livia's neglectful eye—if she and the other children had not burned the place to the ground!

Gavorial closed his hand around Camden's forlorn figure, then rose to his full height, standing so tall that his head vanished into the cavernous darkness of the chamber's ceiling. But instead of turning to leave, the stone giant faced Hrodmar and motioned toward Brianna.

"If you will bring the queen, it's time we left this place," he said. Although the stone giant was speaking to Hrodmar, his voice filled the chamber like a knelling bell.

Tavis uttered a silent curse. When Gavorial had

convinced Camden to abdicate peacefully, the firbolg had hoped the giants would cause no trouble. Now, the scout was glad he had elected to stay hidden until the pair were safely gone. His arrow already nocked, Tavis drew his bowstring back, but did not fire.

In the center of the chamber, Earl Wendel was the first to recover from the shock. He took a hand axe from his belt and stepped in front of Brianna, glaring up into the darkness that hid Gavorial's head.

"What do you mean by this treachery?" As the earl spoke, he motioned for his fellows to gather around. "We won't let you take our queen without a fight!"

"Then you'll die!" chortled Hrodmar.

The frost giant raised his foot to begin kicking earls aside, but Gavorial held out a restraining hand.

"There's no need for violence," the stone giant said. Then, addressing Wendel, he said, "But you and the other earls must understand: a promise was made, and it will be kept."

Wendel scowled up into the darkness. "Why?" he demanded. "Goboka's dead!"

"But the Twilight Spirit is not," Brianna added.

"Quiet!" Hrodmar boomed. The frost giant kneeled down.

Tavis braced himself, waiting for Hrodmar to lower his head just a little bit more.

Hrodmar stretched a hand over the earls, reaching for the queen. "Don't talk about the spirit!" he ordered. "That name is not for humans to hear!"

"Why not?" Brianna asked. "What is there to hide in the Twilight Vale?"

"Quiet!"

To emphasize the consequences of ignoring his demand, Hrodmar slapped his hand down on an earl's head. The man did not even cry out, but simply collapsed to the ground in a jumbled mass of bones and flesh.

Tavis clenched his teeth, reminding himself that even if he had loosed his arrow, it would not have saved the man—or Brianna. To do that, he had to kill the frost giant, and to kill the frost giant, he had to wait for the proper shot. Somehow, that knowledge did not make it any easier to keep his fingers on the bowstring.

Gavorial stooped over and regarded the frost giant with an air of impatience. "Was that truly necessary?" The stone giant looked to Brianna, then said, "If you know of the Twilight Spirit, then you must also know that none of us have any choice except to obey him. Now, will you come along quietly—or must Hrodmar kill more of your earls?"

Hrodmar leaned forward to stretch his hand over Wendel's head, giving Tavis a clear view of a cavelike ear canal. The scout loosed his arrow. The shaft hissed through the air, then disappeared into its target.

Hrodmar roared in pain and cupped a hand over his ear, almost crushing several earls as he crashed to his side. He thrashed madly about for a moment, banging his head against the floor. Several pieces of stone facade crashed off the walls, then the giant finally fell silent and died.

Tavis stepped from the shadows with his second arrow nocked and drawn. He did not fire, for Brianna had instructed him to leave one giant alive. "Gavorial, I suggest you take the king and leave."

The stone giant glared at Tavis thoughtfully, showing no surprise or shock at the firbolg's sudden appearance. "Even you cannot make such a shot twice in a row, Tavis Burdun."

Despite his words, Gavorial drew himself up to his full height, so that his head would be concealed in the shadows above.

"That first arrow was just to let you know we're not making idle threats," Tavis said. He trained his second arrow on Brianna's chest. "This one is for Brianna."

"I see," came the stone giant's voice.

Brianna looked up into the shadows. "Do you?" she asked. "I have no idea why your spirit wants me, and I really don't care. What's important is that he understands this: Tavis Burdun hits what he aims at—and if the Twilight Spirit sends anyone else to abduct me, it will be the Queen of Hartwick that Tavis targets."

"A profound strategy," Gavorial said, genuine admiration in his voice. "The spirit has no use for a dead queen."

The stone giant slowly backed to the exit, then paused beneath the looming arch and bowed to Brianna. "I leave you in peace," he said. "And let this warning be my parting gift: Constantly be on guard, for there are many giants, and sooner or later they must all answer to the Twilight Spirit."

With that, Gavorial pushed through the huge doors and disappeared from sight. Tavis breathed a long sigh of relief and lowered Bear Driller. He fired the arrow into the floor, and it shattered into a hundred pieces.

"Long live the queen!" the scout yelled.

He repeated the words, and when the earls joined in, the cheer was as thunderous as the voice of any giant.

Epilogue

"So now what?" asked Avner. The youth stood on the ramparts of Castle Hartwick, looking across the Clearwhirl's eastern channel. In the distance, the stone giant Gavorial was disappearing into the dusk, the former king of Hartsvale gripped securely in his hand. "Now that you're the queen, what's going to happen to us?"

Brianna laid a warm hand on the youth's shoulder. "I don't know," she said. "What do you suppose should happen to you?"

The boy cast an apprehensive glance over at Basil. "What do you think?" he asked. "We did steal those books, you know."

The verbeeg scowled. "Stealing implies personal ownership, which, as you know, is a rather archaic concept—especially among my people," he said. "Besides, books are no good unless someone's using them. They shouldn't sit endlessly on some shelf."

"That's not a very good answer," Tavis said.

Basil scowled. "Very well, then," he said. "I suppose we shall have to return them to Earl Dobbin's family."

Avner looked up at the scout. "Is that okay with you?"

Tavis shook his head sternly. "Hardly," he said. "Returning what you have stolen is a good start, but I don't see how that alone will discourage you from trying it again."

Avner scowled. After all he had gone through, it hardly seemed fair to punish him for something he had done in what felt like the ancient past—but he resisted the urge to say so. He knew Tavis well enough to realize that complaining would only make matters worse.

"I've thought of just punishments," Brianna said. "Basil, the royal libraries are a mess. Your sentence shall be to clean and organize them."

The verbeeg's eyes lit up. "With pleasure!" he said. "How many volumes do you have—approximately?"

"We have exactly two thousand three hundred and twelve," Brianna replied. "And I should warn you that the one thing we do possess is a complete list. If even one comes up missing—"

"They won't," the verbeeg promised. "Who needs to steal when he can borrow?"

"What about me?" Avner asked, hoping his punishment would be something just as fitting.

Brianna smiled. "Once your arm is better, I think you should stay here to clean out Blizzard's stall—for a year."

"A year!" he gasped.

"Is something wrong with that?" Tavis inquired.

Avner quickly swallowed his shock. "No, of course not," he said. "I was just thinking that a year will be a long time, away from you and Livia and the others back at the inn."

"I don't think you'll be missing them at all," said the new queen. She clasped Tavis's arm, then added, "I intend to keep all of you very close at hand."